THE EMBLEM THRONE

RUNES OF ISSALIA, BOOK II

JEFFREY L. KOHANEK

FALLBRANDT PRESS

ISBN: 978-1-949382-10-5
PUBLISHED BY JEFFREY L. KOHANEK and FALLBRANDT PRESS
www.JeffreyLKohanek.com

Print edition produced in the United States

For my readers.
Without you, Brock's journey would have ended long ago.

BOOKS BY JEFFREY L. KOHANEK

Runes of Issalia

The Buried Symbol: Runes of Issalia 1

The Emblem Throne: Runes of Issalia 2

An Empire in Runes: Runes of Issalia 3

* * *

Runes of Issalia Boxed Set

* * *

Heroes of Issalia: Runes Series+Rogue Legacy

* * *

Rogue Legacy: Runes of Issalia Prequel

Wardens of Issalia

A Warden's Purpose: Wardens of Issalia 1

The Arcane Ward: Wardens of Issalia 2

An Imperial Gambit: Wardens of Issalia 3

A Kingdom Under Siege: Wardens of Issalia 4

* * *

Wardens of Issalia Boxed Set (April 2014)

* * *

ICON: A Wardens of Issalia Companion Tale

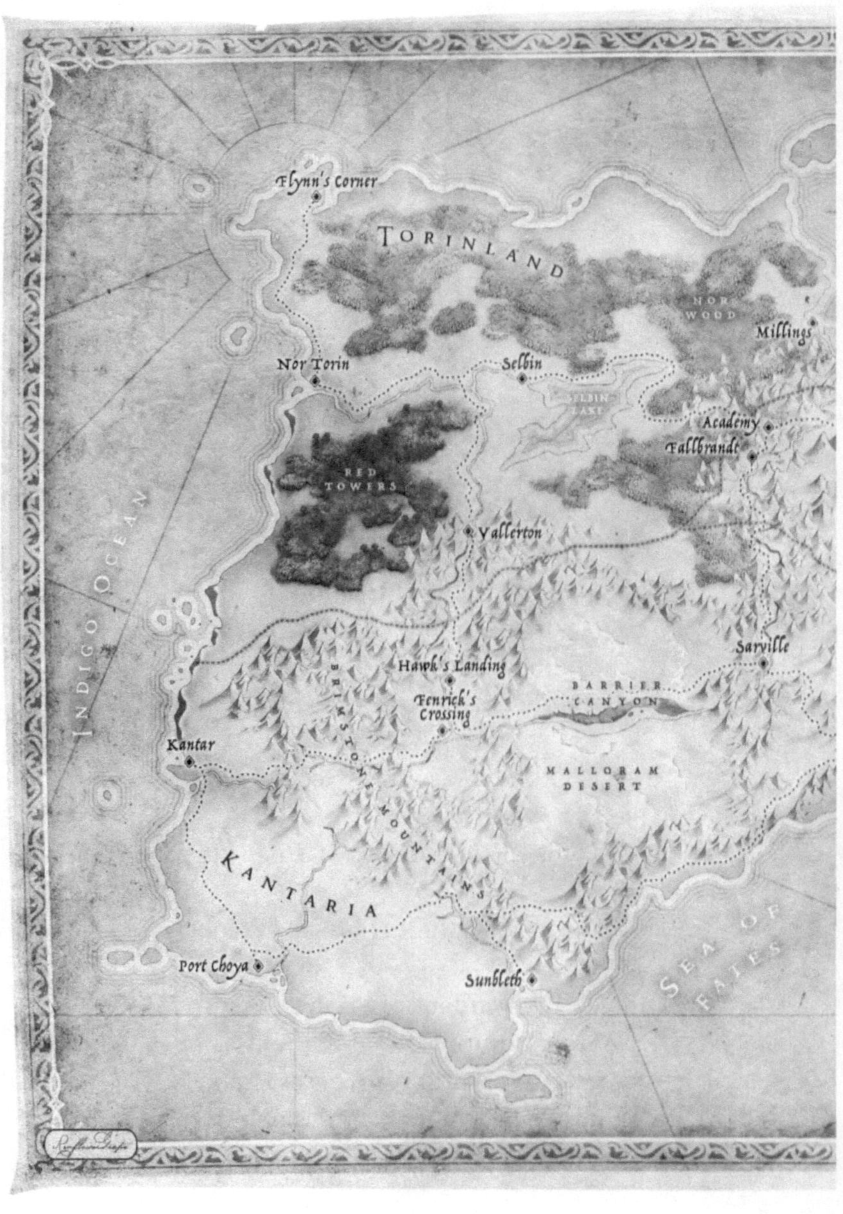

Flynn's Corner
TORINLAND
NOR WOOD
Millings
Nor Torin
Selbin
SELBIN LAKE
Academy
Fallbrandt
RED TOWERS
Vallerton
INDIGO OCEAN
Sarville
Hawk's Landing
BARRIER CANYON
Fenrick's Crossing
BRIMSTONE MOUNTAINS
Kantar
MALLORAM DESERT
KANTARIA
SEA OF FATES
Port Choya
Sunbleth

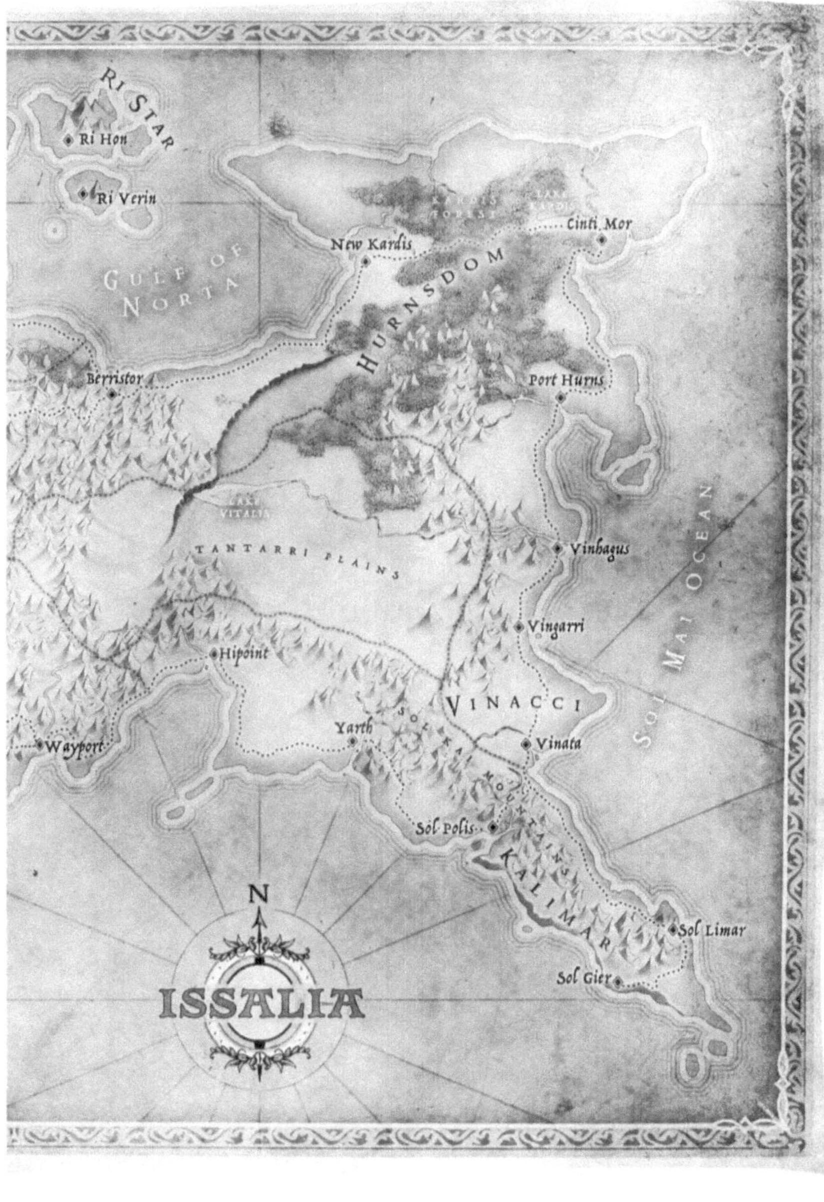

RI STAR
Ri Hon
Ri Verin
GULF OF NORTA
New Kardis
HURNSDOM
Cinti Mor
Port Hurns
Berristor
TANTARRI PLAINS
Vinbagus
Vingarri
Hipoint
VINACCI
Vinata
Yarth
Wayport
SOL MAI OCEAN
Sol Polis
KALIMAR
Sol Limar
Sol Gier
N
ISSALIA

PROLOGUE

Byland Hedgewick climbed the narrow ladder, his arthritic hands protesting as he gripped each wooden rung. Stretching an arm out, he grabbed a thick book from the top shelf and began his descent.

With his feet firmly on the floor of his office, he inspected the volume marked *Methods of Interpreting Prophetic Visions*.

He gave a satisfied nod and pushed his spectacles back into place. Turning toward the door, he lifted his purple cloak from a hook on the wall and secured it about his shoulders. With cloak donned and textbook cradled in one arm, he shuffled out the door.

The hallway was quiet – calm before the storm of activity that would mark the daylight hours. Hedgewick strode purposefully past neighboring offices and the side entrance to the renowned Academy Library before reaching the heavy wooden door that led outside.

A flash of brisk morning air was a shock to his senses, instantly eradicating any drowsiness remaining from his troubled slumber. The clear sky above the eastern mountains glowed a bright blue as the rising sun pushed the darkness of night westward. He descended the steps and marched across the lawn as sparkling frost crunched beneath the soles of his boots, leaving a trail of frost-free footprints on the path.

While crossing the lawn, Hedgewick surveyed the construction of the west wing. The effort had begun in late spring and was now almost complete as the workers raced to finish before the first snowfall. The new wing would soon house female students. Hedgewick shook his head in amazement. The concept of women in the Ministry seemed an oddity, but it was certainly a time of change. Recent events had required the Ministry to alter its views, and opening Academy doors to women was just one shift among many.

Stacks of stone blocks stood near the tower that was to terminate the wing. Rounding the circular walls of the tower, Hedgewick found the small portion of the outer wall that remained incomplete. He expected the builders to fill the opening by day's end. In fact, he counted on it.

With effort, he lifted his leg high enough to step into the opening, grunting as he hoisted himself into the tower. Straightening to stand, his free hand went to his lower back and rubbed at the pain. He'd never been fit or agile, but the years were taking their toll and anything physical had become a challenge. Hedgewick examined the interior of the tower to get his bearings.

The circular room was over sixty feet in diameter with the interior doorway standing opposite from the gap in the wall. A spiral staircase occupied the center of the room, rising from the baths in the cellar below up to the three stories that would eventually exist above. He turned toward the open section of wall and closed his eyes to recall his vision. In his mind's eye, he found it an exact match.

Approaching the opening, he craned his neck around the stone bricks to peer past the inner wall. There was access to the gap in between, just below eye-level. Due to the cold winters at the Academy, they built the walls in two layers, divided by an air gap designed to insulate the interior from the temperature outside. That gap would become the home to his secret.

Hedgewick pulled the heavy book from under his arm. Holding it with both hands, he opened the outer cover to reveal the real book hiding beneath.

His thoughts wandered as he stared at the starburst-shaped rune embossed on the cover. Scenes of death and destruction danced in his head as he relived the prophetic vision that had put him on this path. He had no choice. It was the right thing to do. It was what Issal required him to do.

He flipped the cover open and read the messages he had written the night before. Giving a nod, he gently closed the book. It would have to do.

Hedgewick reached into the gap and inserted the book into the wall, wedging it just beyond view. He stepped back and exhaled. It was done. With a sense of relief, he paused to stare out at the valley.

The frost on the field of long grass glistened in the morning light. Fresh snow on the surrounding mountain peaks reflected the rising sun. The leaf trees hosted a variety of colors, ranging from green to red as they prepared to bare their branches prior to winter. Thin trails of smoke snaked upward from the town nestled along the dark lake at the far end of the valley. It was a beautiful and tranquil scene.

Hedgewick suddenly remembered the time. He was definitely going to be late.

Crouching low, he clumsily climbed down and hurried across the lawn to the main entrance. He ascended the stairs as rapidly as his body would allow, pausing to catch his breath before opening the heavy door.

He hurried across the central hall, his footsteps echoing in the open space as he headed toward a branching corridor. In his rush, he collided with a serving woman rounding the corner.

"Sorry, Master. Please forgive me." The woman stammered while gathering the linens she had dropped.

"No worries, my child," he said as he continued walking. "It was my fault."

He found the doors to the Hall of Masters already closed. Pausing, he pulled out a small cloth and padded beads of sweat from his forehead. After stuffing the cloth back into his pocket, he squeezed the handle and opened the door.

Three long rows of tables ran the length of the room, filled with cloaked men. At the two outer tables sat prelates, visiting from cities across the newly formed empire. Their red cloaks were like bright stripes framing the dark purple cloaks of the academy masters at the middle table. Everyone was facing the table upon the dais, opposite of the doors.

High-Marshal Zurandus and Arch-Prelate Selbin sat at the ends of the short table. At well over six feet, the man standing between them towered over the room.

Headmaster Hardig's height was accentuated by his position upon the three-foot tall dais. The tall man, dressed in the silver cloak of his office, was addressing the Enclave as Hedgewick slid into an open seat at the middle table.

"...and so, I am pleased to inform you that the Cleansing is nearly complete." Hardig said, leaning forward with his hands pressed against the table. "We are committed to this effort. Everyone in this room was part of the decision. We must show resolve and see it through."

Hardig glared at the Enclave members before him, his intense brown eyes scanning the room for signs of dissension. The time for those sentiments had long since passed.

Standing upright, he continued. "High-Marshal Zurandus has been leading the effort to cleanse *Chaos* users from the Holy Army." He gestured toward the military leader. "High-Marshal, would you please report your progress to the Enclave?"

Hardig took his seat, allowing the high-marshal to take the spotlight. Zurandus stood, the shiny metal plates adorning his white leather armor reflecting the incoming sunlight. While not as tall as Hardig, he was a massive man. At just over six-feet, he had a barrel chest and broad shoulders, further enhanced by the padding of the armor. His bare arms showed tan skin stretched tight over bulging muscles from his shoulder plates to the leather bracers wrapped about each forearm.

The high-marshal's deep voice rumbled throughout the room. "I'm here to report that all Arcanists among the Paladin ranks have been eliminated." This revelation caused murmurs to buzz through the hall. He paused, waiting for the crowd to quiet. His brow furrowed as he resumed.

"Careful planning and a well-executed operation left us with few casualties. Their ranks had been thinned considerably from the war, leaving them easier to dispose of than anticipated." Pounding his fist on the table, Zurandus shouted to the room. "The Holy Army is now pure, ready to support the Empire without the taint of *Chaos*!"

The audience cheered, encouraged by this victory. The proud high-marshal nodded and returned to his seat. As the cheering subsided, the headmaster stood to address the enclave. Sunbeams streaming through high windows shone upon his angular face.

Hardig nodded toward the man on his right. "Thank you, High-Marshal. Once again, the Holy Army has proven its value to the Ministry and to the Empire." He turned, gesturing toward the man on his left. "Arch-Prelate, will you please present your update to the Enclave?"

Arch-Prelate Selbin's white hair and beard were a fitting match to his red-trimmed white cloak. Leaning hard into the cane he held, the senior leader rose and addressed the room as Hardig took a seat.

"Thank you, Headmaster." Selbin nodded toward Hardig.

The Arch-Prelate turned his gaze to the Ministry leaders in the assembly below. Although his aging body was beginning to fail, his eyes remained alert. Sharp wits had always been his best assets, and the years had leant a strong sense of wisdom to his arsenal. Nobody doubted that those assets remained as effective as ever.

"Children of Issal, we all are. None among us is perfect. Yet, we are said to be reflections of his likeness. Therefore, not even Issal is perfect. *Chaos* is his imperfection. The destruction and horror wrought by *Chaos* during the war cannot be forgotten by those who witnessed it."

He looked around the room with solemn eyes. "As the shepherds of man, we've taken upon us the responsibility to protect humanity. Often-times, that means protecting man from himself. In this case, we protect man from the lure of *Chaos*. While the task before us may be distasteful, we do what we must for the survival of mankind and for the betterment of the Empire."

The hall again erupted in applause, the sentiment striking a chord with the Enclave. His words provided validation to the chosen course. As the room quieted, he continued.

"With a heavy heart, yet a clear conscious, I can confirm that we have eliminated all Arcanists from within the Hierarchy. While not as schooled in the arts of destruction as their military brethren, there were more of them remaining." Sadness reflected in his old eyes as he surveyed the room. "Even with the advantage of surprise, our losses were heavy. Many good men were taken from us, their sacrifice ensuring that *Order* would win the day and would allow mankind to thrive without the threat of *Chaos*."

There was no applause after this announcement. The room was silent as Selbin shuffled to his chair, the man leaning on his cane as he sat. Hardig put his hand on the old man's arm and their eyes locked, resolve reflecting in their mirrored gaze. The Headmaster stood to address the hall.

"We now move to the last area of concern – how to prevent *Chaos* from returning." He smiled. "I'm pleased to report that we've devised a constructive use for divining and will be incorporating it into a new ceremony. Under a newly instituted law, each Empire citizen will undergo a Choosing ceremony shortly after birth where they will be assigned a vocation rune, marking them for life. Above all else, this ceremony will enable the Ministry to identify and quarantine any individuals with latent *Chaos* ability. This will ensure a *Chaos*-free future for man and will do so without the Ministry being forced into any future act of genocide."

The crowd clapped at this, but with far less energy. His mention of genocide struck too close to home, touching on thoughts they had buried deep.

Hardig continued, "This new divining ceremony will not only weed out *Chaos* but will also ensure that the Empire thrives. We'll begin training our Ecclesiast members in this new method immediately."

Another round of applause followed. When it quieted, Hardig spoke once more.

"For the last order of business, I call on Master Hedgewick."

All eyes turned toward Byland as he slid his chair out to stand. Swallowing hard, he absently pushed his spectacles up and addressed the room.

"I have an update." He began in a hoarse voice before coughing. He cleared his throat before trying again. "I have an update regarding the issue of *Chaos* in the histories."

Taking a breath, he continued. "Agents scattered about the continent have been collecting references of *Chaos*. We've received submissions from as far off as Kalimar, although it still lay in ruins from the war. These books, including everything from the Academy Library itself, have been destroyed. In a few generations, nobody will even know that *Chaos* ever existed, let alone how to harness it." The hall erupted in applause again, saving him from speaking any longer.

Hedgewick sat down, his armpits now damp. He pushed his glasses up, his hand shaking as he did so. The Masters near him smiled and clapped him on the back as he smiled weakly in return. A sense of unspoken confidence hung in the air. *Chaos* was gone forever, or so they thought.

Byland Hedgewick knew better.

PART I

GHOSTS OF THE PAST

1

Nothing. Ashland Pym felt nothing. She opened her eyes and shook her head as she turned toward Brock, whose face appeared orange in the flickering light of their campfire.

"You can't remain calm like you do when channeling *Order*. *Chaos* requires emotion," Brock explained. "Fear and anger work best. When you tap into that emotion and close your eyes, you should sense an external force, an energy all around you. Reach for that energy and draw it in until you've absorbed as much as you can. When it feels as if you're about to burst, open your eyes and pour the energy into the rune."

Ashland nodded that she understood. She just needed to do it somehow. Numerous attempts the previous evening had yielded nothing, but it had been a long day of travel and she had been too exhausted to focus. She hoped tonight would be different.

Knowing that she needed raw emotion, Ashland's thoughts drifted back to when Corbin had tried to kill her just a few weeks earlier. In her mind, she relived the experience, her stomach twisting in anxiety as he strapped her to the metal press. Fear and desperation began to overwhelm her as he cranked the press, crushing her head between the plates. She latched onto the fear, her heart pounding as the terror of the memory resurfaced. Shifting her focus, she recognized a frantic energy just beyond her reach. She pushed hard, stretching toward it. Tension held her back for a bit before breaking. A raging torrent of energy poured in, filling her until she feared she would explode.

Her eyes opened to focus on the rune carved into the log. She released the energy and it flowed out like a waterfall. The symbol began to glow an angry red as a wave of exhaustion struck, leaving her feeling chilled and empty. After pulsing, the rune dimmed to black.

"You did it! I knew you could do it." Brock shot her a smile. His smiles made her feel happy, even special. "Now let's see what happens."

With a grunt, he shoved the downed tree off the long log marked with the rune. The tree bounced like a coiled spring when its branches hit the ground. Freed from the weight of the tree, the log began floating upward. Ashland gawked as the log bumped branches and spun when it collided with the trees overhead and rose into the night sky until she lost it beyond the light of their fire.

"That was amazing!" Benny exclaimed. "I wonder how high it'll go."

Brock wrapped his arm around Ashland's shoulder. "See, I knew you could do it."

Ashland smiled at the sense of accomplishment. She glanced around to find Benny, Cameron, and Lars staring into the evening sky.

"I can't believe it's real," Lars turned toward Brock. "This is what you did to the catapult that caused it to launch the ball so far?"

Brock looked over at Lars. "Yes, but that was different. That rune made the catapult more powerful, while the rune Ashland used here simply makes things super light – apparently even lighter than air."

Lars turned toward the night sky again. "Will it keep going all the way to the stars?"

Benny laughed, reaching up to pat his tall friend on the shoulder. "I don't think so, Lars. Those stars are millions of miles away. Plus, the effect won't last long." He paused, looking up at the night sky. "No, it should continue to rise for a while until it's no longer lighter than the air around it. The wind will blow it far from here, and then it will drop as it returns to its normal weight. Hopefully, it doesn't drop on anyone when it comes down." He grinned and bobbed his head at the idea.

A worried expression shone on Brock's face as he turned toward Benny. "I hadn't thought of that. I figured it would be a safe rune for practice, and I never considered that the log might drop quickly as the effect wore off."

"I'm sure it'll be fine, Brock," Ashland said, giving his hand a reassuring squeeze. "It's done now anyway. There's nothing we can do about it."

He leaned in for a kiss, the softness of his lips contrasting the firm muscles of his fit body. When he pulled away, her eyes opened to find his intense green eyes gazing back at her.

"Are we done playing so I can eat?" Cameron asked – his first words since a previous complaint of being hungry an hour earlier.

Benny laughed. "You're always hungry. We'd never get anything done if we always had to feed you first."

Lars laughed heartily and slapped Cam on the back. "He's got you again, Cam."

Benny walked over to the fire and inspected the jackaroo roasting on the spit they had fashioned. With all sides now darkened to a golden brown, the smell of fresh-cooked poultry filled the air.

"You're in luck, Cam. The bird's done," Benny declared with a nod. "Can you grab that end so we can take it off the fire?"

Cam eagerly looped around the fire and gripped the other end of the stick that skewered the large bird. He and Benny hoisted the bird, walking a few feet before leaning it against a tree to cool. The others began claiming seats on the logs surrounding the clearing, eager to eat. Since it was a warm summer night, they kept a comfortable distance from the heat of the fire.

Lars drew his knife and began carving sections of the bird for each of them. Brock brought Ashland a hot slab of meat sandwiched between two halves of a hard roll. With her mouth watering from the savory smell, she took a bite. The meat was juicy and complemented the chewy bread. It was a welcome change after a day of eating trail rations. She was thankful that they had decided to buy the jackaroo before leaving Fallbrandt the day prior.

Ashland glanced around the camp, observing her companions as they ate. All four boys were quiet, focused on their meal until Benny broke the silence.

"If we get an early start tomorrow, we should be in Selbin in time for lunch. After we get a hot meal, I'm going to the temple to surprise my father." He pushed his rectangular spectacles back into place. "Are you guys staying for a day, or are you planning to continue on?"

Ashland glanced toward Brock, who glanced at Cam before answering. "I think we'll just restock and continue west. We still have another two days of travel beyond Selbin before we reach Nor Torin."

"Same here." Lars said. "Heck, I'm not even stopping in Selbin for lunch since my folk's farm is just an hour beyond the city. My ma will have something delicious ready for me."

Lars stared into the night with a smile after the mention of home cooking. Among Brock's friends, the big guy with curly black hair was the most difficult for Ashland to read. While often jovial, he also appeared a bit guarded.

"Can I ask a question, Lars?" Ashland asked. When Lars shrugged, she continued. "You mention your parents owning a farm."

He nodded. "That's right."

"I assume that means that they're marked by *artifex cultor* runes."

He nodded again.

"Are you the only person in your family marked with the rune of Issal?" she asked.

Lars stared at her, silent for a moment before speaking. "My ma had a brother who was marked with an *Order* rune, like me. He also went to the Academy." Lars stared off into the night for a long pause. "I met him once, when I was ten summers old. He looked the part of a hero in his Paladin armor. He let me hold his sword, although I could barely lift it. I wanted to be just like him." Lars stared into the fire. "He died in a skirmish with the Tantarri a year later."

"I'm sorry to hear that, Lars." Brock said and the group fell to silence as they resumed eating.

Ashland searched the faces of her travel companions. She was still getting to know Brock's friends, but she liked what she saw in them so far.

Brock's roommate, Cam, seemed as loyal as a friend could be. The tall blond boy didn't talk much, but he appeared honest and friendly when he did speak. Having an imposing friend like Cam was reassuring. She certainly would not want to be on his bad side, not after seeing him soundly defeat every opponent in the Arena Championship duels.

Other than a similar sense of loyalty, Benny was the opposite of Cam in every way. With a short and soft build, he would intimidate nobody. However, he had already proven to be among the smartest students at the Academy, and his talkative enthusiasm helped to balance Cam's quiet nature.

Ashland noticed how they gravitated toward Brock, happily following his lead. They formed a tight group who supported each other, which made her happy to be among them. She felt a brief pang of regret for not allowing anyone to become close to her until she met Brock. She now knew what she had missed.

Her gaze shifted to Brock, and she found herself again appreciating his handsome appearance. Brock's short brown hair stood tall on his head before tipping to the side. His chiseled face mirrored the lean muscular frame of his body. He glanced at her, smiling when their eyes met. A wave of happiness welled up inside of her. She didn't know how he did it, but Brock had a way of making others like him.

Brock leaned close and spoke quietly. "Now you know how *Chaos* feels and how different it is when compared to *Order*."

Ashland nodded. "Yes. *Order* is so calm and peaceful. *Chaos* is crazy, even frenetic. *Chaos* is like a herd of stampeding horses while *Order* is more like a frozen lake."

Brock laughed. "I think you get it now." His laughter died down and he became serious. "Since you've now made it work, it will become easier. We can practice together, getting better at both *Order* and *Chaos*. Who knows how it might help in the future? After all, if I hadn't been able to use both, we'd both be dead instead of Corbin."

Ashland stared into his eyes, her thoughts mirroring his. The Archon's son took what Brock had considered a petty rivalry and twisted it into a life and death struggle. Trapped beneath a heavy beam and helpless to act, Brock was forced to watch as Corbin crushed Ashland's skull, killing her. Brock's desperate use of *Chaos* to charge himself with a *Power* rune enabled him to break free and kill Corbin. Backed by the *Power* augmentation, he then used his own force of *Order* to bring Ashland back to life. As far as they knew, it was the first time *Order* had brought someone back to life. The unique circumstances made it likely. Her thoughts returned to the present and she resumed her dinner.

By the time she finished eating, the fire had dwindled to orange coals. Exhausted from a day of travel, the group spread out around the fire to find a comfortable spot to sleep, although comfort was an overly generous term when sleeping on the ground.

Resting her head on Brock's chest, she snuggled up to his neck. Typical of when she was near him, everything felt right in the world. It was as if she saw life through a different set of eyes, helping to heal the scars of her past. She might never forget them, but she could overcome them.

With her head rising and falling with the breath filling his lungs, she drifted asleep.

2

Benedict Hedgewick waved to his friends, smiling as they waved back before turning toward the gravel road ahead. With their backs facing him, he noted how Cam's head towered above Brock's and Ashland's by a solid foot, making the other two appear smaller than they were. At six and a half feet, Cam's muscular frame struck an imposing image. When the trio rounded a bend, the woods surrounding the road obscured them from Benny's view.

Benny's gaze shifted to look out over the lake. Large enough that he couldn't see the far shore across the widest parts, Lake Selbin was an intrinsic part of his childhood. Over the years, he had caught his fair share of fish from its shores. On hot summer days, he and Jimmy would find refuge in those cool waters, where they would swim and play as if they didn't have a care in the world. He tried not to think about Jimmy too often. Memories of his childhood were mostly pleasant, but such thoughts often led back to the night Jimmy died. Although six years had passed, he missed his friend dearly and the pain resurfaced upon thinking of him. Benny closed his eyes and listened to the rhythmic sound of the waves lapping against the shore. After finding a bit of peace, he opened them and released a sigh.

Returning to Selbin was bittersweet. So many positive memories overshadowed by a singular horrible event. It was unfair that one small mistake could forever alter his life and the lives of those he loved. Leaving for the Academy had allowed him to bury the pain and live without the ghosts of the past for almost a year. With his return to Selbin, those ghosts began to creep back into his consciousness.

Shaking his head to clear it, he turned and began making his way through town. As he strolled the busy gravel streets, he took comfort in the familiar sights around him. Shop owners waved as he passed. The counting house where he had worked for five years appeared the same as ever, its weathered wooden façade overdue for a fresh coat of green paint. After passing the counting house, the imposing building looming over the road ahead caught his attention.

The Selbin Temple was among the few buildings not made of wood. Built upon a hill, the pale brick structure towered over the homes and shops in the area. Benny ascended the stone steps and entered the cool environs of the temple.

After passing beneath the arch of the open doorway, he stopped to observe the empty rows of benches encircling the glow-stone altar at the center. Colored beams of sunlight filtered through the stained-glass panels in the small domed ceiling high above. He circled the room toward a side door.

"Benedict?" a voice called from behind. "Is that you?"

Benny turned, a grin splitting his face when he recognized the man.

"Hi, Minister Nassim. I'm back from the Academy."

As the man approached, a smile emerged from the depths of his thick white beard. "I noticed the apprentice cloak," Nassim said. "Congratulations."

Benny nodded in reply. "Yes. You're looking at the Academy's newest apprentice Engineer."

The minister nodded. "As I expected. You were always too clever for your own good. Perhaps your cleverness can now be properly channeled."

Benny's smile faltered as Nassim reminded him of what his cleverness had done. Those thoughts made him think of his father.

"Is he here?" Benny knew he didn't need to say who *he* was.

"Yes." Nassim's face showed concern. "He's always here. Never leaves."

"How is he?" Benny asked, afraid of the answer.

"Oh, he has his bad days, but they're now rare. I'm sure he'll be happy to see you." The old man's tone sounded reassuring.

"I suppose he's in his apartment then?" Benny asked.

The minister nodded. "He usually is. Best of luck, Benedict."

Benny turned to pass through the side door, entering the multi-level building attached to the temple. He knocked on one of the two doors on the main level. With his stomach aflutter, he waited for it to open. After a minute, he heard the bolt slide and saw the knob turn.

The door opened to reveal what remained of his father. Patches of sparse hair grew here and there on the man's otherwise bald head. His good eye focused on Benny but the clouded one stared somewhere beyond. The rippled leather-like skin covering half of his head appeared just as bad as Benny remembered. As he recognized Benny, half of the man's mouth broke into a smile while the other half barely moved.

Benny's father held his arm out. Benny shuffled in and hugged him, closing his eyes as he imagined his father from before the accident. After a moment, he released his arms and wiped the tears from his eyes.

His father nodded. "I'm so glad you came back for summer break. It's good to see you in an apprentice cloak, too. Congratulations."

Benny smiled. "Thanks Pa. I made apprentice Engineer."

"I knew you would, son. You're the smartest person I know." He awkwardly shuffled backward. "Come in so we can sit and have a chat."

Limping as he walked, the man squeezed the handle on his wooden leg with each step. The artificial limb that Benny had invented three years prior still appeared to function as intended. With the handle attached to the stump of thigh remaining, a squeeze of his fist triggered an actuator that flexed his fake knee with each step. He shuffled across the room to his chair, lowering himself into it. Benny followed and took a seat on the adjacent sofa.

"I brought some gold, Pa."

Benny extended his hand toward his father, who stared at the pouch dangling from it. After a long moment, the man spoke.

"Benny, the past is the past. Put it away and leave it there. You don't owe me anything." His father's functional eye locked with Benny's gaze. "I have everything I need here. This apartment is paid for, you saw to that. I'm still useful enough to be an asset to the temple, so they feed me. I'm content with my life now. I miss your mother as much as you do, but

I've made my peace with it. When my time here ends and Issal takes me, I'll join her. Until then, I'm going to continue living the best I can."

His father leaned forward and pushed Benny's outstretched hand back toward him. "Keep the gold, Benny. Use it to build a life for yourself. You've only seen twenty-two summers. While you may be a bit old for an apprentice at the Academy, you're quite young in the scheme of the world. Most of your life lies before you. Do what you can with it. I wish you to be happy, and your mother would've wanted the same. The time for guilt has passed, Benny. Embrace life and make it your own."

With tears in his eyes, Benny nodded. He wanted to leave the past behind, but the screams remained in his memory.

3

"There it is," Cam smiled as he gazed toward the city below. "Nor Torin."

Brock's eyes drank in the beautiful vista as they descended the hill toward Cam's hometown. The sun hovered at the western horizon, painting the clouds orange and red above the dark ocean waters beyond the brick walls surrounding the city. With the tall trees surrounding it, Brock wouldn't have even been able to see the city if not for the elevated height of the approaching road. When he commented about the size of the trees, Cam mentioned the imposing groves that grew south of the Torinus River, called *The Red Towers* due to the color of the wood and incredible height of the trees. Cam explained that some trees had trunks wider than most roads. Brock found it difficult to believe, but Ashland confirmed it, having seen them herself as a child.

Brock and Ashland followed Cam into the city as the trio passed through the eastern gate and walked down busy streets lined with shops, inns, and vendor carts that reminded Brock of Kantar. Some vendors were packing their carts as they finished the day's business before heading home, while citizens on foot milled about, carrying bags of goods as they avoided the occasional horse or wagon passing by.

Upon reaching the heart of the city, they came upon a brick wall surrounding the citadel. The Nor Torin Citadel was a squat, blocky building built of a dark stone, making it a stark contrast to the pale stone and towering construction of the Kantar Citadel.

They looped around the south side of the citadel wall to circumvent the restricted area. After a quarter mile, the wall ended and the street turned north. Turning at the fountain outside the western citadel gate, they resumed their journey and the downhill slope increased as the road descended toward the docks. While scanning the view of the harbor, Brock noticed something odd south of the river.

"Cam, what's that?" he asked, pointing south.

Cam turned to where Brock pointed. "Those are the shipyards. Most of the ships on the west coast were built in those yards."

Several sizeable structures occupied the shipyard, each of which cradled a partially built hull. Men scurried about the area, carrying lumber and scaling the scaffolding that surrounded the cradles.

As the city's western wall came into view, Cam led them down a side street and up a short flight of stairs that led to a three-story house. Cam opened the door and stepped inside.

"Hello? It's Cam! Is anyone home?"

A sitting room with a brick fireplace waited just inside the entryway. As they entered the room, the smell of spiced sausage and boiled cabbage teased Brock's senses and left his stomach growling. A tall blond woman came around the corner, wiping her hands on the tan apron she wore. Her face lit up when she saw Cam.

"Cameron! You're back!" She cried as she embraced him in a hug.

"Yeah, but just for summer break," Cam's voice sounded muffled by her hug. "School starts again soon, so we need to leave in twelve days."

Brock smiled when watching the emotional reunion of mother and son. Amazingly, the woman didn't look small next to Cam, which was rare for a female. She released her hug but kept her hands on Cam's arms as she stood back to look at him.

"I see an apprentice cloak. You make us proud." She nodded before her smile became a frown. "But you look as if you're wilting away, Cam. Haven't they been feeding you?"

Cam smiled. "I keep telling them that I'm hungry."

Brock grinned. "I can vouch for Cam, Mrs. DeSanus. He doesn't talk much, but he's sure to let others know when he's hungry,"

The woman's eyes glanced from Brock to Ashland before returning to her son. "Cam, are these two your friends?"

Cam nodded, "Yes."

Brock chuckled at Cam's typically understated response. "I'm Brock, Cam's roommate." He extended a hand toward her. "And this is my girlfriend, Ashland."

Cam's mother ignored his hand, instead bending to give Brock a hug. "It's wonderful to meet you, Brock. Please call me Janis." Releasing him, she turned to give Ashland a hug. "Hello, my dear."

Ashland responded as the taller woman released her. "Thank you so much for allowing us stay with you for summer break."

With an arched brow, Janis tilted her head in question. When he shrugged, she turned to address Ashland again.

"We're happy to have you, but we are a bit tight on space. Ashland can sleep on the third floor in Cam's old room." Janis turned toward Cam. "You and Brock will have to squeeze in with your brothers. It will be crowded but it's only for twelve days, so I think you'll survive."

Cam nodded in response.

The door opened, and a large man entered. Brock had to do a double take, glancing at his roommate before his eyes returned to focus on the newcomer. If the man's hair had been a bit lighter, he could have been Cam's older, slightly heavier twin.

The man's face broke into a grin. "Cam!"

He gave Cam a bear hug, thumping him on the back soundly before letting go. "Congratulations on making apprentice." He glanced toward Brock and Ashland. "And who are these two?"

Not waiting for Cam to respond, Brock held his hand out to the man for an introduction.

"I'm Brock, and this is Ashland."

"Pleasant to meet you," the man said as he shook their hands. "I'm Cameron's Father, Cassius." He then hugged Janis as he sniffed the air. "Dinner smells wonderful. I'm starving."

She smiled and waved for them to follow. "Dinner's ready. Come and eat before the boys get home and eat it all."

They followed Janis into the kitchen, where a table with six chairs occupied the middle of the room. Janis circled the table to approach the fireplace, where he donned a pair of heavy gloves and removed the kettle from the flames.

"Cam, please run upstairs and grab an extra chair for your friends," she said as she set the kettle on a small stone table.

Cam ran upstairs, while Janis scooped wet cabbage from the kettle into a bowl. As she prepared the food, Cassius pulled three plates from a shelf and placed them on the table to join the four already residing there. By the time Cam was back with the chair, seven places were set. A bowl of cooked cabbage and a plate of sausages waited in the center beside a full loaf of bread.

"Please sit and eat." Janis said as she removed her gloves.

They heard the front door open, followed by the sound of two male voices arguing.

"…telling you that I unloaded far more than you did today."

"As usual, you're dreaming if you think you did more work than me, Jake."

Two young men came around the corner into the kitchen. Brock couldn't believe it. They were both even bigger than Cam.

"Cam! Come here, Puppy!" One of them said, closing the gap to give Cameron a bear hug.

The other was right behind him. "Hiya Cam!" His hug lifted Cam right off the floor.

Despite their brown hair and green eyes, the two young men were obviously Cam's older brothers. Their faces appeared identical to each other and were close matches to Cam's, but with a *laboris* rune rather than the Order rune that marked the rest of the family. The twins both stood a bit taller than Cam and were each at least fifty pounds heavier. The five massive bodies of Cameron's family crowding the kitchen made the room seem smaller than it actually was.

"Puppy?" Brock asked.

Cam's brother nodded, smiling. "When Cam was little, he used to follow us around like a lost puppy. The name just kind of stuck."

"That's enough, boys. Leave your brother be for now. Can't you see that he's hungry from his journey?" Janis said, taking control of the situation. "Everyone grab a chair and let's eat."

Bodies scrambled around the table as they all took seats. With food piled high onto plates, they all dug in. Brock smiled, noting how the amount of food on both his and Ashland's plates paled in comparison to the others.

The conversation during dinner was light and sporadic. Once the food was gone, the chatter increased with Cameron's brothers, Jake and Julius, doing much of the talking as they rattled on about their day of working at the docks. Here and there, they would take a playful jab at Cam, who would simply shrug it off.

About an hour after nightfall, Cam's father declared it time for bed and they dispersed. Cam led Brock and Ashland to the small bedroom on the third floor. Brock bid her goodnight and followed Cam back down the stairs. Within Julius and Jake's room, two pallets on the floor filled the gap between their beds.

"It looks like our Puppy has come back to sleep at the foot of our beds again, hey Jake?" Julius said, with a chuckle.

Jake nodded. "It sure looks that way. If he's good, maybe we'll get him a treat too."

Cam didn't respond, but his face darkened and his lips turned down at the edges. He lay down on one of the pallets, drew the blanket up to his chin, and closed his eyes. Brock followed suit and slid into his makeshift bed. Once everyone was settled, Jake covered the glowlamp and everyone fell quiet. As Brock rested on the pallet, he thought about the evening, sensing an underlying tension beneath the apparent friendly surface.

4

Cameron DeSanus found himself unable to sleep. Anxious to leave and return to the school, he tossed and turned and finally gave up when he noticed that night had given itself to twilight through the curtain-covered window.

After leaving home a year prior, his outlook and confidence had slowly, yet surely changed – expanding as he evolved as a person. He now longed to be back at the school. Until his return to Nor Torin, he hadn't truly recognized how uncomfortable it was to be with his family.

On the outside, his brothers appeared jovial and their jokes harmless, but there was always an unspoken tension. The two older boys found subtle ways to put Cam down, making him feel as if he were less than he was. Over the past twelve days, he felt himself drawing inward – a turtle retreating into its shell.

Cam's father made it worse. Marked with an *Order* rune, Cam always knew he was destined to follow in Cassius' footsteps. Unfortunately, those were huge shoes to fill and Cam wondered if he'd ever measure up to the man he resembled. Leaving Nor Torin was the only way to put it all behind him.

Eager to leave, Cam slipped out of bed, packed his things, and found himself downstairs before everyone but his mother. When he walked into the kitchen, she greeted him as she pulled a heavy pan from the fire.

"Good morning, dear," she said as he entered the kitchen. "Breakfast is ready if you're hungry."

"Thanks, Ma."

Cam held his plate out as she scraped eggs and a couple sausages onto it. He sat at the table and began eating when his father walked in.

Cassius appeared strapping in his leather uniform. As captain of the elite guard for the city prelate, he certainly looked the part. The man gave his wife a kiss before he filled a plate with food and joined Cam at the table. The two sat in silence, eating while Janis prepared another batch of eggs.

Cam stared at his plate as he gathered his courage. "I'm leaving today, Pa. We have to get back to the Academy."

His father looked up from his plate, his eyes meeting Cam's briefly before Cam lowered his.

"I expected you'd be leaving any day now. The Academy asks a lot of you, but you'll be a better man for it." Cassius nodded. "You'll find yourself a captain in the Holy Army before you know it."

Cam shrugged. The subject made him uncomfortable.

The rumble of feet descending the stairs saved him from having to speak. He prayed that it was Brock and Ashland but found it to be his brothers instead.

"You're up early, Puppy," Jake said.

Julius followed him in. "We were surprised when we woke and you were out of bed."

Cam nodded. "We're leaving today so I wanted to have a solid breakfast before an early start."

His brothers nodded in silence, grabbed plates, and began piling food on. Cam assumed that they wanted him gone as badly as he wanted to leave.

The room fell quiet as Cam's brothers shoveled food into their mouths as if they were on a mission. With plates soon empty and bellies full, Jake and Julius stood to leave.

"Bye, Cam. Have a good trip back to school." Julius said.

Jake waved, "Bye, Cam."

They headed out the door, off to work.

Cassius stood and gave Janis a kiss. "Bye, dear. I may be home a bit late. Prelate Yaris is holding court today."

"I'll be sure to save some dinner for you.".

Cam stood to say farewell to his father. Cassius unstrapped the belt holding his longsword and held it out toward Cam.

"What's this?" Cam asked.

"It's your birthright, Son. I want you to have it."

"I can't take your sword, Pa. You need it for your job," Cam replied hesitantly.

"No. I need *a* sword for my job. I'll get another from the citadel armory." His father pushed the sword belt against Cam's chest until Cam grabbed it. "This sword is meant for greater things. You'll need it more than I will." Cassius embraced Cam, thumping him on the back. "Keep up the good work, Cam. We know you'll make us proud."

Cam nodded, not knowing what to say. The sword belt remained clutched to his chest as the sheathed weapon dangled to his thighs. His father nodded to him and turned to leave. With turmoil causing his stomach to churn, his gaze followed the man's back as he slipped out the door. Cam examined the sword in his hand, feeling thankful that it had been given to him after his brothers had left. Worth more than his parent's house, the famous weapon was now his to carry. But was it a prize or a burden?

Although Nor Torin was fading into the distance behind them, Cam found his thoughts to be troubled. He had always known that he was destined to be a paladin, but it never bothered him much before. Now he found himself trapped, as if life were squeezing all the choices out and forcing him to follow a narrow path of someone else's making.

"Cam?" Brock's voice broke the silence. "Can I ask you a personal question?"

Cam glanced over and gave the smallest of nods.

"I sense that something has been bothering you since we first arrived at Nor Torin. You've been even quieter than normal, and you seem… troubled." Brock turned toward Cam. "What is it?"

Cam walked in silence for a bit before responding, trying to find the words.

"I hoped that things would be better, that being away for a year would help." He shook his head. "But it's just the same as always."

"Is it your brothers?" Brock asked. "They pick on you quite a bit."

"That's part of it," Cam nodded. "They aren't happy. They think they should be Paladins. They're probably right, but their runes say otherwise."

Brock nodded. "So, they're jealous of you. They want to be in your shoes, but they're stuck working at the docks instead."

Cameron nodded.

Brock continued. "They pick on you to compensate for the feelings they're hiding. They try to bring you down rather than support you."

Cam nodded again.

After a silent moment, Brock spoke again. "There's something else, isn't there?"

Cam shrugged.

"It has something to do with your father?" Brock asked.

Cam nodded.

"What is it? He appears to support you and is clearly proud of you."

"Exactly. That's the problem," Cam replied.

Brock's brow furrowed. "Why?"

"He's always been that way toward me. However, he doesn't give my brothers the time of day."

"He favors you then." Brock nodded. "I expect that compounds their jealousy, and they take it out on you like it's your fault."

"To make matters worse, he gave me his sword." Cam tapped on the hilt at his waist.

"I was wondering about the longsword. I assume it's an exceptional weapon then?" Brock asked.

Cam sighed. "My father was in the Holy Army for fourteen years, and he made a name for himself. Paladins don't have to wait long to hear his name and stories of his heroics. They often refer to him as the model that new paladins are to emulate. He won this sword in a duel in Sol Polis, against a man previously named the best swordsman in the world. The sword is a famous weapon, hundreds of years old."

After a moment of consideration, Brock asked, "Are you afraid that you won't measure up to your father?"

Cam's eyes remained downcast as he walked, unsure of how to respond.

"Cam, you were the best fighter in the whole school in your first year. By the time you become a master paladin, you'll surely be among the best ever," Brock sounded earnest. "Regardless, I think you should focus on being yourself. Make your own name on your own terms. Don't try to be your father. It seems like an empty pursuit to me. How will you ever be happy trying to be someone you're not?"

Cam shrugged. He wanted to accept Brock's advice, but his path felt so narrow. He didn't know which scared him more, stumbling from the path or continuing down it to discover where it led.

5

Despite a long day of travel, the scenery slid past Ashland as she struggled with her looming decision. She had put it aside on their way to Nor Torin, knowing they'd be passing this way on the return trip. About an hour before sunset, they neared the road to Vallerton, and she found herself forced to make a choice. Realizing that she didn't know when she would come this way again, she summoned her resolve and broke the silence.

"Would it be alright if we took a little detour?"

Brock turned toward her. "What is it? You've been distracted all day."

She shrugged but wasn't surprised. They had only been together for half a year, but he knew her too well.

"There's a farm I need to visit, about an hour south of here."

Brock glanced at Cam, who shrugged. He then turned back toward her. "That should work out fine. Provided we get an early start, we should still reach Selbin mid-day tomorrow to meet Lars and Benny. However, we better hurry since night will fall soon."

Without even asking why, Brock and Cam had accepted her request. She smiled, feeling thankful for their understanding.

They turned south toward Vallerton, and continued in silence. Over the next hour, the thick trees gradually gave way to rolling fields surrounded by railed fencing. Herds of cattle and sheep feasted upon the long grass that grew there. Through the dim light of dusk, Ashland spotted a cluster of buildings across an open field. As they neared the complex, her anxiety steadily increased, twisting her insides. By the time they reached the driveway, her stomach was a knot.

As she walked toward the farmhouse, a man's voice called out.

"Can I help you?"

She turned to find a man with a thick mustache and a wide-brimmed hat, leading a horse toward a brown barn.

"Yes." Ashland angled toward the man. "I'm looking for a couple who works here. Their names are Landon and Ashley."

The man nodded. "Yes, they're working in the fields, but they should be back anytime."

She bit her lip as her stomach fluttered. "Is there somewhere we can wait? I have something important to tell them."

The man's brow furrowed and he stood in silent consideration before responding.

"I suppose you could wait in the shed. You'll find it right behind the barn."

"Thank you, sir." Ashland said before leading the way around the building.

The shed was a tiny dilapidated construction, badly in need of repair. A knock on the door went unanswered, so Ashland tested the handle and found it unlocked. Opening the door, she entered a shed that was smaller than her room at the Academy. The room seemed to shrink even further when Brock and Cameron entered, their bodies crowding the meager open space not taken by the table, two benches, and bed that furnished the tiny building.

Not speaking, they silently observed the cramped surroundings. The summer heat within the small room left the air stuffy and Ashland thankful that she wore light clothing.

Approaching footsteps drew her eyes to the door. An extended moment of anxiety stretched as Ashland waited for it to open. The knob turned, and her heart caught in her throat when she saw two familiar faces enter the room.

"Oh, Ashland!" Her mother cried as she embraced Ashland with a tight hug.

Her father wrapped his arms about both women and the three shed tears in silence. After a minute, they separated and Ashland wiped her eyes dry.

"I'm so happy that you're still alive." Ashland said. "I feared that something had happened, that I wouldn't get to see you."

Ashley glanced down at Landon's leg.

"What is it? Did something happen to your leg, father?" she asked.

Landon nodded. "A bull got me 'bout a year back. Busted my knee good, and now it doesn't work so well." He shrugged. "I get by, though."

Ashland took a breath, and grabbed her father's hand. Closing her eyes, she found her center, her source of Order. Embracing the cool calmness, she extended herself to find the Order within him. Wrapped within the cool blue serenity was a pulsing red wrongness – torn ligaments that had never healed. She grabbed ahold of his force of Order and coaxed it to heal the torn tissue. In her mind's eye, she witnessed the tissue reforming, melding back together.

She opened her eyes as her father gasped for air and a shiver racked his body. With wide eyes, he puffed air to regain his breath. He looked at his leg in wonder, bending it to test it.

"That's amazing." He stared down at the leg with an edge of awe in his voice. "It doesn't hurt at all." His eyes met hers. "So, you did it? You're a student at the Academy?"

She smiled. "Yes, Pa. I've been training there for two years now. In one more, I'll be a master ecclesiast – a healer."

With moisture in her eyes, Ashley gripped Ashland's hands. "My daughter, a healer in the Ministry." Smiling, she wrapped her arms around Ashland again.

When her mother released her, Ashland glanced at Brock and Cam. They both had their eyes cast down, obviously feeling uncomfortable. She realized that she forgot to introduce the boys.

"Mother, Father. This is my boyfriend, Brock." Ashland grabbed his hand to pull him closer.

"Pleased to meet you, Mr. Pym, Mrs. Pym." Brock held his hand out.

Ashland's mother pushed his outstretched hand aside embraced Brock with a hug.

"Pym?" Landon asked.

"Um…sorry Pa. Pym's my last name at the school," she shrugged.

Her father nodded and shook Brock's hand once he escaped Ashley's embrace.

"And this is Cam, Brock's roommate at the school." Ashland said, completing her introductions.

"Please, sit." Her mother said, gesturing to the small table.

Brock, Cameron, and Ashland squeezed on a bench at one side of the table. Her mother and father sat on the other side.

"Are you hungry?" Ashley asked.

"Yes, ma'am."

Ashland and Brock laughed. Those were the first words they'd heard from Cam in hours.

Ashland pulled a rogue strand of hay from her shirt – remnants from a night of sleeping in the barn loft. While better than sleeping on the ground, the hay was itchy and made her sneeze. She turned and waved one last time as her parents mirrored the motion. Leaving them again had been difficult, emotional.

"How long has it been?" Brock asked as she caught up to him.

"What? How long?"

Brock nodded as he grabbed her hand. "Since you've seen them. Obviously, it's been a long time."

Ashland's mind cast back into her past, before her life changed. She recalled fond memories of a childhood filled with love, despite their constant battle with poverty. Her voice was quiet when she spoke.

"I haven't seen them since I was ten, when I left to train for the Academy."

"Eight years?" Brock asked. When she nodded, he gave her hand a squeeze. "It must have been difficult."

She bit her lip as she considered her response. "The first years were… particularly hard. Things got a little better when I arrived at the Academy. Then, you showed up last year and things have been far better ever since."

She flashed him a smile. He smiled back, squeezing her hand again.

"I noticed that they're Unchosen," he said. "How did they save enough to help you, to get you in?"

She realized that Brock was being careful not to be too specific, since Cam was with them. Other than Tipper, nobody except Ashland knew that Brock was Unchosen, marked with the fake rune that he used to get into the Academy. Besides Brock, only Ashland's parents knew the truth about her.

Ashland walked in quiet and stared at the gravel road as she sought for the right words. The truth was a bitter thing sometimes, but it also gave her the life she now had at the Academy – her life with Brock.

"Remember the man we saw last night? The one with the horse?" She glanced at Brock, who nodded in response. "He runs the ranch, working for a wealthy man who lives in Selbin. The man in Selbin…owns my parents."

Brock's brow furrowed. "Owns? What do you mean *owns them*?"

She sighed. "To get the gold required, they agreed to ten years of indentured servitude."

Cam, who had been listening quietly, spoke. "Indentured what?"

"Servitude. It's like selling yourself to become a slave until you pay off a debt." Ashland felt a pang of guilt when she thought of their sacrifice. "The landowner agreed to give my parents the gold if they agreed to work for him from dawn until dusk for ten years. In return, he agreed to give them food, water, and shelter. As you can tell, that equates to the bare minimum needed to survive."

Ashland knew that her parents had forfeited their own hopes and dreams so she could pursue hers, to give her a better life. Although she felt guilty about it, she couldn't blame them. She wouldn't want her child stuck in that life either. It's why she refused to allow anything to come between her and success. She couldn't let them down like that, not after what they had done to ensure her future.

6

Benny gritted his teeth and tightened the last nut. With a grin, he stood back to admire his work, basking in the familiar satisfaction of having created something. He couldn't wait to show his father.

He grabbed the handles and rolled the contraption out of the stable, across the yard, and straight to the ramp he had installed the previous week. With a grunt, he pushed it up the ramp to the back door of the temple apartments. Once inside, he went directly to the second door and opened it.

His father looked up from his book and removed his reading spectacles. The man sat upright in the chair, his good eye squinting at Benny.

"What's this?" His father asked.

"This is my latest invention," Pride rang in Benny's voice. "It'll make it easy for you to get around town."

"Around town? You mean go out?"

Benny sat on the sofa beside his father's chair. "Yes, Pa. You need to get out and live life. I realize that your leg makes it difficult to get around, so I made this so for you."

Turning his head, Benny gazed at his creation. After purchasing a chair identical to the one his father now sat on, he added two wheels on a shortened wagon axle and two smaller wheels on swivels to the front. The result was a padded wooden chair on wheels.

His father stood, rising slowly. Grunting with each step of his fake leg, he crossed the room to inspect the contraption. When he drew close, he rocked it back and forth to test the wheels. He shuffled into position and sat in the chair, causing it to roll backwards with the momentum.

"You can use the rails I added to the wheels to turn them." Benny said, rising to stand near his father.

The man put his hands on the rails, causing the chair to roll when he tested them. Pushing on one wheel while holding the other still, he was able to make it spin. Benny's father looked toward him, the normal side of his face breaking into a grin.

"I like it, Benny."

Benny's heart soared as tears clouded his vision. He wiped the moisture from his eyes and cleared his throat.

"I'm glad you like it, Pa," he said. "It's what I've been working on since I returned to Selbin."

"I was wondering what you were up to," his father said. "I should've known it was another crazy invention."

Benny chuckled and gave his father a sad smile. "I'm sorry Pa, but I have to leave. I'm to meet my friends at Alfred's for lunch before we set off toward Fallbrandt."

The man nodded. "Don't worry about it, Son. I'm glad that you came to visit, but you have to make your own life now. Live it well."

Benny bent to hug his father. When he stood, he wiped tears away before pushing his spectacles back in place.

"Take care, Son. Be your own man, but be the best man you can be."

Benny nodded. "Thanks Pa. You take care too. Make sure you get out and live life. Don't just stay cooped up in here."

His father nodded. "You have a deal."

Benny smiled and turned toward the door. After grabbing the pack from the hook on the wall, he shot one last look back in the room and met his father's good eye before he pulled the door closed. He stopped outside the door and collected himself before exiting the building.

As he crossed town, he thought about the visit. His father was right. Benny needed to stop allowing the past to affect him. It was time move on – time to live for the future.

The familiar sights he passed seemed happier and appeared brighter than before. The old counting house was a pleasant place to work, not just the place where he'd earned enough coin to pay for his father's apartment. The people he passed smiled and waved. Rather than seeing the boy who had caused the death of his mother and best friend, he now believed that they just saw one of their own, returned to visit.

When Alfred's Inn came into view, Benny found himself whistling a happy tune. The sun overhead made the day cheery, while the cool breeze off the lake moderated the midday heat.

He entered the inn, his gaze scanning the place for familiar faces. There were many, mostly town-folk he'd seen countless times over the years. Among them, he found his new friends and approached their table.

"Hi, guys. You made it," Benny said with a grin.

"Hi, Benny," Brock replied. "We were wondering if you were coming."

Benny's grin widened. "Of course I'm coming. I have to return to the Academy. My future awaits."

7

The surrounding trees parted to reveal buildings clustered along the road ahead. As the group entered town, the road came to an intersection, and they turned north. Glancing east, Brock was able at catch brief glimpses of the lake between the buildings. A boy, just a few years younger than Brock, ran from glowlamp to glowlamp, activating them in the dim light of dusk. People completing their business for the day milled about on the streets of Fallbrandt. A sign depicting a headless woman with her arms spread wide came into view, prompting a spike of anticipation within Brock. The miles he and the others had traveled made their last visit to The Quiet Woman seem far longer than twenty-two days. As a result, he found his pace quickening as he approached the inn and led the others inside.

The dining room was busy, the tables filled with local women. Six men occupied one rogue table in a corner, making them the only men in the room other than the waiter and bartender. Pausing as he scanned the room for an open table, Brock found no openings and headed for the bar.

"Hi, James," Brock said as he sat on a stool.

The bartender spun around and flashed a smile, his teeth perfect and almost too white. "Hi, Brock. Back from your trip to Nor Torin already?"

"Yep. We're back, and we're hungry. We haven't missed dinner, have we?" Brock asked as Ashland grabbed the stool to his left.

James shook his head. "No. You're just in time. Garret and Tipper should be bringing it out any minute."

"Great. I'm starving," Benny grabbed the stool to Brock's right and thumbed toward Cameron. "And don't even get this one started about food."

As Cam took his seat, Lars laughed and clapped him on the back. "He's got you again, DeSanus."

James quickly wiped the bar clean. "I assume you're all thirsty as well. Could you go for some wine?"

Brock nodded. "Yes please. Wine for everyone."

James nodded and stepped away as Brock turned to survey the room.

Dory sat at her usual table, entertaining friends and patrons. Her gaze shifted toward Brock, showing instant recognition. Rising to her feet, the curvy inn owner weaved her way through the crowd, her long brown hair framing the inviting smile on her handsome face.

"I'm happy to see you, Brock," She leaned in for a hug, releasing Brock before turning her attention to Ashland. "I'm glad you're back safe and sound, dear."

"It's great to be back, Dory."

"Will you be staying the night?" Dory asked.

Brock nodded. "We'll need two rooms, and we will leave tomorrow after breakfast."

Dory smiled. "Wonderful. Please do stop by and say hello to the ladies after you've eaten."

"I will," Brock replied.

She glanced toward the kitchen. "Ah, Tipper and Garrett are bringing the food out."

When he turned toward the bar, Brock found a full glass of red wine waiting. Looking toward the kitchen, he saw James emerge with a tray of full plates. The bartender looped behind the bar and delivered a plate to each of them. The steaming meat pie smelled delicious.

The group ate in silence, eager to consume the hot meal after spending the past two nights eating trail rations. As they finished eating, Tipper slipped behind the bar to join James.

"Hi, Brock," Tipper said, sporting a toothy grin.

"Hi, Tip." Brock grinned back at his friend. "Are you working all night?"

Tipper nodded. "Yeah. Among other things, I'll have to help clear the tables and then wash the dishes. I had a small break so I thought I'd come say hello."

Brock shrugged. "I guess we'll have to catch up in the morning, then. It won't be a late night for us. We're exhausted."

Tipper nodded, shifting his focus. "Hi, Ashland. Are you taking care of Brock? He'd likely kill himself without us watching out for him."

She smiled. "Yes, Tipper. I'm sure he'd find a way to blow himself up if we weren't around."

"Wait a minute. I'm not that bad," Brock said, laughing.

Tipper grinned as he grabbed their empty plates. "So you say, Brock."

As Tipper spun to return to the kitchen, Cam reached out and grabbed his arm. The thin blond boy raised an eyebrow. "Do you need something, Cam?"

Cameron nodded. "I'm still hungry."

"Ah, ha!" Lars laughed, smacking Cam on the back as Cam grinned sheepishly.

The thick pines of the surrounding forest retained the chill of the prior evening and kept the road shaded from the morning sun. Brock put an arm around Ashland and pulled her close as they walked north.

"It was great to see Tipper and Libby again." Ashland said.

"Yeah." Brock agreed, reflecting on the conversation with the couple over breakfast. "They've become quite close. I wouldn't be surprised if they declared themselves married sometime soon."

"What do you mean, *declared* married?" Lars asked.

"They're both Unchosen, Lars. The law won't allow them to truly get married, at least not by the Ministry," Ashland replied. "The most they can do is pledge themselves to each other and declare themselves husband and wife, even though the Empire will never acknowledge it."

"I don't get it." Confusion was apparent on Lars' face. "I knew that Unchosen were treated differently but that doesn't seem right."

"It isn't right," Brock agreed. "They have just as much right to live their lives as anyone else. Somehow, it needs to change."

Benny turned toward Brock. "You're right, Brock. Maybe when we're Masters, we can do something to change how things work."

Lars snorted. "You're about as likely to change the seasons. The Empire's been around a long time now. How can we hope to change things that have been the same for so long?"

"You never know, Lars," Brock replied. "Eventually, it has to change. Maybe it'll be in our lifetime."

Ashland leaned into Brock and squeezed with the arm she had about his waist. "I hope so."

Brock smiled and gave her a quick kiss on the cheek

The morning suddenly became brighter, causing him to look ahead. The forest opened to reveal an expansive lawn, stretching out before them. Two miles long and nearly as wide, the lawn boasted a wall of thick pines that surrounded fields of knee-high yellowed grass. A row of trees lined the road, casting long shadows away from the morning sun positioned between two eastern peaks. A massive structure loomed at the far end of the field. Although the building had been Brock's home for a year, he was still learning new things about it.

Consisting of many smaller buildings connected together, the Academy had a disjointed appearance. The long wings housing the students stretched outward from the core, making the building appear as if it were reaching out to hug the lawn before it.

Brock glanced to the east, toward the empty competition field. The view reminded him of the Catapult Challenge from the previous fall and the infamous launch their catapult had made. He turned his gaze on the tower that terminated the Girls' Wing at the western end of the school – a tower that stood over two miles from the catapult launch point. Again, he relived the amazement that the catapult had launched a heavy metal ball that far. Although unaware of what he had done at the time, he now knew that he had used Chaos to charge a *Power* rune that was carved into the siege engine. His thoughts drifted, reflecting on how the fateful incident had led them to find the book on *Chaos* hidden in the walls of the damaged tower. If he had never found the book, he would not have learned what *Chaos* was or how to harness it. Without his ability to wield *Chaos*, he and Ashland would now be dead at the hands of Corbin Ringholdt.

His gaze found Ashland and a stream of joy bubbled inside when she smiled back. He was routinely amazed that he had somehow earned the attention of this amazing girl. The connection they had was something deep, something special. *I love you,* he sent. She smiled. *I love you too,* she replied in his head. Interesting. *What else can I do with telepathy?* Brock wondered. He closed his eyes and pushed some very inappropriate thoughts toward Ashland.

Hearing her gasp, he opened his eyes to find her mouth hanging open, shock apparent in her eyes. She swatted him.

"You're so bad, Brock Talenz," she said, laughing.

He chuckled. *Yes, this telepathy thing could be useful.*

His focus shifted back to their destination, now a half-mile ahead. A group of students climbed the stairs to the central hall before disappearing inside. He expected students to be arriving throughout the day today, since returning students were to arrive prior to sundown. However, new students were due the following morning.

When they entered the building, they found two small lines leading to staffed tables. One table had a sign marked *Apprentice* and the other had one labeled *Adept.* Brock and the other boys stood in the apprentice line, while Ashland joined the line with the other adept-level students.

After a few minutes, it was Brock's turn to check in.

"Hi, Monica." Brock said to the blond girl sitting at the table.

The girl pushed her glasses up and smiled shyly. "Hi, Brock. Welcome back."

She flipped through her papers, located his name, and looked back up at him. "Would you like your own room? We have fifteen singles remaining."

Brock shrugged. "No. I'd rather keep my roommate from last year. His name is Cameron DeSanus." He thumbed toward Cam. "He's right here, checking in with me."

Cam nodded with a grin. Brock smiled back, knowing that Cameron preferred not to be alone. He turned back to Monica, who was making a notation.

She called out to the male student standing behind her, "Room 2024."

"Actually, can we have a room at the end of the hall? One by the lounge?" Brock asked.

She shrugged. "Sure. Make that room 2099."

The boy ran off toward the cart of keys. Moments later, he returned with two keys tied to cords. Brock grabbed both keys and handed one to Cam.

"Thanks, Monica. You're the best," Brock flashed a smile.

The girl smiled back. "Thank you, Brock."

"Come on, Cam." Brock said, waving his roommate along as they made their way to their new room on the second floor.

8

Benny woke early, excited to begin the new school year. After dressing and taming his mop of brown hair, he snuck out into the hallway, careful not to wake Parker. He crossed the hall and put his ear against the door. Hearing nothing inside the room, he decided that Brock and Cam were still asleep. Rather than waking anyone, Benny strolled down the hall to the stairs and descended to the ground level. He decided that it was a bit early for breakfast and instead made his way through the main hall to step outside.

Stars above twinkled in the sky as the first inkling of the coming daylight began to lighten the eastern horizon. Birds tentatively chirped in surrounding trees in anticipation of dawn's breaking. The still air left the valley serene in the dimness of twilight.

Benny noticed someone on the lawn below. He had expected to be alone, but felt a twinge of excitement at the opportunity to speak with someone. After descending the stairs and crossing the lawn, he approached the person.

"Who's there?" he heard a familiar voice cry from ahead.

"It's Benny, Master Nindlerod. Benny Hedgewick."

"Hedgewick? Oh, yes." The man nodded as Benny came into view. "Welcome back, Mister Hedgewick."

"Thank you, Sir. I'm glad to be back." Benny indicated the tripod standing beside the man. "What's with the telescope?"

"What? Oh, this?" Nindlerod patted the device. "I've been using it to track the planet."

"Planet? You mean in the sky?" Benny asked.

"Yes, it's getting closer." The master engineer nodded. "Come see for yourself."

Benny leaned in to look through the lens. A gray-tinted sphere popped into view, lines swirling upon its surface. He stepped back and found the instrument pointing toward the brightest object in the early morning sky.

"Soon, it will be lost in the bright haze of the day sky." The old master said. "Come spring, it should reemerge in the evening sky and will appear to our naked eyes as it does now when peering through this telescope."

Benny frowned at the old man, his brow furrowing. "I've never heard of this planet. How can this be?"

Nindlerod shrugged. "I'm not sure, sonny. Perhaps it's always been there, just moving on a different plane than our planet and rarely coming near ours. After a month of research, the only reference I can find comes from hundreds of years ago. I'm assuming that this is what they saw, since the man who noted the object was never able to identify it."

Benny looked up and found the sky noticeably lighter than when he had first slipped outside. The song from the birds had increased, soon to reach a crescendo as they welcomed the day.

"Thanks, Master Nindlerod," Benny said. "I'm going to get some breakfast before I head to Engineering orientation. Will you be there?"

The man turned toward Benny. "What? No, not me. I am still working with the novices." Nindlerod's head shook as he spoke. "Master Shim will now be your instructor."

"I guess I'll see you later, then." Benny turned and walked back toward the building as the light of dawn brightened the sky above him.

After grabbing some eggs, a biscuit, and a piece of sausage, he sat at a table in the Dining Hall. Just when he had cleared his plate of food, Brock and Cam joined him with Ashland arriving soon after. Even Parker sat at the table, since he was no longer bound to follow Corbin around. Finally, Lars showed. Of those in their group, he was the only boy who had opted to room alone. There were far fewer female students, so the girls all had rooms to themselves.

Their conversation revolved around questions of their new roles as apprentice students. Even Ashland, who had spent much of her time assisting Master Varius the previous year, was curious to discover what her new role involved. She explained that Varius was now instructing the upper-level students and no longer required an assistant with there being far fewer apprentice and adept Ecclesiasts than there were novices.

The bell rang, and they each went to their own destination.

Benny made his way to the Engineering wing, entering the classroom across from the one he had spent so many hours in the year prior. Glancing around, he counted more than thirty other students in the room. He grabbed a seat at a workbench and waited for orientation to begin.

A minute later, the bell rang and a hefty man with over-sized features waddled into the room. His purple master's cloak swished side-to-side as he walked to his desk. In an attempt to cover his balding crown, his brown hair was combed from one side to the other. Thick sausage-like fingers adjusted his small round spectacles as he addressed the class.

"Welcome, apprentice and adept Engineering students." He spoke with a thick tongue, making it challenging to understand. "Today, you begin the next stage of your journey toward master engineer."

The man shuffled closer to the class, and those in the front soon learned that his thick tongue included a bit of saliva overspray.

"My name is Master Shim. I will be your primary instructor this year. In this room, we will focus on the advanced principles of physics, strength of materials, fluid dynamics, and scientific theory. You will meet here every other morning to cover those topics. On the mornings when you are not meeting here, you will be heading to the foundry for training with our skill experts, who will help you to perfect your skills in metal casting, metal forging, woodworking, glass blowing, and more. By year-end, the apprentices will be advanced in these skills and the adept students will be experts."

He smiled, nodding. "Now, for the fun part. The afternoons will be yours to design and build anything you can envision. The inventions you create may well improve the welfare of the citizens of the Empire. We only ask that you give way to any novice-level instruction occurring in the Foundry."

Benny smiled at the thought of having so much free time to dream up new creations. With full access to Foundry resources, he could create anything. He just needed to decide which idea to tackle first.

9
___

Cam couldn't take his eyes off the red-haired girl. The tight white vest and tan breeches of her sparring outfit enhanced the long, lithe body underneath. He redirected his gaze toward Master Kardan, and he tried to concentrate on what the man was saying. The other thirty-five apprentice paladins stood in a line to Cam's left and right, mirroring the adept students in the line across from them. Kardan paced between the lines as he spoke to the group. Cam found his gaze continuously shifting back to Tegan.

A trickle of sweat ran down Cam's brow, stinging when it entered his eye. His shirt was damp with perspiration, proof of the effort expended in the warmup exercise he had just completed.

"Listen up!" Kardan shouted. "Grab your headgear and sparring weapons and find a partner. Let's work some of the rust out of your system after a month lazing about."

Cam and the other students scrambled to get their gear. With his wooden sparring sword in hand and helmet tucked under an arm, Cam hurried across the floor to where the adept Paladins had gathered. His eyes found the splash of bright red hair just before a helmet slid down to cover it. As he approached, he gathered his courage and spoke to the girl.

"Tegan?" he said, his voice sounding unsure.

She turned toward him, and her eyes examined him up and down. "Cameron." Her brow arched in question. "Are you here to break my leg again?"

He recalled the last time he had faced her, defeating her on his way to becoming Arena Champion. He hadn't meant to break her leg – it just happened in the flow of the duel.

Nervous, Cam stammered. "Um…I…No. I mean, I was hoping you would spar with me."

She smiled. "I was just teasing. There is actually nobody I'd rather *not* spar with."

Cam's mouth dangled open, unsure of what to say.

The devious smile slid off her face as she released a sigh. "However, if I want to get better, you're my only choice." She began walking away, speaking over her shoulder. "But I'm warning you that I hate to lose. I hate it."

She stopped in an open area, not far from where he stood. He stared at her, baffled.

"Unless you hope to catch some flies, close your jaw and get over here." She waved her two wooden short swords about. "Let's do this."

10

Brock nodded in response to the request. "I understand. I'll do my best."

Master Varius nodded, and a gracious smile crossed her face. "Thank you, Brock."

She raised her voice to address the small class. The twenty-six students included every apprentice and adept ecclesiast at the school.

"The thirteen students who raised their hands will each be assigned healing duty with one of the other thirteen. This will pair one experienced healer with one student still attempting to develop the ability. Once Brock submits the schedule tomorrow, you are to follow it and attend the Paladin classes as healing support whenever scheduled. When that schedule conflicts with your daily session here, you must get notes from a student who attended class. Do not take healing duty as an excuse to fall behind."

With her hands clasped behind her purple-cloaked back, the Master Ecclesiast strolled down the aisle dividing the room. Brock stared at her from behind, watching stray brown hairs dangle below the bun that held the majority of her hair in place.

"Healing will continue to be a major focus of your training throughout the year. However, now that you are officially ecclesiasts in training, there is something else I need to share with you."

Turning about, a serious and heavy weight held within her brown eyes as she scanned the room. "The adept students in the room have heard what I am about to say, but it bears repeating." She continued talking as she walked toward the head of the classroom. "You've been introduced to the art of divining. In fact, I believe that each of you has exhibited skill in this area."

"You also know that divining is the ability used during a Choosing ceremony, where we determine a newborn's potential and assign them a life vocation. In a few weeks, we will go over the details of the ceremony, training you how to perform the process."

She stopped at the front of the room.

"But first, we will cover the most important part of the ceremony. It involves a new symbol, one for which you are to remain forever vigilant – for it is evil."

A murmur of concern and disbelief ran through the room.

The Ecclesiast Master nodded. "Yes. I said *evil*. The rune I'm about to show you is nameless and must remain nameless. All you need to know is that you must always watch for this rune and when you recognize it, you are to halt the Choosing ceremony. The child must not be marked with a vocation rune but instead must go Unchosen."

She stepped aside and gripped a corner of the sheet hanging on the wall. With a flourish, she tore the sheet away to reveal a tapestry depicting a rune of a red starburst with four major points and four smaller points sewn into a solid black background. As Brock had expected, it was the symbol for *Chaos*.

Varius gestured toward the tapestry. "Remember this symbol, for wherever you find it, evil follows. Among the most important missions of the Ministry is to prevent this evil from returning. We do so by seeking it within each child we divine, ensuring that those who have it remain Unchosen." She clasped her hands at her waist. "Do not kill them or do anything else so overt. Doing so would only cause panic and rebellion among the population."

Her intense brown eyes scanned the room in a moment of grim silence.

As Varius spoke, internal conflict began to roil within Brock. He knew the truth of *Chaos* and the power it possessed. It was part of him. It was part of Ashland. Regardless of what Varius or the Ministry might think, he refused to believe that the ability was evil. He certainly wasn't evil, and Ashland was among the best people he knew.

Yet the Ministry was asking him to be among those who would ensure that children with this ability remain Unchosen. Concern about the situation rang within his mind. *How can I force others to live that life? How can I place them in the same hopeless position that I have fled?*

The thought led Brock to another question. *Did every Unchosen have the innate ability to channel Chaos?*

11

The whirling song of Cam's fluted blade slicing through the air filled his ears. He lunged with an arcing slash. Spinning, he chopped downward at another enemy. With a twist, he dodged an overhead strike and drove the sword tip through his foe. Another enemy jumped forward, and Cam led with a feint followed by a redirected attack based on the anticipated response of his attacker. With speed and precision, the well-balanced longsword shredded surrounding enemies as their lifeless bodies littered the turf around him.

"You know you're not supposed to have a real blade yet, right?"

Startled, Cam spun toward the voice.

"Careful, I wouldn't want you to slice off any important parts," A smirk tugged on the corner of Tegan's full lips. Her eyes flicked down to his bare torso.

"Um…sorry. You startled me. I thought I was alone," Cam tried to regain his composure – a difficult task when he was around this girl. "How did you find me?"

He had intentionally gone into the woods to practice alone. The small glade in the heart of a copse of trees seemed an ideal location to brandish his sword in private. He had shed his shirt due to the warmth of the afternoon sun.

"Maybe you're not the only one who knows about this spot," she said, circling him as she spoke. "Then again, maybe I followed you out here."

Cam frowned. *Why would she do that?*

"Let me look at the blade." She held out her hand.

He passed the blade to her, hilt first. She lifted the sword and tested its balance.

"Longswords aren't my thing, but this is a beautiful weapon." She examined the rune stamped into the fluted portion of the blade, just above the hilt. "I bet it's worth a fortune. Did you steal it?"

"What?" Cam's brow furrowed. "No. My father gave it to me."

She nodded. "I've heard of him. Cassius DeSanus. There are stories."

Cam shrugged. "I've heard them."

"I'm sure you have." She eyed the blade again. "It's a named blade, isn't it?"

He nodded again. "Yes. *Silencer.*"

She nodded. "Is that why they called your father *The Calm*?"

Cam shrugged. Talking about his father always put him in a mood.

Tegan flipped the sword, deftly catching the blade with one hand to hold the hilt toward Cameron. He reclaimed the sword and slid it back into its scabbard.

"It must be difficult," she said.

"What?"

She slid closer. "Being your father's son."

Squinting, he stared into her intense green eyes.

She smiled. "If it helps, I can't imagine anyone else even hoping to live up to that standard. You're the one student who'd have a chance."

"Um…thanks."

Her hands suddenly thrust out, striking his bare chest and causing him to stumble back a step.

A grin stretched across her face. "Take the sword off so we can fight."

"What?" Cam asked.

She raised an eyebrow. "Are you afraid I might beat you?"

Flustered, Cameron stammered. "Well, no. It's just…" He released a sigh. "Fine."

He pulled the belt off, and tossed the sword into the long grass. When he looked up, she was in a ready stance. The corners of her lips turned up slightly, reflecting her confidence. He didn't want to fight her as his heart pulled him in another direction.

She leapt up and spun with a high kick. Cam ducked and watched her warily when she landed. She lunged toward him, throwing a punch that he easily dodged. With a tight spin, she flipped her hips and kicked backward, striking him in the stomach. Cam bent with the blow to absorb it. She leapt again and her leg flashed toward his face. He twisted to avoid the strike, while wrapping his arm under her leg to lift it high. Rather than falling on her back, Tegan pushed off Cam with her other leg and flipped backward to land on her feet.

Smiling, she paused a moment. Cam took a half-hearted swing at her smug grin. She dodged and grabbed his wrist. Twisting her body, she pulled hard on his arm and flipped him over her back. He landed hard in the long grass with the girl on top of him. Straddling his mid-section, she pinned both of his wrists in the long grass. He stared up at her pretty face, not even trying to resist. With her eyes locked onto his, she drew closer.

When their lips met, his eyes drifted closed. The kiss was intense, passionate, and wonderful. He had often wondered what it was like to kiss a girl. There were times when he had wanted very badly to try it, but his shyness always won out. No other girl had intrigued him like Tegan. To kiss her was a dream come to life.

As the kiss lingered, his body reacted – the pounding of his heart sending desire coursing through his veins. When she lifted her head and their lips parted, they were both breathing heavily. Sporting a grin, she began to unlace her top. Cameron's day had suddenly become very interesting.

12

B rock opened the door to his room and found himself alone. It appeared that Cam was still out training somewhere. He set his pack on the bed and then bent to dig a thick book and some notes from the desk drawer. Exiting his room, he strode to the entrance of the apprentice lounge. As he expected, he found Benny bent over a table while Parker and Lars were lounging on nearby sofas. There were perhaps a dozen other boys scattered about the room.

Walking to the rounded brick wall that housed the stairwell in center of the room, Brock pulled a hot kettle from beneath the caffe filter and found it half-full. He grabbed an empty cup from the counter and filled it with the steaming liquid.

As he neared the table where Benny was working, Brock noticed Benny sketching on a sizeable sheet of paper. He craned his neck over Benny's shoulder and tried to determine what his friend was drawing. It reminded Brock of the Hedgewick Roller invention from the previous spring but with a lot of extra parts.

"Is this your latest creation?" Brock asked.

Benny's head popped up and turned to face Brock. "Oh, hi Brock," His head bobbed as he spoke. "Yes, it's a new invention I'm working on."

"I don't suppose you'll tell me what it does?"

Benny shook his head. "Nope. It will remain a secret until its ready."

"Don't bother, Brock. You won't get anything out of him." Lars' voice came from behind Brock. "We've already tried."

Brock turned around. "Hi Lars. Hi Parker. What are you guys reading?"

Parker held his book up for Brock to see. The title read *Empire Civil Laws, 1447 Edition*. "As you can see, I'm having too much fun for my own good."

Lars chuckled. "Yeah, me too. I'm reading over equipment care and supply rules." He smiled, his eyes lighting up. "Budakis asked me to be one of his assistants for the year. I guess the one he had arranged hasn't returned since leaving for summer break."

"That's great, Lars," Brock said, stepping closer to the sofa. "But we're almost two weeks into the school year. I'm sure Budakis hasn't been fond of being limited to one assistant."

Lars chuckled again. "Not at all. I spoke with Jasmine, his other assistant. She told me that he's been ill tempered. She's thankful about my coming in to help."

Brock nodded. He knew well how irritated Budakis could be when things weren't going as expected. Pulling a chair out at the far end of Benny's table, he set his book, notes, and cup of caffe down before taking the seat. Pursing his lips, he blew air over the steaming cup before taking a sip. The bitter drink was hot, but thankfully didn't burn his tongue. He preferred it with sweet milk, but that wasn't an option in the lounge.

After pulling back the cloth cover from about the thick book, Brock stared at it as his fingers traced the gold rune embossed in a dark red cover – a rune that he now knew was forbidden. He slipped the cloth cover back on and flipped the book open to read the messages inscribed inside – messages he knew by heart. On the left was a message written in mysterious runes and foreign text. The opposing page contained a message he could easily read – one he had memorized. It had taken him days to determine that the two messages were identical. It still amazed him that someone scripted this message to him, knowing he would find it two hundred years later. The fact that Benny's ancestor wrote the note was just as amazing. The man had experienced a major prophetic vision, seeing something in the distant future. Brock and Benny were still trying to understand what was behind the prophecy. While it had become clear that learning to use *Chaos* was important, they had no idea why. Brock was doing his best, but it was slow going. At the same time, he remained careful not to let anyone outside of his small group of friends know about his abilities or about the existence of the book.

"Have you made any progress?" Benny asked after seeing Brock with the book, knowing quite well what hid beneath the cloth sleeve.

"Yeah, but the translation still comes along slowly," Brock flipped through the volume until he reached his marked page. "You know what we discovered about the rune for *Light* with the log in the woods. When we were staying with Cam in Nor Torin, we tested that same rune on safer things while indoors."

Brock smiled, remembering one of those tests. "Ashland stayed in Cam's room, which is in the third-floor attic of his parents' house. One night, we tested the *Light* rune on a pillow shortly before going to bed. It floated up and wedged itself into the peak of the ceiling. Over an hour later, I was lying in bed trying to fall asleep and I heard Ashland cry out. I ran upstairs to find her sitting upright in bed with the pillow beside her. She said that had just drifted to sleep when the pillow fell, landing on her face and scaring her."

Benny laughed.

"So, we know how long the effect lasts," Brock explained. "The next chapter introduced a rune that behaves completely opposite. *Heavy* makes something many times heavier than normal. We tried it on a piece of driftwood near the docks of Nor Torin. Afterward, I couldn't lift it or even move it."

Benny nodded. "Interesting. I wonder how it works from a physics perspective. Does *Chaos* increase the gravitational effect of the object, or does it actually change the mass?"

Brock shrugged. "I have no idea. I just know it works." Brock's eyes lit up. "We found something else about *Chaos*. I had Ashland test the *Heavy* rune on a sheet of paper. Afterward, we could still lift it, but the paper was as heavy as a brick." Brock smiled. "Just to see what would happen, I applied my own charge of *Chaos* to the same piece of paper."

Benny's eyebrows shot up, causing his spectacles to twitch. "What happened?"

Brock chuckled. "I knew you'd be interested. After I charged the sheet of paper, the table it was resting on crashed to the floor, its legs shattering."

"Ooo. That *is* interesting. It sounds like the effects stack on one another." Benny chewed on his lip, deep in thought. "I wonder if the second effect is added to the initial one or if it's multiplied."

Brock's eyes narrowed. "What?"

"Well, if the first charge makes the paper a hundred times as heavy as normal, does the second charge make it two hundred times heavier, or does it make it 10,000 times heavier?"

Brock shrugged. "I don't know, Benny."

Benny was thinking hard now. "Were you able to determine if your use of *Chaos* differs in strength from Ashland's?"

Brock shrugged again. "I'm not sure. I guess that's something we can try to figure out, though."

"Hi, guys."

They looked up to find Cam grinning at them, his blond hair disheveled.

"Hi, Cam," Brock said. "You look like you just woke up or something. What happened?"

Cam's grin increased in size. "Something wonderful."

Brock recognized the look on Cam's face, a look he knew well. "It's a girl, isn't it?"

Cam nodded, still smiling.

"Tegan?"

Cam nodded again, his grin somehow growing even wider.

"Really? Benny flipped that huge stone block all the way up there?" Ashland asked in disbelief.

"Yep. You should have seen how excited he was." Brock grinned, remembering the day from early spring. "He launched three others, with fifteen minute breaks between each, before the effect began to fade."

Brock gestured toward the pile of massive stone blocks that Benny had fired from the quarry to the adjacent hillside. He wondered if anyone had come out to the quarry since. If so, they were likely quite confused by the scene.

"What rune did you use?" She asked.

"*Power*," he replied. "As you can expect, it's quite useful and is one you want to memorize."

Ashland slid closer, wrapping her arms around his shoulders. "Is that what we're working on today?"

Brock smiled, "No. I have something else in mind today."

His hands gripped the small of her back as he leaned close for a kiss. When their lips parted, he stared into her enchanting blue eyes. A stray curl of brown hair dangled down on her forehead, partially obscuring the fake rune of *Order* that marked her. She absently flicked the hair aside as she stepped away.

"Well, I assume it involves something other than you having your way with me," she said with a coy smile.

He laughed. "Yes. Although I could be persuaded…"

"Oh, no. Stay focused lover boy," she said, laughing.

"Fine. I discovered another rune and thought it was time to test it." Brock drew a piece of paper from his pocket, unfolding it to reveal a rune he had sketched the night prior. "This rune stands for *Brittle*. I think we can both guess what it does, but I needed somewhere to try it. A rock quarry seemed like a suitable place."

Walking to the nearest stone block, he set the paper on top of it. The top of the stone reached Brock's waist, its length twice its height. He reached into a pocket and removed the metal bolt he had taken from the Foundry. With it, he began scraping the rune into the surface of the stone. While Brock worked, Ashland watched intently until he had the symbol drawn to match the image on the paper.

He scooped up the paper and looked at Ashland.

She gave him a nod. "You first."

Brock glanced around to ensure they were still alone before taking a deep breath. Needing emotion, such as fear or anger, he focused on the fact that Unchosen had no rights or options for a better life. He then thought of how the Ministry refused to heal Unchosen, allowing those like his mother and aunt to die for no reason. Anger began to stir within. Holding tight to the anger, he also could sense the storm of *Chaos* all around. Drawing in as much of the frenetic energy as he could hold, he opened his eyes and poured the energy into the rune. It glowed bright red, pulsing briefly before fading. With the emotion and energy expelled, a cold wave of exhaustion washed over him.

He smiled at Ashland. "Would you do me the honor?"

Her brow furrowed. "Do what?"

He smiled. "Someone has to hit it to see if it breaks."

She glanced at the stone and shrugged. Stepping closer, she gave the stone a gentle kick with her boot. The block disintegrated, crumbling into a pile of fine sand that buried their feet as it slid outward.

Ashland giggled. "That's amazing."

Brock nodded. "This could be useful. Would you like to try?"

She nodded. "Absolutely."

13

———

There was one Ecclesiastic skill that ran the risk of exposing Brock and Ashland as Unchosen. With their relationship now widely known, it surprised no one when the couple repeatedly paired up for in-class divining practice. However, Brock worried that their lack of interacting with others might arouse suspicion.

When Master Varius declared that they were finished covering divining and the details of the Choosing ceremony, Brock felt relieved. A glance toward Ashland confirmed that she shared the feeling. What Varius had revealed during the past weeks left Brock unsettled. While he found it easy to extract a rune from within a person and imprint him or her with it, marking that person for life, the process upset him. Varius seemed quite convincing when she explained why the Ministry dictated which rune each citizen was assigned, rather than imprinting them with whatever might be the strongest inherent trait. She preached that Ecclesiasts had an obligation to the Empire and its citizens and that controlling the number of individuals assigned to each profession balanced natural ability with the Empire's need for certain jobs, making the Empire better for everyone.

Brock then remembered that he had been left Unchosen simply because of his ability to channel *Chaos*. Even if he had been given a rune, it would have been of the Ministry's choosing rather than from his own desires. He wondered if people choosing their own path in life would lead to a better world. Having passion for a job surely had to yield better results than being forced into a career.

He blinked, trying to clear his thoughts and focus on what Varius was saying.

"However, while telepathy is a useful skill, it is also exceedingly rare," she said. "In the few cases recorded, every instance involved two people who were very strong with *Order* and who had established a tight emotional bond."

The ecclesiast master paused and her gaze settled on Brock and Ashland.

"Interestingly, the limitations and potential applications of telepathy are still not fully known. While we've proven that distance has no impact, we don't yet know the limits of what is possible to share over this connection. Is it just language, or can they share images or even feelings?" She paced before the class as she spoke. "We would very much like to work with another pair of individuals who have this ability. It would enable the Ministry to experiment and document any new findings.

"Have any of you ever experienced anything like what I have described?" Again, Varius stared at Brock and Ashland.

A sense of dread washed over Brock. He sent a mental message to Ashland. *Don't respond. Don't even look at me. Let's keep this private.*

She responded. *Agreed. I have a bad feeling about telling anyone.*

Brock was careful not to show his relief. He stared back at Varius, his face void of expression. After a long moment, she continued with the lesson by detailing instances where telepathy had impacted events in the history of the Empire.

Distracted by an internal sense of foreboding, Brock half-listened to what she was saying. The impression nagged at him until the bell rang.

"Do you want to grab lunch with me?" he asked Ashland as they walked out the door.

She smiled. "I'd love to, but I have to run back to my room first. Can you meet me at our table in a bit?"

Brock nodded. "Sounds perfect."

She hurried ahead and was soon swallowed by the mass of students in the central hallway. With time to burn as he waited for Ashland, Brock opted to lean against the wall and wait for the crowd to clear.

He found himself thinking about what Varius had said about telepathy. It had been quite useful to Brock and Ashland on a personal level, but he had never considered that it might be utilized on a larger scale. There were times when instant communication across great distances would be useful and might even save lives. However, the very thought of being separated from Ashland made his heart ache.

Realizing that the hallway was now empty, Brock began his walk toward the dining hall when he noticed Master Pretencia heading his direction from the Hierarchist Wing. Their gazes locked, and Brock saw hatred burning in the man's eyes.

"Mister Talenz." Pretencia said, forcing Brock to stop and acknowledge him.

"Hello, Master Pretencia." Brock said, trying to sound friendly.

"I've been watching you, Talenz. I know in my heart that you are a murderer and a fraud." The man came to a stop just a few feet away.

Brock didn't know how to respond. "What do you mean, sir?"

"You murdered Corbin Ringholdt."

"Sir, you must be aware that Headmaster Vandermark found me innocent. It was proven that Corbin was in the wrong, and I was only defending Ashland and myself," Brock explained.

Ignoring Brock, the master hierarchist continued, "When I look at you, I see someone who does not belong. You skirted the rules, bending them to suit your needs. Mark my words, I will find a way to expose you and have you expelled."

Pretencia turned and walked away, leaving Brock alone. As the man departed, Brock realized why he had felt a sense of dread.

14

Cam emerged from the changing room, unsure of what to expect. The past month had been that way, ever since his first interlude with Tegan. She was beautiful, yet bold. Passionate and unpredictable. His stomach twisted in anxiety of what she might do next, yet his heart raced at the mere thought of her.

He stopped in the middle of the arena floor, dimly lit by the late-day sun coming through the glass panels in the ceiling high above. He glanced toward the stands and nodded toward Brock and Ashland. Tegan had asked him to be sure to have a healer present. He had found two. The three of them were alone within the building until the door from the girl's changing room opened.

With her hair tied back, Tegan held her sparring helmet under one arm and wooden sparring swords in the other. Cameron's heart began to pound as he watched her long, lithe legs stride confidently across the open floor. Rather than wearing the traditional sparring vest and trousers, she wore short brown leather shorts and a matching leather vest, leaving her flat mid-drift exposed. Tegan looked stunning.

She stopped just a few feet from him, flashing a devious smile. "Are you ready for this?"

Cam somehow pulled his focus from her body and mustered a response. "I don't even know what *this* is."

Tegan pulled her helmet down over her head. "This is about redemption, Cammy." With a naughty smile, she bit her lip. "I've had my way with you a number of times now, but not in the arena. Not for real. Losing to you in the championship still irks me. It's time for a rematch."

"You want to fight me here and now because of what happened last year?" he asked.

She smiled again, holding her short swords up. "Yes."

Cam stared at her as he searched for a way out of her bizarre plan. Deciding she wouldn't take no for an answer, he released a sigh and slid his helmet over his head.

"Let's do this."

Cam raised his wooden longsword and she attacked, spinning with her leading sword high and the following sword low. He slapped the high one away with his shield and blocked the other with his sword. Countering with a stab at her mid-section, he only found air as she dodged to the side.

Now caught in the flow of the fight, Cam forgot that he was fighting the girl of his dreams. Swinging, blocking, dodging, and countering all came naturally in a rapid rhythm. Back and forth, they exchanged blow after blow with neither gaining an advantage. Tegan's speed and agility made her a difficult target. Her ferocious fighting style required Cam to react rapidly with little opportunity to attack.

As the minutes wore on, Cam felt the dampness of sweat building under the metal helmet. He remained poised, concentrating on the duel as he waited for her to make a mistake.

After blocking a swift series of strikes from Tegan, Cam swung his wooden sword low, trying to catch her off-guard or knock her off-balance. She jumped and flipped backward over the sword as it swept beneath her. When she landed, she thrust hard at his exposed side. Cam had anticipated the move, having seen her use it before. Her swords slashed in vain as he spun away with his shield arm outstretched. The shield clanged off her helmet with a glancing blow, causing her to stumble. In a moment of concern, Cam let his guard down and took a step toward her. She dipped low and slammed her sword under his shield arm and into his ribs, cracking them as air shot from his lungs and a grunt escaped his lips. Pulling his shield arm in tight to protect his wound, he stepped backward.

Smiling, Tegan lowered her swords. "Got you."

He nodded. "Yeah. I think I broke some ribs."

Cam turned to find Brock and Ashland descending the stairs from the stands. He walked across the floor to meet them, each breath like blades piercing his lung.

"That was a pretty spectacular duel," Brock said as he drew close.

"Yeah. It could have gone either way," Ashland said. "I think you may have some broken ribs, Cam."

Cam nodded, holding his side tenderly.

"What about you, Tegan?" Brock asked. "That shield hit to the helmet made quite a racket."

Tegan yanked her helmet off, her wet red hair sticking to her face. "Just a bit of a headache."

Ashland placed her hand on Cam's bare arm. A moment later, Cam's body shook with a chill, and he gasped for air. Thankfully, the deep breaths no longer hurt.

"Thanks for the healing." Cam said as she stepped away.

Brock held out an apple. "Sorry, but this is all I have on short notice."

Cam grabbed it and took a bite.

"Thank you two for coming to watch," Tegan said. "Thanks for healing him, too. We're done here now, so you can leave."

Brock shrugged. "It was no problem. We'll see you guys later."

Grabbing Ashland's hand as she waved goodbye, Brock led her toward the stairs. Cam continued to nibble at the apple, now half gone.

Tegan turned toward him with a smirk. "Lovely duel, Cammy. Thanks for agreeing to it and for putting effort into it."

He shrugged and continued to eat.

"Well, I'm going to take a bath. I stink." Tegan turned to walk away.

Cam finished off his apple as he stared at her backside strolling toward the changing room. The door to the arena sounded, echoing in the voluminous space as Brock and Ashland departed, leaving Cam and Tegan alone. She stopped and turned back toward him.

"Aren't you coming? Bathing alone is quite boring." She spun and continued toward the baths.

Cam considered her words briefly before he followed along. He never knew what this amazing girl was going to do next.

15

The Foundry Yard behind the school was quiet. As Brock crossed the ample gravel space between the Foundry and the outbuilding, his eyes drank in the beautiful view. The high peaks above the valley now had a coat of white snow, glistening brightly in the afternoon sunlight. The dark green of the pines along the mountainside below gave way to the oranges, yellows, and reds of the leaf trees. Since it was just his second autumn at the Academy, the sight still amazed him. However, with winter almost upon them, many of the leaves had already abandoned their branches.

Rounding the corner of the outbuilding, he glanced up at the stall numbers he passed until he found his destination at the far end of the building. The doors to the stall were twice the width of the others. Whatever Benny was working on, Brock decided that it must be significant. He knocked on the doors, hearing Benny's reply from inside.

"Just a minute."

Brock waited outside, hearing shuffling noises inside as his friend unlocked the door. It swung open to reveal a smile stretched across a familiar face.

"You made it. Thanks for coming to help me test it, Brock."

"I still don't even know what *it* is, Benny." Brock gestured toward the stall. "Aren't you going to let me in?"

"Oh, yeah. Come in." Benny shuffled aside to let Brock pass.

Brock scanned the length of Benny's latest contraption. Like a larger version of the Hedgewick Roller, it had wheels and pedals but also had pale sheets of animal hide pulled tight over long sections that stretched across the extra-wide stall. Two wooden rods ran to hinged panels at the rear of the thing. Pale, hollow, bamboo poles framed the contraption, giving the appearance of a skeleton made of wood. Rather than having two wagon wheels like the roller, this device had three much smaller wheels.

"It's awesome, isn't it?" Benny said, caressing the frame.

"It's something," Brock replied. "But I'm not sure what that something is."

Benny held his arm out. "You are looking at the Hedgewick Flyer, the world's very first flying machine." He smiled and rocked his elbows side-to-side in excitement.

Brock mouthed the words *flying machine* as it began to sink in. The long skin-covered sections were wings. Two sets of massive fan blades were mounted at the rear of the unit, each with a rod connecting to a cam at the back. When Brock's gaze fell on the two seats with foot-cranks, realization struck.

"Oh, no. You're not getting me to fly in this thing with you," Brock waved his hands in a crossing motion. "We'll crash and be killed."

"But I need you, Brock," Benny pleaded. "From what I've calculated, we need two of us to get enough wind speed. Even then, it might not be enough."

"Why me, Benny?" Brock exclaimed. "Why can't someone else help you with your crazy ideas?"

Benny stepped closer. "Logic, Brock. It comes down to weight. The more this thing weighs, the more lift and speed I need. I could only make the wings so long and still fit them in here. Besides, I don't believe that we can go fast enough to compensate for more weight. I need someone who is light and strong. I need you."

An internal struggle waged inside of Brock. He wanted to help his friend, but he didn't want to die while doing it.

"Let's say I help you," he said, pointing a finger in Benny's face. "You have to make sure we remain low so we don't plummet to our deaths."

Benny nodded. "Done."

"That's not all, Benny," Brock said. "I'm going to get Ashland so that she can heal our broken bodies when we crash."

"*If* we crash, Brock. *If*," Benny replied. "But, don't worry. I already thought of that. I asked her to wait for us in front of the school. Cam and Parker should be out there with her. We just need to push the flyer out front to meet them."

Well, at least Benny was aware of the risk and had thought about injury. He *had* spent many hours over the past six weeks building this thing, and he deserved to know if it worked. Resigned to the task ahead, Brock released a long sigh.

"What do you want me to do?"

A crowd had gathered, eager to witness an event of such importance. Once word got out about Benny's strange contraption, it spread like wildfire, drawing most of the Academy students. Not occupied by classes since it was Seventh Day, a throng of students lined the sides of the road before the school. Seated in one of the wooden seats, Brock tried to ignore the fluttering within his stomach as he waited. He glanced toward the seat beside him and found Benny sporting a grin, his eyes alight with excitement.

"Remember that you can crank as fast as you want now," Benny said. "When your feet stop, the pedals will stop, but the blades will continue spinning."

Brock nodded. Benny was proud of the design improvements he had made since the Hedgewick Roller. In addition to altering his design so the rotating blades would spin freely even when the pedals stopped turning, he had made the gearing such that one rotation of the foot-crank generated numerous rotations of the fan blades. While it made the cranks harder to turn at first, it would help tremendously once they had some momentum.

Redirecting his attention to the road leading to Fallbrandt, Brock observed the crowd of students lining the path before them. Their excited chatter bespoke of their hope to witness the first-ever flight of man. Peering past those students, nearly a mile away, he spotted

Ashland. She was standing in the road, her distant form appearing tiny as she began waving her blue cloak in the air.

"That's the signal," Benny said with an excited tone. "Let's go!"

Cam and Parker began pushing the flyer, its wheels squeaking as it rolled down the road. Brock began pumping his legs, straining as the pedals on the foot-crank spun faster and faster. Benny grunted as he mirrored Brock's actions, and the spinning fan blades behind them began making a whirling noise. The machine continuously increased its speed as it rolled downhill and it soon outpaced the foot speed of the two boys who had been pushing.

Brock pumped his legs hard, moving them as fast as he could. The fans spinning behind him buzzed noisily. The vibration of the hard wheels on the gravel road caused Brock's teeth to chatter as he bounced on the wooden seat. When it seemed they had reached top speed, Benny pushed upward on the two levers, tilting the panels at the rear edge of the wings.

Brock's heart skipped a beat when he felt a floating sensation hit him. Lifting off the ground, the flyer tilted side-to-side. Benny adjusted the levers to steady the thing as it weaved left and right, drawing danger-ously close to the trees that lined the roadway. Jumping up and down, the spectators cheered as the flyer sped past them.

Benny shouted. "Keep cranking! We need more speed!"

The peddles spun so fast that Brock's feet were a blur and sweat beaded on his forehead only to evaporate in the fast-moving air. The flyer rose higher and leveled two stories above the ground. It was fright-ening, yet exhilarating. A grin broke on Brock's face as the cheering students below them sped past.

He turned and noticed Benny puffing, his cranks slowing. The ground drew closer as their speed decreased, so Brock peddled even harder. His thighs were on fire, and he was beginning to tire. He real-ized that he couldn't keep this up much longer, and Benny was fading fast.

The flying machine dropped suddenly, the ground rushing toward them as they smashed into the road on two wheels. One wheel broke off, causing the flyer to turn sharply into the long grass of the lawn. The contraption caught, stopped fast, and launched both boys from their seats. Brock landed on his hands and rolled onto his back with the momentum. Black spots clouded his vision, while pain shot through his head when it struck the ground.

He lay on his back with his palm on his forehead, blinking as he tried to clear his vision. The sounds of yelling and screaming filtered through the fog that clogged his brain. Feeling groggy, he sat upright and turned to find Benny a few strides away, squirming on the ground as he cried in pain.

Ashland ran past Brock to kneel beside Benny.

She probed his shoulder, causing Benny to cry out. "You broke your collarbone, Benny," she said. "I have to set it before it can be healed." She turned toward Brock. "Can you help me?"

Brock nodded and rose to his feet. A crowd began to gather as they ran in to discover the fate of the fallen flyer and its crew.

"Grab his right hand." Ashland said as she wrapped her arms around Benny's torso. Brock complied, nodding when ready. "Now pull hard on his arm."

Taking a deep breath, he pulled hard. Benny's scream drowned out the sound of bones scraping together, although Brock felt it through his grip on Benny's arm. Benny's eyes rolled back and his head fell limp.

Ashland laid him down gently. "I think he passed out from the pain."

She put her hand on Benny's forehead and closed her eyes. A moment later, his body shook and his eyes shot open. Benny sat up, gasping for air.

Ashland dug into her cloak pocket, removed a hard roll, and held it toward him.

"Here, Benny. This will help with the hunger," she said.

"Thanks," Benny breathed heavily as he grabbed the roll and bit into it.

Ashland stepped close to Brock and put her hands on his arms. "Are you all right?"

Brock nodded. "Yeah. I have a headache, but nothing's broken." He turned toward the remains of the flyer. A mob of students had clustered around the downed contraption. "Well, besides that."

Ashland hugged his arm and pulled him closer. "I'm glad you're safe. I was so scared. When I saw you guys crashing, I think my heart stopped for a moment."

Brock nodded. "I was a bit scared, too."

Benny climbed to his feet, pausing his chewing. "We did it though, Brock. We flew!" Excitement lit his eyes, now taking ahold of him.

Brock snorted. "I guess."

"We did. We must have flown at least a thousand feet." Benny nodded as he reaffirmed his statement.

"Sure, we flew. However, we couldn't keep the thing in the air for long. It's too much work." Brock nodded toward the wrecked contraption. "Plus, landing really hurts."

Benny stared at the flying machine, his eyes scanning the damaged contraption. "Good point. I need to work on this. Help me wheel it back to the school."

16

———————

A cheerful tune echoed in the empty hallway. Brock's shadow repeatedly pivoted around him as he passed the periodic glowlamps mounted to the wall. It was rare to venture into this part of the Academy after dark, especially alone. His whistle was an attempt to make the eerily still halls feel more cheerful, more alive. When he stopped whistling, silence filled the gaps between the rhythmic tapping of his boots on the tiled floor.

When Brock reached the door, he knocked softly. From inside, a familiar voice bid him to enter. As he gripped the doorknob, a ripple of dread washed over him. Was it his imagination, influenced by the eerie setting, or was it something more?

He took a breath to calm his nerves, opened the door, and slipped inside to find Varius sitting at her desk. The nimbus of the glowlamp beside her created an island of light within the dark classroom.

"Ah, Brock. Thank you for coming," she said, rising to her feet.

Brock crossed the room to meet her. "Your note said it was urgent."

She nodded. "Yes. You see, something disturbing has come to my attention. It appears that the Academy has been a victim of deception." She held a piece of paper up, waving it. "This is a letter, written by a master who graduated from this very institution. This master claims to have never heard of the student who is said to have his support in a writ of recommendation."

She paused for a brief moment before continuing. "The man who wrote this message is from Port Choya. His name is Master Snod."

The sense of dread that had been hovering over Brock became a shock of icy cold fear. Snod was the name Brock had used as a reference when applying the Academy, never dreaming that the man might be contacted regarding the subject.

A wrenching motion jerked his arm backward, pushing his hand between his shoulder blades as a thickly muscled arm wrapped about his neck. Brock winced at the pain in his shoulder as his elbow was twisted further than it was meant to bend.

"Hold him tight, Eldarro." Varius smiled as the academy enforcer gripped Brock tightly. "Don't move, Brock. We will get to the bottom of this right now."

Varius approached and placed her palm on Brock's forehead before closing her eyes. Brock held his breath in fear as he realized what she was doing…what she would find.

Her eyes flashed open as she recoiled in horror. A moment later, the horror turned to anger. Brock's face snapped sideways from the force of her slap. He blinked and worked his jaw, it stinging with pain.

"How dare you? You filthy Unchosen! How dare you come into this righteous institution, into my own class, under a veil of deception?" Varius panted in anger. "I believed in you. I stuck my neck out for you."

She struck him again, causing his eyes to water. He squeezed them tight to blink away the tears. When he opened them, she had calmed.

"You could have been among the greatest Ecclesiasts of all time. Such a shame." She shook her head. "But we cannot allow the taint of *Chaos* to threaten the beauty of *Order* or the welfare of the Empire. You're the type of lying filth that proves why The Hand must forever exist."

Her eyes shifted past Brock. "Eldarro, put him to sleep."

The thick muscled arm around his neck tightened, the man's grip on Brock's wrist falling away as Eldarro wrapped his other arm around Brock's his head. Brock struggled for air, pulling hard on the thick arm around his neck. Try as he might, he couldn't break the enforcer's strong grip. His vision narrowed, blackening as he flailed weakly. Thoughts of Ashland were his last before everything went dark.

Brock woke to darkness. His head pounded with a throbbing headache. He found himself lying on his side, his shoulders aching. When he tried to move his arms, he discovered them shackled together behind his back. He rolled over and fell off the bed, hitting the floor hard and driving the breath from his lungs. Brock winced in pain as he gasped for air. When his lungs refilled, he lifted his head to look at his surroundings and noticed the soft light of a glowlamp emitting from the small window in the door to the room. Having been in the cell before, Brock recognized where he was and knew that the Infirmary doubled as a jail.

He was in trouble. Varius knew that he had entered the Academy under false pretenses. Worse, she had determined that his rune was fake, which was a penalty punishable by death. He needed to escape.

Rolling to his stomach, he pulled his knees beneath him and stood. Sharp pain shot up his arms when he pulled hard on the iron shackles, trying to free them. The attempt left deep gouges and yielded only bloodied wrists. Without having his hands free to draw a rune, using *Chaos* was impossible. He closed his eyes and took another approach. *Ashland!* He paused and tried again. *Ashland! I need help!*

He waited for a response, hopeful that she was awake. Her voice sounded within his head. *Brock? What is it? What's wrong?*

A spark of hope flamed. *Something bad. Varius discovered that I'm Unchosen. Eldarro has me locked up in the infirmary. Hurry and get help to come free me.*

He waited for her response. After a moment, he heard her voice again. *I'll be there as soon as I can. Let me know if anything changes.*

Brock breathed a sigh of relief. Help was coming. He just hoped it would come soon enough.

Noises outside the door disturbed the silence. Excited by the thought of Ashland coming to free him, Brock crossed the small cell to peer through the window. His heart sank when he realized it was Eldarro and Varius.

"The carriage is ready, and the driver is on his way." Eldarro said.

"Perfect," she replied. "Let's get him loaded and sent on his way before anyone wakes. I'll let those at the mine know to expect him in a few days."

He heard Eldarro respond. "I'll pull the carriage up to the back door, and he will be in it when the driver arrives."

Footsteps sounded, followed by a door opening and closing.

A shadow fell over the window as Varius stepped close.

"Don't worry, you'll be out of there soon," she said to Brock.

"Where are you taking me?"

"Somewhere you can't cause trouble. You can still be an asset to the Empire but on our terms. *The Hand* will see to it." She smiled.

Hearing her mention a mine reminded Brock of what Minister Samson said when he kidnapped Tipper back in Kantar. Samson had mentioned a mine as well.

"I can't tell you how disappointed I am," Varius said to him. As she spoke, Brock saw movement behind her. "Since you were able to fool me, there may be others. Once you're gone, I'll have to take a closer look at some other students, starting with your girlfr...."

A *clang* sounded, and the woman crumpled to the floor in mid-sentence. Cameron stood behind her, holding his father's sword. Ashland stepped past him, close to the window.

"Brock! We'll get you out. Where are the keys?"

Brock shouted through the glass. "Eldarro probably has them. He slipped out the back door and should be back any moment."

Cam nodded and disappeared in the direction Eldarro had gone. Moments later, Brock heard Eldarro enter, followed by a brief scuffle. Not long after, Cam entered his line of vision and handed the keys to Ashland. After a few attempts, the lock clicked open. Brock moved back as the door swung inward and Ashland darted in to wrap her arms around him.

"I was so scared. I'm glad you're safe."

"Um...can you please unlock my wrists? They're killing me." Brock replied through the curled hair covering his face.

She released him. "Sorry."

He spun about, and she removed the metal shackles using one of the keys. Brock rubbed at his raw wrists as he exited the small cell, stepping over the form of the unconscious Varius.

"Thanks, Cam. That was close," Brock said.

Cam shrugged. "No problem."

Brock smiled at seeing Cam behave as calm and understated as usual. He looked down at Varius and realized that they needed to do something with her and Eldarro. Inspiration struck and he grabbed the shackles from Ashland. He knelt and removed Varius' purple cloak before shackling her hands behind her back.

"Cam, please cut me a couple long strips from the cloak." Brock then nodded toward Ashland. "Find another set of shackles for Eldarro."

He glanced down at Varius and noticed the dark spot of bloodied hair where Cam had struck her. Something she had said bothered him. Curious, he parted the hair along the back of her neck. In the pale blue light of the glowlamp, he could just make out a dark mark hidden among the brown roots – a mark in the shape of a hand.

"Here you go." Cam handed Brock the two strips of cloth.

Brock lifted Varius' head, wrapping the cloth around it so it gagged her open mouth. He tied it tight behind her head and then stood as Ashland approached with another set of shackles.

"Good. Let's get Eldarro locked up," he said.

Two minutes later, they had Eldarro shackled and gagged just as they had done to Varius. Brock removed Eldarro's purple cloak and handed it to Cameron.

"Put this on," Brock said to Cam. He nodded when Cam donned the cloak. "Now put the hood up and drag Eldarro outside to put him in the carriage."

Cam shrugged, pulling the hood up and then reaching under the enforcer's arms to drag him outside. Brock ran back, lifted Varius over his shoulder, and carried her to the door.

Cam opened the door and whispered. "The driver just arrived."

Brock handed the unconscious form of the master ecclesiast to his roommate. "When you get her in the carriage, tell the driver to be on his way. Try to sound like Eldarro."

Cam nodded and closed the door behind him.

Brock turned to Ashland, who slipped in close to hug him. As he stood with his arm around her, he realized that everything had just changed. His stay at the Academy was over.

17

Cam glanced about the room and found himself surrounded by sleepy but familiar faces. Benny rubbed his weary eyes while Lars leaned back and yawned. The yawn became contagious as it passed on to Parker. Cam resisted the pull of an oncoming yawn as he attempted to remain alert for whatever was about to come. He turned toward Brock and Ashland, who sat together atop the desk in their crowded room. The darkness beyond the window behind them informed him that night lingered, although dawn would be breaking soon.

Brock cleared his throat. "Thank you for coming. Since you are my closest friends. I want you to know that I value your friendship, and I would never intentionally deceive you. However, I thought that I had no other option."

He glanced down and gathered himself. "I've been portraying myself under false pretenses." He tapped the *Order* rune on his forehead. "This isn't real."

Confusion clouded the faces in the room.

"What do you mean, Brock? I'm pretty sure I'm not imagining it," Benny noted.

Brock sighed. "What I'm trying to say is that I am Unchosen. This rune is fake – body art created by an artist in Kantar."

The room fell silent. Nobody made a sound for a long moment until Benny whistled. "That's a heavy secret you've been carrying, Brock."

Brock nodded. "Trust me, I know." He looked around the room. "If you've never lived as an Unchosen, it may be difficult to understand the hopeless existence we're expected to accept. The Empire puts you on a path devoid of personal dreams, and they make it almost impossible to find an honest means to earn a living. Unchosen often are forced to thievery, whoring, begging, and other unsavory or illegal means to earn the coin needed to survive."

All eyes were downcast, the air in the room ripe with discomfort.

Brock continued. "Rather than being stuck in a dead-end life with little hope, I paid to be marked with the rune of *Order* and found a way into the Academy. You see, my mother and aunt both died from a common disease. I came here to learn to heal so I could save the next person who was in need, even if that person was Unchosen."

They all knew it was illegal to heal Unchosen. That particular law had always seemed odd to Cam, but now he found it ridiculous and cold-hearted.

"As we became friends, I wanted to tell you the truth, but I couldn't find a way to do it without exposing you to repercussions should I get caught." Brock let out another sigh. "I'm telling you because I now realize that your mere association with me puts you at risk. Unfortunately, that risk is very real after what happened tonight."

Brock dropped off the desk to stand. "Varius sent me a note earlier tonight, requesting that I meet her in her classroom. However, Eldarro was also there with her. He snuck behind me and held me so Varius could divine me. When she did, she discovered the truth."

Cameron nodded, understanding. Now he knew what had happened and why Ashland had sought him out to help free Brock.

"Varius and Eldarro locked me up with a plan to send me away forever. Luckily, I was able to contact Ashland so she and Cam could come save me. Bound and gagged, Varius and Eldarro are now riding in the same carriage they had intended for me. I don't know where they're heading, but it will buy us some time. Hopefully, it buys us a few days. You see, Ashland and I must leave the Academy."

Benny nodded. "You definitely need to leave, but does Ashland have to leave too?"

Ashland responded. "I belong with Brock. Where he goes, I go." She smiled at Brock before continuing. "But there is more. Like Brock, I'm also Unchosen and am here under a false identity and a fake rune."

Benny looked at her, his eyes narrowing. "And you two can both use *Chaos*."

Brock nodded. "It's something I determined a few months ago. The reason people go Unchosen is because the Ministry is weeding out those who can channel *Chaos*. When divining, if the symbol for *Chaos* is seen, the child is left Unchosen."

Benny's face lit up as he stood. "You mean that all those Unchosen out there might have the ability to channel *Chaos*?"

Brock shrugged. "I'm not sure, Benny, but that's my guess."

Benny whistled again as he plopped back on the bed, shaking his head.

Brock gaze met each of their eyes for a moment. "You are my close friends, so I wanted you to know the truth. I'm sorry that your association with me has put you at risk. Now that you know what's at stake, I'm inviting you to come with us."

Lars spoke. "Leave the Academy? Where would we go? What's your plan, Brock?"

Brock sighed. "I'm not sure yet, Lars. At this point, survival is the first step. I'll figure out what comes next after we're away from here."

"Are you sure it's necessary to leave? What will happen if we stay?" Lars asked.

"I don't know. Perhaps it won't be an issue, and you'll be allowed to continue on your path to becoming a master paladin."

Benny spoke again. "If the Ministry has been hiding this secret for so long, they must feel strongly about it. I believe that they'll do anything to keep it a secret. The risk to any of us who remain here is real." Benny looked about the room. "Regardless, I don't want to be part of the Ministry any longer. I've always hated how they've treated Unchosen. Knowing that their motivation is simply to prevent the use of something as amazing and useful as *Chaos*, I want no part of them." Benny stood and placed his hand on Brock's shoulder. "I'll follow you, Brock. You're the best person I've ever known. I don't know where we're going, but it'll be better than remaining here."

Brock smiled and gripped Benny's shoulder in return.

Cam glanced at his friends as he thought through these new revelations. If he left, he'd never be a master paladin. But would that be so bad? It was his father's dream, forced upon him. He'd never felt like he controlled his own destiny. Perhaps it was time to be his own man.

Rising to his feet, he gripped Brock's other shoulder. "I'm with you, Brock."

Lars laughed. "I'm in. I never liked it here anyway."

Parker nodded. "My father's going to hate this. I love it." He smiled. "I'm in."

Brock nodded, still serious. "Thank you all, but we have a long road ahead. We need to pack up and leave before dawn." Turning, he glanced out the window. The first inkling of pale light was showing over the mountains. He turned back to face the group. "That leaves us with maybe a half hour." He turned toward Lars. "Do you have a key to the armory?

Lars nodded. "Yeah. All paladin assistants get one."

Brock nodded. "Perfect. You, Parker, and I are heading to the armory to get a few weapons. The rest of you, get your things packed and meet me outside the main entrance."

Cam grabbed the heavy cloth-covered book and stuffed it into Brock's pack. He glanced around the room one last time, now clear of their belongings. Shouldering his pack along with Brock's, he emerged out into the corridor and locked the door. He rushed down the hallway, fearful of someone spotting the longsword strapped to his waist.

After running down the stairs, he crossed the central hall without seeing a soul. Hurrying down the corridor, he raced to the stairs beyond the library and he ran up to the third floor. As he reached the top, someone came around the corner. He jumped back in reaction, coming to a fast stop.

"Cam! You startled me," Ashland said as she held her hand to her chest. "Where are you going? We're supposed to meet out front."

Cam nodded, stepping around her. "I need to speak with someone. I'll be right down."

Ashland nodded knowingly. "Tegan."

He flashed a quick smile before turning to rush down the hallway. Stopping at the eighth door on the right, he knocked softly and waited. When there was no response, he knocked harder.

A long moment passed, one that caused him to look down the hallway, nervous of somebody catching notice. The door flew open, startling him.

Tegan stood in a thin white shift, rubbing her eyes. Her red mane was a mess. She appeared glorious.

"Why are you here so early, Cam?" she asked.

"Can I come in?" he asked, anxiously.

She stepped back, allowing him in and closing the door after he slipped by.

"I have to leave," he said to her. He had never been much for words, finding it easier to get straight to the point. "I want you to come with me."

Her brows furrowed. "What are you talking about?"

Cam sighed. "I'm leaving the school." His eyes locked with hers. "Not just me, but a few others as well. I was hoping you might come with me."

She stared at him as if he were crazy. "You want me to leave the Academy halfway through my last year? I'll be a master in six months."

Cam moved in close, taking her hands. "I know this is a difficult decision. You see, I love you. I want to be with you, Tegan."

She chuckled. "I like you, Cam. We have fun together. However, there's no way I'm leaving the Academy to go gallivanting off with you to who-knows-where."

Cam was silent. He had said it, told her that he loved her. She had laughed in response. He swallowed hard and stepped to the door, glancing at her one last time.

"Go back to bed, Tegan. Goodbye."

Cam pulled the door closed and released a sigh. Heartbroken, he stared at the floor until he remembered that the others were waiting. He hurried down the hall, now eager to leave the Academy far behind.

18

Rays from the sun streamed between the peaks to the east to shine upon the front of The Quiet Woman. A layer of frost glistened in the shady areas but quickly melted in the areas lit by direct sunlight. The frost crunched beneath Brock's footsteps as he approached the inn. He opened the front door and entered as the others followed.

Finding the dining room empty, Brock led his party to a table before making his way to the kitchen. As expected, Saul was busy preparing breakfast for the patrons who would soon arrive.

"Hello, Saul," Brock said as he entered.

"Brock! Is good to see you," the heavy man chortled. "Been a long time since you been in Saul's kitchen."

"Thanks, Saul. I'm not alone, though. When Tipper and Libby join us, we'll need food for eight. More if you expect other guests."

The heavy-set cook nodded. "Saul has you covered, my friend. The food will be ready soon."

Brock nodded, passing through the kitchen and out the back door. He crossed the frost-covered ground toward the apartment behind the stable. His heavy knock on the door echoed in the quiet yard.

Tipper's tired voice came from inside. "Who is it?"

"It's me, Tip. Let me in," Brock said through the door.

He waited until the door cracked open and a familiar eye peeked through the opening.

"Brock?" Tipper asked.

"Yes. Let me in. We need to talk," Brock said seriously.

The door swung open, and Brock stepped inside. Libby was in the bed with the covers pulled up to her neck. Brock turned toward Tipper, who stood in his smallclothes.

"I'm sorry to wake you," Brock said. "Tipper, I'm leaving the Academy, and I think you and Libby had better come with me."

Tipper looked at Libby, who had lifted her head. He turned back toward Brock.

"What happened?"

Brock sighed. "Something significant. I'll explain while you two get dressed." He turned away from them, facing the door as he began recounting the events of the prior evening.

Brock hugged Dory, thanking her for the food and water. He was going to miss her and the staff at the inn, and he told them he hoped to be back someday. Stepping outside to join the others, he squinted in the bright sunlight. When he glanced into the blue sky above, he noticed a star shining despite the bright blue sky surrounding it.

"That's odd," he said, pointing at the sky. "You don't usually notice stars during the day."

Looking up into the heavens, Benny responded, "It's actually a planet. I ran into Nindlerod at the beginning of the school year, and he was looking at it through a telescope. Back then, you could see it just before dawn. He said it would continue drawing closer to us until it appeared in the morning sky."

Brock nodded as he reflected on his conversation with Nindlerod in mid-summer. The man had been tracking a planet, stating that it was drawing closer. It was odd to be able to see it during the day though.

Turning toward the others, Brock surveyed the group. Prepared for the cool weather ahead, they were dressed in coats and plain travel cloaks, none opting to wear their blue student cloak. Cam's longsword dangled from his hip, while the great sword Lars had taken from the armory rested snugly within the baldric strapped to his back. Parker, with a longbow and full quiver, and Brock, with his metal-reinforced staff, were the only others who were armed.

"Is everyone ready?" Brock asked.

Nodding heads gave a silent reply. He gripped his staff in one hand while taking Ashland's hand in the other and began walking east.

"Where are you going, Brock?" Tipper asked. "The roads out of town are that direction." He pointed southwest.

Brock nodded. "I know, Tip. That's why we're going east instead. Anyone looking for us is likely to check either the road heading west toward Selbin or the one that runs south down to Sarville. Dory told me about an old trail that cuts east through the mountains. It sounds like the best way to avoid attention."

They cut through town and down a narrow road that skirted the north edge of the lake. Small waves lapped the rocky shore just south of the road, while thick stands of trees stood to the north. After a mile, the road turned from the lake, narrowing as it cut a path through the trees. Birds tweeted cheerfully from the bare branches of the leaf trees, oblivious to the problems and struggles of man. The group walked in quiet, tired from having so little sleep. Conflicting emotions churned inside of Brock, torn between the loss of what might have been and the excitement of what the future might hold.

Tipper caught up to Brock, breaking the silence. "So, this *Chaos* thing you told me about. You said that Libby and I might be able to do it too. Is *Chaos* what you used to heal my leg when I fell off the roof last winter?"

Brock smiled. "No, Tip. Healing comes from something called *Order*. It's kind of the opposite of *Chaos*."

"Well, what can *Chaos* do then?"

Brock snorted. "I'm still discovering that myself. All I can tell you is what I've seen it do so far."

Tipper nodded. "That's fine."

Brock recalled that Tipper had already seen it in action. "Remember when we were trapped in the cave with the bacabra? Remember how I made the boulder come to life and attack the beast?"

Lars' voice came from behind. "I saw a bacabra once. It was at sunset, near the shore of Lake Selbin. Luckily, I was across the bay with a good quarter mile of water between us. Even from there, the massive beast appeared fearsome."

Tipper nodded. "It was fearsome alright. I thought we were dead until the boulder attacked it." He addressed Brock. "That was *Chaos*?"

Brock nodded. "Yeah. I didn't know it at the time, but that's what it was. Another time that you've heard about was when we won the Academy Catapult Challenge. Remember how our catapult launched a heavy metal ball over two miles? That was caused by *Chaos*, though I was unaware of what I had done."

Tipper's eyes narrowed. "So, you're saying that *Chaos* can somehow bring things to life and can make things fly further?"

Brock smiled. "Close. *Chaos* can be used in different ways. Each use is determined by the symbol applied when channeling it. The symbol defines the effect it has. With the boulder, I somehow brought it to life or animated it. With the catapult, I used a symbol called *Power*. According to Benny, it increases the energy of whatever it's used on, making it many times more powerful."

Tipper nodded again. "I think I get it. But what happens later? You said the Academy Engineers couldn't make the catapult work the same way."

"Well, the effect lasts for a short time. From what Benny and I tested, the potency is noticeably diminished after an hour and is fully dissipated within two hours," Brock explained.

Tipper looked back at Libby, who had been listening in quiet. "So, you'll teach Libby and me how to use it?"

Brock smiled. "Sure, Tipper. It might come in handy at some point to have more of us able to use it. After all, who knows what lies ahead?"

PART II

DARK HORIZONS

19

B rock gazed out at the valley that had been his home for more than a year, now partially darkened with shadows cast by the mountains to the west. From his vantage point atop the mountain pass, the Academy appeared far smaller than normal. Surrounded by tall mountains on three sides, the open fields of the lawn stretched south of the school, split down the center by the tree-lined road to Fallbrandt. His gaze followed the road until it was swallowed by the dark forest, thick with pines.

Farther south, the road reappeared as it wound through the town that encircled the western banks of Lake Fallbrandt. The glass-like surface of the lake gave the illusion of a window to a slightly darker version of reality – one that reflected a blue sky populated by fluffy white clouds that slowly drifted past. Along the north shore, Brock spotted the road they had taken along the lake and where it entered the woods, narrowing into a winding path that ran up to a saddle straddling two mountains.

He turned toward his companions, who had paused to rest upon the rocks and fallen trees strewn about the clearing. Although thousands of feet above the valley floor, the elevation where they now rested paled in comparison to the surrounding peaks. Here, the air felt crisp despite the mid-afternoon sun. Knowing they were on the cusp of winter, Brock was intent on escaping the mountains before the first snowfall. Travel, at that point, would become far more difficult…and more dangerous.

"We should get moving," Brock announced. "I'd like to reach the bottom by sunset. It will be a bit warmer down there at night."

"Thank Issal that we now go down," Lars grumbled. "I've had enough of uphill to last a while."

Parker patted Lars on the shoulder. "That's because you're carrying the most weight."

Lars' brow furrowed. "My pack is about the same as yours."

"I wasn't talking about your pack." Parker grinned.

Lars took a swipe at Parker, who dodged and scooted away.

Cam chuckled. "Enough messing around. Let's get moving."

The group shouldered their packs and gathered along the trail. With everyone ready, Brock led them down the winding path toward the valley floor, still unsure of where it would lead.

The narrow trail weaved among dark pines and bare leaf trees, through long grass and thick underbrush, continuously heading downward. Cool air clung to the shadows of the forest canopy, ensuring that Brock never broke a sweat despite the weight he carried, or the energy he exerted with his urgent pace.

After two hours of steady descent, the ground began to level. Pushed by the need to put more distance between them and the Academy, they pressed on for another hour until the dying light forced the issue.

Brock stopped and turned to face his trailing companions. "We're almost out of light. It's been a long day, and the Academy is now many miles behind us. Let's seek a place to camp for the night."

"Sounds great to me," Benny remarked. "My feet are killing me."

They resumed their trek, scanning the surrounding woods as they walked. A grunting noise emerged from a nearby thicket, and a wild boar burst from the brush. Beady black eyes and yellowed tusks flashed toward Brock as the animal charged. Covered with short brown hairs, the beast stood as tall as Brock's waist and outweighed him by hundreds of pounds. It took less than a second to realize that a collision could be fatal.

Brock leapt to the side and swung his staff at the beast's snout. The metal-plated end connected, redirecting the boar's path so it missed

Ashland and trampled through rumberry bush. Startled by the attack, cries and shouts of alarm rang through the group.

"Everyone get back." Brock moved forward to get the boar's attention.

The boar spun about and shook its head with an angry snort. With a tremendous shake that ran down its body, it snorted again and snot blew out its stubbed nose and onto the thick tusks. A grunt followed and it rushed toward Brock. He took two steps toward the beast, planted his staff into the turf, and leapt into the air – the vault launching him over the boar as it ran past.

Brock landed and lifted his staff, ready for another pass. A glance revealed Cam and Lars advancing with their swords drawn, but they were too far away and the beast was focused on Brock.

The boar snorted in anger, dug with its hooves, and launched into another charge, directly for Brock. Two rapid *twangs* sounded, followed by *thuds* as arrows impaled the boar's thick neck. The boar crashed face-first on the trail, forcing Brock to leap aside to avoid it as tumbled into the undergrowth.

Brock glanced down at the animal and then turned to find Parker with another arrow nocked and ready.

"Thanks, Parker. That was becoming a bit scary." Brock wiped sweat from his brow.

Parker shrugged as he slid the arrow back into his quiver. "No problem. It's nice to be able to use one of these," he held up his longbow, "for something besides target practice."

Now able to get a better look, Brock stared intently at the dead boar. It was an imposing animal, with tusks nearly a foot long. Short brown spiky hair spikes covered its body, the dirty skin beneath containing folds at the joints.

Lars strode in closer and peered at the boar. "It's a bit like the pigs on my pa's farm." He scratched his head in thought. "I've never seen any move this fast, though. Besides, our pigs don't have weapons like that on their face."

Cam leaned in, now interested. "Pig? Are you saying that we could cook this, and it'll be like eating pig?"

Benny laughed. "It sounds like Cam is hungry again. This thing has to be five hundred pounds. It might even be enough to fill Cam's belly."

Lars laughed and slapped Benny on the back. "He's got you again, Cam."

~

Within a small clearing surrounded by thick woods, the camp stood less than a hundred feet from where Parker had shot the boar. While the others set up camp, Lars skinned and dressed the animal right there on the trail. By the time Benny had a fire started, Cam and Lars sidled into camp carrying two sections of the animal. They skewered each section with a branch and suspended them over the fire using branches lashed together into makeshift supports. The scent of roasting boar taunted the group as they prepared the camp for their brief stay, resulting in grumbling stomachs and watering mouths as they frequently glanced toward the dinner to come.

Nightfall was soon upon them, and the fire became an island of light among the darkness of the surrounding woods. Exhausted from little sleep and a long day on the trail, they ate in silence. The cooked boar was delicious, tasting much like pork. To have the luxury of such a meal while traveling in the wild was a treat that all appreciated heartily. The roasted beans that accompanied the meat were purely to add variety since the quantity of food was of no concern. Everyone ate more than their share, somehow trying to compensate for the trail rations that they were destined to eat in the coming days.

Though everyone consumed more than their fill, half of the meat they had cooked remained. Lars pulled a sheet of tanned hide from his pack and wrapped it around a section of the leftover pork, stating that it would help to preserve the meat so they could eat it the next day. He stuffed it into his pack and sat on a log to watch the fire with the others.

Scattered around the dancing flames, the group rested in silence. Ashland snuggled against Brock with her head on his shoulder and his arm around her. Lars cleared his throat, breaking the peaceful moment.

"Brock? Where are we heading? Do you know?"

While Brock often found himself amazed at the way his friends relied on him for guidance, it was too much to expect them not to have these questions in their heads. Lars was merely the first to voice them. Brock did his best to sound confident with his response.

"The first thing to do is to get clear of the mountains. We're now deep into autumn. The leaf trees are bare, and snow could hit any day. We're not equipped for that kind of weather, so we have to clear the mountains before winter hits."

Pausing to construct his thoughts, Brock continued. "After that, we head south. Again, to avoid snow and cold weather. The climate to the south is warmer, especially at lower elevation, so that's the best bet. That is, unless anyone else has a better idea."

In the orange light of the flickering fire, Brock's gaze scanned the faces of the group. His companions looked to one another, silent but for shrugs and nods.

After a moment, Lars nodded as well. "Makes sense. But, then what?"

Brock sighed. "I don't know, Lars. I know that I'm done with the Academy. I also know that I can't change the past. For now, I'm just trying to look forward. I'm hopeful to find a future out there somewhere. If you believe in me, I just ask that you give me a little time."

Again, Lars nodded. "Fair enough."

"In the meantime, maybe you all should ask yourself what it is you want to do." Brock's gaze swept from person-to-person. "What do you want from life?"

Nobody responded, the camp falling silent other than the crackling of the fire. The conversation was over and had gone far better than Brock had hoped.

Tipper voice emerged from nearby. "Brock, when can Libby and I start learning about *Chaos*?" There was an eager edge to his voice.

Brock smiled upon hearing the familiar tone from his friend. With both Tipper and Benny in the group, they had enough enthusiasm to fill a stadium.

"If we're able to stop a bit earlier tomorrow, we can work on it then. By tomorrow night, we should be beyond the reach of anyone who's looking for us. From there, we can afford to slow our pace."

Tipper nodded and slipped his arm around Libby. "Sounds good to me."

. . .

The day after the boar encounter was largely uneventful as they followed the trail along the valley floor, heading southeast. Shortly after noon, they came across a small bubbling creek and stopped to refill their water skins. At the creek, the trail turned south and continued in that direction until they stopped to make camp for the evening. Having consumed the boar meat during lunch, they had to resort to trail rations for dinner. Once finished with dinner, Brock and Ashland worked with Tipper and Libby as they attempted to channel *Chaos*. After two hours without success, they decided to join the others and get some sleep. Although Brock assured them that they could make it work with more practice, he realized that their possession of the ability was only a theory until proven otherwise.

Rising with the sun the next day, they ate a quick breakfast and resumed their journey. Soon, the elevation began to rise as the trail led them toward another saddle. The sun was high overhead by the time they crested the top and caught their first glimpse of what lay beyond.

While the mountain slopes remained wooded, the forest was far less dense than the hills and valleys behind them. Where the ground leveled at the base of the mountains, the trees gave way to grassy plains. The sea of grass extended southward for miles until the plains met another line of distant mountains. When Brock looked east, the grassy fields extended for endless miles toward the far horizon.

To the north of the plains stood the line of mountains from which they were now emerging. The mountains extended along the western edge of the plains until they wrapped around the south edge, many miles away.

"How far do you think it goes?" Benny asked, looking out at the fields below.

"I have no idea, Benny," Brock replied. "This must be the Tantarri Plains."

Benny nodded. "The Wailing War happened down there, wherever the upper plains meet the lower plains."

Brock thought about the war, trying to imagine the armies of man fighting the evil force of the Banished Horde. *Chaos* had been involved, somehow. Whatever happened, despite the integral role *Chaos* played in winning that war, the Ministry chose to bury its existence and hide it away forever. The reasoning behind that decision remained a mystery.

Tipper stopped beside Brock and rested a hand on his shoulder. "It's another new adventure, Brock. If we keep going like this, eventually we'll see the whole world together."

Brock grinned. Tipper had a way of making him feel better. "Could be, Tip. Could be."

Cam's voice rose up from behind the group. "Since we're stopped anyway, can we eat now? I'm starving."

20

"You don't understand, Tip. It won't work unless you can generate a strong emotion," Brock explained. "*Chaos* is out there, everywhere around you. But, for some reason, it can't be accessed unless you're filled with fear or anger."

Tipper nodded. "I understand. However, saying it and doing it are totally different. I'm tired from walking all day. It's hard to even think, and you want me to get all full of anger when I'm not even angry."

Brock realized that Tipper was right. With the need to trigger emotion in Tipper, Brock set his mind to the task. He glanced from Tipper to Libby to Ashland as he contemplated the situation. The peaceful swishing sound of the chest-high grass surrounding them reminded Brock of the ocean. In fact, the setting was too peaceful, making it even more difficult for Tipper to tap into emotion. Brock needed to do something drastic and unexpected.

"You're right, Tipper. Let's try something new."

Brock withdrew his knife from his inside coat pocket. Grabbing Tipper's hand, he pulled it toward him and sliced across Tipper's wrist. Bright red blood began to spurt out.

"Argh! Why did you do that?" Tipper cried while trying to stop the blood with his other hand.

Brock wiped his knife clean on the long grass before sliding it back into its sheath. "I'm motivating you, Tip. You're about to bleed out. Unless you channel *Chaos* right now, you're going to die."

"Are you crazy?" Tipper screamed. "You're going to let me die if I can't make this work?"

Brock glanced toward Ashland, who remained calm. However, Libby's face had turned pale, her eyes wide as she stared at the blood.

Brock nodded. "Embrace the fear, Tip. Use it and try again."

Tipper swallowed hard and closed his eyes. After a few moments, his eyes flashed open and he stared at the small rock centered at the circle of their feet. In the dim light of dusk, it was easy to see the rune on the rock illuminate with a crimson hue, the glow pulsing before fading.

Trembling for a moment, a spray of tiny shards blasted from the rock as it sprouted four tiny legs. Crunching and grinding sounds emitted from the stone as walked toward Tipper.

Brock smiled and looked at the girls. Ashland was smiling, excited at the possibilities of this new rune. Libby's face had somehow become even whiter.

Libby spoke, her voice trembling. "What is it? What is that thing?"

Brock laughed. "It's the same rock we've been staring at for the past twenty minutes, now come to life like a little pet." He pointed to it as the rock rubbed against Tipper's boot. "See, it likes Tipper." He smiled at his friend. "Say hello to your little pet rock, Tip."

Tipper gave a weak grin. "I did it. I really did it." His grin faltered and his eyes rolled back as he collapsed into the long grass.

Brock ran over to him. "I totally forgot he was bleeding."

Kneeling beside Tipper, Brock closed his eyes and found his center. Within his mind, Brock searched within Tipper until he found a cluster of angry red symbols roiling about. He seized upon the *Order* within Tipper to smother and dissolve the symbols. The arm in his grip shook with a violent shiver as the symbols faded. Opening his eyes, Brock found Tipper struggling to reclaim his breath. The boy's lungs filled and he visibly calmed, gasping as if he had just run a mile. Brock smiled at his friend and helped him to his feet.

"Sorry, Tip. I forgot about your wrist. You must have passed out from the blood loss."

Tipper gave him a grin. "Don't worry, Brock. It worked. I was able to sense *Chaos*. As you described, it was this hot energy everywhere all around me. I pulled it in until it I thought I'd explode, and then I pushed it into the rune." He stared at the small stone as it circled his feet. "And now the rock can move. I did it!"

Tipper turned toward Libby. "You have to try it, Lib!"

She shook her head. "Oh, no. I'm totally creeped out right now."

Brock laughed. "Don't worry about it. You can try tomorrow night. I'll figure out something less creepy."

Libby nodded. "And you're not going to cut me either, right?"

Brock nodded. "Right. We'll figure something else out for you. Come on, let's join the others."

Taking Ashland's hand, he led them toward the nearby tree line. The orange light of the fire, just beyond the first layer of trees, was guiding beacon. They had decided to set up camp in the trees rather than the open fields, thinking it would offer better shelter from the wind and be safer than starting a fire within the long grass. Brock shuddered at the thought of those fields catching fire.

Brock glanced toward the pale aura behind the silhouette of the dark mountains to the west. That light would soon fade and stars would dot the evening sky.

Upon reaching camp, Brock walked past Lars, who was running a whetstone over the huge blade of his great sword. The blade sat across his lap as he honed the edge.

Benny knelt beside the fire, cooking the jackaroo that Parker had shot earlier in the day. The first two birds bursting from the long grass had startled the group. Expecting others, Parker quickly had his bow out with an arrow nocked. When they came across this one, it tried to take flight but crashed to the ground seconds later, an arrow piercing its breast.

Parker and Cam sat on a log across from where Benny rotated the makeshift spit. As Brock emerged into the light, Benny glanced up and greeted him.

"How did it go? Did they get anywhere tonight?"

Brock nodded. "Tipper was able to make it work. Now he knows what to do and just needs practice. Tomorrow, we'll try again with Libby."

Tipper walked past Brock with Libby in tow, both taking a seat on a log.

Tipper sniffed the air, commenting, "Mm mm. Smells good, Benny. When can we eat? I'm so hungry, I'm shaking."

Benny leaned closer to the fire, examining the roasting jackaroo. "I think I can take it off the fire in a few minutes."

Brock dug into his pack. "Sorry, Tip. I totally forgot how hungry you'd be after I healed you." He pulled a small bag filled of nuts out and tossed it to Tipper. "Here. This will help."

Tipper caught the bag and eagerly poured some nuts into his mouth.

A few minutes later, Benny declared dinner ready. As usual, Lars took the bird aside and began slicing sections off. Although the meat was a bit chewy, the bird was delicious. Brock knew that finding fresh meat for dinners would make their food supplies last longer and make traveling more bearable.

Lars suddenly yelped and jumped to his feet.

"Argh! What's that?" He pointed toward the ground.

In the orange firelight, Brock could just make out what had startled Lars. He laughed as Lars backed away from the animated rock, no bigger than his fist, as it shuffled past the massive boy.

As if in a trance, Benny approached the living stone, squatting to get a better view. "Would you look at that? Just look at it! It's amazing!"

"He's mine. I made him with *Chaos*," Tipper said proudly.

The stone walked right into the fire and over the hot coals as it headed toward Tipper.

"Interesting," Brock muttered.

Libby spoke again. "I still think it's creepy."

"It's super creepy." Lars shivered as a chill ran down his spine.

"If you want, I can make one for you, Lars," Brock said with a smile.

The big guy shivered again. "No thanks." Lars patted the rock he had been sitting on as he reclaimed his seat. "I prefer my rocks to just stay dead."

"How do you know yours hasn't been brought to life?" Ashland said with her brow raised.

Lars yelped again as he scrambled away. Everyone laughed.

21

—————

Like tiny ships sailing across an open sea of grass, the upper bodies of Brock and his companions bobbed above the long shoots as they journeyed southward. Carrying a biting chill, the blowing wind caused the expanse of grass to dance around them. A gray blanket of clouds, one that had the look of snow, obscured the sun and made the wind feel even colder.

The wall of mountains that formed the south horizon still appeared distant even though they had been walking for hours. Lacking any visual sense of progress left Brock imagining himself walking on a wheel, it spinning freely beneath him but never actually taking him anywhere.

A tickle at the base of Brock's head became a tingle and grew to a surge of dread, the sensation giving him a chill and sending his heart pounding. He stopped abruptly, causing Ashland to collide into his back.

"Why are you stopping?" Parker asked as he walked past.

"We need to turn around. Now." Brock grabbed Parker's shoulder and pulled him back.

As he reversed direction, four heads rose up from the long grass, each head shaved bald but for a single black topknot. Spinning, Brock realized that a small force surrounded them. Thirty warriors appeared from the long grass, some with swords drawn while others had nocked arrows aimed in their direction.

Cam and Lars quickly drew their swords, standing ready as Parker drew an arrow from his quiver.

Brock shouted. "Stop! Nobody move."

A man wearing a leather vest stepped closer, breaking apart from the others. A brown leather headband with a peak in the front held his long black hair in place. In addition to being the lone warrior with a full head of hair, he had body art covering his tanned face and arms. He stopped a few strides away, crossed his muscular arms, glared and at Brock with contempt.

"You Imperial swine are trespassing on Tantarri land," he growled. "You are under arrest. Surrender your weapons or you die." His words were thick, with an odd accent.

Brock's mind raced. With a dozen arrows pointed at him, he would never have enough time to channel *Chaos* even if he had a plan. If anyone made the wrong move, they'd be dead in seconds. Seeing no other option, he tossed his staff at the foot of the man who addressed them.

"What are you doing, Brock?" Lars asked.

"Look around, Lars. How many can we kill before we die?"

Cam tossed his sword and Parker dropped his bow. Moments later, Lars sighed and followed suit.

The man put two fingers in his mouth and whistled loudly. More Tantarri appeared from the tall grass and ran in toward them. Rough hands began searching his body, finding his knife sheath inside his coat pocket and tossing it into the growing pile of weapons. They grabbed his wrists, yanked them behind his back, and bound them together with rope. Hearing an approaching rumble, Brock turned to the east as a herd of horses crested a small rise a half-mile away, led by a bald Tantarri on a gray stallion.

Once finished binding the wrists of Brock and his friends, the Tantarri pushed them into a line. The approaching horses slowed and came to a halt. Two Tantarri grabbed Brock and shoved him toward forward, causing him to stumble briefly. He glanced back, surprised to notice feminine facial features, although she had a single black topknot and shaved head like the others. Looking about, he noticed that many of their captors were women. She shoved him roughly toward the horses.

After leading him toward a brown mare with a flowing black mane, two sets of hands hoisted him onto the animal, draping him stomach-down over its back while they strapped him to the saddle. From his inverted viewpoint, he craned his neck to find Ashland being strapped to the saddle of a piebald mare. When their eyes met, Brock sent thoughts Ashland's way. *We will be fine. We'll figure something out.* She smiled, the look becoming a wince as her horse burst into a trot.

Brock's horse followed the others, his stomach bouncing uncomfortably against the saddle as the grass shoots swatted against his dangling head. The world hung upside-down, mountain peaks below the grass, pointing down toward the sky, it all bouncing past in a rapid blur. With blood running to his head, the pressure soon evolved into a headache – a headache that was among the least of his worries.

22

B rock's ribs were on fire, and he felt as if he had been bouncing on the horse for days although barely an hour had passed. With the sun obscured by the gray clouds, it was difficult to know the exact time. The ground below his head eventually changed from long grass to green scrub dotting red-tinted dirt. The rhythmic clopping of hooves somehow became soothing, numbing his mind. He'd have fallen asleep if the position wasn't so uncomfortable.

The ground tilted and gravity began pulling him sideways as the horse headed uphill. Craning his neck, he could now see a drop-off just a couple feet beyond. They appeared to be climbing along the wall of a narrow canyon, the drop to the canyon floor below steadily increasing to an alarming depth. Anxiety twisted his stomach as his mind conjured unwanted images of the horse making a misstep and tumbling over the edge.

When the trail grew wider, Brock craned his neck about and found a rock wall separating them from the canyon. The horses turned and he caught a brief glimpse of a stone city built into the side of the mountain. A rock wall suddenly obscured his view as the horses entered a cave.

Within the deep shadows of the tunnel, the horse slowed to a stop. Still draped over the animal, Brock waited as the other horses settled into place. Rough hands untied the bonds that strapped him to the saddle.

Those same hands grabbed him under his arms and yanked him from the horse. He was careful to lift his legs when they dropped off the beast, extending them once he was vertical. With his feet beneath him, Brock hunched over as he tried to loosen his cramped and sore stomach muscles.

He looked around and saw Benny, Ashland, and Parker standing with Tantarri holding them. Two warriors pulled Tipper and Libby from their horses, pushing them toward the other captives. Due to their size, it took longer to get Lars and Cam off their animals. With everyone dismounted, the Tantarri guards herded them into a smaller cave opening.

Elaborate drawings decorated tunnel walls that stood three strides apart. The scenes appeared to tell a story, but they passed too rapidly for Brock to grasp the context. After rounding a bend, the walls opened to reveal an open gallery. Torches along the walls cast orange flickering light upon the uneven ceiling. Coals burning in a stone brazier lit the heart of the cavern, spreading a glow to the surrounding area. Their captors ushered them into the heart of the cavern and then jerked them to a stop as the man who had led their capture crossed the cavern and disappeared into another tunnel.

Brock examined their surroundings as he waited in silence. The cavern appeared natural, the torchlight failing to penetrate the dark recesses of a ceiling two stories above. While more than thirty people stood in the cavern, it could hold four times that number.

Turning toward his companions, Brock found fear reflected in their eyes. He felt the same way. His mind raced, grasping for a way out of this mess, seeking a piece to a puzzle he didn't understand. He noticed that half of the Tantarri warriors held him and his friends in place while the others stood back, ready with bows and long curved swords in their hands. The odds of surviving a fight were slim and left him with little choice.

An older man and the warrior who had led their capture soon emerged from the tunnel, followed by a female Tantarri warrior. Judging the lead man's build and gait, Brock decided that he must have been a fearsome warrior in his youth. Even now, Brock would not want to challenge him. Similar to the younger man standing to his side, body art covered the older man's tanned skin. He wore a leather vest and leather pants like the others, but with the addition of colored strips of cloth hanging down his back like a cape. A jewel-encrusted leather headband held his gray-peppered black hair back. The red and blue gems on the headband formed a symbol that was vaguely familiar to Brock – a symbol of import, yet one of mystery.

The three stopped a stride before the captives. Brock glanced at the Tantarri woman to the leader's side, seeing that she also had a peaked leather band holding her long black hair in place. Black leather cut to fit her form left her arms, midriff, and thighs exposed. The hilt of the sword strapped to her back stuck up over one shoulder and a matching hilt joined the dagger strapped to her hip. With dark eyes sporting a hawk-like gaze, she was beautiful and fearsome at the same time.

The man who had led their capture spoke, his voice echoing in the cavern.

"Father, these Issalians were caught trespassing on Tantarri land. We found them near the wood along the upper plateau."

The older man nodded, responding with the same odd accent. "I see, Juran. Were they armed?"

Hearing movement, Brock turned as four Tantarri stepped forward and tossed the confiscated weapons into a pile. Brock's staff bounced and rolled across the cave floor before coming to a stop beneath the Tantarri leader's foot.

The man stared at the small pile of weapons. "Armed and on Tantarri land. They could be spies or perhaps assassins. Regardless, the punishment is death."

Brock couldn't hold back any longer. "Sir. We mean you no harm. We didn't even know we were on your la…"

An explosion of pain struck Brock's face, his head turning sharply from the force of the slap. Tears from his watering eyes made the room a blur. He blinked to clear them.

Juran spoke angrily, his face close to Brock's as hatred burned in his dark eyes. "You are not to speak, imperial swine. You have no right to address the head clansman. When the Ministry declared war on the Tantarri, you forfeited any rights to negotiate."

The head clansman put his hand on the man's arm. "Peace, Juran. We will not resort to murder. We are not the Ministry. We will lock them away for the night, and they will be executed in the morning per Tantarri law." The man addressed Brock. "You see, even if what you say is true, and you had no ill intent, we are at war with your Empire. According to the rules of war, as the Ministry has so clearly established, we will execute those who trespass on our lands. Do not blame us young man. Your Ministry is to blame. Their treachery has left us no choice." He then gestured with a finger. "Put them in the pit. They die at dawn."

The head clansman reversed direction, the long colored strips of cloth flowing behind him as he retreated into the tunnel. Juran gave Brock one last hateful glare before following his father. The girl eyed the group for a brief moment before turning to follow the others.

The two Tantarri guards who were holding Brock spun him around and dragged him toward a tunnel entrance cut into the side of the cavern. He noticed his pack and the others piled along a cavern wall just before he entered the tunnel.

The corridor curved in a slow arc before opening to another gallery. A single torch flickered on the wall, making shadows dance on the walls and the high ceiling, its light failing to penetrate the deeper recesses. Looming below was the focal point of the room, dark and forbidding. A narrow ledge encircled a hole in the floor ten strides across, the unknown depths of the pit consuming any light attempting to enter.

Two Tantarri began to uncoil a thick rope as they lowered it into the dark opening. Once unwound, they backed away from the edge.

"Climb down." A Tantarri commanded as another cut the bonds from Brock's wrists.

Without having any choice, Brock stepped to the edge, grabbed the rope, and began lowering himself into the hole. He glanced down again to find nothing but darkness below. His heart raced when he thought of falling some incredible unknown distance. He tried to calm himself by shifting his focus, concentrating on the placement of each foot as he descended into the black abyss.

23

A s Lars reached the pit floor, Cam and Brock helped him get his footing. The moment his hands released the rope, it began to rise. Brock peered up at the distant pit opening as a pair of hands pulled the rope up. When the rope cleared the rim, the hands disappeared and it became quiet.

Lowering his eyes, Brock peered into the darkness, seeking the faces of his companions. The indirect light of the single torch above was just enough for him to perceive shadowed forms standing about him, the mood as black as the surroundings, lacking the light of hope. A long moment of quiet held them captive, silent but for the breathing of the captives. How many breaths remained for them? Morning waited merely hours away.

Lars spoke, breaking the silence.

"You have to get us out of here, Brock." Lars sounded angry, desperate. "We're in here because of you. I can't stay in this tiny dark hole." His voice rose to a shout. "You have to get me out!"

Tipper stepped between Lars and Brock. "Relax, Lars. Brock has a plan. He always has a plan."

Brock had begun working through a plan the moment he reached the bottom. The outline of an idea was forming, but he needed a little more time.

"We can't do anything yet," Brock did his best to sound calm. "It's around dinner time now. We must wait a few hours for them to fall asleep. That's when we get out of here." He reached out, fumbling about until hand found Lars' thick shoulder. "Until then, try to relax."

Lars remained still. Even the breathing seemed to cease as the pit fell to silence. A long moment stretched as Brock waited for his reaction.

"Fine. We wait for a couple hours," Lars grumbled and turned away.

Tipper patted Brock's shoulder and moved aside as Ashland's hand found him. She wrapped her arm around his waist. *I'm scared.* She said in his head.

He closed his eyes and sent his thoughts back to her. *I'm scared too. The Ministry has created an enemy here and that makes us guilty by association. Words aren't going to work, so we must escape. We have nothing to lose in trying since they plan to kill us anyway.*

Do you really have a plan? she asked.

I'm working on it, he replied.

Brock rose to his feet and wiped the dirt off the seat of his trousers. "It's time. Wake up."

The group began to stir, although Brock was unsure if anyone had actually slept. He certainly couldn't sleep, not with their lives in the balance. Time had passed at an achingly slow pace while he watched the pit opening, high above him. Having seen nothing but the flickering torch dancing on the uneven cave roof, he decided it unlikely that there were any Tantarri waiting at the top.

Brock turned to focus on his friends, searching for their faces in the darkness. "After a much consideration, I think I've devised a way out of here."

After a pause, he revealed his plan. "Ashland is going to use *Chaos* on me so I can float up to the cave above. Once there, I'll lower the rope and you guys can climb out."

"Is that safe?" Ashland asked.

Hearing the concern in her voice, he squeezed her hand to reassure her. "I used *Chaos* on myself once and it worked."

"But you were also rendered unconscious for days," she noted.

Brock nodded. "True. However, other circumstances may have caused that. Regardless, it's a risk we have to take. Lars is right. I'm the one who got us into this mess. I'm the one who has to get us out."

Ashland sighed. "What am I going to draw with? How am I going to see the rune in this dark pit?"

Brock dug into his inside coat pocket, pulled a small tube out, and began shaking it. A soft blue light bloomed from the glowstick, illuminating the pit.

Lars growled, "You had light the whole time we've been down here?"

Brock nodded. "Yes, but I couldn't risk using it. I didn't want them to take it away. The fact they didn't take it when they searched me means that they didn't know what it was or they just didn't find it." Brock smiled. "Regardless, this little prize is going to save us."

He lifted the glowstick high and smashed it into the rocky pit floor. The thick glass broke, sending a splash of glowing blue powder to the ground. Brock lifted his shirt, and tapped his torso as he addressed Ashland.

"Draw the rune on my stomach using the glowstone powder."

She nodded, bending to grab the intact end of the glass tube. After pouring the glowing powder from the tube into her palm, she dipped her index finger into it and began tracing the symbol on Brock's skin.

After a minute, she stood upright. "I think it's ready. How does it look?"

Brock examined the rune. "It's missing a line right here."

"Oh, right." Ashland bent to add the mark. "There. It should be ready."

Handing the remains of the tube to Benny, her eyes met Brock's.

He nodded to her. "Do it. If we don't escape, we die in the morning. The fear of that thought should be enough."

She nodded and closed her eyes. Brock's stomach twisted, his heart racing as he prepared for what was coming. After a minute, her eyes flashed open, revealing crimson power glowing within them. Having never noticed it before, Brock leaned closer and stared at the sparking energy that arced about her pupils, as if tiny thunderstorms raged within. He glanced down at the rune as it began to glow, pulsing before the glow faded. When his gaze shifted back toward Ashland, he found her eyes returned to normal.

His body began to tingle, his muscles twitching for a moment. His stomach flipped, feeling queasy as he began to float. After rising upward a foot, he sank to lightly tap the cave floor.

"I didn't float all the way up." Brock noted, confused.

Benny responded. "Your clothes might be too heavy. Take your coat and boots off."

Deciding that Benny was correct as usual, Brock held onto Ashland as he pulled a boot off. When the first one came free, began to rise. He let go, pulled the other one off, and removed his coat as he drifted upward. The moment he dropped the coat, he began rising faster.

The walls of the cave slid past as he rose higher and higher. A swipe of his hand on the wall spun him around to face upward. Emerging from the mouth of the pit, he floated up toward the high ceiling. He extended his arms, bracing himself as he collided into the uneven rock dome. It felt odd to rest against the ceiling – gravity gone mad, the world turned upside down. Spinning to look down, he spotted the coiled rope in a pile near the tunnel entrance. He squatted with his legs with his feet against the rock ceiling, focused on his target, and extended them in a burst.

Anxiety twisted his innards as he plummeted far faster than anticipated. Starting at a height of thirty feet, a headfirst drop could be lethal. The knot in his stomach began to loosen as his speed slowed. By the time he reached the rope, his momentum had dwindled to a slow drift. He grabbed ahold of the rope as his momentum began to reverse, using it to keep himself from rising. After pulling his legs down to the cavern floor, he twisted the upper portion of the rope around one calf to use as an anchor. He then began feeding the thick coil of rope into the pit. His heart raced in fear as he thought of the Tantarri discovering him before he could free the others.

"We have it, Brock." Tipper's voice came from the depths below when the rope reached the bottom.

"I'm ready!" Brock braced his feet against two ridges in the rock and gripped the rope with both hands. "Send Cam first so he can help pull others up."

. . .

Brock's armpits were damp with nervous sweat. The process of getting everyone out of the pit took longer than he had hoped, and the constant threat of being caught made the wait excruciating.

Cam, Parker, and Tipper made it to the rim with little problem. Benny struggled a bit but made it with some help. Libby was unable to get far on her own, requiring the boys at the top to hoist her up. However, Ashland had no such issues. Pride hummed within Brock at her surprising strength of body and will. Despite his aversion to the pit, Lars surprisingly opted to go last, and it was a struggle to get him out. His weight required all of them to pull in unison. When he finally cleared the rim, he lay on his stomach, panting heavily.

The burning need to make haste prompted Brock to prod his friend along. "Lars, I know you're tired, but we have to leave. Now."

Lars nodded and grunted as he climbed to his feet.

Brock turned to Ashland, who still had his coat and boots tied to her back. "Can you keep my things for a bit? I doubt that running would even work with me being this light, so I'll have to float along for now."

She nodded. "Sure. Grab on."

He gripped her gray travel cloak and unwrapped his leg from the rope. Released from their anchor, his legs began to float toward the ceiling.

"Let's go grab our stuff and get out of here." Brock said from his odd position, floating above Ashland. "Cam, you lead."

With a nod, he headed down the tunnel, toward the gallery where their belongings had been stored. Ashland and Brock followed with the others trailing behind. From time to time, Brock's foot would hit the roof of the tunnel and he'd push off so he'd float horizontal again. The bruises and scrapes on his heels were nothing to note with what they faced.

They rounded the bend and approached the spacious cavern. It was far darker than before, with just two torches lighting the open space. Cam paused and glanced at Brock, who nodded, anxious to escape the situation. They entered the gallery and ran for their weapons, still piled in the middle of the cavern.

A shout sounded from behind. "Stop or you die!"

Brock spun toward the voice, and Ashland's cloak slipped from his grip. His arms flailed about as he attempted to reach her, but he lacked any sense of control and floated upward, beyond her reach. He winced in pain when he collided into the rocky ceiling, with its uneven surface jutting into his back.

From his position high above the room, he easily spotted the dozen Tantarri warriors stationed along the wall near the tunnel that led to the pit. The warriors' eyes reflected fear, their bows aimed at Brock.

Rapidly approaching footsteps drew Brock's attention toward another tunnel entrance. Ten Tantarri, armed with curved swords, emerged in a run and surrounded Brock's friends. Juran ran in behind them, slowing to a stop as he addressed his captives.

"I don't know how you managed to escape the pit, but we were prepared to stop you if you did." He crossed his arms in an arrogant stance. "Death still waits for you at sunrise."

A Tantarri bowman shouted. "Juran! Beware! Above you! They have dark magic!"

Juran looked up and saw Brock for the first time. With wide eyes, he backed away. His look of shock transformed into one of pure hatred before issuing the command. "Shoot him. Kill him!"

"Juran, no!"

Everyone turned toward the woman's voice. Stepping from the mouth of the tunnel was the same woman who had accompanied the head clansman earlier.

She approached Juran, shaking her head. "You cannot kill him, Juran. You must honor the prophecy." Her hand rested on his arm. "If he dies, so does our hope."

Juran's face was a cloud of frustration. "Puri, it cannot be. How can one of the treacherous Imperials offer hope for the Tantarri? If we let him live, he'll betray us."

Puri shook her head. "No, brother. Not every one of them has a lying heart. You know Elder Duratti's words as well as any. The portent appeared in our morning skies just days ago, and now the outsider who can fly is here in Mondomi." She glanced up at Brock. "It cannot be coincidence. He is the one." She turned toward Juran. "The days of the prophecy are upon us, and the fate of the Tantarri hangs in the balance."

Juran stared at her, frustration apparent on his inked face. A long moment passed before he relented.

"Fine. You deal with them. I'll have no part of their treachery." He thrust a finger toward her face. "But when they betray you, do not come crying to me."

Juran stormed off, disappearing into the tunnel.

Puri called to the Tantarri. "Put down your weapons." She looked up at Brock. "We will not harm you. Please accept our apologies for your harsh treatment. You are now our guests and will be treated as such."

Brock sensed something good within this woman. She did not exude the same hatred as her brother. He coiled his legs against the ceiling and launched himself down toward the others. The speed of his drop slowed as he approached the ground. He reached out to grab Cameron's outstretched hand, bringing his legs down so he could stand. Ashland grabbed his other hand to help hold him down.

He turned toward Puri, who stood almost a head taller than Brock. Although her brown eyes were intense, her smooth cheeks showed that she was younger than he had first assumed. She also displayed far less ink on her skin than her brother did.

Puri bowed to him. "I am Puri, first daughter of Turan, head clansman of the Tantarri. Welcome to Mondomi."

24

Brock woke as the hammock swayed from Ashland shifting her position. He lifted his free hand to swipe the sleep from his eyes, blinking to clear them. Ashland's mess of brown curls tumbled across his chest, where her head remained. She had fallen asleep atop of him to help prevent him from floating away, which he didn't mind in the least. Any reason to be close to her was enough for him.

Like him and Ashland, the others slept in the row of hammocks hanging within the man-made cavern. A single torch in the tunnel outside flickered, sending dim light through the seams in the curtain hanging in the doorway. Here inside the mountain, Brock felt disconnected from the day, unable to determine if the sun had yet risen.

He looked down at Ashland and gently touched her cheek. Stirring, she lifted her head to look up at him. She smiled, her eyes still sleepy. He smiled back. *I love you.* He said to her in thought. *I love you more.* She said, her smile growing.

He chuckled. "Is this a contest?"

She closed her eyes and rested her chin on his chest. "Yes. Sorry, but you're losing."

"I find that hard to believe. I'm pretty sure I love you as much as anyone could possibly love anyone else," he said as he stroked her hair.

Her eyes flickered open. "That's nice, Brock. But I still love you more."

"Are you guys done with the mushy talk yet?" Benny grumbled. "It's making me ill."

Brock laughed. "Yeah. Sorry if we woke you."

Benny sat up, his hammock swinging from the motion. "I was already awake, trying to figure out what time it is."

"I know what time it is." Cam said from the hammock just beyond Benny's. "It's time to eat. I'm starving. After eating just one meal yesterday, I think I can eat a whole cow."

Benny replied. "I had better go warn the Tantarri to hide their cows. Cameron's on the loose and he's hungry."

Lars' bellowing laughter filled the cave, joined by the laughter of others in the group.

"He got you again, DeSanus! Ha! Hide your cows!" Lars said, laughing even harder, his hammock swinging wildly.

As the laughter died down, brighter light coming from the tunnel redirected Brock's attention. A Tantarri man pulled the curtain, entered, and placed a torch in the sconce secured to the wall. A woman carrying a large pot followed him.

"Your breakfast is served," she said as she set the pot on the long table located near the door.

Another woman walked into the room and set a towel-covered basket beside the pot. Two others followed, one carrying two pitchers and another with a basket filled with bowls and utensils. A minute later, the table was set and the group of Tantarri bowed before leaving.

Ashland sat up and set the hammock swinging. "At least you're not floating away anymore."

"Yeah." Brock sat up. "Thank goodness it finally wore off. It felt bizarre to be all floaty. I wouldn't want to do that outside without anything above but open sky. At least, not without some weight on me."

Everyone abandoned their hammocks and claimed seats on the benches that lined both sides of the long table. The biscuits in the basket were warm, fluffy, and delicious. Lars scooped steaming porridge from the pot and plopped a clump into each bowl before passing it along. While Brock was not a fan of the mushy dish, he was too hungry to care. Starved from the lack of food the day prior, they ate in silence as they focused on filling their stomachs. The plates were mostly empty when another visitor appeared.

All eyes turned to the familiar face at the doorway.

With a bow, Puri addressed them. "Good morning, guests. I hope you slept well." She directed her attention toward Brock. "Master flyer. If you have finished your meal, my father would like to speak with you."

Brock glanced at Ashland as he climbed off the bench. "Yes, Puri. Let me put my boots on, and I'll join you."

After slipping his feet into the boots, he gave her a nod to indicate he was ready. The Tantarri woman bowed to the others and then turned to leave. Brock followed her down the narrow corridor, lit by a flickering torch at each intersection. They reached an open room with branching tunnels, one with a descending stairwell and another with a rising stairwell. Puri led him to the one that went up, following a winding stone staircase that brought them to a spacious terrace. Unlike the other parts of Mondomi that he had seen, the terrace was open to the outdoors. The cliff on the opposite side of the narrow canyon consisted of red and brown stripes, brightly lit by the morning sun. The ceiling above appeared to be a natural rock overhang that extended for hundreds of feet, providing shelter from the sun and rain. Puri led Brock across the upper tier of the terrace before descending three steps to the lower tier, where the head clansman waited.

Puri stopped a few strides from the man, gesturing for Brock to continue. He sidled up to the short stone block wall that surrounded the terrace. Imitating the man standing beside him, Brock put his hands on the waist-high wall to gaze out at the scene beyond.

Below the terrace, a small city made of stone bustled with activity. Horses pulled carts filled with supplies along narrow streets. Women tended clothing lines strung on the rooftops. Children played in a plaza, running and laughing. Men and women filled buckets of water from a fountain at another plaza. A third plaza located upon building rooftops waited just below where Brock stood. The upper plaza was empty other than a lone craftsman who sat on a bench, carving a wooden totem. A natural rock wall, perhaps ten feet tall, surrounded the outer edge of the city to obscure it from view from the canyon floor beyond.

Brock was stunned. How had this city been constructed into the side of a mountain? The very thought of carving this much stone was beyond comprehension.

"It's amazing, wouldn't you say?" the man beside Brock asked.

"Yes…um…sir. I've never seen anything like it."

He turned toward Brock. "Please, call me Turan. You are not of my people, so any other term would be inappropriate."

Unsure of what to do, Brock imitated Puri's bow. "I feel privileged to meet you, Turan. My name is Brock Talenz."

Turan smiled. "Manners. This is good. I hoped that you would not be difficult." He stepped away from the wall. "Come with me."

Brock followed as the man spoke. Puri trailed them both at a distance.

"We Tantarri have lived here for four hundred years." His arm swept out in a gesture toward the city. "This place is our home and is quite special to us. You and your companions will be the first outsiders to visit this place and leave alive. Ever."

Brock swallowed hard. The Tantarri had meant to kill them, but something happened to change their intentions. He sensed that he was about to discover what it was.

Turan led him to a tunnel that snaked upward, speaking to Brock as he made the ascent. "Every head clansman for the past four hundred years has dreaded your coming. We have remained wary of the signs, waiting for your arrival. Now that you have arrived, the fate of my people rests upon your shoulders and mine. My role is to ensure you have what you need to succeed. Yours is to have the wits to find the correct path and the will to survive."

Brock had no idea what the man was talking about. "I don't understand."

The man paused, glancing at Brock with sad eyes. "Soon, you will."

Turan led Brock up the winding stairwell and into a small cave. A thin beam of light streamed through a single opening opposite from the entrance. Looking through the narrow opening, Brock realized that they were directly above the terrace they had just vacated.

Shifting focus, his eyes settled on an old man sitting cross-legged on the floor. Blue-colored smoke emitted from a small brazier next to the man. The smoke swirled about, filling the small room with an odd sweet scent.

Turan addressed the man. "Elder Yuranni." He paused as he gave a shallow bow to the old man. "The portent hovers above us in the morning sky, warning the Tantarri of what is to come. The Duratti Prophecy comes to fruition." He gestured toward Brock. "I present to you the outlander who can wield the lost magic. May fate smile upon him and the quest to come."

The small man raised his head, his eyes looking upon Brock. Despite the slight stature of the ancient man, Brock sensed the weight of wisdom in his dark eyes. A gust of wind whistled through the narrow window and teased the man's wispy white hair, causing it to dance and his long white beard to ruffle

The man gestured at the floor before him. "Please, sit, my son."

Brock sat across from the man. The brazier stood to one side, the blue-tinted smoke filling Brock's lungs. He soon began to feel dizzy. The old man beckoned with his fingers, and Brock leaned close. Yuranni's palm settled on Brock's forehead, and the man closed his eyes. After a few moments, his eyes flashed open, and he nodded.

"He is indeed the outlander from my vision. I sense the lost magic within him and life magic as well."

The old man stared into Brock's eyes with frightening intensity. Brock felt light-headed, and the room began to spin. Yuranni's skinny arm shot out to grab Brock's wrist. The man's eyes rolled back and Brock's vision blurred to white.

Brock drifted in the white, all floaty and weightless. As if a fog were lifting, an image materialized before him. He found himself high above the Tantarri plains, a battle raging below him. Paladins from the Holy Army fought against waves of giant creatures. The Tantarri rode in on horseback, attacking the evil army from the side, but it was clear that the enemy was too many. Time lurched, the evil army replaced by scattered human corpses littering the grassy fields. Among the broken bodies of Paladins and Tantarri warriors, he found only a scattering of enemy remains.

The image blurred again, revealing a city of stone built into the side of a mountain. Lonely streets of blood-soaked stone were a harsh reminder of the joy and hope that used to dominate the now dead city.

Leaving a trail of corpses behind, the dark army had moved on. Brock knew they could not be stopped. Humanity was doomed, destined to be but a memory. He began to cry as the last threads of hope inside him severed. Mankind would be no more.

His vision cleared, and he was back in the small cave. The old man before him sat with his head bowed. Brock wiped the tears from his face, trying to get his emotions under control. *Was that a dream?*

The old man lifted his head, locking eyes with Brock. "No, it was not a dream. It was a vision of the future."

Choked up, it was difficult for Brock to speak. "How did you do that? It was so vivid, so real."

"It is called dream weaving." The old man gave a small smile. "I must confess, this is not the first time you and I have shared a dream."

Brock's brow furrowed. "What do you mean? We just met."

"The world of dreams does not require physical proximity. It is possible for a practiced Dreamweaver to locate someone, though they are a great distance away, and share a vision within their dreams. Even someone whom they have yet to meet." Yuranni glanced up at Turan before looking back toward Brock. "About a year and a half ago, I experienced a vision of great importance - what you call prophecy. Driven by this vision, I entered the world of dreams to locate the person from my vision, seeking to implant a rune within his mind, for without my interference, the lost magic would never return." The man folded his hands in his lap and leaned back. "Though we had not met, my vision gave me an impression of your spirit, your essence, which I located through the world of dreams. I then entered your dream, presented myself in the image of your god so you would not question the message, and imprinted the rune into your mind."

Brock's eyes grew wide as he remembered the dream he had the night of the banshee attack at Glowridge Pass.

Yuranni nodded. "You know of what I speak."

"Yes. I know of it." An inkling of wonder rang within Brock's voice as he tried to grasp the concept.

"And I expect that the rune helped you in some significant way?"

Brock nodded, thinking back on how charging the rune with *Chaos* had animated Hank's corpse – a corpse that attacked the banshee before both fell over the cliff edge. "Yes. Without it, I would have been killed." He then remembered the encounter with the bacabra. He had used that same rune to bring a boulder to life. "In fact, it saved me twice."

Yuranni nodded. "The vision warned that we were doomed unless I took action. Though it is against our beliefs to insert oneself into another's dreams, I found that I had no choice. I apologize for the violation."

Brock didn't know what to say. His thoughts recalled what Yuranni had revealed.

"What about the vision you just showed me?"

The old man sighed. "The night after I entered your dreams, I had a vision of hope, matching an ancient prophecy that the Tantarri hold dear. Each night since then, I have instead had some variation of the terrible vision I just showed to you. These visions all relate to the same prophecy, one that Tantarri Elders have witnessed countless times over the past four centuries. "

"It's not just the Tantarri, is it?" Brock stammered. "I saw…I felt everyone dying. It would be the end of everyone."

The old man nodded. "That is correct. All of humanity will fall to this evil force."

"I don't understand," Brock said. "Why show it to me?"

"The weight of responsibility is heavy, but there are some who seek it like a drug. They seek power, seek to control others." The old man paused, his eyes softening. "Sometimes, responsibility seeks out the person. When this happens, forces unknown see in a person what is required. Some quality within makes them special. Perhaps it is courage. Perhaps it is strength of will. Perhaps something else. I believe it is a strong sense of compassion. After all, isn't caring the most desirable quality in a leader?"

Still not understanding, Brock asked a different way. "I still don't understand what this has to do with me."

"To understand, first you must understand how true prophecy works." The old man explained. "Imagine you toss a stone into a pool, sending ripples across the peaceful surface of the water. Now imagine the water to be the calm of life magic, what you call *Order*. When a world-changing event occurs, it is like the stone dropping into the peaceful pool of *Order*, sending ripples outward, even into the past. Those with the ability of true prophecy encounter these ripples in the form of visions. Since these events are in the future, there are variations in the outcome, dictated by people's actions leading up to the event itself. You see, our future is not pre-determined, it is the result of a convergence of what might happen and the choices we make."

Brock nodded, confirming that he understood. "So you are saying that this vision is one of many possible futures, which means there are other possible outcomes."

"It is good that can think with reason." Yuranni gave a nod and a small smile. "I have seen similar visions of this event hundreds of times. All but once, I have witnessed the same heartbreaking outcome."

Brock gritted his teeth, holding back his growing frustration. "So, there is hope, but it is slight. What can we do?"

Elder Yuranni looked up past Brock. "Turan, did you bring the Duratti scroll?"

Brock glanced up at Turan, who pulled a roll of yellowed paper from his belt. Unrolling it, he read out loud.

"And, so, many generations after the War of Wails, a portent will appear in the morning sky. Look for the star that shines during daylight, for it marks the return of the great evil. Within days of this warning, an outlander will appear on Tantarri lands. You must bring this outlander to the mountain home. Misguided by distrust, you will attempt to imprison him though your deepest pit cannot hold him. You will know him when he walks above where others tread, for he is blessed with the lost magic."

Turan glanced at Brock before continuing. "The Tantarri must watch for him, share these words, and keep him safe. This outlander marks the *Reditus*, the return of the lost magic. In all possible futures I have envisioned, the coming enemy destroys everything unless they face the might of the lost magic. Even then, the path to survival is a narrow thread stretched across a deep chasm."

Brock thought about the words, about the term *lost magic. They must be referring to* Chaos. While there were others who could now use it, everything had started with him. His mind was racing, trying to understand.

"So this prophecy, you're saying that it describes me." Brock realized it was difficult to argue, based on the specifics described. "Where did you get this?"

Elder Yuranni spoke. "It was written by my ancestor, Elder Duratti, roughly four hundred years ago. He was the first of the Tantarri elders and was the first to experience visions of this event. Like me, he had hundreds of prophetic visions, all but a single instance ending in despair. The prophecy you just heard are the words he wrote after his vision of hope." Yuranni paused, frowning. "Since his passing, his ancestors have seen many times that number, never again seeing this single path to an outcome of survival. That is, until the night I entered your dreams."

Brock swallowed hard. Four hundred years was a long time for these people to wait. One vision resulting in survival among thousands ending in doom spoke to poor odds. Although disheartening, giving up hope was outside his nature.

"Let's say I believe you. What can I do? I can't stop an army, I'm just one person."

Turan spoke again. "There is more in the prophecy. Listen closely."

He unrolled the scroll again and located the passage needed. "Guided by a single warrior of the head clansman's line, this outlander must lead a quest for secrets hidden within a throne marked by runes. Guard the outlander well, for the quest will be fraught with peril and death. With this prize in hand, they must free the lost magic and meet the armies of evil in the heart of Tantarri lands when the portent reaches the evening sky. Should the quest fail, the end of humanity is certain. Of this fate, there can be no doubt. This vision is the greatest truth I will ever record."

Turan paused, glancing at Brock and then at Puri before continuing. "There was more to my vision, though I know not what it means." He read, unrolling the scroll to reveal the bottom. "The outlander must close the world's wound and stop the bleeding before it's too late. He must also seek the truth and set it free, for the lost magic hides within a web of lies. The coming days will be dark for mankind. Remember, when the portent shifts to the evening sky, death will roll across the plains of Tantarri."

Turan lowered the scroll, his eyes locking with Brock's.

Brock turned from Turan to the old man on the floor across from him. "I don't understand. What do these things mean? What am I to do?"

Yuranni nodded. "It is much to consider." He glanced to Turan then back to Brock. "We have had centuries to think on this and yet have little to offer in guidance. We instead must place our hope in you to find the answers. Even the vision I experienced myself was clouded, leaving an impression of hope without the details that Duratti recorded."

Brock tried to come to grips with the words that Turan had read to him. Where to begin? He recalled the vision again. It felt so real, the sorrow lingering.

"This is difficult to digest." He said, his gaze shifting from Yuranni to Turan and back. "I agree that something must be done, but I have no idea what I am to do. Please tell me that I don't have to do it alone, that my friends are allowed to join me."

The elder spoke again. "Yes, your companions may join you. As the prophecy notes, one of Turan's children must join you as well, or the quest will fail."

Brock looked toward Turan, who glanced at Puri.

"I want to go with them, Father. I am as skilled a warrior as Juran," she said. "He has been leading Clan Halatti since you became head clansman. I, however, have no defined role. In addition, Juran remains blinded by his hatred." She nodded in conviction. "I am the logical choice."

Turan stared at Puri, his brow furrowed as he considered her words.

Brock interjected. "The prophecy mentioned seeking a throne of runes. We haven't seen kings, queens, or thrones for centuries. How am I to find a throne I know nothing about when it's been lost for hundreds of years?"

"I regret that I have no answers. Nor can I guess at what wound must be closed or at what truth must be set free," Yuranni replied. "You must rely on your own council in these matters. We place our faith in the choices that you and your companions make. The actions of man, the guidance of free will, and the gift of hope are the best weapons against a dark prophecy."

Brock muttered "Why me?"

Yuranni laughed. "I would ask the same question if I were in your shoes. This is not a fanciful tale of some *Chosen One*." He laughed again. "From what we have been able to determine, one simple thing hinges on the survival of humanity. Somehow, you are triggering the return of the lost magic. According to the prophecy, we cannot survive the coming days without it. Keep that in mind, and I believe you will find your way."

Brock couldn't believe this was happening.

His thoughts drifted back to how he had gained the false rune of *Order* when trying to pursue a better life by entering the Academy to become a Master. Everything had been going well until Varius discovered his deceit, forcing him to flee the school. Now, Brock and his friends had the hopes of a nation, and perhaps of all humanity, relying on them. He still didn't know what they were supposed to do or how to get it done. *How did I end up in this mess?*

25

Turan left Brock alone with Puri and sent a warrior to fetch Brock's friends. Brock leaned against the block wall of the terrace and stared down at the busy city below, his mind elsewhere as he struggled to come to grips with what had been revealed.

He turned around, looking up as he searched for the window to the old man's room. After a moment, he spotted the opening and was surprised at how well it blended with the rock. His gaze lowered, shifting to find Puri studying him with her dark eyes. Feeling self-conscious from her intense glare, Brock spoke to break the tension.

"Why does your brother hate me, Puri?" he asked. "What have I done that he wants me dead?"

Puri sighed as she stopped beside Brock and leaned on the short wall. "He doesn't hate you. You are just a convenient target for his hatred. He sees you as the enemy who betrayed him and broke his heart."

She turned toward him, her eyes searching his face. "What do you know of the Tantarri?"

Brock shrugged. "Truthfully, very little. The Ministry shares almost no information about the Tantarri with Empire citizens."

"Then, I will start at the beginning." She rested her elbows on the short wall, her gaze directed toward the city below. "Long ago, the clans came to the plains in search of refuge. There, they found fertile lands to feed their cattle. They also found herds of wild horses, but not just any horses. They were the fastest and most beautiful animals anyone had ever seen. Among them was a glorious white stallion, who led the largest herd. It was then that the head clansman, Garamon the Great, declared these lands to be our new home. Smitten with the beauty of the lead stallion, he vowed to tame the animal and become one with its spirit. The clans moved about the vast plains, relocating periodically so their cattle could feed on fresh grass. Their travels followed the herd of wild horses. Each time they drew close, Garamon would attempt to befriend the white stallion, knowing that the horse was the key to gaining the trust of the herd. Days became weeks, weeks became months, months became years, and still Garamon pursued the wild white stallion but was never even able to touch the beautiful animal. Two years after he had initiated his pursuit, Garamon followed the stallion and his herd into this very canyon." She gestured toward the sunlit canyon walls before them. "The horse led the head clansman and his party up the narrow trail along the canyon wall. There, he discovered an abandoned city of rock, hidden from view."

She paused, looking at Brock as he digested her story. "But that was not all. The wild herd led Garamon down a long tunnel that opened to a secret valley filled with lush grass and a spring-fed lake. Surrounded on all sides by steep cliffs, the tunnel was the only path to this hidden valley, which Garamon named Viridian. This is when Garamon knew he had truly found a home for the Tantarri, naming the rock city Mondomi, which means *home in the mountain.*

"Within Viridian, the lead stallion finally allowed Garamon to approach. With a slow and steady hand, Garamon greeted the beautiful creature. Amazingly, when he grabbed the stallion's mane and mounted its back, it did not rear nor bolt. Instead, it remained calm and ready. With a thrill in his heart, Garamon bid the stallion to a trot, then to a gallop. Soon, they were racing across the green fields of Viridian, riding faster than man had ever traveled before.

"Garamon named the stallion Primus and proudly led the herd out to the plains to meet his people. When the clans saw Garamon approaching upon the white stallion, followed by the herd of wild horses, they were amazed. This is when they named him Garamon the Great. He led the Tantarri here to Mondomi, where we have lived ever since."

She smiled. "This is the legend of the Tantarri. How much is true, I do not know. What I can tell you is that the Tantarri raise the fastest horses in the world. Our horses are a great resource, much desired by your Empire. This resource allowed the Tantarri to exist peacefully and independently from the Empire for centuries. That is, until twelve years ago when Archon Ringholdt demanded the Tantarri join the Empire and share the herds for the benefit of all. Of course, the clans refused. Since then, the Tantarri have been at war with the Empire. Two years ago, we believed the war was nearing an end after a Ministry emissary approached to arrange a meeting with our leaders. When the Tantarri emissary, led by Juran, met with the Ministry, they were attacked. That act of betrayal further damaged the relationship while taking the lives of key members of the Tantarri. One of those lives was Juran's wife, Minurri."

Brock nodded, now understanding. "Juran hates the Ministry for their betrayal and for the death of his wife. He hates me because he sees me as one of them."

Puri nodded. "I'm glad that you can think logically. Since much rides on you, it gives me hope." She smiled.

"Wow. Thanks," he replied, sarcastically.

"Brock!"

Turning about, Brock smiled when he saw Ashland descending the steps and crossing the terrace, trailed by the others.

"I'm so glad you're safe," she said as she approached.

"Yeah. I'm fine." He glanced at Puri. "I have some…new information. It appears we now have a mission, but our future has become far more dangerous."

Ashland was staring at him with an odd look on her face. Benny slid in next to her, squinting through his spectacles while leaning close to Brock's face. Parker, Cam, and Lars all stepped closer, looking at Brock over Benny's shoulders.

"What is that?" Benny said, pointing at Brock's head.

Ashland's eyes narrowed. "It's another rune, Benny." Her focus shifted from Brock's forehead to his eyes. "Did you know you've been marked with a *Chaos* rune?"

Brock was confused, trying to digest her words. "What are you talking about?"

She touched his forehead. "*Chaos*. Its right here, embedded into your *Order* rune."

He glanced at Puri, who replied. "You did not know this? When Elder Yuranni touched your forehead, it appeared as was foretold. It marks the return of the lost magic, the magic needed to defeat our coming enemy."

Brock put his palm against his forehead, his mind racing. *Yes, life is definitely going to be more dangerous.*

"You mentioned a mission. What mission?" Benny asked.

Brock turned toward Benny and refocused on what was before him. "There is a prophecy that mentions me, mentions us." His gaze swept across his companions as he spoke. "Something bad is coming, and we have been tasked with a quest that could stop it. Failure could mean the end of everything, of everyone." He paused, thinking about the gravity of his statement. His brow furrowed. "Apparently, I need your help to find some throne of runes."

"The Emblem Throne?" Parker asked.

"What?" Brock frowned at Parker.

Parker glanced around and found expressions ranging from curiosity to bewilderment. "The Emblem Throne. You know. The song you sing during knucklebones."

"Knucklebones?" Lars asked. "What are you going on about?"

Everyone stared at Parker, waiting for a response. "Nobody else has played knucklebones?"

Heads shook in response. Parker shrugged, explaining.

"It's a game you play, kind of like dice. However, it relies on quickness and dexterity rather than luck. I used to play it with my friends in Sol Polis when I was a kid."

Brock's brow furrowed. "What's this have to do with a throne of runes?"

Parker sighed in response. "While playing knucklebones, we sing songs and play to the beat. One of the songs is called *The Emblem Throne*. Listen."

Parker began slapping his thigh to a beat, nodding his head as he sang.

"People lie when they feel they must, though they hide behind truthful tone,
Scheme and cheat those who trust, but no lie may pass The Emblem Throne,
With runes gracing the rising sun, behind a seat of Tallinor's own

Gifting him with eyes of truth, no lie may pass The Emblem Throne."
Parker grinned. "There's more, but you get the idea."
Brock nodded. It was a thin lead, but it was something. "So where is this throne and who is Tallinor?"
Parker shrugged. "Tallinor was the King of Kalimar, hundreds of years ago."

Pulling the curtain back, Brock held it to allow Ashland to pass before he followed through the doorway. A single torch on the wall illuminated the empty room with their friends still on the terrace eating lunch. Ashland had asked him to join her for a private moment, setting Brock's stomach flipping between hope and anxiety.

She glanced toward the swaying curtain before meeting his eyes. "I didn't want to say anything in front of the others, but are you sure we should do this? We know nothing about these people, and now you're asking us to run off on some crazy quest based on the words of an old man."

Brock sighed. "I know it sounds outlandish, but you weren't there." Stepping closer, he gazed into her eyes. "These people can wield *Order* in ways unknown to us. I suspect they know things about *Order* that the Ministry doesn't. I'm not sure how he did it, but this Elder Yuranni showed me a vision. It was of the future, or at least a possible future. Death and destruction swept over the land, obliterating everything, even this city in the mountain. Everyone, every single person on the continent, died in this vision." Brock felt the emotion of the vision creeping back in. The sorrow. The heartache.

Ashland's eyes searched his. "You appear convinced. Whatever it was, it must have been compelling."

He nodded. "There was something about the vision and the prophecy they read to me. I could sense the truth of it. Whatever's coming is ominous. I can feel it building, somewhere out there. We have to find this Emblem Throne. If we don't, I'm afraid that we will lose everything." He wrapped his arms around her waist. "Part of me wants to take you and run off to hide somewhere, but I'm afraid it would just delay the inevitable for us while also dooming everyone else."

Ashland's eyes drifted closed as she leaned in for a kiss, opening them when she pulled back. "I love the idea of running away with you, but the Brock I know couldn't live with himself knowing that he abandoned everyone."

Brock smiled. "You're probably right." He paused, thinking about their discussion. "Nobody has said it yet, but I'm sure others will be questioning this plan as well. For now, they're happy to be alive and to know that we are soon leaving. Once we are away, the questions will come, and I might need your help in convincing them to give this a chance."

Ashland nodded. "Of course I'll help." She smiled. "We're in this together."

Brock kissed her again. Looking back toward the closed curtain, he found that the tunnel outside remained quiet. His focus shifted, eying the hammock they had slept in.

"We have a few minutes alone." A smile crept across his face. "The hammock looks like it could offer some interesting possibilities."

A smile lit her face. "Brock Talenz, you are so bad." Glancing at the hammock, her smile took a devious turn. "Let's hurry before the others come back."

26

———————

Cam had done his best to bury thoughts of Tegan, trying to focus on the future rather than the past. However, when he looked at Puri, he couldn't help but think of the fiery red-haired girl. She and Puri shared much in their physical stature and the way they carried themselves. However, Puri had an exotic nature that made her unique.

Sitting at a table with his friends, he remained quiet as they bantered in conversation during the dinner. Cam ate because he was hungry, but his eyes continually searched out the table where Puri sat with other Tantarri leaders. It was obvious that the Tantarri respected her. He felt unsure if it was because her father was head clansman or her skill as a warrior. Perhaps both.

"Cam, do you want another slice of beef?" Ashland asked as she held the platter toward him.

"Sure. Thanks."

He slid a thick slab of meat on his plate before passing the platter to Lars. Cam cut a section and took a bite, finding the meat juicy and flavorful. It went well with the boiled vegetables and flatbread served alongside it. The wheat ale provided was also delicious. He took another drink, enjoying the sweet hint of pumpkin that reduced the bitter aftertaste.

As Cam ate, he scanned the faces of his companions. Smiles and laughter surrounded him, and everyone appeared in good spirits – the Tantarri feast a welcome distraction from the dangerous quest before them. His eyes landed on Brock, and the new rune on his friend's forehead. After a lifetime of seeing familiar vocation runes, it was startling to see the red starburst of *Chaos* stamped within the blue-tinted symbol for *Order*. It would be difficult for Brock to go unnoticed. Cam did not understand what had happened, but he knew it was significant. Whether for good or bad, things had changed forever. He had the feeling that the future would require him to support Brock more than ever.

Loud beats began to thump throughout the city, causing Cam to seek its source. He glanced down toward the Tantarri in one of the plazas below. All eyes were focused up past where Cam and his friends sat. He followed the direction of their gaze, turning toward the terrace overlooking the city, two stories above the rooftop plaza where Cam and his friends sat.

The drumming stopped, and the city fell quiet. Turan appeared at the short wall surrounding the terrace, raised his arms, and addressed the people below.

"Good evening, Tantarri nation." His voice carried amazingly well, echoing off the angled rock overhang above. "Thank you for joining in this feast. It is well that we pause and enjoy what we have, for the path the Tantarri travel is about to turn."

"As foretold long ago, the *Reditus* has come. The lost magic returns." The announcement sent a buzz throughout the city. Turan waved his arms to urge quiet.

"Yes, it is true. Tomorrow, a select group of Tantarri warriors will escort our outlander guests to the border of Tantarri lands. From there, my daughter will join the outlanders on a quest of great importance. The fate of the Tantarri hangs in the balance, determined by the success or failure of this quest."

Turan waved a fist high, pumping it. "However, the Tantarri will not sit idle waiting for the outcome. Instead, we will prepare for the future and the war that will surely come to our lands. I speak not of the pitiful disagreement we have with the Empire. No, this war will rival, or perhaps even surpass, the War of Wails. There cannot be doubt that war will come; it is merely a matter of time."

He held his arms wide, a welcoming gesture. "But this evening is not about war and death. Tonight, we celebrate life. I urge you to enjoy your-selves this evening, for tomorrow we begin our preparations. When the war comes, you will be asked to do everything in your power to preserve the lives and freedom of those you love."

A deafening cheer rose up, vigorous enough that Cam felt the energy of it within his chest. Turan turned from the edge of the terrace, disap-pearing from view.

A Tantarri woman came to the table with a pitcher, refilling mugs with the pumpkin-spiced ale. With his mug refilled, Cam took a deep drink and wiped the orange-tinted foam from his lips.

The loud beats of the drums began again, accompanied by the strum-ming of something sounding much like a lute. Looking for the source of the music, he spotted a group of Tantarri on a nearby rooftop. The sound of pipes joined in, filling in missing notes. A Tantarri woman, standing upon the rooftop, began to sing.

Cam had heard music in taprooms in Nor Torin, which often involved a man with a lute singing some rhyme as he strummed. However, he had never heard anything that sounded like this, filled with joy and energy. Glancing around, he noticed Tantarri everywhere were rising to their feet and dancing to the beat.

Ashland's eyes lit up. "It's wonderful." She grabbed Brock's hand as she stood. "Come. Let's dance!"

Brock laughed. "How can I say no?"

The two ran out and joined the dancing Tantarri on the rooftop plaza. Ashland's smile glowed, Brock laughed as they dipped, danced, and spun with the music. Cam watched them for a bit, deciding that they danced well, far better than he could.

"They are not bad."

He turned, surprised to see Puri claiming the seat that Ashland had just vacated. Her intense brown eyes followed the dancing couple.

"Um…Yeah," he replied, anxiety now brewing in his gut.

Puri's eyes flicked toward Cameron. She looked him up and down, appraisingly. The way her eyes measured him made him uncomfortable. He swallowed hard, unsure of what to say.

"You must be a great warrior among your people," Puri noted.

Cam's eyes shifted to determine if she was addressing Lars, but he was busy talking to Benny.

Cam cleared his throat. "Well, I was training to be one." He found himself sweating. Why did she make him so nervous?

She leaned forward and rested her elbows on the table, her piercing eyes locked on his.

"I examined your weapons before we returned them to you. I saw the rune on the blade you claimed. The Tantarri know this blade. If you are not a great warrior, did you steal it?"

Cam's face clouded over. "No, I didn't steal it. That would be wrong." He calmed himself before continuing. "My father gave it to me."

Puri nodded. *"The Calm."*

Cam raised an eyebrow. He shouldn't be surprised. His father was well known, and he'd been in skirmishes with the Tantarri late in his career with the Holy Army.

"Yes."

Puri eyed him again. "You are among a great line of warriors then." She smiled, nodding. "That is good." She glanced toward the people dancing. "Would you like to dance with me?"

Cam glanced at Brock and Ashland and frowned. "No."

Dancing did not appeal to him, expecting he would do poorly. His eyes flicked back to Puri to find her eyes narrowed at him. He held his hands up in appeal.

"Sorry. It's not...I just don't dance...sorry."

Her eyes softened. "I see." Her gaze returned to the dancers as she spoke. "Among the Tantarri, everyone dances. It is part of us, as is the music we play."

Cam nodded. "Again, sorry."

She smiled. "If you don't dance, perhaps you'd like to do something else with me?"

Cam's heart began to race. "What did you have in mind?"

She stood, grabbed his hand, and pulled him to his feet. Her eyes scanned him from head to toe. When her gaze met his again, a smile spread across her face.

"Come with me. I'll show you. I think you'll like it."

27

———

Watching Puri as she dressed, Cam appreciated her lithe and fit form. The evening with her had been wonderful, even therapeutic. His torn heart now had been patched over, in the process of healing. In many ways, Puri was Tegan's equal. In some, she was far superior. As Puri laced her leather vest, she spoke to him.

"You need to get moving. We are to leave within the hour."

Realizing she was correct, Cam sat upright, which caused the hammock to swing. He flipped his legs over the side and dropped to the stone floor. The hard surface felt cold beneath his bare feet as he gathered his clothing. He glanced toward Puri and found her leering in his direction.

"What?" he asked.

"Men are not alone in their ability to appreciate the form of another," she flashed a devious grin.

Cam felt a flush of embarrassment as he pulled his tunic over his head. Once he was dressed, Puri drew the doorway curtain aside and waved Cam forward. He ducked as he stepped through, careful not to hit his head. Having made that mistake the previous evening, the lump on his head was a painful reminder that still hurt.

She led him along a narrow corridor, down a flight of stairs, and approached the room where his friends were staying. Puri drew the curtain aside, and he slid past her. Heads turned in their direction, more than one face showing a brow raised in question. Feeling his cheeks flush again, Cam glanced at Puri to gauge her reaction.

Seemingly unaffected, Puri addressed the group. "It is good that you are awake. I feared that you might find yourself ill from partaking in last night's feast."

Brock smiled weakly. "We've had better mornings. However, a messenger was just here and reminded us to prepare for an early departure."

"This is helpful." She nodded. "Gather your things and meet me in the receiving hall. It is the cavern where we first met."

Puri turned and ducked out the door without giving Cam a second glance. He stared at the settling curtains as he listened to her footsteps fading. While he had a wonderful night with Puri, he had no idea what it meant. *Does she like me or did she just seek me out for the personal contact?* Cam decided that he might never understand women.

Shaking his head to refocus, he crossed the room to gather his belongings. By the time he had his sword belt strapped and pack shouldered, everyone was ready to go.

Brock's gaze swept the room, briefly making eye contact with each of them. "Is everyone ready?" Everyone nodded, and he walked toward the doorway. "Let's go."

Cam and the others followed Brock as he ducked through the curtain. They traveled down the rock tunnel and down a flight of stairs to another tunnel. When they entered the cavern where they first met Puri, they found her waiting with her a sword strapped to her back, long dagger at her hip, and a loaded saddlebag in hand. Nine other Tantarri warriors stood beside her, armed with weapons and supplies.

"Follow me." She waved them forward.

As Puri led them to the opposite tunnel, the other Tantarri warriors trailed behind the group. The tunnel brought them to a much wider tunnel that opened to the canyon sky in one direction. Puri turned the other direction, leading them deeper into the mountain. Since the tunnel was quite broad, they walked in a clump rather than in a trailing column. After a quarter mile, the tunnel revealed light beyond a curve ahead.

To Cam's amazement, they emerged from the tunnel into a hidden valley surrounded by steep cliffs on all sides. The rising sun was just emerging above the high cliffs to the east, brightly lighting the western half of the valley. The scene thrived with life, green and lush despite it being winter. A single lake lay near the center, its calm surface reflecting the bright sky above. Herds of horse and cattle crazed peacefully in the fields, feasting on the long grasses. It was gorgeous.

Three Tantarri men were waiting for them. Puri approached the men, speaking with them before one of them turned and whistled. A small herd of horses came running from around a rock outcropping. Whites, browns, blacks, and spotted piebalds trotted over to the man who had whistled. He stood calmly among the horses as they surrounded him.

Puri returned and addressed Cam and his friends. "Please listen carefully. You are to spread out in this area. You may touch a horse with your hand if it comes close, but do not move your feet. Once a horse picks you, we will tell you its name. You are to take a few minutes to become friends with your horse while we prepare to have it saddled."

Tipper appeared confused. "Do you mean that we choose a horse?"

Puri shook her head. "You do not choose a Tantarri horse. A Tantarri horse chooses you."

Tipper's brow furrowed in confusion, reflecting Cam's own thoughts. The others began to spread out and Cam followed suit. The Tantarri man who had called the horses passed through the group and made another high-pitched whistle. The horses began to wander among Cam and his friends. After a number of horses passed him, a tall male piebald stopped a step away. The animal sniffed at him before nuzzling him with his nose. Tentatively, Cam reached up to pet the horse's forehead. He glanced around to find the others speaking to the horses who had approached them.

"Hi, boy." Cam spoke to the animal, trying to figure out what to say to a horse. "You're a pretty horse."

The horse whinnied and shook its head with a snort. Startled, Cam backed away a step. A Tantarri man approached with a saddle in hand.

"His name is Gigamont. He is quite proud," the warrior said as he hoisted the saddle onto the horse's back. "I would not call him pretty again if I were you."

Cam considered another approach while the man secured the saddle. "Hello Gigamont. My name is Cam. I would be honored if a glorious steed such as yourself would consider me as a rider."

The horse nuzzled Cam's neck and stamped a front hoof twice.

The Tantarri warrior stepped back, finished with the saddle. He nodded to Cam. "Much better. You will get along fine."

As the man moved away, Cam stepped beside Gigamont. Placing one foot in the stirrup and one hand on the saddle horn, he hoisted himself up into the saddle.

"Where's the bridle?" Brock asked from astride the red roan that had chosen him.

That's when Cam realized there were no bridle or reins.

Puri responded, shaking her head. "Tantarri do not use bridles."

"How do we steer the horse?" Parker asked.

She smiled. "You'll see."

28

Ashland moved gingerly, wincing as she sat upon the downed tree. Having not ridden a horse since her first year at the Academy, one day in the saddle left her sore - every movement hurt from her ribs down to her feet. She glanced over at Libby, who gritted her teeth in pain as she sat beside Tipper. Those two were in misery together, neither having ever ridden before. Libby had opted to ride with Ashland rather than attempting to ride on her own. To the girl's credit, she never complained despite receiving the worst of every bump coming through the saddle.

Tipper, on the other hand, complained to Brock throughout the day. The two boys had shared a horse as well, but Tipper was sure to let Brock know how much every movement hurt. At one point, he even accused Brock of purposefully making it as bad as possible. Brock laughed it off, claiming to be at the mercy of the roan they were riding.

A small groan slipped from Brock as he sat beside Ashland,

"My thighs are sore," he said. "Using them to guide the horse is taking a toll on me."

She nodded in response. When Puri had explained that they had to use pressure with their legs to guide the horse, Ashland had been skeptical. While she was no longer a skeptic, squeezing with her legs throughout the day left them very sore.

Puri stood from her seat among the other Tantarri and circled the fire toward them.

"You outlanders ride worse than I had feared," she said, shaking her head. "Now, you all sit here and complain about pain from riding. I do not understand how you can go through life without experiencing the joy of riding every day. If you rode more often, there would be no pain."

Brock laughed. "It's not that easy, Puri. Horses are very expensive. In the Empire, only the wealthy own horses for riding. Yes, traders own workhorses to pull their wagons, but those horses are a business investment and aren't meant for riding. The rest of the population might dream of owning a horse, but it's a dream that will likely never happen." Brock gestured toward his companions. "Luckily, most of us here attended the Academy, or we'd have never learned to ride at all."

Tipper snorted. "You guys are lucky. After never riding a horse before, I now hurt so much, I can't walk."

Puri shook her head. "You outlanders are strange."

Benny, who had been uncharacteristically quiet, responded. "It is a matter of perspective. What you think is strange, we might find normal. Trust me, there are many things about the Tantarri that we think are strange."

Ashland nodded. "That's true. Perhaps we should learn more about each other, and then our differences won't seem so strange."

Puri stared at Ashland for a long moment before giving a nod. "The words you speak are wise." She sat on a log and stared at Brock and Ashland. "What should I know then?"

Ashland started, not prepared for the direct question. Brock responded instead.

"You make a mistake if you judge us by the actions of the Ministry. While they govern us, they represent their own agenda, not ours. The citizens of the Empire are just people. We all have hopes and dreams. We want to love and to be loved. While we might prefer to go about our lives in peace, many of us also realize that we need to work together and support each other for a better tomorrow. We know that compassion breeds compassion and that hate, selfishness, and contempt lead to bitterness and an empty existence." Brock looked her in the eye. "Do we sound so different?"

Puri and the other Tantarri had listened intently as Brock spoke. As he finished speaking, Ashland noticed that they were nodding along with each statement.

Puri shook her head. "No. We are not so different." She smiled. "I'm glad to know you, outlander."

Brock winced. "Please, call me Brock."

She smiled. "All right, Brock."

As they traveled southward, the forest growth thinned. When they camped for the second night, it was in a hollow near a creek. The surrounding country consisted of pines scattered among dry scrub that grew in the reddish dirt and rock pervading the hillsides.

Mid-morning the following day, they crested a saddle and found a canyon surrounded by steep hillsides. Upon seeing man-made structures at the east end of the canyon, Ashland stared at it and tried to make sense of what it she saw.

A tall brick wall ran across the canyon from north to the south and a road coming in from the west ran up to the gate in the center of the long wall. While a handful of buildings occupied the interior of the compound, it was nowhere near the number normally found in a city. People within the compound were moving about in single-file lines, going in and out of the shadows of the cliff that encapsulated the compound. Ashland had never seen anything like it.

"What is it?" Benny asked.

Puri shook her head. "I do not know. We are now well beyond Tantarri lands. I was instructed to look for an Empire road that runs along the coast and to take it eastward, but that is still miles south of here."

Brock spoke, his brow furrowed. "It's like a small city, but why is it so empty inside? Why such a massive wall for so few buildings? Yet, no towers or a keep exist, so it cannot be a castle."

Ashland thought the very same thing. It was an odd sight. She glanced about for answers but found nothing but shrugs and blank stares.

"This may be dangerous, Hitarri," Puri said to the leader of their escort. "You'll need to stay with us a bit longer. The road to Kalimar cannot be far."

Hitarri nodded. "Yes, Puri."

She raised a hand and waved them forward.

With Puri in the lead, the horses repeatedly turned in switchbacks as they made their descent toward the canyon floor. After fifteen minutes of steady decline, the ground began to level.

Ashland looked toward the compound and found that the wall spanned the width of the canyon. Standing over two-stories tall, men armed with bows patrolled the top of the wall. The gate opened, and a group of twenty armed riders rode out on horseback. It was clear that the riders meant to intercept them when they reached the road.

Puri called out. "Be wary. We will flee west if they attack." She turned toward Hitarri. "You must delay them so we can escape."

Hitarri nodded in response, his expression grim.

The approaching riders came to a stop and waited. As they neared the group, Ashland recognized one of the riders. A stab of fear struck when she realized who it was.

"Eldarro." She heard Brock mutter.

Eldarro stood in his stirrups. "You!" he exclaimed as he pointed toward Brock. "Get them!"

Puri shouted, "Go!"

The horse beneath Ashland and Libby launched into a gallop. She thanked Issal for her firm grip on the saddle horn or she and Libby would have surely flown off in an instant. Libby's arms tightened about Ashland's midsection as the horse shot across the open ground and down the road heading west. A glance to the side revealed Brock and Tipper riding beside her. Ashland turned the other way and found her other companions holding tightly to their saddles as they followed Puri on the lead horse. Craning her neck, she glanced backward to see enemy riders and horses tumbling to the ground in a cloud of dust, Tantarri arrows sticking from them.

Ashland turned to face forward as they sped down the gravel road, creating their own trail of dust. Without a doubt, this was the fastest she had ever traveled. She prayed that the horses would hold out long enough for them to escape.

~

Ashland leaned into Brock with her eyes closed, enjoying the comfort of his embrace. She lifted her head from his shoulder and stared into his eyes.

"What was that place?" she asked him.

He looked off toward the road with eyes narrowed in thought. "I've been thinking about that. It has walls like a city, but it's too empty to be a city. Eldarro and those men rode out from it, so it has something to do with him. Varius mentioned sending me to a mine, and I think that's what we saw."

She nodded. It made sense. "For a mine, it sure has a lot of security."

"True. Maybe what's inside is valuable." His brow furrowed in thought. "Or maybe the security is to keep the people inside, like some sort of prison. A prison for Unchosen."

Their eyes met, both thinking about what it meant. After a moment, Brock's gaze shifted to the side. Ashland turned to see what had caught his attention and realized that Puri was returning. When she reached the small alcove where they had stopped, she had a grim look on her face.

"We cannot take the coastal road." Puri said, shaking her head. "They have sent another group that way to cut us off. They are waiting just east of here."

"If we follow the coast west, we'll end up in Wayport," Parker suggested. "From there, we could take a ship to Sol Polis."

Brock nodded. "True. It might cost more, but it should be just as fast as riding. Maybe faster."

Puri's face clouded. "A ship?"

"Do we have any other choice?" Ashland asked.

She looked toward the others, in search of a response. Everyone remained quiet.

Finally, Puri nodded. "Fine. Let's go."

She mounted her stallion and waved for others to do the same. Once they were all mounted, she led them from the alcove, onto the road, and kicked her horse into a gallop. Prepared this time, Ashland held on tightly as her horse raced after Puri's and headed toward the place she dreaded most.

29

———

The sun was high overhead when Wayport came into view. As they crested a small rise, Ashland looked upon the port city tucked against the Sea of Fates. Although it appeared peaceful and innocent from here, she knew better.

They continued down the Greenway at a trot, through the heart of the valley that led to their destination. Scattered farms and other buildings dotted the countryside. Traffic upon the road steadily increased – farmers' carts, oxen-towed wagons, workers on foot, and an occasional dog or pig. By the time they approached the city gates, the road had grown thick with activity.

Ashland found Parker's horse passing hers as he made his way to the fore, beside Puri.

Parker turned and spoke aloud. "I've been here a number of times. If you'll follow my lead, I will secure us accommodations. It may take some time to locate a ship heading to Sol Polis."

Brock nodded. "That would be great, Parker. Just let us know what to do."

"Good." Parker nodded. "First, let's dismount and break into smaller groups. Horses are expensive and attract attention. A group this size will surely warrant notice."

Puri gave a short whistle and the horses came to a stop. They dismounted, each rider standing beside their steed as Brock addressed the group.

"Lars, Benny, and Ashland will take their horses and follow Parker. Tipper and Libby can go with them since they have no mounts. Cam, Puri, and I will keep a distance behind as we follow."

Everyone nodded in confirmation. While Ashland preferred to remain with Brock, she could guess why he had placed her in separate group. She glanced back at him, noting his new rune. *You should hide your forehead People will notice.* He nodded and pulled the hood of his cloak up.

Parker turned toward Puri. "How do we lead the horses without a bridle?"

Puri smiled. "Just place your hand on Tallidad's neck and begin walking. He will follow."

With a shrug, Parker placed his hand on the stallion's neck and began walking horse toward the gate, the horse following along as if tethered. Likewise, Ashland placed her hand on her mare's neck and followed Parker into the city. The moment she passed through the gate, her stomach twisted in anxiety. After burying the dark years she had spent in Wayport, she felt them clawing back to the surface, threatening to drown the peace she had found since she met Brock.

The stable boy appeared confounded by horses lacking a bridle. After stern instructions from Puri, he told her he understood how to treat the horses. Ashland glanced back at the boy as they walked away. He appeared bewildered as he watched the untethered horses chew on the provided hay. She understood his doubt. It was hard to believe the horses wouldn't wander off.

Parker opened the back door to the inn and held it for the others as they entered. Ashland nodded thanks as she slid past him and walked down a hallway that led past the stairs to the upper levels. The hallway brought them to a taproom, currently occupied by the lunch crowd. With half of the tables open, it wasn't difficult to locate a long table that could seat the group. Ashland slid on a bench beside Brock, who still had his hood up. With both long benches full, Parker grabbed a chair and set it at the head of the table before taking a seat.

Moments later, an older woman with graying brown hair approached. "Hello. Welcome to *Gulley's Inn*. I'm Charlotte, but you can call me Char. What can I get for you?"

Parker took the lead. "We need four rooms, with one of them large enough for three. We will also need meals for the nine of us."

Char began counting on her fingers, calculating the cost. "That will be two silvers and two coppers per day, but ale will cost you extra."

Parker nodded. "Done." He turned toward Benny. "Benny, please pay the woman. Give her some extra to cover the ale."

Benny had a pained look on his face as he pulled out his coin purse. He handed the woman three silvers before flashing Parker a bitter look.

Char pocketed the coins, smiling. "I'll be right back with some roasted lamb and potatoes."

When she walked away, Parker leaned close and spoke to the group. "After we eat, Benny and I will search for a ship bound for Sol Polis, one that can accommodate us."

Benny winced. "I get the suspicion that this little trip is going to cost me."

Brock laughed. "It isn't our fault that you're the one with all the gold."

The pained look resurfaced on Benny's face. "I earned my gold through hard work."

"What?" Brock was incredulous. "You earned most of it by placing bets on us in last year's arena duels. The rest was from an invention that we helped you build and test."

"Well, I guess I didn't have any plans for it anyway." Benny sounded dejected.

Ashland smiled. It felt good to have this friendly banter surrounding her.

The banter continued throughout their meal. Once finished, Parker and Benny departed on their mission to find transportation. The rest of the group followed Char upstairs to settle into the rooms they had rented.

Tipper and Libby took the first room. Ashland smiled when Puri pulled Cam into the next room. The third room they came to was larger, with three beds.

Brock turned to Lars. "Go ahead and take this room to share with Benny and Parker. We'll take the last one."

Lars entered the room, dropped his pack on the floor, and plopped onto the nearest bed.

Char led them up another set of stairs to the room at the end of the third-story hallway. She opened the door and let them inside before giving them a smile and pulling the door closed

Ashland set her pack on the end of the bed and glanced around the room. The quaint space felt homelike, furnished with a vanity and a bed designed for two. Brock crossed the room and pulled the curtain back to reveal the view outside.

The window faced south, toward the bay. Streaks of bright aqua blue shone among the darker blue waters of the sea. The white sails of ships crossing the bay stood bright in the sunlight as gulls circled above, in search of food over the busy docks. One thing spoiled the amazing view, the one thing that drew Ashland's attention. She swallowed hard, trying to keep her emotions in check as she stared at the dark stone structure of the Wayport Temple.

The group chatted in friendly conversation as they waited for dinner to be served. Ashland ran her hand through her hair, now almost dry. Like most of the others, she had seized the opportunity to bathe during the afternoon and found that it felt wonderful to be clean again. She had begun to smell a bit too much like a horse for her own liking.

As the others talked, she attempted to remain engaged, to stay in the present. However, her dark past lingered in the background, like a shadow just beyond view. Brock asked her what was wrong, but she shrugged it off. She should have known he would notice, despite her attempt to hide her discomfort. The sooner they were away from the city, the better.

When she saw Parker approaching with a smile on his face, hope bloomed inside of her. He plopped into the chair at the end the table and addressed the group.

"Good news, folks. We found a ship that can take us, and we leave at noon tomorrow."

Lars clapped Parker on the back. "That is good news! I knew you were the man for the job."

Benny slid onto the bench opposite from Lars. "Yeah. Great," he grumbled.

Brock put an arm around Benny. "What's wrong? Aren't you glad to be on our way?"

The pained look reappeared on Benny's face. "Yeah, but it cost *so* much."

Lars leaned in. "How much?"

When Benny didn't respond, Parker grinned, "Two gold Imperials."

While Lars whistled, Ashland winced. That was a lot of money.

Parker spoke again. "The price includes passage and food for the horses. Unfortunately, we are limited to two cabins, so we'll need to squeeze a bit. If we can get out of here safely, I think we can endure cramped quarters for three days."

Brock nodded. "Splendid job, indeed. Thanks for making this happen." He clapped Benny on the shoulder. "Sorry about the gold, Benny. I'm sure you'll invent some scheme that will make you rich again."

Although Benny's nod appeared dejected, a small smile tugged on the corner of his mouth. Ashland suspected that spending the money didn't hurt him as much as he let on.

Char approached the table with a tray filled with tankards of ale. She passed the drinks out to the group before retreating to fetch their dinner.

Brock held his mug high. "Let's toast to Benny and Parker. Thanks for getting us a ship, guys. We're off to Sol Polis tomorrow."

Mugs tapped each other over the table as the group toasted to the two boys. Ashland smiled despite the anxiety stirring within her, something that would remain until she left the city behind.

After a long night of tossing and turning, Ashland gave up when she saw light coming through the window. She slipped out of bed, careful not to wake Brock as she dressed. Using the washcloth and small bowl of water on the vanity, she quickly washed. Rather than attempt to tame her curly locks, she pulled her hair into a bun and slipped out the door.

When she descended the stairs, the dining room was empty other than Char, who sat at a table looking over some papers. As Ashland approached, the woman glanced up and smiled.

"Good morning, dear. I hope you slept well."

"Good morning, Char." Ashland gave a brief smile. "Actually, I slept horribly. It's not the bed. It's...something that's been bothering me."

"Oh my, dear." She nodded toward the chair across from her. "Please sit. We can talk about it if you like. Sometimes it helps to get it out."

Ashland sat across the table from the old woman, trying to gather her courage. She swallowed hard and forced herself to explain how she felt.

"There's something...something I dread. I feel helpless about it and am afraid to even think about it. Being here, in this city, makes it worse. I don't know what to do."

The old woman's kind eyes stared at Ashland before giving a nod.

Char reached out and took Ashland's hand. "Gulley was my husband. He bought this place over thirty years ago. It was run-down back then, but he fixed it up and built a profitable business. Three years later, he died. His heart just gave up on him. He was a big man with a bigger heart, but not a strong one."

She leaned back, her eyes distant. "When he died, I was lost. I had always relied on him. He ran the business, bought our supplies, set our prices, and managed the money. All I had done was serve tables. I'm marked with the rune for the job, but I didn't know what to do, so I closed the inn down." She sat upright. "After a month of wallowing in pity, I made a decision. I didn't want to be the victim." She shook her head. "I decided that I couldn't let Gulley down. I was stronger than that. He had given me the tools to succeed, laying out how everything needed to be done. I just needed to take charge and make it work. Now, here I am, thirty years later still running this inn and making a good living. In a couple years, I will sell it and retire to a quaint home near the city, not having to work another day in my life." She smiled at the thought.

Ashland forced a smile in return as she considered the advice. Char was right. She had the tools she needed. It was time to address her fears and stop being the victim.

30

———

Ashland took a calming breath and entered the temple. While the morning air was warming outside, it remained cool inside the brick building. Rows of benches surrounded the dais located in the heart of the space. Colored shapes of light shone brightly upon the walls as sunlight streamed through the stained glass panels of the dome above, glinting off the gold-gilded symbols embossed within the walls.

Since it was still early, the building remained empty. Patrons would soon arrive to pray and to give offerings to Issal, but for now, it was peaceful and quiet. Ashland stopped before the glowstone altar and closed her eyes for a moment of reflection.

"Can I help you, child?" A voice came from behind, a voice she recognized immediately.

She turned to face the man. "Hello, Uncle Tyrin."

The man's brow arched in surprise. "Ashland!" He stepped closer. "My favorite niece and pupil has returned. How are you?"

Tyrin appeared much the same as she remembered. Curly brown hair still puffed at the sides of his balding head, although much of it had gone gray. His narrow face accentuated the graying brown mustache draped below his bulbous nose. Although the man had a lean build, he stood a head taller than Ashland and his long, wiry frame held more strength than one would guess. Of that, she knew well.

"I'm with some friends, passing through the city," she replied. "I thought I would stop by the temple while I was here."

Tyrin's eyes scanned her again. "I do not see an Academy cloak upon you. Were you unable to get in?"

Ashland shrugged. "I did get in, but it didn't last. I'll not be an Academy Master after all."

His eyes narrowed, his lips drawing a thin line. "Perhaps we should adjourn to my apartment to discuss this further."

Not waiting for a response, he grabbed her wrist and led her toward the rear of the temple with his purple cloak billowing behind. Ashland's heart was thumping and her vision remained unstable. She grasped for the resolve she had found deciding this course, but unbridled fear threatened to break loose from its pen and trample her will. *You can do this. You must do this*, she told herself.

They exited the temple and entered the adjacent apartments. Tyrin opened the door to his room and waved her forward. She walked inside and found the room looking much the same as she remembered. It did seem a bit smaller now, though. For that matter, so did he. She realized how much her perspective had changed in the past three years. There was a time when this city, this temple, and this man were all she knew.

Tyrin stepped closer and put his hands on her shoulders. "What did you do? If you were accepted, why are you not at the Academy now?"

She looked him in the eye as the heat of anger battled with the fear inside her. Anger at what he had done to her.

"I decided that I'll not be a party to their lies. Much like you, the Ministry hides cruelty and deceit behind a thin veil of pure intentions."

The man's expression changed, hardening. One hand released her shoulder, wound back, and flew toward her face. When it stopped short, he looked down to find her arm blocking his. Rage lit in his eyes as he screamed at her, resorting to intimidation.

"Why do you resist me? You know what it will get you!"

"I'll bend to your will no longer, Tyrin." Ashland was firm. "You are wrong to abuse your position like this, using Issal's name as a shield while inflicting pain on others. It is evil, Tyrin. Promise me you'll stop, and Issal might forgive you."

Raw fury clouded the man's face as it contorted. "How dare you!"

His fist flashed toward her and stopped dead in her palm.

His eyes grew round. "How?"

She squeezed and Tyrin screamed, the bones in his hand crunching and snapping as blood oozed down his wrist. He fell to his knees, gasping for air. Ashland let go, turned, and stepped away.

She had expected satisfaction, but his whimpering cut into her heart and inflated her guilt. Not having the stomach for cruelty, she took a breath to steady herself. With closed eyes, she recalled memories long buried.

Her ten-year-old self had been full of hope and wonder and trust when she first arrived at Wayport, sent to Tyrin to act as her guide and guardian. He took that trust and twisted it. Behind a fake smile and smooth words, he had used fear and violence to control her. That fear now fueled Ashland's anger for what he had done – for the years of happiness Tyrin had denied her.

Hearing him move behind her, she spun about as he struck at her with a cold fire iron, the same fire iron that he had used countless times to burn her for little reason. Her hand flashed up, snatched the iron from the air, and yanked it from his grip. She tossed the iron aside, driving it through the thick wooden door. With a twist, she slammed her boot heel through his knee. Tyrin screamed in pain and collapsed to the floor, his eyes saucers filled with fear. She stood over him, telling herself it was about justice and not revenge. The truth lay somewhere in between.

With her heart pounding in her ears, Ashland stared down at her tormenter. He lay curled into a ball, clutching his ruined hand to his chest and crying like a baby as blood pooled beneath his destroyed knee.

"For six years, I suffered as you stole every bit of joy from my life." Ashland spoke with the heat of anger at the thought. "I was a child, Tyrin, and you were to train me and take care of me, not beat me upon every misstep. With my actions, I sentence you to the life you deserve, knowing what it's like to be crippled by fear and pain."

The door burst open with a thud. Master Herrin and Minister Jerrold entered the room. Herrin glanced down at Tyrin then up to Ashland.

"What happened?" The old man sounded horrified. "What have you done to him?"

Ashland's tone remained calm, yet commanding with an edge of anger. "I've done what you cowards should have done long ago. His reign of tyranny ends today. He'll hurt others no longer."

When she attempted to walk past the two ministers. Jerrold made the mistake of trying to stop her. With a flick of her wrist, she slammed the man against the wall and he crumpled to the floor, unconscious.

Her eyes flashed toward Herrin, who backed away in fright. "Go on and heal him, Herrin, just like you healed me countless times after Tyrin went too far. You may have healed my scars from sight, but they remained beneath, festering and causing more pain than you'll ever know." She moved closer to him as the man cowered in fear. "You're as bad as him, you know. You knew what was happening and did nothing to stop it."

After staring at him a moment longer, Ashland turned and stepped over the prone form of Minister Jerrold. She paused at the door to look back at Herrin.

"Like I said, you may heal Tyrin. However, he will never be the same. I hope the world is just a little better for it."

As she walked down the hallway and into the temple, she looked down at her hand as she walked toward the exit. She'd have to wash the blood away, along with the *Power* rune she'd drawn on the other hand.

Emerging outside, she stepped out into the sunlight and paused atop the stairs. She closed her eyes and took a deep breath to calm her nerves. When she opened them, she began descending the stairs before stopping abruptly. Her eyes locked with Eldarro's, who was standing just two steps below. Recognition instantly turned from surprise to anger as he stared at her.

He lunged out, his hand gripping her arm. As he pulled her toward him, she braced her feet against the steps and pushed against his chest. Her *Chaos*-charged strength launched the much larger man backward, causing him to smash into the armed men who were following close behind. The six guards in the vanguard took the brunt of the impact and tumbled to the ground with Eldarro on top.

Ashland leapt from the stairs and hurdled the entire group to land in the street thirty feet away. She dashed off, weaving her way through the crowd. Careful not to hit anyone for fear of injuring them with her chaotic strength, she wiggled her way through and darted into the first alley. Shouts sounded from the street behind her as she bolted down the narrow corridor.

When she emerged from the other end, Ashland pulled her hood up and melted into the foot traffic on the busy street. Keeping pace with the flow of people around her, she resisted the urge to look backward, hoping that her plain gray cloak would blend with the people surrounding her. Two blocks later, she made another turn and *Gulley's Inn* came into view. She glanced backward just before reaching the building – and when she did not see her pursuers – approached the door and entered the inn.

Ashland crossed the taproom and pulled her hood back as she approached the table where her friends sat eating breakfast. Her eyes caught Brock's, his smile melting when he saw her expression.

"What happened?" Brock asked.

"It's Eldarro. He's here with some men," she replied, her heart still pounding from the encounter.

Brock stood to approach her. "Are you hurt? Do you need healing?"

She glanced down at her bloody hand. "No. I'm not harmed."

Parker stood and addressed the group. "Our plans have changed. We leave now. Get your things and meet at the stable in five minutes."

As the others stood and made their way for the stairs, Brock stepped closer. When Ashland looked into his eyes, she saw concern.

"You're not telling me everything," He lifted her non-bloodied hand, clearly noting the rune drawn on it.

Ashland grew angry. "Leave it be, Brock. I don't want to talk about it." She paused, calming a bit when she realized that he was trying to help. "I just needed…I needed to deal with something from my past. The rune was necessary for my protection. It also enabled me to escape from Eldarro."

Brock stared into her eyes before nodding. "Just as long as you're alright."

He gave her a smile, which she mirrored, thankful that he didn't press further.

Ashland believed that what she had done was necessary, but it was horrible at the same time. She didn't want to talk about it. In fact, she now found that she wished to forget the whole incident.

31

Cam gazed at Puri while she waited for the horses to cross the planks connecting the dock to the ship cargo hold. Ignoring curious onlookers, she focused on the animals entering the ship without the use of a bridle to guide them. Perplexed and amazed expressions reflected upon the faces of surrounding sailors and dockworkers watching the scene unfold. When the last horse crossed, the sailors pulled the planks and secured the cargo door. The sailors then reset the planks to run from the pier to the ship's deck to allow Cam and his companions to board.

Having spent a fair amount of his early years on the ships at the docks at Nor Torin, pleasant memories resurface when Cam stepped on board, touching a part of him he'd forgotten. While his older brothers were busy loading ships, Cam would often play on board, pretending he was a famous captain or a pirate. Sometimes the ship captains allowed him to remain aboard for short day runs in the area. However, he had never actually been out to open sea, a dream that lay just beyond reach until now. A smile crossed his face as he looked out at the sunlit blue waters.

He turned toward the planks, ready to help the others step aboard. Benny's face reflected the excitement that Cam felt. Tipper's did as well.

Brock, Ashland, Lars, and Libby appeared curious. Parker acted as nonchalant as ever, which was understandable since he had sailed numerous times before. However, the look on Puri's face was starkly different. If Cam didn't know better, he'd swear the strong-willed woman's eyes showed fear.

Her hand gripped his firmly as she stepped on-deck. With her aboard, the captain called for his crew to pull the planks and ready the ship.

While the others made their way to the bow, hugging the rail as they waited in expectation, Cam and Puri lingered behind.

"Are you feeling well?" Cam asked, concerned.

Puri looked at him, her eyes flashing anger. "Of course. Why would I not be well?"

Cam shrugged. "Well, I assume you've never been on a ship before. It's a new thing, and sometimes new things are scary."

She shook her head. "Nonsense. It isn't that it's new. It's just unnatural. Men and horses were meant to be on land, not water. That's why we have feet and hooves and not fins."

Cam nodded but suspected that she was afraid and wouldn't admit it. He liked Puri, but she still confused him. Tegan had confused him as well. Glancing toward the bow, he saw Brock at the rail with one arm around Ashland. Cam felt a pang a jealousy. Those two appeared to have a special connection. It must be because Brock understood women. Cam thought, *Maybe I should have Brock explain them to me.*

The captain issued a command, and a sailor began to coil the thick rope that had held them to the mooring. The ship drifted away from the long wooden pier, turning toward the open water.

The captain called out again "To your marks!"

Cam noticed two men scramble up the foremast near the bow of the ship. He turned to find others scaling the rigging on the main mast and mizzenmast. Other men scurried around the deck, getting into position and grabbing lines.

The captain bellowed again. "Unfurl the courses! Let go the clew lines! Let go the buntlines! Sheet the sail!"

The men above worked with precision as the lowest sail on each mast expanded to a white sheet, rippling in the breeze. They then climbed to a higher position in the rigging, ready for the next sail as the captain's voice called out again.

"Unfurl lower topsails! Let go the clews! Let go the buntlines! Sheet the sail!"

After unfurling the lower topsails, the men climbed even higher.

"Unfurl upper topsails! Hoist the yards! Let go the downhauls!"

Craning his neck, Cam gazed at the upper topsail rising along with the long wooden pole that held it. Once in place, the men climbed to the very top of the rigging. Once more, the captain called out.

"Unfurl topgallant sails! Hoist the yards! Let go the downhauls!"

With all sails ready and waffling loosely, the men shot down the rigging to return to the deck. The crew on the deck pulled lines tight, securing them to cleats on the deck and rails. Cam turned toward the stern and saw the captain standing on the quarterdeck. The man nodded and said something to the short blond woman who stood at the wheel.

The ship turned again. The sails above rippled loudly until snapping full. They picked up speed, and the pier behind them began shrinking into the distance.

A smile bloomed on Cam's face, having always enjoyed the rush he experienced when sailing. He turned toward Puri, who appeared even worse than before. The bow rose up as the ship left the calm of the harbor, hitting the breakers just beyond. He smiled again at the rush and turned toward Puri, excited to share this experience with her. Her tanned face had turned white. One hand covered her mouth, and she ran to the rail. He waited for her to finish retching before approaching her.

"Is there anything I can do to help?" he asked, genuinely concerned.

Anger flashed in her eyes. "I'm not weak."

Cam's brow furrowed. "I can't imagine *anyone* believing you are weak."

The anger in her eyes cooled and she nodded. "I find being ill difficult to accept. We Tantarri are taught to be strong."

Cam's hand cupped her shoulder. "Trust me. We are all aware of your strength and courage. Anyone can get seasick. It isn't a choice. You just need some time to get used to the ocean and then you'll feel better."

Her dark eyes locked with his in a moment of tension. Cam hoped she saw his sincerity. When she gave a brief nod, he smiled.

The ship dipped low, rising high before dropping again. Cam saw Puri's face whiten further. She leaned over the rail and emptied the remaining contents from her stomach.

"Welcome aboard," a deep voice bellowed.

Cam turned to find a tall man crossing the deck toward them. The man wore a red leather vest over a tan long-sleeve shirt, cinched at his waist by a thick black leather belt. Serving dual-purpose, the belt also supported dark brown trousers tucked into his black leather boots. A black brimmed hat with a single white plume rested atop his head, the feather dancing in the wind like a miniature sail. His short-trimmed dark beard framed a handsome face with enough lines to indicate many more years of experience than his guests.

The man introduced himself. "Well, met. I'm Captain Sinclair." He smiled as Cam shook his hand. "Welcome aboard *Star Dancer*."

"Thank you, sir. I'm Cameron." Cam looked over at Puri, who seemed to have recovered somewhat. "This is Puri."

Sinclair took Puri's hand, bowing as he kissed it. "Welcome aboard. It's a pleasure to have such an exotic beauty on my ship," He grinned as his gaze scanned her up and down.

Puri's eyes narrowed. "I am not a toy. I am a warrior. If you or any of your men try to touch me, you will regret it." Her tone contained a fierce edge, the threat a challenge she dared anyone to accept.

Sinclair held his hand up. "Sorry. I meant no offense."

"Sinclair!"

Cam turned to see Parker approaching.

"Thank you for launching early," Parker shook the man's hand.

Sinclair smiled. "Thank you for the extra silver marks. We were already loaded, so leaving early was of little inconvenience."

Parker nodded toward the others as they gathered around him. "Would you mind showing us to our cabins so we can get settled?"

With a nervous glance toward Puri, Sinclair responded.

"Yes. Come along, then," he said, waving them to follow as he headed for the stairs.

Cam looked at Puri, who continued to stare daggers at the flamboyant captain's back.

He cleared his throat and spoke to her. "I think you scared him."

She turned toward him with a hopeful look. "Do you think so?"

Cam nodded, which earned him a smile. "All right, then. Let's go check out our cabins."

Cam followed her toward the steps, deciding he'd never understand women.

32

Gulls overhead circled in search of fish driven by the ship cutting through the deep blue salt water. The ocean breeze cooled and dried the sweat on Cam's brow as swiftly as it emerged, while the deck below his feet rose and fell with the rhythm of the waves.

The crew of *Star Dancer* watched in silence, but Cam ignored them, along with everything else. Losing focus could result in a lost limb or a quick death.

He held his sword low, ready to counter. The attack came, forcing him to spin beneath and swing at his enemy's legs. He rose to block, countering again with a quick strike to take out another enemy. Twisting, he dodged an attack before spinning with a backhand stroke followed by a slash at a foe on his other side.

Another enemy dove into the fray and Cam turned to parry before slicing with a return strike. One foe went down, instantly replaced by another. On and on they came at him. Over and over, they fell to the might of his blade.

"You're holding the tip too low when you pause."

He turned to find Puri emerging from the stairs. Her eyes drifted to his bare torso, covered with a coat of sweat gleaming in the sun.

"What?" he asked.

She smiled and moved closer as he lowered his blade. "Holding your blade like that might be easier on your wrists, but being lazy is a good way to die."

Cam's eyes narrowed. "What are you saying?"

In a flash, she had her blade free from the baldric on her back and held it before him.

"You should hold your blade higher, like this. That way, you have coiled energy in your wrist and are always ready to strike."

Cam nodded. What she said made sense. He lifted his sword, matching her pose.

Puri nodded. "Good."

He dodged as her sword flashed past – close enough to feel the moving air brush past his shoulder. Spinning, he prepared for another attack.

She grinned and held her sword ready. A slash arced toward his mid-section, which he blocked – the clang of the striking swords ringing loudly in his ears. Her blade twisted to slash at his other side, which he also blocked. He sliced upward toward her, but she spun away with her sword coming around, leveled at his neck. Ducking, he lunged with a thrust that she twisted around as she spun about to face him again. Puri attacked with a series of swift slashes. Despite her repeated attempts, he blocked each before jumping backward to create space.

With both breathing hard, they stared into each other's eyes. She had a slight edge on speed, much like Brock. He knew that he had an edge on strength. If he wanted to beat her, he needed to use his power as an advantage. Just as he worked out a strategy, she lowered her sword and smiled.

"That was fun. You are not bad for an outlander."

Confused, Cam lowered his sword. "Um…thanks."

He turned toward the sound of applause and found Sinclair approaching as he clapped soundly. The other sailors who'd been watching echoed Sinclair, clapping heartily until Sinclair held his hand up to still them.

"That was quite a performance," Sinclair said. "I haven't had such skilled duelists aboard my ship before. It was truly a treat to watch." He gave a deep bow before turning toward Puri. "You are a most skilled warrior, Miss Puri."

Puri's eyes narrowed at Sinclair and she responded with a brief nod.

Sinclair redirected his attention to Cam. "When I first saw you practicing with the sword, I thought it perhaps just for show. After your fierce exchange, I can see that you are truly a force, Mister Cameron."

Cam nodded. "Thanks, Captain."

Sinclair smiled and patted Cam on the shoulder as he walked past, on his way to the cabin below the quarterdeck.

Cam glanced up to the small woman guiding the ship. She nodded to him when their eyes met. It surprised him that the captain entrusted someone so young with steering the large vessel. He then spotted Parker and Benny in deep discussion at the rail behind her.

When his gaze returned to Puri, she was sheathing her long curved sword.

Cam nodded toward the weapon as he sheathed his own. "The Tantarri seem to favor that type of sword. I'm not familiar with it."

Puri's brow arched in surprised. "The sabre? You don't have this weapon in your land?"

Cam shrugged. "Not that I've seen."

Puri shrugged. "It is the sword I know, designed for quick strikes and excellent for slashing. It works quite well from atop a horse."

Cam reflected on her statement as he bent to retrieve his shirt. It was easy to imagine how the light single-handed weapon would be effective for cavalry. When he looked in her direction, Puri was again openly leering at him. With a flush of embarrassment, he pulled his shirt over his head.

He suddenly recalled her seasickness. Now two days into their journey, Puri had spent almost the entire time in the cabin she shared with Libby and Ashland.

"You appear to have recovered," he noted.

"Yes. I am much better, now." She gestured toward the quarterdeck. "I see two of your companions, but where are the others?"

"I believe that Lars is taking a nap," Cam replied. "Brock, Ashland, Tipper, and Libby went somewhere to practice *Chaos* runes."

"*Chaos*?"

"I think it's what you call *lost magic*."

Her brow raised. "The others can use the lost magic?"

Cam nodded as they began walking toward the quarterdeck. "Yes.

Brock thinks it'll be important for them to learn. Ashland is already quite proficient, but Tipper and Libby are new to it."

He climbed the six steps to the quarterdeck with Puri following.

"Hello, Cam." Benny smiled.

"For a minute, I thought she was trying to kill you down there," Parker said.

"You outlanders know nothing," Puri said as she reached the deck. "If I wanted him dead, he'd be dead."

Cam hoped her comment was in jest, but she appeared serious.

Benny and Parker laughed, deciding it was a joke. After laughing a moment, Benny spoke.

"Tenzi here was explaining how the ship uses the wind for sailing. I find it quite interesting."

"Tenzi?" Cam asked.

The short woman steering the ship gave a small bow before turning back to the wheel.

"Did you know that the ship can't sail directly against the wind?" Benny's excitement showed as he spoke. "Instead, they have to go at an angle, turning frequently if they are running a coarse into the wind."

Parker nodded, as if it were obvious.

Cam nodded as well. "I know a bit of how it works. I've spent a fair amount of time on ships in Nor Torin's harbor."

Puri grumbled. "I still think it's unnatural. Men were not meant to be on the water."

Tenzi turned toward the taller woman. "Sailing is the most natural thing there is. It's a dance on the ocean with the wind as your partner." She sounded bemused as she spoke. "To sail, you must embrace the mother wind, bending to her will as she propels you across the sea."

Puri stared at the shorter woman. "That's fine as long as she propels you across the sea and not into it."

33

B rock climbed the steps from their cabins onto the empty foredeck. Above the bow, the eastern sky glowed as it prepared to welcome the sun. He glanced backward, and saw Ashland's gorgeous face glowing in the pre-dawn light. The wind blew her curly brown hair back, making it look a bit wild. She flashed him a smile, which he returned.

Grabbing her hand, he pulled her toward the bow. They latched onto the rail as the ship rose and fell in time with the waves below. With the voyage about to end, this was their last chance to watch the breaking dawn together.

Having grown up along the west coast, Brock had seen the sun set into the ocean waters countless times. Until this voyage, he had not even glimpsed the sun rising up from the ocean. The previous two mornings, he and Ashland had risen before the others to watch the sunrise together. Unlike the previous dawns, today they found a silhouette of land against the brightening horizon.

Minutes later, a sliver of light edged over the landmass to the east. The sliver soon evolved into a ball of fire floating above the horizon. As the sun rose into the heavens, the coast ahead began to take shape.

In the distance, tall towers thrust toward the sky above the city of Sol Polis. The city spread out along the coast, unable to remain captive within the walls that had attempted to define it. Brock had heard that the capital was colossal, but he never expected it to be this sprawling. Sol Polis appeared bigger than Kantar and Nor Torin combined

The harbor was teeming with life as smaller craft set sail to the north and south, hugging the coastline. Two ships the size of *Star Dancer* launched, their sails being unfurled as they drifted from the pier. Moments later, they had captured the wind and sailed out of the harbor, one heading north, the other turning south.

Brock glanced toward Ashland, who appeared radiant in the bright light of the rising sun. He heart leapt every time their eyes met. *I love you.* He thought to her.

I know. How could you not love me? She replied, cracking a smile.

He laughed, turning toward the city that was their destination. Despite the steep odds of their quest succeeding, a confidence remained inside him. With Ashland by his side, he felt as if he could do anything and the odds became irrelevant. Of course, he was quite happy to have the support of his friends as well.

As the ship closed the distance to the docks, others from their group began to join them. When Sinclair called the men to their marks to lower the sails, Brock's companions were all at the bow and eager to dock.

As the sails were drawn, the ship slowed. By the time all sails were furled and secured, the ship was less than a hundred feet from the pier. A man ran along the long dock, waving a flag as he neared an open mooring. Sinclair called out orders, and Tenzi steered the ship toward the designated berth. Men along the rail tossed thick lines to workers on the pier. With the lines secured to the thick posts rising above the dock, Tenzi turned the ship to slow the last bit until the secured ropes pulled tight. After straining on the ropes for a moment, the ship relented and settled into its mooring.

Sinclair resumed barking out orders, sending the sailors scurrying about the ship. When Brock noticed Sinclair crossing the deck toward them, he drew his hood up over his head. He had been careful to keep his new rune out of sight during the voyage. It was something he would have to remain mindful of in the future.

Parker greeted Sinclair with an extended hand. "Good morning, captain. True to your word, we arrived here safely and on schedule."

Sinclair took Parker's hand and gave a deep bow. "T'was my pleasure good sirs and pretty lasses."

The man was smooth with his words. A little too smooth for Brock's liking.

"My men will have the ship ready for you and your mounts to disembark in moments," Sinclair said. "You should retrieve your things so you are ready to depart." He followed the words with a small bow and spun to retreat across the deck.

Parker turned to the group. "You heard him. Let's get our things and get off this ship. Once the horses are unloaded, we'll head into the city."

They followed Parker, descending the stairwell to their cabins. The six boys crammed into their tight quarters and collected their items from their bunks. Brock emerged in the narrow corridor, pausing to wait for the girls to exit the room next door. When they returned to the deck, they found that planks had been set for them to cross to the pier.

The sailors then opened the cargo doors and set planks for the horses. Puri blasted a loud whistle. Moments later, her white stallion emerged and crossed the planks to where she waited. The other six horses followed across and down the pier as Puri escorted the animals to shore.

Sinclair followed the process with a furrowed brow before shaking his head in wonder.

"I've heard stories about the Tantarri, but I always thought them to be exaggeration." The captain adjusted his hat. "I now believe that they may have been understated. I've never seen anything like it."

Parker smiled. "Yeah. It makes for interesting travel." He shook Sinclair's hand. "Thanks for the hospitality and the safe passage."

Sinclair smiled, bowing his head slightly. "Thank you for the gold. It made the trip one of profit where we would have otherwise merely broken even."

As the group began walking toward shore, Sinclair called out. "We'll be here for a few days. Come find me if you need passage back to Wayport!"

Brock was happy to be back on solid land. He didn't hate the sea, but he didn't like being trapped in such a small space for three days. The smooth way that Sinclair spoke also irritated Brock, making it seem as if the man were trying to sell him a bird promised to lay eggs of gold.

After traversing the length of the long pier to the dockyards, they came upon Puri and the horses. She stood in the middle of the small herd, speaking quietly before emerging to address Parker.

"You must find us a place with food and water for the horses. The access they had on the ship was limited, and they are hungry."

Without a hint of surprise at Puri's statement, Parker nodded and waved for the group to follow. The brick storage buildings along the waterfront soon gave way to tightly packed houses that lined the road on both sides. People and carts filled the street, traveling in and out of the city. After a few hundred feet, they passed through the west gate and into the walled portion of Sol Polis.

The streets inside were even busier, bustling with activity. In fact, every street in this city appeared equal to the busiest street in Kantar. Within minutes, Brock caught sight of four different steam carriages. After seeing two others in his entire life, to find four in such proximity left him wondering how many others existed within the city.

The shops and homes inside the walls appeared in better condition than those at the outskirts. Brock's gaze drifted beyond the nearby buildings to land on the cylindrical towers of the citadel, which reached toward the morning sky. The citadel was located in the heart Sol Polis, similar to Nor Torin. Unlike Nor Torin's squat rectangular design, this citadel resided upon a hill and had a gloriously elegant appearance.

Distracted by the beauty of the citadel, Brock realized that he had fallen behind the others. He hurried along, careful to keep his hood over his head as he searched the crowded street. When he spotted Cam's blond hair above the throng of people, he weaved through the crowd and caught up to the group as they entered a narrow alley.

Parker led them into a gated yard just off the alley. A walking path cut through the yard, passing a stable as it led to an impressive three-story house. While Parker held the gate open, a boy in his early teens emerged from the stable.

"Welcome back, Master Parker," the boy said before addressing the group. "Hello everyone. I'm Niles. I'm here to care for your horses. Welcome to the Thanes Household."

Parker clapped the boy's shoulder. "Hello, Niles. We'll be staying for a few days. Please care well for our steeds."

Niles smiled as he pocketed the silver Parker handed him. "Yes, sir!"

He moved toward the first horse, frowning.

"Um. Where's the bridle?"

Puri loomed over the boy, her stance a threat unspoken even before her words rolled out. "They are never to be bridled. Do you hear me?"

Niles backed away, nervous. "Yes. Sorry. I just haven't seen a horse without a bridle before now."

Parker stepped between them. "Don't worry, Niles. If you want the horse to follow you, just put your hand against its neck, like this."

Parker placed his hand on the horse's neck and began walking with the horse in tow.

Niles smiled, nodding. "No bridles. Got it."

Cam slid close to Puri and whispered in her ear. Her look softened and she nodded.

Niles put his hand on one horse, leading it to another and walked both toward the stable. The other horses followed behind, causing the lad to giggle.

Parker clapped his hands and turned toward the group. "All right, then. Let's go inside and get some food. Cam is starving." He flashed a grin at Cam.

Lars and Benny burst out laughing as they followed Parker into the house.

PART III

THE BREAKING STORM

34

Conflicting emotions warred within Parker Thanes at the thought of returning home. While he had never been close to his Father, Parker had never outright defied him either. His mid-year departure from the Academy had changed things, for better or worse.

After years of dreaming about living his own life rather than the one his father defined, Parker had finally done it. Since coming to the decision to flee the school with Brock and the others, he had enjoyed every moment, feeling free for the first time. However, in returning to Sol Polis, he would have to face the consequences of his decision.

When he led his friends into the building, he found Agatha in the kitchen. After a moment of shock at seeing him unexpectedly, she greeted him warmly and set to making a meal for the visitors. Parker was confident that she was up to the task, having dealt with surprise guests countless times during her tenure as the household cook.

Passing through the other kitchen door, he led his friends to the dining room, urging them to seat themselves around the long table while he exited to the room beyond. A smile lit upon Parker's face when he entered the receiving hall and saw another man in his father's study. Here was a man he was quite happy to see.

"Hi Pockets," Parker announced. "I'm back."

The man spun about to face Parker. True to his name, he had one hand tucked into a pocket of his long black coat. The other adjusted his rounded spectacles as he focused on Parker. The man's bushy gray eyebrows furrowed for a moment before a smile spread across his rounded face.

"Master Parker! You have returned."

Parker crossed the room to shake the man's hand. "Thanks, Pockets. I believe I just said that, though."

"Well, yes, sir. I believe you are correct." The man nodded. "However, must you continue to call me Pockets?"

"Sorry, Pinkus. I'll try to remember." Parker was well aware that the name irritated the man. "Is he around?"

Pinkus shook his head, the sunlight from the window reflecting on his bald pate. "No sir. He's at the citadel, not due back until this evening."

Parker felt relieved to have a few more hours before he had to confront his father. Perhaps the extra time would help him determine the best approach.

"In that case, I want you to come and meet my friends."

"Friends, sir?" Pinkus asked. "You brought others?" He escorted Parker from the study.

Rather than respond, Parker crossed the receiving hall and opened the door to the dining room. He moved aside and held it for Pinkus as he watched the man's face.

The room was abuzz with conversation, quieting when they noticed the newcomer at the door. Pinkus blinked a few times before he recovered himself.

"Welcome to the Thanes Household." He bowed to the room. "I'm Pinkus, Master Thanes' manservant."

Parker introduced the group and Pinkus nodded with each introduction.

"We need a place to stay while in the city, Pinkus," Parker added. "I was hoping to stay here. Assuming that father will take us on, can you prepare rooms for us?"

Pinkus nodded. "It would be my pleasure, Master Parker."

As the man exited through one door, Agatha entered through the other with a tray filled with food. The smell was wonderful and Parker's mouth began to water. After three days on a ship, a cooked meal would be a treat. He just hoped that his father would take the news well, or they would have to find another place to stay.

With the others safe in their rooms, Parker descended the stairs to the first level. Resigned to the task, he entered the study to wait for his father. His timing was perfect as he heard the man enter through the kitchen moments later. Parker scooped up the glowlamp from his father's desk and shook it vigorously, lighting the room a blue glow. He set the lamp down as his father entered the receiving room.

Coming into the light, Parker noticed his father wearing the white and red cloak of his office. The man's hard eyes glared at Parker, showing no reaction. After a long moment, Parker spoke.

"Hello, Father."

"What are you doing here, Parker?"

"Something has come up. Something more important than my career in the Hierarchy."

His father snorted. "I can't imagine what that could be."

Parker nodded, aware of his father's belief that Parker's career was everything. After all, he had made it clear that he thought his own career was everything.

"I'm on a mission, Father. Something is coming. Something that could be the end of us all." Parker tried to sound convincing. "My mission is to prevent that from happening."

His father stared at him before responding. "You really believe that?"

Parker nodded, somewhat surprised that he did believe it.

"It still doesn't answer why you are here."

"I need your help, father. I need to get a couple friends and myself into the citadel basement. We're seeking something."

"Friends?" The man asked.

Parker nodded again. "Yes. They came with me from the Academy. They're upstairs. I was hoping we could stay here a few days, just until we retrieve what we came for."

His father stepped closer. "What then? Will you return to the Academy and finish your training?"

This was it. The outcome of this conversation hinged on Parker's response. Should he confront his father and tell him that he was finished living under the man's thumb? Or should he tell the man what he wanted to hear? He swallowed hard, prepared to do what he must.

"Yes, Father. Of course, I'll return to the Academy." Parker smiled through the lie. "What else would I do with my life?"

The man's eyes narrowed before he nodded. "You and your friends may stay here. I'll see what I can do about getting you inside the citadel."

He then turned, walked to the stairwell, and faded into the darkness. The man's footsteps echoed within the study as he ascended to the second floor and entered his room.

The conversation had gone far better than expected, yet Parker felt as if he had missed something in the exchange. Whatever it was, he hoped it wouldn't to come back to haunt him.

35

"What are we doing here, Brock?" Lars complained, pushing his empty plate aside. "I still don't understand why we're doing this. We fled the Academy to no longer be pawns of the Ministry and now you have us acting as pawns for the Tantarri."

Brock sighed and set his fork down on his plate. He absently adjusted the strip of cloth tied around his head as he considered his response. Knowing that the question would come eventually, he had put some thought into how to approach it.

"Don't you think I realize how crazy this seems? Don't you think I've questioned the whole thing over and over?" Brock stared Lars in the eye. "Why should we listen to an outlandish vision that some random Tantarri recorded hundreds of years ago? Why should we follow the man's directions and embark on a ridiculous quest to find some unknown secret hidden in a throne lost centuries ago?"

Lars nodded as Brock spoke, likely having those same questions himself. The others remained quiet as they followed the exchange from their seats at the dining table. Brock's gaze swept around the room, searching their faces before continuing, finding expressions ranging from confidence to curiosity to doubt.

"It's quite possible that the quest will be pointless and we are chasing our own tails for no reason." Brock said with a slow nod. "However, what if the prophecy is true? What if we are teetering on the brink of destruction, the end of humanity? If it is true and we do nothing, it could be the end for us all. What would you have us do, Lars? Do we not at least try?" He allowed the question to hang in silence for a moment. "On the other hand, if we are near the end and do nothing, at least we won't have to live with the guilt for long."

Lars' face clouded, clearly not liking what he was hearing.

Benny interjected. "What else have we to do anyway, Lars? When we left the Academy, we left the defined path behind. From that moment, our future has been completely open. This quest will fill our future for a short time. If it turns out to be pointless and there's nothing to fear, we can go on with whatever life we choose for ourselves."

Parker nodded in agreement. "I agree. I say we continue with the quest for a bit yet and see what the future holds. Whether the Tantarri prophecy is real or false, we'll soon find out."

Lars looked at Parker, his eyes then shifting to Brock before he nodded. "Fine. You win, Brock. We continue on for a while and see what happens."

Brock reached over to clap Lars on the shoulder in silent thanks. The motion of the door opening drew his attention as a middle-aged man entered from the kitchen. The man had a bundle of black cloaks with blue piping in his arms.

"Hello, everyone," the man said, his gaze scanning the room. "I'm Cedric Thanes, Parker's father."

As soon as he said it, Brock saw the resemblance. The man had the same tall, thin build as Parker. His graying hair still held some of the dark brown that pervaded Parker's scalp. Although there were lines about the man's eyes, they were an older version of Parker's own brown eyes.

"Hello, Father," Parker stood to greet the man.

Cedric pushed the bundle toward Parker, who reached out to take it.

"What's this?" Parker asked.

"Clerk cloaks. Three of them," Cedric replied. "It's the best I could do. These should get you into the citadel. I suggest that you go just after sunrise, when most people are entering. What you do once inside is your own problem."

Parker grinned. "Thank you, Father. Would you like to join us? We are just finishing up dinner."

Cedric shook his head. "No. I'm off to my study. I need to finish drafting a document that must be ready for the Archon by morning."

The man gave them a brief nod before departing.

Parker turned to look at Brock. "This will be risky, Brock. In order to get in, we'll will have to be unarmed. We have three cloaks. Who comes with us?"

Brock nodded. "You guys heard him. It will be dangerous, and I expect the penalty for trespassing in the citadel will be stiff." His gaze swept across the table, his eyes meeting those surrounding him. "This job requires us to look the part. If we are to be city clerks, I think Benny best suits the role. Plus, his over-sized brain might be more useful than muscle for this outing." He looked at Benny. "Will you join us, Benny?"

Benny gave a grin. "You know I will, Brock. We'll find that throne and whatever is inside it."

36

Brock and Benny followed Parker outside before descending the steps to the cobblestone street at the front of Parker's house. Turning east, they walked toward the citadel, its tall towers looming above the city. Still covered in shadow, the streets were coming to life as skies above brightened. Dawn would break soon and mark the moment when the citadel doors opened.

With only two blocks to travel, they soon approached their destination. They climbed the stairs to join the people assembled outside the gate and waited in the shadows of the tall walls.

A distant bell tolled. Moments later, a bell in the towers high above them rang in response. The gate swung open and guards called for those entering to do so in single file. Shuffling his feet as the line inched forward, Brock's pulse began to quicken and his stomach took a queasy turn. Five long minutes passed before they reached the front of the line and a guard standing beside a scribe waved them closer.

"Hello, sirs." Parker said to the two men.

"Names and your business at the citadel." The scribe said, holding his pen ready.

Parker smiled, ready with his practiced response. "Parker Tannis, Benedict Hedding, and Brock Takkins. We are new clerks from Wayport, come to learn how things are done here at the capital."

The scribe jotted down information on the clipboard, his tongue sliding back and forth across his lip as he wrote. When he nodded, the guard waved them in. Brock noticed that his nerves left his armpits damp despite the cool morning weather.

They crossed an open plaza occupied by statues and sculpted shrubs at the center, the plaza paved with square blocks of stone, each a stride across. Others were crossing the plaza, many heading in the same direction as Parker, who appeared confident as he led them toward the massive building in the heart of the complex. As they approached, Brock admired the row of high arches at the front, supported by rounded alabaster pillars. Following another group with similar cloaks, they climbed another set of stairs and passed under the arches.

A set of double-doors led them from the exterior hall into the spacious interior hall. A fountain in the heart of the open space ran freely, flowing around a tall statue of Issal. Terraces high above overlooked the hall, illuminated by sunlight pouring through the glass-paneled ceiling four stories above. People scurried about, with many disappearing down corridors connected to the room as they headed toward other parts of the building.

Rather than walking across the open hall, Parker made a sharp right toward a narrow stairwell with Brock and Benny a step behind. A quick descent brought them to a level with branching corridors, dark but for the pale blue light emitted by glowlamps mounted to the wall at wide intervals. Parker followed the central corridor, not slowing as he spoke over his shoulder.

"There's supposed to be another stairwell leading down from this level. That's what we must find."

Closed doors lined the corridor, leaving Brock wondering which door hid the stairwell they were seeking.

"Do you know where you're going, Parker?" Brock asked. "How do you know it isn't one of these doors?"

Parker turned and gestured toward the nearest door. "These rooms are apartments for the clerks. They tend to work long hours and often sleep down here rather than commuting." He pointed ahead. "We need to reach the older part of the keep, beneath the heart of the citadel. Once we get there, we'll start checking doors."

Brock nodded and followed as Parker led them down the corridor.

The hallway soon came to a short flight of stairs, bringing them down a half-level. At the foot of the stairs, the walls dropped away to leave an open space filled with desks, some occupied by clerks already busy writing under the dim nimbus of a glowlamp. The scattered lamps in the dark room gave an illusion of the desks floating in space.

Feeling self-conscious, Brock tried to appear nonchalant as he followed Parker across the room to the opening at the other end. They entered the dark corridor, which terminated at a pair of double-doors. Parker paused at the doors, glancing back at Brock before he pushed one open.

A slight creak echoed as they passed through and into the dark space beyond. The door closed behind Benny, leaving them blind with no lamps lighting the way.

Benny grabbed Parker's arm. "Wait a minute. I'll be right back."

Without pause, Benny slipped through the door they had just entered. Blind in the inky darkness surrounding him, the thumping of Brock's pulse sounded in his ears as he anxiously waited for Benny's return. Moments later, the door opened, and Benny appeared with the soft blue light of a glowlamp in each hand. He passed one lamp to Parker, who nodded. Shaking it briskly to increase the light, Parker headed down the corridor. Brock slipped behind him with Benny and at the rear.

"The stairwell should be somewhere near here," Parker said quietly.

"I have an idea," Benny said.

Benny tapped his lamp against the stone block wall, the clink of the glass on the rock echoing in the corridor. He did it again, harder. The third time, the glass broke, scattering sharp shards across the floor while the base of the lamp remained in Benny's hand.

"Do you have to be so loud?" Parker asked in a whisper.

"Sorry," Benny said. "I need the powder from inside the lamp."

"What?" Parker asked.

Benny smiled, rocking his shoulders. "You'll see."

Benny walked past Parker to the first hallway door. He poured just a bit of glowing powder out. When the powder settled on the floor at the bottom of the door, Benny shook his head and moved on.

He repeated this process at each door they passed before moving on. Parker and Brock watched in confusion, following along. Just when

Brock had enough of Benny's quirky behavior, something changed. Nine doors in, the powder floated to the floor and was drawn through the gap under the door, disappearing from sight.

Benny smiled at Brock. "This should be it."

He squeezed the handle and opened the door. Sure enough, there was a dark stairwell leading downward.

Parker clapped Benny's shoulder as he passed by. "Good job, Benny."

Brock threw his arm around Benny and gave a quick hug. "I knew those brains would come in handy."

The light from Parker's lamp was a beacon that Brock followed down into the darkness. The dampness of the air increased noticeably as they descended. Stone blocks of a different material now marked the walls, appearing to be of older construction than the structure above. Brock counted the stairs during their descent, which totaled thirty-six steps – enough for two stories. They followed the dark corridor at the foot of the stairwell and found themselves before a set of heavy double-doors.

Parker stopped at the doors and glanced back in question. Brock sensed something beyond the closed doors, a quiet tension that left an itch at the back of his skull. A sense of trepidation washed over him, causing his stomach to twist in anxiety. Just as he was about to tell him to wait, Parker pushed the door open and entered the room beyond.

The musty air thickened further beyond the heavy door. Parker held the glowlamp higher so they could better inspect their surroundings. Broken relics occupied the room, covered by cobwebs and a thick layer of dust. Despite the sense of trouble lurking within him, Brock felt a spark of hope. The throne might be among this refuse.

Brock and Benny followed as Parker weaved his way down the aisle before them. Brock's eyes scanned objects as they passed, finding an ornate wardrobe with a broken door, an unloaded ballista, an odd glass sphere mounted upon a pedestal, a wooden chest with a rusted lock, and other assorted objects along the right side of the aisle.

As Brock turned toward the opposite side of the room, he noticed a faint light beyond a set of double doors that stood partially open. Reaching out, he grabbed Parker's shoulder and pulled him to a halt.

"What's that ahead?" Brock whispered, pointing toward the doorway.

When the light grew brighter, a shock of ice-cold fear wiggled down

Brock's spine. A moment later, a glowlamp entered the room, held by a familiar face.

"Father? Why are you down here?" Parker asked.

As guards began to follow the man through the doorway, Brock realized the source of his uneasiness.

"I'm doing what I must, Son." Cedric's tone sounded resolute, with a twinge of regret.

A dozen armed guards fanned out to the sides of the man, some drawing swords. A female guard holding a glowlamp entered the room, accompanied by a man dressed in gold-embroidered white clothing and a shimmering gold cloak. The woman was tall, perhaps the tallest woman Brock had ever seen. Her muscled arms were bare from her padded shoulders to the metal-plated bracers strapped to her forearms. The cloaked man stood taller than the woman, perhaps even taller than Cam. Gray peppered the man's black hair, including the short-trimmed goatee that framed his grim smile.

Parker's father spoke again. "Don't bother trying to run, Parker. We have men posted in the corridor above the stairwell behind you." His expression was firm, harsh. "You're little quest is over."

"Please, sir," Brock pleaded. "We just wanted to find the Emblem Throne and retrieve something hidden inside it. We meant no harm."

The man in the gold cloak laughed. "The Emblem Throne?" He turned to Parker's father. "You were correct, Cedric. A fanciful quest indeed." The man's gaze fell back on Brock. "The Emblem Throne is a myth, merely existing in the words of a children's song. Even if it were real, the Kings of Kalimar never lived in Sol Polis. Sol Limar was the capital back then. Not only are you idiots to believe in such a stupid quest, but you went to the wrong city!"

The man laughed again. It was not a pleasant sound. As the words sunk in, Brock realized that he had led his friends into a trap and they weren't even in the right city. The trust that they had put in him now felt unjustified. A wave of guilt washed over him, sour and distasteful.

As the laughter died down, Cedric nodded toward Brock. "That's him, Archon."

Another dagger of dread thrust through Brock when he realized whom he faced.

Archon Ringholdt smiled a smile bereft of humor. "Very good,

Cedric. Very good." The man stepped closer to Brock, his intimidating female bodyguard mimicking him. "You may have fooled the Academy, but you can't fool me. I know you murdered my son."

With those words, the last tendrils of hope remaining within Brock evaporated. The Archon's arm extended and he pointed toward Brock.

"Arrest them!"

The guards advanced to surround the boys. Without any weapons nor a plan as to how *Chaos* might help him, Brock gave no resistance when the men grabbed his arms. Ringholdt moved closer, stopping just a stride away as he glared down at Brock.

"Even if I can't officially charge you with murder, you were caught trespassing in the citadel. To do so while I am here can be construed as an attempt on my life, which is an act of treason." A smug smile crossed the tall man's face, reminding Brock of Corbin. "The penalty for treason is death."

"Father, how could you?" Parker pleaded.

Ringholdt gave Parker a knowing grin. "Don't worry lad, your father has negotiated your safe release. Of course, that release will not occur until you've been escorted back to the Academy to complete your training." He glanced at Parker's father. "Cedric has assured me that you were manipulated into some fanciful quest. He's convinced me that once you are away from these bad influences, you'll become yourself again and will focus on your studies and career."

The tall man's gaze shifted toward Brock, oozing contempt. His dark eyes narrowed and he reached toward the bandage around Brock's forehead. With a quick yank, he tore it off.

Ringholdt's eyes grew wide. He gasped and stumbled backward. "That rune! It can't be!"

The moment passed and the look of shock evolved to one of rage.

"Take them to the dungeon. The others will be there shortly."

He turned to leave, stopping beside Parker's father. "Arrange for your son to be taken to Wayport. See that he is away no later than tomorrow. The others are to be executed for treason."

The man stormed out the door, his gold cloak billowing behind him as the woman with the glowlamp quickly followed.

"Why, Father?" Parker pleaded.

Cedric appeared grim. "I'll not have you throw your life away for nothing. You're going back to Academy to complete your training. These others who you call friends are nothing but a distraction. They don't care about you. If they did, they wouldn't have lured you here in the first place."

Tears streamed down Parker's cheeks. "I can't believe you betrayed me, Father."

"You betrayed me first, son," Cedric sneered. He turned, addressing the guards. "Take them to the dungeon."

37

Rough hands pulled Brock down the dark corridor, gripping his upper arms hard enough to leave bruises. Brock's mind was elsewhere, trying to grasp the gravity of the situation. A pang of fear twisted within when he realized that Ashland and the others were in danger. He closed his eyes and reached out to warn her. Ashland responded that he was too late. The city guards had rushed the house moments before and had shackled his companions after a brief, but violent struggle.

He opened his eyes and focused in an attempt to keep his bearings. They turned down another hallway, which led to a door that opened into a dark room with a single glowlamp resting upon the desk in the corner. Heavy wooden doors lined the otherwise barren brick walls.

A mountain of a man with a thick brown beard waited within the room, leaning against the desk as he twirled a ring of keys around one finger. With a grunt, the man stood upright and approached one of the closed doors. After unlocking it, he stepped aside, and the guards holding Brock violently shoved him into the dark cell. Stumbling, Brock reached out to brace himself as he collided with the cold wall. He spun about and the door slammed shut, the sound like a thunderclap in the small cell. A key slid into the lock. The subtle click of the lock engaging sounded more ominous than thud of the door that preceded it.

Brock put his face against the small barred opening in the door, a narrow window to the light beyond. Guards rudely shoved Benny and Parker into neighboring cells and locked them within. The guards who had been their escort departed, leaving the one with the keys behind. The man walked to the corner, plopped down into the wooden chair and crossed his feet upon the desk.

For a while, Brock heard nothing but his own breathing. He swallowed hard, his mind churning as he contemplated his options. Approaching footsteps soon drew his attention toward the doorway to the corridor outside. The sound grew louder until another group of guards emerged and shoved Cam through into the room. Brock's tall friend had a black eye and a split lip. All three guards appeared as beaten as Cam, their faces bloodied and swollen. They unshackled his hands from behind his back and pushed him into a dark cell.

Each of Brock's companions was ushered through the room and locked into his or her own cell. Brock searched each familiar face to determine if they were well. Similar to Cam, both Lars and Puri were bound in shackles until they were within their cell. Lars had a lump on his head while Puri had a hastily bandaged gash on her upper arm. Tipper and Libby both appeared shaken, but they were unharmed and unshackled.

Not seeing Ashland among them, Brock feared that something had happened to her. A wave of relief hit when she passed through the door and appeared unharmed. Her eyes searched the room, finding his just before the guards pushed her into a cell and locked the door. With the prisoners locked away, the guards filed out the door, again leaving the keeper of the keys behind.

As the man reclaimed his seat behind the desk, Brock turned from the door. Sitting upon the pallet that was to be his bed, Brock put his mind to the task of escaping.

~

Are you sure you want to do this? Brock asked.

Yes. It's the only way to ensure our escape without killing the man or having him call for help, Ashland replied.

Brock closed his eyes and gathered as much *Chaos* as possible before opening them and pouring the energy into the *Power* rune. The glow briefly lit his cell in a red light before pulsing and fading.

I'm ready. Do it now, Brock sent.

"Hey, big guy!" Ashland called out. "Can you come here?"

Brock moved close to his cell door and peered through the bars. The recent shift change resulted in a different guard now on duty. Surprisingly, this man was even bigger than the last.

The guard stopped eating his meal, rose to his feet, and approached the door to Ashland's cell.

"What do you want?" the man asked.

"I'm starving. If you give me some of your food, I'll give you something in return." Her tone was one of unsaid invitation.

"What could you give me? You're a prisoner."

A moment passed before Ashland responded, "Does this give you any ideas?"

The guard smiled as he peered through the bars into Ashland's cell.

"Very nice," the man nodded. "But how do I know you're not trying to escape?"

Ashland's voice came from the cell again. "Here. I'll turn my back and you can shackle me when you come in. You just have to promise me some of your food when you're finished."

Brock heard the jingling of keys as the man unlocked the cell door. When the guard stepped inside her cell, Brock did his best to remain calm. Seconds passed, seeming like hours, until he heard Ashland. *Hurry, Brock!*

He thrust his hands against the door. His *Chaos*-enhanced strength blasted the door off its hinges, spraying splinters in all directions as it slammed into the opposite wall.

"What was that?" the guard exclaimed.

Brock darted into the cell and swept the man aside. Although the man was twice Brock's size, he slammed into the wall as if he were made of rags and crumpled to the floor, unconscious.

Ashland's back was facing him, her wrists shackled behind her. Brock bent to retrieve the man's ring of keys. Careful to be as gentle as possible, he used the smallest key to unlock Ashland's wrist. As the shackles fell to the floor, she spun to hug him. Not wishing to injure her with his chaotic strength, he kept his arms to the side. After a moment, she loosened her arms and gave him a smile. He returned the smile, relieved that she was safe. She stepped back and his smile grew wider upon seeing her in her shift.

"The man was right." Brock nodded, grinning. "Very nice indeed."

She laughed and shook her head as she pulled her tunic over her head. "You are so bad, Brock Talenz."

"Are you guys done with the lovey-dovey yet?" Benny pleaded from his cell. "Some of us would like to get out of here."

Brock held the keys out to Ashland. "You take these and lock him in here before you free the others. I'll keep watch until you're done."

She nodded and took the keys. Brock crossed the room to the doorway and poked his head out, relieved to find the corridor empty. He turned back to watch Ashland free the others. Libby ran to Tipper, hugging him fiercely. Benny rocked his elbows in anxiety. Cam and Lars each grabbed a cudgel from the desk, ready to use them as needed. Puri appeared ready to eat lightning. Parker's eyes met Brock's when he emerged from his cell.

"I'm sorry that this happened," Parker said. "I never imagined that my father would betray me, betray us."

"Don't worry about it, Parker," Brock replied. "Go grab that lamp. We'll need the light to retrace our steps." As Parker grabbed the lamp, Brock addressed the others. "I'll take the lead. It should be night outside now, so we should be able to slip out without running into trouble. Now, let's get out of here."

With Parker and the lamp a step behind, Brock darted down the corridor. Retracing the route they had taken to the dungeon, he led them through the depths of the keep. They crossed the room filled with old relics, passed through the double-doorway, and ascended the long flight of stairs. After running down the dark corridor at the top of the stairs, they passed through the underground office where the city clerks worked, only to find the room dark and the desks empty. Up the short flight of stairs and down the long corridor they went, turning at the end to head toward the stairwell leading up to the main hall. Brock slowed as he climbed the stairs, hoping that they might remain inconspicuous. Expecting it to be quiet since it was well past nightfall, he was surprised at the flurry of activity within the citadel.

Clearly in a state of panic, people scurried about the open space. A group of guards struggled against the stream of civilians that flowed into the building, eventually forcing their way outside. Not having time to consider what was happening, Brock jumped in line with the guards and followed them outside with his companions trailing close behind.

As Brock led them across outer hall, the noise and hysteria became even more intense. People ran in every direction within the plaza, seeking entry to the buildings inside the citadel walls. The night sky suddenly grew bright as a ball of flames arced over the south wall. The rumble shook the city as an explosion of flames shot up from buildings a few streets away. Brock reached out to stop a man running toward the citadel.

"What's happening? Why's everyone running?"

The man turned to Brock, his eyes frightened. "The city is under attack by monsters! This is the end of days!"

Backing away from Brock, the man turned and ran toward the building. Brock glanced back at the others. From their expressions, Brock knew they heard what the man said.

With a new sense of urgency, Brock ran down the steps and led them across the plaza, toward the gates. As he drew close, he found guards urgently pushing people back as the gates began to close. Brock squeezed past the guards and through the frantic mob as it drew closed. Once outside, he grabbed the thick iron bars and the gate came to a halt, causing the two guards who were cranking it to cry out in pain. As Brock held the gate with his *Chaos*-charged strength, a guard grabbed his shirt and tried to push him away. With a flick of his wrist, Brock tossed the guard into two others who were trying to hold the mob back.

Cam and Lars pushed their way through the oncoming crowd, cutting a path for the others to follow. Once his companions were clear, Brock released the gate and followed their trail as they fought their way through the terrified populace.

38

———————

Upon discovering that his father wasn't home, Parker assumed he was at the citadel and would remain there with the Archon, live or die. When he realized that he might never see the man again, Parker decided that he didn't care. They had never been close, but his father's act of betrayal had severed the last threads to Parker's heart.

Agatha and Pinkus were another story. The cook and butler had been part of the household for decades and felt more like parents to Parker than his father ever had. He urged them to leave the city, but both were adamant that they would remain with the house. As long as the house survived, they would survive. While his companions gathered their things, Parker said some very painful goodbyes. He led the others out into the stable yard and wiped tears from his eyes under the cover of night. With the impending deaths of Pinkus and Agatha, he was losing the only family he'd ever known.

Niles waited anxiously, the horses appeared ready to go.

"I'd like to go with you, Master Parker. That is, if you'll have me," the boy said while wringing his hands.

Another explosion lit the night sky, causing everyone to glance toward the thunderous sound.

Parker nodded as he mounted his horse. "Of course you can join us,

Niles." He reached a hand down toward the boy. "You can ride with me. Grab my hand and get on,"

The boy grabbed Parker's hand and climbed up to sit behind him.

With everyone mounted and ready, Parker kicked his horse into motion and led them down the dark alley. When they reached the street, it was filled with people milling about, the general flow heading toward the harbor. Hysteria had taken ahold of the populace, reducing them to mindless drones running in fright. The basic human need to survive had erased any thoughts of compassion as the mob trampled over anyone who had the misfortune of falling.

Parker and Puri led the others down the street as the horses forced the mob to part. When they reached eastern wall, they found the gate open. Following the throng of people pouring through, they rode down the street toward the pier where *Star Dancer* had docked.

"Look. She's still here!" Benny pointed toward the ship, still in its mooring.

With Parker and Puri leading, the group rode their horses onto the pier, pushing through the mob of those who hoped to escape aboard a ship. When they approached the end of the pier, Parker noticed the crewmembers of *Star Dancer* using poles to keep the crowd from climbing the lines tied to the ship.

"Ho, *Star Dancer!*" Parker called out. "Where's Captain Sinclair?"

A sailor called back. "He's coming up behind you!"

Parker turned and spotted the man's bright red coat trailing the last horse in their group. As the man stumbled past the horses, Parker called out to him.

"Yo, Sinclair! We need to get out of here. Do you have room for us?"

Sinclair stopped, swaying as if on the seas, his eyes at half-mast. A smile lit up on the drunk captain's face.

"Well met, Master Thanes! Thanks for parting the crowd for me. I wasn't sure if I would make it to the ship." He waved his arm and stumbled into the horse beside him. "Of course we'll have you. However, we have an issue with these people in the way."

Parker nodded. That much was obvious.

Brock dismounted and handed his staff to Tipper, who remained upon his horse. "I'll handle this."

Turning to the inland side of the dock, he grabbed ahold of the rail. Still charged by Chaos, Brock pulled a fifteen-foot long plank off the thick posts that held it in place, sending splinters flying from where it broke loose. He then turned toward the throng of frightened citizens, held the rail across the width of the dock, and eased the crowd backward. Numerous men pushed back in an attempt to resist, but Brock continued to move them backward at an even but relentless pace, forcing a cluster of over fifty people down the dock until they were past the midpoint of the ship.

As the dock opened, the crew dropped boarding planks to the deck and to the cargo hold. Puri whistled and her white stallion led the other horses across the planks. As the horses boarded the cargo hold, Parker led the others up the other planks to the deck. When the last horse was on board, the crew kicked the planks into the sea and closed the cargo hold doors.

Brock turned toward Parker. "Go ahead and pull the planks as soon as you're aboard. Don't worry about me."

Puri was the last to board. As she crossed the planks to the deck, Parker called out.

"All right, Brock! Let's go!"

Brock turned and nodded to Parker as the sailors pulled the planks back on the ship. Brock dropped the rail, the heavy plank bouncing on the pier as it settled. He took a couple strides and leapt. Amazingly, he flew thirty feet up into the air, arcing high over Parker with his arms and legs swinging wildly in an attempt to remain upright. The ship's deck croaked a *thump* when Brock landed feet-first before tucking into a roll with the momentum.

Wrapped in a state of awe at what had just occurred, the sailors stopped working and stared at Brock, Sinclair among them. The captain closed his gaping jaw and shook his head to clear it before shouting.

"Come on, you lazy dogs! Get to work! We have a ship to sail!"

As the men resumed prepping the ship, Sinclair turned back to Parker as he straightened his hat. "I know I've been drinking, but I'm not *that* drunk. I've never seen anything like it." He shook his head in wonder. "You are an interesting group. I hope it's lucky. We could use some luck right..."

Sinclair stopped mid-speech as he stared toward land. Parker turned toward the city, his eyes searching for what had caught the man's attention.

"Issal's breath," he muttered at the sight before him.

A wave of dark forms flowed through the streets that lay between the docks and the city wall. High-pitched screams carried across the bay as enemy attackers tore through the crowd. Parker watched in horror as the attackers began pouring through the open gate into the city and down the docks toward the crowded pier. As the enemy reached the people on the pier, he realized that the dark shapes were huge, dwarfing the people they cut down. Despite the increasing the distance from the pier, the sound of screams continued to rise. The sound gave Parker chills, making his hair stand on end. In just a few short minutes, the enemy mowed down all before them. Corpses scattered the length of the pier. The few who still lived thrashed in the sea, having leapt into the dark waters in hope of escaping.

Sinclair recovered enough to call the crew to their marks. The sailors quickly raised the sails, driven by a new sense of urgency. Everyone wanted to be far from the city as fast as possible. Parker looked around and saw other ships both ahead and behind theirs as they fled the city.

Glancing backward, he noticed a couple ships still tied to the pier. Massive silhouettes tore through the ships as sailors leapt into the water, abandoning the vessels. The city lit up again as a fireball arced through the sky to strike a citadel tower. Parker's father was somewhere within the complex. The building where Cedric spent so much of his life was soon to become his tomb. Parker felt a small pang of loss for his father, despite their strained relationship. His thoughts shifted to others he would greatly miss, the people who had played important roles in his life. Closing his eyes, he prayed for Issal to reward Pinkus and Agatha for being good people.

With a slight turn, the sails rippled and snapped taught when they caught the stiff breeze. The ship gained speed as it sailed toward the breakers, leaving the dying city of Sol Polis behind.

39

———

The ship raised up high as it crested a massive wave. Parker stumbled toward the quarterdeck and grabbed the rail to steady himself. When the deck tilted hard to the side, he held on tightly to keep from sliding across it. It leveled and he advanced, blinking at the wind-driven rain pelting his face as he scaled the stairs to the quarterdeck. He hugged the rail and shouted to Tenzi.

"What is it?"

"I don't understand where this storm came from. It's almost…unnatural, like a hurricane despite the season being far too late for one." She frowned. "I need you to get the captain from his cabin."

Hurrying back down the stairs, Parker scrambled toward the Captain's Cabin. He pounded on the door while holding himself steady with his other hand. The intensity of the rain had increased steadily over the past fifteen minutes, now filling the air such that he could barely see the bow. The ship rolled again, tipping to one side before rocking to the other. Deciding that he couldn't wait for Sinclair to answer, he grabbed the knob, gave it a twist, and he fell into the room when the door swung open.

The dim light of the discharged glowlamp on the wall gave shape to the room's interior, allowing Parker to see the prone form on the floor near the bed. He knelt beside the man and rolled him over. Blood covered Sinclair's face. A deep gash glistened wetly on his forehead. He checked for a pulse and confirmed that the man was alive. Parker patted his cheek and tried to wake him. Finding no response, he scrambled out the door and into the pouring rain.

When he reached the quarterdeck, Parker shouted to Tenzi.

"Sinclair hit his head. He's alive, but he's out cold."

Her face reflected a blend of alarm and frustration.

"I guess it's up to me, then."

Tenzi turned toward a cluster of three sailors, standing just below the quarterdeck. "We have to take down the sails before the masts break! The wind's blowing too hard!"

The men nodded and scurried in response. Two of the men ran toward the bow while the third began scaling the mizzenmast rigging. Through the driving rain, Parker watched as other sailors began to scale the two forward masts. The bow rose high again and dropped as it crested an enormous wave. Sea spray drenched the deck, sweeping the feet from beneath two of the sailors. They slid across the deck, wedged against the rail by the heavy flow of water.

Parker remained on the quarterdeck, hugging the rail as Tenzi maintained a firm grip on the wheel. Now soaked through and through, he found himself jealous of his companions, safe and dry in their cabins below deck.

A mighty gust of wind hit, causing the ship to heel hard to one side. A scream sounded as the sailor on the mizzenmast lost his grip and tumbled into the churning waters below. Three of the sails on the mast remained unfurled, stretching under the pressure of the heavy wind.

Tenzi turned toward Parker. "Take the wheel!"

Surprised, Parker jumped forward and grabbed the wheel.

"Just hold it steady! Don't let it turn on you!" she yelled to him before darting toward the rigging.

With practiced ease, she scrambled up the height of the mast. Up and up she went, not halting until she reached the top. Moments later, she had the uppermost sail down before dropping to the next. One end of the upper topsail collapsed but the other appeared stuck. Tenzi climbed on the yard, balancing on it as she ran to the stuck end. Grabbing the rigging with one hand, she used the other to cut the line holding the yard in place. It dropped from under her feet and left her dangling from the rigging.

Tenzi shimmied down to the lower topsail, getting it lowered just before a huge gust struck the ship. She jumped for the rigging and held on tightly to keep from being tossed into the sea as the ship heeled hard. A loud cracking snap sounded, drawing Parker's attention toward the bow. With three of its four sails still unfurled, the foremast broke away from the ship. The two men in the mast rigging fell with it and tumbled into the sea. The mast crashed down hard, smashing the rail and sending splintered wood in all directions. Some of the rigging held for a moment and caused the long wooden shaft to dangle from the ship until the next big wave hit. The bow shot high with the wave, and the last of the rigging broke free to launch the mast over the side and into the sea. A huge wave followed and another sailor washed across the deck through the section with the broken rail, the man's distant scream cutting off as he plunged into the roiling sea.

Parker glanced back up as Tenzi collapsed the last sail. She shimmied down the rigging and landed on the deck beside him before grabbing the wheel. He looked toward the main mast and found its sails now down, the men safely on deck. While the seas remained rough, the ship appeared far more stable with the sails down.

Tenzi shouted to him. "Thanks. Now we just have to ride it out and try not to run ashore."

Parker stared out at the dark waters. With the heavy rain, he could see little other than the whitecaps surrounding the ship. He had no idea how Tenzi would be able to see anything out there. It would be a long night.

With the sails down, the heavy waves continued to toss the ship for hours. The night dragged on as if it would never end. Drenched from the relentless rainfall, Parker could not have been wetter if he was in the sea itself. Eventually, the wind calmed enough to allow them to unfurl the lowest sail on both remaining masts.

He glanced toward Brock, who was returning from Sinclair's cabin.

He and Cam had joined Parker on deck to help fill-in for the five crewmembers who had been lost to the storm.

Parker asked, "Sinclair's still out?"

Brock nodded. "Yeah. I healed him, but he hit his head hard. I have no idea when he'll wake."

Parker wasn't sure what difference it would make. Despite the horrible circumstances, Tenzi seemed to have things under control. At least, as under control as was possible.

His eyes shifted to the horizon over the port side of the ship and noticed the sky growing lighter. Parker peered hard into the murky twilight, trying to see what was beyond the immediate vicinity of the ship. Brock and Cam noticed and attempted to do the same. Parker thought he could discern shapes through the rain, but he was unsure if they were real or tricks played by his wishful mind. Moments later, the sky lightened further, and the dark shapes took form.

A wall of high cliffs loomed a quarter-mile away with jagged rocks poking above the raging sea between the ship and shore. Some of the rocks were mere feet from the ship.

Parker spun toward Tenzi. "Rocks!"

Tenzi turned the wheel hard to starboard as a heavy wave struck. The force of the wave drove the ship toward the rocks, causing the ship to lurch when the hull connected. Parker almost went over the rail, but Cam had a grip of his cloak and yanked him back. A scream sounded as another sailor slipped through the section of broken railing and disappeared into the rough sea. The deck held at a steep angle for a long moment, the hull scraping noisily on the rocks as the ship broke loose from the brief stasis.

Parker glanced back at Tenzi, who was trying desperately to get the ship clear of the rocks. He ran across the deck and scrambled up the steps to the quarterdeck.

"What can I do?" he asked.

She shouted back. "We hit that rock pretty hard. Go below deck and check if we're taking on water."

He nodded and climbed down the stairs before waving for Brock and Cam to follow. Weaving back and forth as the ship rocked, they crossed the deck, climbed down the stairs, and slipped inside. The noise of the storm dimmed when they closed the door behind them. Brock ran into the men's cabin, emerging with a glow lamp as Lars, Benny, Niles, and Tipper looked on. Parker heard Benny shout from the room.

"What's going on?"

Ignoring him, Parker opened the door at the end of the hall and descended to the cargo hold with Brock and Cam a step behind. The smell of feces was overwhelming, informing him that the horses were shaken by the poor treatment.

Parker ran to the bilge hatch and pulled it open. Pale light of his glowlamp poured through the hatch. The surface of the dark water was just inches below the hatch, informing him that the bilge was full and the leak would not stop there. He glanced toward Brock, their eyes meeting in a grim exchange. It was clear that ship wouldn't stay afloat much longer.

Parker closed the hatch and they climbed back to the cabin level. Brock went to warn the girls, while Parker stuck his head into the boys' room.

"Get your stuff and get on deck. The ship is sinking. We don't have long."

Benny, Lars, Niles, and Tipper scrambled to gather weapons and packs as Parker and Cam grabbed their own. When he emerged from the cabin, Brock was leading Ashland, Libby, and Puri toward the deck.

They emerged topside and found that daylight had taken a firm grip, providing a view of the shoreline. Parker scanned the landmass and found a forbidding wall of tall cliffs lining the coast. He ran to the quarterdeck and climbed up to report to Tenzi.

"We are taking on water! The bilge is nearly full!"

Tenzi stared at him for a moment before nodding. "We don't have long, then. I will try to get us closer to land before we abandon ship."

Parker nodded. "What do you want me to do?"

"There's a bucket in the dingy. Take it and start bailing!"

Parker nodded, dropped to the deck, and ran to the dingy. Brock saw him and met him at the rail.

"What's the plan?" Brock asked.

"We need to bail out the dingy. We'll have to abandon ship soon!"

"I'll do it," Brock said as he climbed the rail and jumped over to the swinging dingy.

Parker ran across the deck to meet their other companions.

"We are about to abandon ship." Parker gestured toward the dingy.

Puri glanced at it, then back to Parker. "What about the horses? We cannot leave them."

"What else can we do? They can't fit on the dingy."

She stared at him for a long moment, her face a dark frown when she finally nodded. Turning, she disappeared down the stairs with Cam a step behind. Minutes passed as they stood on deck, watching the dark cliffs to the east. When Puri and Cam returned, her face remained grim but Cam's now appeared haunted.

Parker stepped close to Cam. "What happened?"

Cam looked away, not meeting Parker's eyes. "When we got down there, the water in the cargo hull was waist deep and is rising fast. Puri didn't want the horses to drown, trapped down there, so she gave them a better death I guess."

Parker now understood. He patted Cam on the shoulder but had no words to add. The ship lurched again, causing everyone to stumble toward the bow. Parker spun about to find that they were now just a couple hundred feet from shore. Tenzi had opted to run them aground.

He turned toward the stern as she leapt from the quarterdeck.

"Abandon ship!" Tenzi shouted as she approached the remaining crewmembers. "Grab the captain, and help him to the dingy."

Parker turned to his friends. "To the dingy. Come on," he led the others to the small vessel.

Starting with the three girls, Parker, Cam, and Brock helped the others climb into the dingy as it dangled above the churning water twenty feet below. They were all in the dingy when Tenzi appeared at the rail, trailed by three sailors stumbling under the dead weight of Captain Sinclair. Cam and Lars helped load the unconscious man into the dingy. The remaining three sailors climbed into the fully loaded boat, leaving only Tenzi on the ship.

A wave hit, splashing cold water high enough to soak them. Parker looked up at the ship, now tilting away from the dingy, but he could no longer see Tenzi. Moments later, she appeared and flipped the winch release. The queasy sense of weightlessness hit Parker's stomach as the small craft plummeted to the sea. It struck hard, flattening out the passengers and sending a sailor over the side to vanish into the dark waters. Parker and Cam leaned over the edge, looking to fish the man from the sea, but he never surfaced. A rope from above dropped into the water. Parker to look up again and realized that Tenzi had cut one of the winch lines connected to the dingy. With a leap, she jumped to the other line and shimmied down to the boat. Once onboard, she used her knife to sever the line and turned to the group.

"Get those oars in the water! We have to get to shore, now!"

Mirroring the two sailors, Cam dug an oar from beneath their seats and set the pivot pin in place. Lars had his in place seconds later, and all four oars were set.

Tenzi yelled. "Row at the same time, on my count!" They nodded and she called out, "Stroke!"

Parker's gaze shifted toward the shore as the small boat rose up on a high swell. There was a narrow beach nestled between the cliff sides, hundreds of feet away. The beach disappeared as the swell passed them and the boat dipped low, surrounded by high waves. He glanced back to where the last sailor had fallen, still not seeing the man. He prayed to Issal that the sea would not claim anyone else.

Parker held tight to the rail as the dingy ran aground. Tenzi and the last two remaining sailors leapt from the bow into the waist-deep water. Without their added weight, the bow raised up and the next wave drove the boat forward while those on foot pulled it along. When the wave receded, the hull remained firmly beached against the wet sand.

Cam and Parker each grabbed one end of Sinclair, lifting him over the side of the boat as they passed the captain to the two sailors. Another wave crashed in and caused the men to stumble as they tried to get to dry land. When they fell, they lost grip of their captain. Tenzi grabbed the man's hands before the receding water could pull him from shore. She was able to drag Sinclair across the sand despite being half his size. Parker leapt from the boat to help as another wave hit, the force washing Sinclair further ashore. Seeing that Tenzi had the captain safely on the beach, he turned to help the others from the small boat.

A minute later, the group sat high on the beach, exhausted as they watched the waves crashing along the sandy shore. Parker's gaze searched beyond the breakers to determine what had become of *Star*

Dancer. Nothing but the quarterdeck and two remaining masts stood above the waterline. The ship appeared to have settled into its fresh grave, a quarter mile from shore.

The rain had lessoned significantly since they had boarded the dingy, now wavering between a sprinkle and a fine mist. Cold and wet, Parker prayed for the rain to end.

Using his staff, Brock climbed to his feet and dusted the sand from his bottom before extending a hand to Ashland.

"Come on. Let's see what's here besides sand and rock." Brock said.

She took his hand, standing as others began climbing to their feet.

Tenzi gestured toward the remaining sailors. "Perry, Bart, and I will stay with Sinclair to make sure he's safe."

Parker responded. "Do you want me to stay with you? I'm pretty good with this bow." He patted the bow strung across his back.

"Don't worry about me," Tenzi said. "I'm pretty good with these knives, too."

Parker had seen the girl use her knife, but hadn't noticed more than one. He suspected that she wasn't boasting. Her toughness was among the reasons she intrigued him.

They headed toward the green gap beyond the beach. The pale sands extended hundreds of feet in both directions, terminating against steep cliff walls that towered over the sea.

When they crested the rise of sand, they found a small river emerging from a ravine as it flowed into the sea. Parker sent Issal a prayer of thanks for the fortune of landing near a source of fresh water.

The canyon before them was thick with palms and lush green under-growth. The foliage enveloped a shallow river, dotted with partially submerged rocks. Parker removed his flask and submerged it in the swift flowing water to fill it. Others copied him, refilling their water skins as they observed their surroundings.

Brock turned east. "It appears that the way out is to follow this ravine uphill. Since this river will provide fresh water, we can follow it inland until we find a place to stop and rest. I think we could all use a break after last night. Besides, we can't make it too far until Sinclair recovers."

Parker pointed inland. "You guys scout ahead. I'll go back and help carry Sinclair up here."

"Good idea." Brock nodded before turning east, leading the group up the ravine.

As Parker headed back to the beach, he realized that the rain had stopped. Glancing back at the eastern horizon, he saw a slim beam of sunlight breaking through the gray skies above the ridgeline. The storm was over.

40

Brock raised a knuckle to his eyes and rubbed the weariness out. He was thankful that they had escaped the storm alive but was now concerned about their continued survival. Despite knowing that the attack on Sol Polis and subsequent storm were not his doing, he felt responsible since he led the quest that had put them in this position.

Looking out at the sea, a half mile away, the steady sets of white waves upon blue waters appeared far friendlier than they had an hour ago. Now that the storm had moved on, the sea had settled, and the land had begun to dry in the morning sun. He turned to survey the camp, and spotted Parker and Cam draping clothing from the lowest branches of an umbrella-like tree. A small fire burned in the center of the camp, fed by dead wood gathered from the area. Between the warmth of the fire, emerging sunlight, and the ocean breeze, he expected that things would dry quickly.

After taking a seat upon a rock, Brock began removing his belongings from his pack. He pulled out a bundle, wrapped within his old apprentice cloak. Finding the cloak to be quite wet, he winced at what he might find when he unwrapped it. The cloak fell away to reveal a thick red book with a gold *Chaos* rune embossed on the cover. His fears were realized when he noticed that the edges of the pages were wet. He carefully peeled the wet pages open to where his folded notes were stored. Luckily, the notes were intact, but most of the book was ruined. Finding much of the text and symbols on the pages smeared beyond recognition, Brock's heart sank. The *Chaos* runes discovered thus far might be all they would ever learn. He stared at the two most recent symbols, drawn in his notes – symbols that he, Ashland, Tipper, and Libby had begun memorizing. They could only guess at their effects until they had a chance to test them. Having translated the runes during their journey from Wayport to Sol Polis, they had resisted any experimentation within the confines of the ship. The last thing Brock had wanted was to sink the ship. With the thought, he looked toward the water and saw the ship's masts jutting above the surface at an angle, looking like two toothpicks from the distance. He found it ironic that the ship ended up sinking for a totally different reason.

"The book is in bad shape." Ashland said as she sat beside him.

Brock looked back at the wet book in his hands. "Yeah. The notes survived, but the book is beyond saving."

While staring at the drenched book, the warmth from the sun drew Brock's attention. He looked toward the sky overhead, holding his hand up to block the bright sunlight. There, he found another shape in the heavens. Now a pale ball, the ominous planet could easily be seen in the day. How long did they have before it reappeared in the evening sky?

A survey of the camp revealed that the others had stripped down to minimal clothing as their things dried. Brock's eyes fell on the ship captain. Sinclair was now awake, but still seemed quite out of sorts. The man tried to sit and then promptly tipped sideways to throw up. Apparently, it would take a bit more time for him to recover.

Approaching Parker, Brock spoke softly. "Do you have any idea where we are?"

Parker glanced toward Niles, who shrugged. "No. However, since that way is east," he pointed inland, "we must be somewhere in Kalimar."

Tenzi rose from her crouch beside Sinclair and moved closer. "This is the western coastline of southern Kalimar. I estimate that we're about thirty miles north of Sol Gier."

Parker nodded. "That makes sense. However, getting to Sol Gier will be difficult with the high cliffs south of us."

Brock nodded, thinking. "What about Sol Limar?"

Tenzi's brow furrowed. "Sol Limar? There's nothing there but old ruins. Why would you want to go there?"

Parker smiled. "He has a reason." He turned toward Brock. "Sol Limar should be just about directly east of us, across the peninsula."

Brock nodded. "Thanks to what the crew grabbed from the ship, we have enough food here to get by a bit. I suggest we rest for a few hours and then follow this canyon inland. We'll see if we can scrounge up more food along the way. Regardless, at least we have fresh water as long as we're near this river."

~

Brock hopped across the rocks, over the flowing water of the shallow river. As they traveled inland, the river had gradually become smaller and was now only twenty feet across.

Pausing at the far side, he glanced back to see the others following along in a line. Ashland deftly hopped from rock to rock across the river, giving him a smile as he held a hand out to help her onto the bank. He turned and resumed cutting a path through the damp wood, swinging his staff to push the undergrowth of ferns, brush, and long grass aside.

The sky had begun to dim, with the sun now behind clouds to the west. They had been climbing up the canyon for hours, and their belongings remained damp from the storm.

Brock meandered through the woods, seeking the easiest route while trying to avoid the sloppy red mud that dotted the forest floor. Something burst from the undergrowth and scurried across his path, causing him to jump with a start. It was a large unfamiliar bird. Stopping, he motioned for Ashland to quiet. She stopped and he motioned to Parker, who was a step behind her.

"Crowster," Parker whispered as he slid his bow from his shoulder. He eased an arrow from the quiver and took aim. A *thwap* sounded as the arrow pierced the bird's neck. It stumbled about and flapped its wings for a bit before tumbling into the fallen leaves.

Benny exclaimed from behind Parker. "Whoa! Wonderful shot, Parker."

"Thanks," he said, pulling another arrow out. "Have everyone stay here and remain quiet. There should be others. They typically nest in groups."

Brock and Ashland stood still as Parker slid past them. He took perhaps another ten steps before three more of the birds burst from the brush and scurried in different directions.

Parker's bow followed one of them, firing and hitting it in the breast to knock the bird over. It twitched for a bit before lying still. Parker drew another arrow from the quiver before creeping deeper into the woods. When Brock lost sight of him through the trees, he decided it was time to claim their dinner.

"Benny, grab this bird, and I'll get the one up ahead," Brock said, pointing at the first bird. "Now, the fruit we found earlier won't be all we have for dinner tonight."

Benny nodded and weaved his way through the trees toward the bird. "That's great to hear, because I'm starving. I'm sure the others feel the same way."

After grabbing the second bird, Brock turned toward the others who waited behind him. He waved them forward and followed the route Parker had taken. A minute later, he spotted Parker pulling an arrow from a third bird. Brock pulled the arrow from the bird he carried before handing it to Parker.

"Great shooting. You've fed us again, so expect a lot of love from everyone at dinner tonight," Brock said, smiling at Parker.

Parker smiled back. "I could use a little love right now."

Brock passed Parker and led the group uphill through the forest. He soon noticed a rushing sound ahead, the noise steadily growing louder. Angling back toward the river, he stopped at the bank as the sun broke through the clouds behind him. The beam of sunlight shined upon a tall waterfall, creating a rainbow in the mist rising from the rushing water. It was an amazing sight.

Ashland stepped next to him. "Wow. It's beautiful."

He smiled, putting his arm around her. Shipwrecked and lost in a foreign land, yet Ashland still appreciated the beauty surrounding them. How could he not love this girl?

. . .

41

———

After breaking camp the next morning, they left the waterfall behind to resume their uphill journey. When the canyon leveled to become a saddle, the river split in two small rivulets, dribbling down from the peaks to the north and the south. They stopped to refill their skins one last time before continuing east.

Brock skirted around a peak and led them along a ridgeline, which they followed for much of the day. They ate sparingly, trying to ration the leftover crowster and the sweet fruit they had collected near the coast. It wasn't much, but it was enough to keep them going.

For hours, they hiked, and the miles slid past. When they reached the eastern end of the ridgeline, the sun was low in the sky behind them. Brock paused and surveyed the view, trying to determine the best route. If they wanted to continue eastward, he saw no option but to descend and cross the valley ahead. After taking a drink, he capped his water skin and began seeking a route down.

Motion in a clearing at the valley floor caught his eye. Hope spiked in his chest when he saw a person running across the clearing thousands of feet below, disappearing when the wooded hillside obscured the view. If there were people here, food and shelter couldn't be far away.

Ashland stopped beside him. "What a view."

"I saw someone down there." He pointed toward the clearing.

"Are you sure?" She peered in the direction indicated.

"We are heading that direction anyway. Let's watch the clearing as we descend to see if they show up again."

Brock glanced backward, seeing the others stopping to drink from their water skins. He waved them along and began the long descent.

42

The thick forest offered no view of the valley floor during their decent, but Brock could sense something ahead, something substantial. He could almost hear it, but he had no idea what it was. The irritation began to eat at him, making him anxious. Something inside of him yearned to discover what it was, just to know what could make him feel this way.

Ashland caught up to him, whispering. "Brock, I don't know if this is real, but I feel like there's something ahead. It's...noisy."

He stopped and looked her in the eye. "You feel it too?"

She nodded. "What is it?"

He shrugged. "I don't know, but I hear it. It's so loud that I almost can't think."

The others began to catch up to them, clustering as they stopped to drink from their skins.

"Does anyone else...sense or hear something ahead?" Brock asked.

"I do." Tipper nodded. "Libby does too. We were wondering what it was."

Benny squinted, looking at Tipper then back to Brock. "What are you guys talking about?"

Tipper spoke again. "I don't know, but there is something ahead...a buzzing noise messing with my head."

"Yes. Exactly." Brock nodded. "Nobody else feels…or hears what we are talking about?"

Blank stares looked back at him.

"That's what I was afraid of," Brock said before turning toward Benny. "It has something to do with *Chaos*. I know it."

Benny nodded. "That's why you four can sense it, and we can't."

"I believe so." Brock nodded in return. "I think we had better be careful. Everyone, try to be quiet. No talking until we find out what lies ahead."

They resumed the snaking descent, and the pressure increased in proportion to their decreasing elevation, leaving a clear impression that something powerful waited ahead. When Brock spotted a rocky outcropping where the trees parted and the sky opened, he snuck out from the trees, climbed up the rocks, and lay on his belly as he eased to the edge.

In the failing light of the setting sun, his eyes scanned the clearing far below. The sheer rock wall of the opposing hillside faced him, providing a clear view of the cave at its base. Tall, human-like shapes moved about at the mouth of the cave. Their long black hair and lumbering gait were familiar to Brock. The timbre of a single high-pitched wail echoed through the valley, setting his hair on end. Fear threatened to take over, triggering a cold sweat.

"What was that?" Benny asked from behind with voice oozing with anxiety.

Brock turned his head, whispering. "Hush. Don't make a noise or we're dead."

His companions quieted and turned toward one another with questions in their eyes. Ashland slid beside Brock to get a view.

"What's happening?" she whispered.

Brock pointed toward the cave. "Those are banshees. Dozens of them." Even as he said it, chills went down his spine.

"What? I've never heard of more than one," she whispered. "How can this be?"

He whispered back. "I don't know, but I do know that this is bad. Very bad."

Benny slid in on the other side of Brock. "What's happening?"

Brock kept his eyes on the cave. "Banshees."

Benny shook his head. "That's a lot of banshees. They're big, right?"

"Yes. Ten feet tall," Brock replied. "And there are dozens of them. Maybe more."

A shorter form emerged from the cave, walking out in front of the gathered banshees. This one didn't have the same lumbering gait as the others, nor did it have the same crazy long hair and torn clothing. The shorter one waved an arm, and the banshees broke into a run across the shadow-covered clearing as they headed north. Hoots and high-pitched wails sounded out as the shorter one ran among them. Each wail sent chills down Brock's spine and increased the fear within his gut. Shadowy forms continued to pour from the cave, lumbering across the darkening field. He counted two hundred of the huge beasts before the scene quieted.

"What's that?" Benny whispered, pointing toward the edge of the clearing.

Partly obscured by the trees, Brock saw the glowing red of a shifting shape hovering in the air. The edges of the thing danced in quick jerking motions.

"I don't know." Brock's brow furrowed in thought. "It's almost as if it's alive or something. I…"

Brock heard a buzzing sound as three banshees emerged from the sizzling red curtain of energy, as if materializing from nowhere. The beasts broke into a run, following the others to disappear into the forest at the north end of the clearing.

Brock's throat tightened as a deepening fear gripped and twisted his insides. It all came together at once. The Banished Horde was back. They were back, and he now knew where they came from.

PART IV

VISIONS OF TRUTH

43

"**I** know you're wondering what's happening," Brock spoke in hushed tones to those seated around the small fire. The sense of trepidation surrounding him was palpable, fear reflecting in the eyes facing him.

"I assume everyone has heard of the Banished Horde." Heads nodded when he paused. "Well, they've returned."

"What? How is that possible?" Lars asked. "They were destroyed hundreds of years ago."

"Really, Lars?" Brock raised an eyebrow. "Were you there to witness it? Do you know where they even came from? Can there not be more than those who died in the Wailing War?"

Lars shook his head. "Well, no. But..."

Benny clapped the big guy's shoulder. "It's real, Lars. Brock and I researched them, learning all we could from a book we took from the Academy Library archives last year." He paused, releasing a sigh. "Everything matches. It makes sense, too much sense. What we saw, what you heard, was the Horde. They're back, and now we know what they are."

"We do?" Parker asked, looking from Benny to Brock.

"They're banshees." Brock replied. "Perhaps the term came from a play on the word *banished*. Banished, Banshee. Pretty similar, wouldn't you say?"

Sinclair released a laugh, which sounded forced. "Banshees. They're just a wild tale used to scare children. There's no such thing."

"How can you say that, captain?" Brock asked. "Didn't you see what happened on the docks of Sol Polis? Did your eyes tell you it was just a wild tale?"

Sinclair's gaze scanned the faces circled around the small fire. "That was real? I thought it was just a dream I had after I hit my head."

The quiet night was disturbed when a high-pitched wail sounded in the distance, causing everyone to search the surroundings. Shadows within shadows stirred in the night, fear and terror their names. The darkness had never been more frightening. Another chill caused Brock to shiver, one of many since arriving in the valley. The wail reminded him of the banshee that killed Hank.

"Tipper and I had a run-in with a banshee last year. It was horrifying. The beast was twice my height and had solid red eyes, no whites showing. With pale skin, long black hair, and sharp talons, it was a creature from nightmares. I watched it take a crossbow bolt in the shoulder, barely pausing before it advanced and tossed a grown man aside as if he was a child's doll. Each time it wailed, fear overwhelmed me. Thank Issal that the banshee fell off a high cliff and plunged to its death. Otherwise, Tipper and I would be dead instead."

Parker spoke next, his voice somber. "Sol Polis fell to the Horde. You all saw it. The city is lost. If they could sweep over the largest city in the Empire in mere hours, what chance does the rest the Empire have?"

"To make matters worse, their numbers are growing." Brock pointed east. "We just saw hundreds of them run off to join their dark army."

Cam asked, "Where are they coming from?"

Brock turned toward Cam, a bit surprised to hear his voice. The big guy had been more quiet than usual since the shipwreck. For that matter, Brock realized that Puri hadn't spoken in that time either. He then remembered the horses, and the fate that had befallen them. The horrible, yet necessary, act must be weighing on Cam and Puri.

Brock gestured toward the canyon mouth, toward the field where the banshees had been seen. "They have something out there. More banshees are coming from it." Brock looked to Benny. "I think that thing is where all of the noise is coming from. What is it?"

Benny scratched his head and adjusted his spectacles. "Well, it appears to be some sort of a doorway. They're coming through the portal from somewhere else. I have no idea where from, but I'm sure that's what we saw."

Brock nodded. "I guess that makes sense."

"Brock," Ashland said, drawing his attention. "Earlier, while we were sitting here, I tried to meditate to calm my nerves." She didn't need to explain why. "When I did, I could sense the wrongness of this thing radiating. The discord it was causing made it difficult to find my own sense of *Order*. It's almost like some sort of giant wound that has been torn into our world."

Something clicked within Brock, a puzzle piece sliding into place to reveal a hidden secret.

He nodded. "You're right. It is a wound. A wound that we must close, just as we were told by the Duratti Prophecy." His mind was working through something more significant. "What you feel is the discord of *Chaos*. It is a wound, as all wounds and illnesses are forms of *Chaos* invading our body. This wound is just enormous – a wound in the world itself."

Ashland's eyes grew wide. "Wounds are a form of *Chaos*? I never thought of that, but it makes sense." She nodded. "Now that you say it, it seems so obvious."

"What are you talking about, man?" Sinclair asked. "You aren't making sense."

Brock took a deep breath, preparing to deliver his message. He needed their commitment.

"I'm saying that the Empire and every single person within it will fall to this dark army. You heard Parker. This dark force was already enough to crush Sol Polis. Worse yet, the size of the Horde continues to grow. They're getting reinforcements through this doorway they created." His eyes scanned those facing him. "We are doomed."

Everyone was quiet as a distant wail sounded, contributing to the eeriness of the surrounding darkness.

"Well, thanks for the uplifting talk. I feel quite better now," Sinclair said.

Brock leaned forward. "Since we are doomed if we do nothing, let's do something to stop them. Let's fight back."

Lars glanced around and asked, "How? What can we do?"

Brock's eyes searched the faces before him, highlighted by the dull orange glow of the flickering campfire.

"If we can destroy this doorway, it will prevent more of the Horde from coming through and would limit their numbers to those who are already here." Brock needed to inspire them, persuade them. "It might give us a chance. This isn't a fight about any single city or province, but about the survival of humanity."

A long moment passed before Lars spoke, breaking the silence.

"That sounds like suicide." Then, he smiled. "I like it."

Lars was usually the doubter in the group. With him on board, Brock knew the others would agree. He just needed a plan.

44

The sun hovered mid-way to its apex as the group waited in nervous silence for Cam's return. Thin beams of sunlight streamed through the surrounding trees, the rays like ungraspable threads of hope taunting Brock after a long and sleepless night. He looked toward the hillside where they had camped the prior evening.

Although the mountain obscured the camp from where the banshees gathered, he was glad to find no trace of smoke rising from the small fire they had smothered before sunrise. He didn't want give a reason for the monsters to investigate the narrow ravine despite their purported aversion to sunlight.

Hearing crunching leaves, Brock turned to find Cam weaving his way through the trees. As his friend approached, Brock's heart began thumping in anticipation.

Slowing as he drew close, Cam nodded. "I haven't seen any come through for over an hour. They're huddled within the cave as you guessed, not making a sound."

Brock nodded. "Good. Let's hope they're sleeping. I'll take any advantage we can get right now."

Turning toward the others, Brock spoke louder. "This is your last chance for questions before we begin. Does everyone know what they're to do?"

Heads nodded in reply, their eyes reflecting everything from resolve to terror. Brock wasn't sure which end of the spectrum was appropriate. Perhaps both.

"It starts with you, Lars. Light the first branch and we'll follow you. Stop just before the clearing and then we'll use it to light the others."

He moved closer to Ashland as Lars broke out his flint. "Are you ready?"

Her nod appeared resolute. "Yes."

He forced a smile. "We have each other. We can't lose."

She gave him a shaky smile before closing her eyes. When he moved away to give her space, a tap on his shoulder caused him to turn.

Cam bent and whispered in his ear. "There are a lot of them. Dozens or more. I can't tell how many were in the cave before I began my watch."

Brock nodded, trying not to show the fear clawing inside him. He closed his eyes, seized the fear, and embraced it, opening the door to the tumult of *Chaos* surrounding him. Drawing in as much as he could, he felt as if his eyes would burst from the pressure. He opened them to focus on the *Power* rune scrawled on his hand and fed the raging torrent of energy into it. The exhaustion that normally struck after using *Chaos* lasted for just a moment. As the rune began to glow, a surge of strength flowed through his veins, making his vision a bit unstable. The glow pulsed red before returning to the black of charcoal.

Brock turned to find Lars holding a burning branch as he turned and led the others eastward. Most carried dead tree branches while Niles and Tenzi trailed the group, each carrying cloaks tied into a ball. Brock handed his staff to Libby, who stared down at it with apprehension.

"Stay back with Ashland and hold this until my hands are free. Remember to remain clear of the action." He placed a hand on her shoulder and spoke softly. "Keep Ashland safe, because you're her eyes. Keep yourself safe, too. We need you at the end."

She nodded, fear reflecting in her eyes.

He turned toward Ashland, who nodded that she was ready. They split up and walked to either end of a fallen tree, which had broken off about twenty feet from its base. Brock grabbed ahold of the thick roots, easily lifting the three-foot diameter trunk and tearing the remaining roots from the ground. Despite being aware of his *Chaos*-enhanced strength, it was odd for the tree to feel so light, as if it were a hollow shell. Ashland held the other end with ease, her strength enhanced by a *Power* rune as well. She gave him a nod and they began following the others through the woods.

After walking a quarter mile, the trees thinned. Lars paused at the edge of the woods and used the burning limb to light the branches the others held. With all branches lit – black smoke billowing from the burning ends - everyone turned toward Brock and waited for the signal.

Brock nodded, trying to show confidence despite his twitching nerves. "Go."

Lars burst into a run and led them out into the open. Cam passed him and tossed his burning branch into the mouth of the cave. One by one, the other party members ran to the cave mouth and threw a burning branch inside. Lars, Cam, and Puri then spread out before the dark opening with their swords brandished and ready while the sailors ran toward the far end of the clearing.

After dropping the tree, Ashland ran toward the portal from which the banshees had appeared. Brock watched her as he moved to stand behind the thick tree trunk. The position allowed his first good view of the magic doorway.

The portal was perhaps ten strides across and nearly as tall. Sizzling red energy danced and pulsed at the edges while shapes and colors shimmered within the expanse of the doorway, making his eyes hurt as they tried to follow the chaotic movement. His focus shifted back to Ashland as she seated herself on the ground beside the doorway. She crossed her legs, closed her eyes, and she slipped into meditation with Libby looming behind her.

He turned back toward the cave as Niles and Tenzi ran in with their bundles. They stopped just before the growing fire and hastily worked at the knots tied into the cloaks. Tenzi's came free first and she lifted the cloak high to dump the bundle of leaves tied within. Moments later, Niles dumped a pile of leaves a few feet from where Tenzi's leaves had fallen. They both ran away, darting past Brock as the smoldering leaves began to fill the cavern with black smoke.

Brock glanced to the cliff wall beside the cave and spotted Tipper using a chunk of blackened coal to trace a rune on the rock. Howls and wails of anger blasted from the dark maw of the cave and a dagger of ice-cold fear plunged deep into Brock's soul. Everyone froze.

A massive beast burst through the smoke, holding an arm up to shield the sun from its eyes as it neared the mouth of the cave. With long, twisted black hair and impossibly pale skin, the banshee's torn clothing covered its gigantic ten-foot tall frame. The lumbering gait of the monster covered broad chunks of ground with each step as it stumbled forward. The banshee's arm shifted, allowing Brock to see eyes of solid red. It paused and blasted another bone-chilling wail from a mouth filled with pointed teeth that matched the long blackened talons at the end its massive fingers. Brock felt stuck in place, his head fogged by fear.

The banshee stepped toward Cam, who ran in to meet it. A whirling sound sang out as Cam's silver longsword flashed toward the beast. Brock's head cleared, the fear subsiding even before Cam's blade sliced across the midsection of the tall monster. The banshee looked down in shock as Cam jumped backward. A thump sounded as the monster fell to its knees, attempting to pull its spilling intestines back inside.

Everyone sprang to action simultaneously. Brock bent and lifted the tree, readying himself. Tipper resumed working on the rune, now almost finished. Puri leapt past Cam with a wide slice, taking the head off the eviscerated banshee. As the huge head bounced away and its body tumbled to the side, others began to emerge from the dark smoke within the cave.

Brock shouted. "Step aside!"

Lars jumped back to one side, Puri and Cam to the other, and the path opened before Brock as four more banshees emerged from the black smoke. Brock heaved the tree and it flew toward the cave to smash into the chests of three of the monsters, knocking them back into the fire. The dead tree ignited, the fire latching onto the dead dry bark.

Impossibly, the wails from the cave became even more horrible. As before, Brock's brain felt addled as fear gripped him tight. The sound of Cam's blade whistling through the air sang in Brock's ears and fear's grip slid away. Cam's longsword lopped the hand off the fourth banshee as it took a swipe at Puri. She then lunged and jammed her sword upward into the crotch of the beast, burying it to the hilt. She tried to pull the blade free, but her grip slipped and she stumbled backwards. The banshee howled and lifted its intact arm for another strike. Before the arm could descend, Cam cut through its thick leg just below the knee and the beast fell backward with a howl of pain.

Brock turned toward Libby. "The staff!"

Libby ran closer, tossing it before running back toward Ashland. Brock snatched the staff with one hand and spun toward the cave as two of the banshees freed themselves from the tree. One broke into a run, its hair on fire as it charged toward Lars. Jumping aside, Lars spun about to slam his huge great sword into the banshee's lower back as it ran past. The monster stumbled and fell facedown. Lars climbed on the beast and plunged his sword into its ribcage.

The other banshee burst from the cave and ran toward Brock. Not waiting for it to reach him, Brock leapt toward it. He flew thirty feet up into the air before descending. As he dropped toward the banshee, he swung the metal-plated staff in an underhand arc. The *Chaos*-charged strike smashed into the side of the brute's head. Brock twisted with the recoil, careful to bend his knees and absorb the impact as his feet contacted the ground. When he turned back toward the banshee, it smashed to the ground with its brains oozing from the gaping hole in its head.

When Brock turned his head to check on Tipper's progress, he found his friend standing before the completed the rune. Brock sprinted toward Tipper as the rune began to glow bright red. Slowing when he reached the cliff wall, he turned and shouted to the others.

"Run! Everyone get clear of the cave!"

He turned to find Tipper still staring as the rune pulsed and faded.

Brock shouted, "You did it, Tip. Now run!"

With wide eyes, Tipper turned and bolted. Dozens of angry wails blasted from the cave, the ear-piercing screams building to a nightmarish crescendo. Terror gripped Brock as he stood beside the cave entrance. The fog of fear clouded his mind, locking him into an internal struggle. It became difficult to think, let alone move. Fighting through it, Brock tried to focus. Blinking, he found huge humanoid shapes emerging from the dark wall of smoke from the burning tree. Gritting his teeth, he brought his staff back and thrust it out, driving the metal-capped butt into the rune drawn upon the rock. As soon as it hit, he spun and launched himself from the cave. Landing in a full run, fifty feet away, he distanced himself from the cliff as quickly as possible. A deafening rumble roared toward him as the angry mountain raged in hot pursuit. He felt the force of it in his chest, drawing closer even though he ran faster than humanly possible. As he passed Tipper, he reached out and scooped him into one arm without slowing. Bits of rock from the landslide pelted Brock's legs as he sped away.

In mere seconds, he closed the five-hundred-foot gap to where the others stood watching the scene unfold. Slowing to a stop, he set Tipper down and turned to see the results of their gambit.

The cave was gone, buried beneath thousands of tons of tumbling rock and dirt that stirred a massive cloud of dust high into the air. A fair portion of the cliff had fallen, affected by the *Brittle* rune that Tipper had drawn. Brock didn't know how many banshees remained trapped within the cave, but they were no longer a problem.

He glanced toward Ashland, still sitting in meditation near the shimmering doorway. The pile of debris from the landslide ended just two strides from where she sat. He closed his eyes and thanked Issal that the landslide hadn't buried her as well.

He faced his companions with a nod. "The hard part is over." He pointed toward the portal. "Now we have to protect Ashland until the doorway is closed."

45

The mood of the group mirrored the bright sun high above. With every trace of the banshees now buried beneath the landslide, they just needed to wait for Ashland to finish closing the portal. Examining it as he drew close, Brock found that the opening had shrunk significantly and was now half its original size. He and his companions slowed to a stop before the shimmering doorway.

"When the first banshee came out, I couldn't even move because I was so scared," Lars said to Cam. "But when you attacked it, the feeling slipped away."

Brock's brow furrowed. "I felt the same thing. Until Cam began swinging that singing sword, I was frozen by fear."

Cam shrugged. "It never bothered me. Those banshees are big all right, but they're also slow. As long as you face one at a time, they're not that bad."

"Well, it didn't bother me much after that." Lars said with a smile. "I even got one. Did you see it?"

"You sure did, Lars." Benny clapped him on the shoulder. "You got him good."

Brock stepped closer to Cam. "Cam, let me look at your sword."

Cam handed him the longsword, still smeared with banshee blood. Brock noticed a rune engraved in the fluted blade. He held it closer to

225

examine the rune. Although the symbol was unfamiliar, he believed that it meant something significant.

He handed the sword back to Cam. "There's something about this sword and the rune engraved on it."

Taking it, Cam's eyes narrowed at the blade. "Well, the blade is named *Silencer*. Maybe the name is tied to the rune?"

Benny moved closer to examine the sword.

A buzzing noise sounded and the air sizzled, causing Brock's hair to stand on end. A massive curved blade flashed past him, taking Perry's head off before slicing right through Lars' chest. Horror gripped Brock as the upper half of Lars' body fell away and the lower half collapsed to the ground. Brock would never forget the surprised look on his friend's face as he watched the moment unfold. Everyone stood motionless, locked in a state of shock as blood spurted from the severed remains of their comrades.

"Lars!" Benny screamed in horror.

The buzz returned as another curved blade flew out of the portal, the flash of rotating metal tearing through Niles and Bart, sending body parts and blood spraying about.

Screams and shouts filled the air as people began to scurry from the scene.

"Everyone behind the doorway! Now!" Brock ran to the side of the portal, stopping beside Ashland. The others scrambled from the area, circling around the edges of the doorway. Brock turned toward Libby.

"Draw the rune, right here," indicating the ground before him. "Be sure to point it toward the clearing before the doorway and be ready."

The girl nodded, her brown eyes appearing even wider than normal.

Brock turned toward Cam. "I'm going to help Ashland. I need you to protect us."

Cam glanced at Puri, both of them nodding.

Brock sat beside Ashland and closed his eyes. Taking a calming breath, he began seeking his center. He struggled to locate the cool peacefulness of *Order* through the raging noise of *Chaos* hovering nearby. Once he was able to tap into his source of Order, he reached toward the wound and found a massive storm of red symbols tearing about. He also sensed Ashland trying to calm the storm, surrounding it with the harmony of *Order*. Pushing with his will, he joined her. Even strengthened by the

Power rune, the pressure of resistance was tremendous, a thousand times worse than any wound he had healed.

He heard wailing and shouts but remained focused as he and Ashland pulled at the force of *Order* all about them to close the portal. The symbols began to unravel faster and faster, accelerating behind the momentum of the healing. The pressure dropped away and a loud pop reverberated in the clearing, startling Brock and Ashland to open their eyes.

On the ground before them was the twitching upper half of a banshee, sliced at an angle from the middle of its back to its waist when the doorway slammed shut. The other half was somewhere else – wherever the beasts came from.

Loud wails sent waves of raw terror through Brock. Blocking their eyes from the bright sun, a small group of banshees stood just twenty feet away. Two dead banshees littered the ground nearby. Cam took a wide swing with his sword to keep the banshees at bay. The whistle of the sword cut through the terror, freeing Brock's mind. He grabbed Ashland's hand and scrambled to his feet.

"Everyone get back, behind the rune," Brock yelled before turning to Libby. "Now, Libby! Use your fear!"

Cam and Puri backed away from the four remaining banshees. As they parted around Libby, the rune she had sketched in the dirt began to glow red. It pulsed once and the ground before the rune burst, rippling forward in a tidal wave of earth. The wave smashed through the banshees and swept their legs out as it passed beneath them. They tumbled to the ground awkwardly. Two of the banshees rolled about as the other two climbed back to their feet. Another wave blasted from the rune, pummeling the banshees with torn earth as it tossed them backward and covered them with debris.

Everyone backed away as the shockwaves continued to pound forth, again and again, tearing through the clearing. In less than two minutes, the banshees were beyond the rubble of the landslide and buried beneath layers of earth. Although Libby had proven to be weak in her ability to channel *Chaos* – far weaker than Brock – the *Shockwave* rune proved to be devastating.

Closing his eyes, Brock said a prayer for Lars, Niles, and the sailors, whose corpses were now buried beneath the blasted earth. He opened them as another shockwave blasted across the clearing.

Turning to the others, Brock found looks ranging from shock to sadness. Benny wiped tears from his eyes. Tipper did the same as Libby buried her head in Tipper's chest to cry. Parker shouldered his bow and stared down at the ground, as if trying to avoid looking at the field where Lars and Niles had died. Tenzi glanced up at him with a look of concern in her eyes. Sinclair took his hat off and held it over his heart as he closed his eyes in prayer. Puri sheathed her sword, looking grim. Cam did the same and appeared to be doing all he could to hold the tears back. Brock understood. Of any of them, Cam had been closest to Lars.

Gathering himself, Brock spoke in a solemn tone. "It appears that our friends have gotten a burial. While it isn't a proper funeral pyre, at least they will be left in peace. May Issal watch over them."

He swallowed hard and forced himself to consider what they needed to do next.

"I don't know how long this will last," Brock thumbed back at the shockwaves, repeatedly obliterating everything in their path, "but we're done here. Let's go back to camp and rest for a bit."

Saddened by the loss of their companions, he led the silent group back into the woods. Despite having accomplished the impossible, he didn't feel victorious. An overwhelming sense of dread began to seep inside of him, dread from the realization that he would likely lose other friends in the days to come.

46

Brock blamed himself. After assuming the role of leader, his companions had placed their trust in him, relying on him for guidance and protection. Their success in attacking the banshee hideout had made him confident. That confidence resulted in the death of those he led. The image of the huge blade slicing through Lars flashed before his eyes...again. It continued to haunt him, etched firmly in his mind and was sure to cause future nightmares.

His gaze shifted toward the ground, and he noticed the attack plan he had sketched in the dirt during the early morning hours. In frustration, he jumped up and began kicking the dirt, stirring a cloud of dust as he destroyed the diagram. The result was not exceptional, merely what one would normally expect. Apparently, the effect of the *Power* rune had fully dissipated.

With the burst of frustration expended, he stopped and looked toward the wooded ravine below him. Feeling empty and too tired to cry, his eyes lost focus and he stared numbly into space. A pair of arms appeared from behind, wrapping about his waist. He felt Ashland's body against his back as she hugged him while resting her head on his shoulder. Even before he heard it, he knew she was about to speak in his head.

I'm sad and I miss Lars too, but you need to stop blaming yourself. Lars knew it was risky. We all did. The fact that any of us still live is because of your actions and leadership. Focus on what we have, not on what we've lost.

When he didn't respond, her tone turned to scolding. *Don't let the rest of us die because you feel guilty. We don't have time for self-pity.*

Brock winced at the harsh words. She was right, though. Four members of the group might be dead, but the nine surviving members still needed him. Ashland needed him.

He nodded and hugged her arms to himself. *What would I do without you?*

I expect that you'd get yourself killed. She replied, him sensing her smile through their connection.

She released him and Brock turned to face his companions, who had finished consuming the last meager scraps of food that remained. He realized that not a word had been spoken since returning to camp over an hour earlier. He suspected that they were mourning those who died, as Brock was. Unfortunately, they didn't have the luxury to mourn as they should or more deaths would follow.

Brock cleared his throat, drawing their attention. "Unless anyone objects, we should pack up and move on. We're out of food and our water supply won't last more than another day."

The others stood and began gathering their things. Brock walked over to the trail they had blazed earlier and waited for the others. When everyone appeared ready, he headed down toward the ravine.

Tenzi quickened her pace until she caught up to Brock, walking beside him.

"Excuse me, Brock. I have a few questions," she began.

Brock nodded, trying to maintain composure. "Go on."

"What happened back there?" she asked. "The things I watched you do…I don't understand how it's possible. Was it some sort of magic or something?'

He sighed. Explaining *Chaos* was a challenge.

"I guess it is a kind of magic." He shrugged. "We were using a force called *Chaos*. It's something we discovered about a year back. Thank Issal for that."

After a moment, Tenzi spoke again. "First, you became super strong, tossing that huge tree like it was nothing. Then you began leaping around like some kind of human grasshopper. You made a whole cliff crumble into a landslide, and Libby did something to cause waves of dirt to blast across the field." She paused, shaking her head in disbelief. "What else can you do with it?"

Brock ducked under a branch and turned toward her. "Honestly, I have no idea. We know of a few other things, but I get the feeling that there's far more we don't know."

She walked in quiet for a few strides before speaking. "Well, I'm frightened to think of how things would have gone without you guys. Those…monsters are the scariest thing I've ever seen. If there's an army of them, I can't imagine what we could do to stop them."

Brock thought about what she said. Thousands of banshees would be unstoppable, even with the help of their small group of *Chaos* users. How could mankind survive? He hoped that the answers were somewhere down the road ahead.

The party walked in silence without complaints of hunger, save for the rumbling within their empty stomachs. With nothing to do about it, they found no sense in complaining.

Brock's body shook and quivered with each step, starved of nourishment. He looked up at the puffy cloud that blocked the sun, its rays lighting the outer edges in gold. The sun was at about the same angle as when they left their camp near the banshee cave the day prior. In that time, he had eaten nothing but a handful of berries gathered along the way. Almost two full days had passed since they last consumed a decent meal. To make matters worse, their water supply was now exhausted. *It would be ironic to survive the skirmish with the banshees only to die of malnourishment*, Brock thought

Lifting a heavy leg, Brock climbed up a small boulder that rested atop the ridge they were cresting. His gaze shifted toward the eastern horizon, now able to see the Sol Mai Ocean beyond another line of hills. His gaze drifted to the valley below, thickly populated with leaf trees. He noticed a long gap in the trees along the valley floor, cutting from the south to the northeast. Squinting, he spotted the brown of a roadway between gaps in the trees. His eyes followed it and he paused when he noticed something.

A wagon appeared to have run into a tree, and three people lay on the road near it. He stared hard at the bodies, watching for any sign of movement. Seeing no activity, he turned to face the others as they gathered on the trail behind him.

"There's a road at the foot of this ridge. There's a wagon down there." He pointed toward the brown strip, showing here and there through the trees below. "Let's head that way to see if anyone can help us or if there's anything we can use."

Searching the eyes of those who followed him, Brock found nothing but blank stares. *Has hope deserted them?* Finally, Ashland nodded, followed by Tipper, Benny, and Cam. Brock was relieved that some of them still responded. He hopped off the boulder and started weaving his way down the hillside.

Sapped of energy, they moved at a snail's pace. Even going downhill took more effort than they could muster without forcing each step. Almost two hours passed before they reached the road. Even on the flat, obstruction-free surface of the road, their pace was lethargic, as if their legs moved while their minds slept, lost in the haze of hunger.

They rounded a bend and the scene that Brock had spied from atop the ridge came into view. A covered wagon leaned hard against a tree, missing one wheel. The carcasses of two horses lay beyond the wagon, torn and shredded. The remains of three bloody bodies were strewn upon the road, left in a twisted mess of red, white, and pink.

As Brock neared the site, he was able to identify the bodies as a man, a woman, and a boy. The clothing and size were the indicators, for two of them no longer had a head and the third had no face. Worse yet, their arms and legs had been shredded, chewed to the bone. Flies flitted about the corpses, filling the air with their buzzing. Brock held his hand over his nose against the smell of rotting flesh.

He turned back toward his companions. "I'm going to check the wagon for food and water."

Puri nodded grimly. "I will help."

The others remained silent and kept a distance from the gruesome scene. Brock pulled his extra shirt from his pack and tied it around his head to cover his nose and mouth. Puri found some cloth to do the same. He gave her a nod, and they walked toward the wagon.

As they passed the bodies of the boy and the woman, Brock did his best to remain focused beyond them, having already seen more than he wished. Once past the corpses, he approached the wagon.

Pulling aside the rear flap, he found a number of crates, sacks, and a barrel piled into the lower side of the angled wagon bed. He reached for the nearest crate and slid it toward him. With a grunt, he lifted it from the wagon and set it on the ground. Puri drew her dagger and began to pry the lid. Her fingers slid into the gap she had created, pulling the lid back to reveal the red and green peels of apples.

Despite the oppressive hunger and thirst that gripped him, a fountain of joy bubbled within Brock and he let out an involuntary chuckle. Puri looked at him and nodded.

She turned her head toward the others. "Cameron! Come over!"

Without a word, he ran toward them.

Brock turned back to the wagon and removed a heavy burlap sack. He didn't need to untie it to know it contained potatoes. Despite the grim scene around him, his spirits began to lift. He turned and handed the sack to Puri as Cam arrived to scoop up the apple crate. The two left to join the others as Brock slid the flap aside and crawled onto the wagon bed. Prying the lid from another crate revealed dried beef wrapped in tight bundles. He replaced the lid and pushed against the barrel, finding it heavy with sloshing liquid. Rocking it from side to side, he spun the barrel around to reveal a spigot. Carefully, he worked it loose and clear liquid began to seep from it. He bent and put his mouth to spigot, eagerly slurping the seeping water.

Brock lifted his face from the spigot and pushed it back in place. A delirious giggle emerged as a rush of hope and joy overcame him. Although banshees had murdered and eaten this poor family, they left behind a wagon filled with food and water. He and his friends would survive because of the Horde's horrible actions.

47

———————

With full bellies and water to drink, everyone appeared in much better spirits. Glancing westward, Brock found that just enough light remained in the sky to show the dwindling trail of smoke rising from the funeral pyre.

They had somehow found the will to perform the grim task of building the fire after agreeing that they couldn't leave those people's bodies to scavengers. The poor family had endured enough. At the same time, Puri wouldn't leave the horses to rot either. With reluctance, Brock and Cam agreed to help her push the damaged wagon onto the fallen horses. They then performed the ugly task of placing the dead family's corpses into the wagon bed before lighting it ablaze. While their companions carried the cache of food and water to their campsite, the three watched the fire grow into a raging inferno. When the wagon collapsed on the horses, lighting their flesh, Puri finally nodded. Cam put his arm around her shoulder and walked her toward camp as Brock followed along, guessing that Puri's thoughts were of the horses that they had put to death before the ship sank.

Turning from the pyre, Brock glanced about the camp as his thoughts drifted to the remaining crates and sacks of food. While they had made a sizeable dent in the stores, there was more left than they could carry. When morning came, they would have to fill their water skins and load their packs before leaving the rest behind. It was certainly a better problem than the previous alternative.

Brock put his arm around Ashland as she leaned into him. They stared into the flames of their campfire as the others talked. He suspected that they wanted to focus on anything but the events of the past few days. He couldn't blame them.

Benny stood, grunting as he lifted the crate he had been using as a seat. Walking awkwardly as he carried the weight, he shuffled over and set the crate beside Brock. He released a sigh of relief as he sat back on the makeshift seat.

"Hi, Brock," Benny said. "How are you feeling?"

Brock glanced toward him and noted the concern in Benny's eyes.

"I'm better now that we have food and water."

Benny glanced back toward the smoldering pyre.

"It's a grim business, dealing with the dead," Benny said, his eyes landing back on Brock. "I'm afraid that this is just the beginning."

Brock nodded. Of that, he was sure.

"But that's not what I wanted to talk about." Benny stared into the fire. "I've been thinking about what we've seen, about what we've learned."

Brock remained silent, letting Benny explain what was bouncing around in that tremendous brain of his.

"As we had guessed, the Horde doesn't like sunlight. The assumption was confirmed by how they acted back there."

Brock nodded. "It's a good thing, too. It was a crucial part of the plan."

"Yes, but there's more." Benny looked him in the eye. "When they make those wailing sounds, terror grips my body and freezes my brain all at the same time. When Cam swings that sword of his, it all washes away."

Brock nodded. "Yeah, that's exactly what I felt as well."

"That leads me to my next conclusion." Benny sat upright, ready to reveal his findings. "The Horde can use *Chaos*."

Brock realized that the statement was more of a confirmation than a revelation, internally acknowledging that Benny was correct.

Benny continued. "First, that doorway was created by *Chaos*. In order for it to exist in the first place, I assume that the Horde somehow made it.

Second, I think that the fear we experience when they scream is also *Chaos*-induced. Somehow, Cam's blade is able to dispel the effect. It protects him as the user and when he swings the sword, it frees the others in the area from this supernatural fear."

Brock nodded. "Benny, I think you're right on both accounts."

Benny smiled. "Thanks, Brock. That leaves me with some questions, though."

Brock raised an eyebrow. "Only some? I have dozens of them."

Benny rocked his shoulders as he stared at the fire. "Remember that smaller banshee? The one we saw the first night? He was leading the others, and they responded to him." Benny turned to look Brock in the eyes. "The others appeared to be mindless beasts. I wonder what makes him different. I also wonder if there are others like him."

Brock turned the idea over in his head. *Could the smaller one be the key? If so, why?*

Benny continued. "I also want to know how it's possible for Cam's blade to cancel active *Chaos*. From what we've seen, *Chaos* spells last for just an hour or two. *Chaos* hasn't touched his blade in months or years, perhaps longer. Accordingly, there must be a way to create a permanent effect."

As Brock thought about it, he decided that Benny's theory made sense.

"You're right, Benny. There must be a way. I wonder if the book we found covered that information. If so, I guess we'll never know now."

Looking into the flames of the fire, Benny nodded. "Yeah. I'd sure like to know how it works though. With it, we could do amazing things."

Brock glanced back over at his friend, wondering what ideas were bouncing around in his head.

48

Benny hated feeling scared and useless. In the past week, he had watched his friends save the day again and again while he cowered in fear.

First, he had shut down when they were locked in the citadel dungeon. While he had hoped that they might find a way out, he had played no part in it and had simply followed along.

As they had fled the city, his companions secured their path out of the citadel and to the ship, herding Benny along like a frightened lamb. Aboard *Star Dancer*, it became even worse. When the huge storm began to toss the ship about, he huddled in his safe, dry cabin and prayed that they wouldn't sink while Parker, Cam, and Brock helped keep them alive.

Once safe ashore, he had contributed nothing as others found food and water, started fires, and made the key decisions that kept the group alive. When attacking the banshees, his part had been nothing more than throwing a single burning branch into the cave before running.

Fear was the problem. He felt trapped by it, as if a cocoon of fear had wrapped around him, threatening to smother him from existence. Fear had gripped Benny for days, coming to a deafening crescendo with the wails from those horrible banshees. Ever since, the echoes of those wails had filled his dreams. The memory of the fear set him on edge even during the day. He hated it.

Despite attempts to focus on anything else, his uselessness in the face of fear kept bubbling back to the surface. Deciding that was through with being afraid, he focused on being strong and brave. It was time to put his fears to rest.

While Benny struggled with his own inadequacies, the others seemed to be in better spirits. With food in their stomachs, water to quench their thirst, and the low winter sun lighting their way, the dark days since leaving Sol Polis appeared to be behind them. Now traveling down the open roadway, the miles passed more rapidly. The sun was still above the horizon when they caught their first glimpse of a long forgotten city, hiding within the trees beside the road. As Brock led the party through the shadows beneath the canopy of foliage, the view of the ruins opened up before them.

Broken pillars stood outside the city, joined by crumbling arches bathed in orange light. Gaps stood from broken wall sections, offering a view of what lay beyond. Buildings, beaten and broken and decaying with age, were covered in ivy, moss, and debris. Fallen structures built upon a mound backed to a high ridge that overlooked the ocean to the east and the city to the south. Benny tried to imagine the city in its former glory, alive and thriving before the Horde crushed it. He wondered if Sol Polis might one day be rebuilt or if its future was as bleak as the one before him.

Brock stopped in the shadow of the trees and stared at the ruins. "This must be Sol Limar. We can camp here and search the city tomorrow."

Sinclair responded, placing his hand on Brock's shoulder. "Hold on a minute. I realize that we sailors have some fanciful tales, but it's fairly well-known that this city is haunted."

Brock turned toward Sinclair with one brow raised. "Haunted? Are you referring to ghosts? I find it ironic that you did not believe in banshees but now you tell me that you believe in ghosts."

Tenzi sidled beside Sinclair. "What the captain is saying is true. At least, it's what all the sailors say. Nobody who enters the dead city returns. It's why they never rebuilt." She paused and looked down.

"They say it's possessed by restless spirits – those who died here at the hands of the Horde."

A chill ran up Benny's spine, causing an involuntary shiver. He shook his head to clear it. Fear was *not* going to own him.

Brock frowned at them both as he considered their words. "Is there anything to back these stories? Has anyone seen one of these evil spirits?"

Sinclair glanced at Tenzi, then back at Brock. "Well, other than stories of people entering the city and never being seen again, I guess not."

Brock nodded. "Would you agree that there are other possible explanations for people entering and not returning?"

Sinclair turned to Tenzi again, who shrugged. "Well, of course."

Brock patted Sinclair's shoulder. "While I don't completely dismiss the possibility of evil spirits, we should assume that something else is the cause for these disappearances."

As Benny watched Sinclair's face, he sensed the man's doubt despite nodding in agreement. Seeming satisfied, Brock turned to address the others.

"We know that the Horde is out there somewhere." He waved toward the northwest. "Thus, I think it best if we set up camp just inside the walls to hide us from view. Does anyone object?"

After receiving no response, Brock spoke again. "All right. Let's find a suitable spot to build a fire. While we eat, I'll explain what we need to do tomorrow and why."

Benny knew what and why. Somewhere in those ruins is an ancient secret, waiting to be discovered. Or so he hoped.

The fire had almost burned itself out, now barely more than orange coals. Upon nightfall, the temperature had dropped to leave a damp chill in the evening air. Wrapped within the warmth of his travel cloak, Benny rested comfortably with his head on his pack.

However, sleep did not come easily. Thoughts of evil spirits kept creeping into his head, causing him to open his eyes and stare at the glow of the coals to ground himself. After a minute, would close them to try again.

A howl sounded in the night, and his eyes flashed open. Another sounded, closer this time. He sat upright, his eyes searching the darkness surrounding the camp. Some of his companions rose to their feet.

"What was that?" Parker whispered.

"I've heard that sound before." Tipper said, looking at Brock.

Brock nodded. "Bacabra."

Chills shook Benny's spine again. The tentacles of fear wrapped around him and squeezed the air from his lungs.

Brock spoke louder. "Everyone up. Arm yourself if you can. Gather around the fire and keep your back to it."

As she rose to her feet, Benny noticed knives in Tenzi's hands. "What's a bacabra?"

Tipper responded. "It's another creature from your nightmares."

Brock nudged Tipper with his staff. "Hush, Tipper. You're not helping." He turned toward Tenzi. "A bacabra is like a dog, but four times larger than any dog you have seen. It has strong jaws and sharp claws. Don't let it get close to you."

"Um…thanks." Tenzi said.

Benny's eyes darted about, searching the night for signs of the beast. The remains of the city wall stood just twenty feet beyond the orange coals of the fire. They had opted to camp about a hundred feet from a break in the wall, where it had collapsed over the years. He glanced backward into the dark ruins, toward the silhouette of a tall mound not far from where they were camped.

A howl sounded, coming from near the break in the wall. Staring hard into the dark opening, Benny's eyes strained to see if anything lurked in the shadows.

Then, something moved, something massive. It blasted a howl, far louder than the previous ones. The sound caused the cold fear to resurface from within Benny.

Not waiting for it to attack, Cam and Puri began to stalk the beast. It held its ground, its massive head tilting toward Cam, to Puri, then back to Cam. Evil red eyes reflected in the dim light of the coals, sending another chill down Benny's spine. A deep growl rumbled and Benny's hair stood on end.

With incredible speed, the beast leapt toward Puri. She dove as Cam's blade sliced toward the bacabra. The whirling sound of the blade loosened fear's grip from Benny's heart. The beast landed hard, rolling awkwardly as its severed front leg tumbled to the ground beside Puri.

Oddly, a whimper sounded from the bacabra as it tried to stand on its remaining three legs. As it rose to its feet, a shape appeared from the darkness. Leaping onto the bacabra's back, Tenzi landed with a knife in each hand. Both blades sank deep into the beast's neck, causing it to lurch and collapse as she rolled off into the long grass.

Cam and Puri approached the downed bacabra, but it did not move.

Another howl sounded in the distance, followed by others in the opposite direction. More bacabra stalked the night, coming toward them.

Brock shouted. "We need a more defensible location. Everyone to the mound in the center of the ruins. Go!"

Benny didn't even remember turning to run. It just happened. Driven by fear, he weaved his way through the rubble. Past imposing stone blocks and fallen brick walls, he ran. Up crumbled stairs and through fallen arches, he ran. He focused on the mound ahead, seeking it as a symbol of hope and safety.

He hit the hillside at a run as more howls sounded from behind. They were drawing closer.

Reaching the top of the hill, he scrambled over a broken wall, trying to reach safety. Somewhere ahead, there had to be safety.

Benny spun about, his eyes searching the darkness. He could vaguely see the others approaching as they navigated the ruins below. Howls sounded near the wall, redirecting his focus back to their camp. There, dark silhouettes of twenty or more bacabra lurked, sniffing and circling. Fear twisted Benny's gut and tightened his throat. He stepped backward, and the ground dropped beneath him.

Air blasted from his lungs as he landed hard on his stomach. Sliding feet-first on his belly, he desperately tried to grab ahold of something to stop his rapid descent. The surface he was sliding down suddenly ended. His arms flailed in the darkness, legs kicking in the air as he fell. Fear seized his faculties, fear of falling some incredible distance to an unspeakable death.

At impact, everything went black.

49

B rock's breaths were rapid, his pulse thumping in his ears as the dark ruins of Sol Limar slipped by. He paused to look back and saw Cam and Puri behind him – his other companions somewhere ahead. As the couple ran past, Brock noticed dark shapes gathering at their campsite. Noses lifted toward the sky and howls echoed in the night. There had to be a dozen bacabra. Maybe more.

He turned and ran, catching up to Cam and Puri as they reached the hillside. They scrambled to the top and stopped before the broken wall before turning and readying themselves for an attack.

Dark shapes slipped through the ruins below – a flash of black fur over here, the scratching of claws on stone over there. As the first beast rushed up the hill, Cam and Puri engaged it. Another followed closely behind, heading toward Brock. When the bacabra leapt, Brock jumped to the side and swung hard with his staff as the beast flew past. The staff connected with a rear leg of the creature, which caused it to stumble in the rubble of the fallen wall.

Not giving it a chance to recover, Brock swung the staff around and connected with the same rear leg. The leg swept from beneath the beast, and it crashed to its hip with a yelp. Closing another step, Brock slammed his staff down on top of its head. The metal-capped end struck hard, and the bacabra collapsed.

Breathing heavily, Brock glanced toward Cam and noticed a dead bacabra on the rubble between him and Puri. A growl drew his attention toward the hillside as another bacabra emerged from the ruins and raced toward him. A whizzing sound went past, followed by a *thwap* and a second *thwap*. Brock dodged as the beast crashed to the ground where he had been standing, dead with an arrow poking from one eye and a knife from the other.

Brock spun about to find Parker and Tenzi standing side by side beyond the broken wall. One had another arrow ready while the other held a knife by the tip, ready to throw.

"Thanks," Brock spun toward the city below and searched the darkness as he prepared for the next attack.

A bright white light suddenly lit up the night, revealing their surroundings. The bacabra below began to yelp, their red eyes squinting as they backed into the shadows. Now able to see clearly, Brock counted more than a dozen others retreating from the mound and fading into the night.

Turning, Brock raised a hand to block the brightness of the light. He squinted, able to make out a female figure standing below the light.

What did you do? He sent to Ashland.

I tried the other new rune. It turned out to be rather bright I think. She sent back.

Brock laughed. "Have I ever told you that I love you?"

He heard her voice from behind the bright light. "Yes, but I could always hear it one more time."

50

Benny ducked under a branch as he ran after Jimmy. Weaving through the trees, their footsteps trampled the ferns covering the forest floor, joined by the laughter that filled the air. Jimmy disappeared through a thick cluster of pine boughs, the branches springing back after he passed by. Benny held his hands up to protect his face as he squeezed between the pines.

The sky opened to reveal the old rock quarry below them. Jimmy squatted at the edge and eased himself onto the steep bank. As Jimmy slid down into the pit, Benny sat at the edge and prepared to do the same.

The thrill of speed tickled his stomach as Benny slid down the slope into the pit. His foot hit a rock, and he stumbled headfirst. Luckily, Jimmy was there to catch him, saving him from scraped hands or worse.

As Benny stood upright, he straightened his spectacles and flashed his friend a smile. Jimmy nodded toward the far end the quarry before turning and running in that direction. With a giggle, Benny scrambled after his friend.

Downward they ran, hopping over the crumbled rocks scattered about, remnants that didn't survive excavation. Benny guessed that every stone block that built the Selbin temple had come from this old quarry.

Jimmy stopped at the rear of the pit and stared at the wall of rock before him, fifteen-feet tall and three or four times the width. Dark metallic veins streaked here and there among a vast field of pale stone. As Benny came to a stop, he put his hands on his knees and gasped for air.

"That must be what old Bitters was talking about," Jimmy said as he pointed toward a thick vein in the rock. "He was right when he said it appeared like a darker version of silver."

Benny nodded as he tried to catch his breath. He wasn't nearly as athletic as Jimmy. "Yeah." He took a breath. "That's it alright."

Benny pulled his pack off his back and withdrew the jar he had brought. With a twist, he removed the lid as he spoke to Jimmy.

"Use the pick and try to break some off. Be careful not to hit with a glancing blow. We don't want any sparks."

Jimmy nodded while lifting the pick he had borrowed from his father. "Here goes."

The pick flashed in the sunlight as it struck the dark streak of rock. A crack formed. He swung again, and the crack widened as a small piece fell to the ground. The third strike embedded the tip of the pick in the crack. With a twist and pull, Jimmy broke off a chunk the size of his fist. Benny was ready for it, holding the jar beneath it to catch the sparkling chunk of rock. His breath caught in Benny's throat and a jolt of fear twisted deep inside as the rock rattled inside the jar. Luckily, nothing happened.

Jimmy moved closer and looked at their prize. "Do you think it's enough?"

Benny nodded, capping the jar. "From what Bitters told us, this is more than enough."

"I just hope you know what you're doing," Jimmy cautioned Benny. "This stuff sounds dangerous."

The scene wavered, shifting. Benny glanced to the side and saw Jimmy standing beside him. Just beyond, his mother was busy making dinner in the kitchen. His father sat near her, whittling a small statue of Issal from a chunk of wood. It amazed Benny how the man could so deftly create something from nothing.

"Are you sure this is safe, Benny?" Jimmy whispered.

Benny nodded as he stared at the small glass vial. "It will be fine. There's just a tiny bit of powdered rock in here. When it lights, it should flash a green flame as Bitters described."

Jimmy nodded. "You're the brain here. I trust you."

Benny set the larger jar down on the living room table and held the vial up in one hand. He glanced at his friend, who nodded. Sensing the oncoming thrill of discovery, the thing that Benny loved most, he inhaled and tossed the vial into the fireplace. Involuntarily, he stepped backward in anticipation of what would happen. It was a moment frozen in time, etched within his memory.

The cool breeze coming off the nearby lake came through the window behind Benny, cooling his neck. Jimmy stood beside him, holding his hands to his ears as he looked on in anticipation. His Father remained focused on his intricate carving while his mother removed a fresh loaf of bread from the oven. It was a moment to remember, followed by a moment he wished he could forget.

The vial burst, a blast of green flame lashing out. The concussion launched Benny through the open window. Stunned, he stumbled to his feet as green flames turned orange. Despite the ringing in his ears, he could hear his mother screaming.

"Benny! Benny!"

He took a step toward the building and saw his friend through the open window. Jimmy was lying beside the jar that held the rest of the rock and powder. The table the jar lay beside was on fire, burning angrily, with the flames spreading rapidly. Benny's eyes grew wide as he stared at the jar. Fear gripped his insides, twisting them hard. Lost in a haze of fear, he backed away a step as the house exploded.

Pain surged through Benny's shoulder. He hit the back of his head and everything went black.

. . .

His mother called his name.

"Benny!"

How can she call me? She is dead, killed in the explosion – an explosion that was my fault. Sorrow racked his heart, aching from the loss of her and Jimmy.

"Benny!"

Benny's eyes opened and blinked tears away. It was dark.

"Benny!" He heard in the distance.

He tried to sit up and cried out from the sharp pain from his shoulder when he put pressure on his right arm. His collarbone was broken again. His head hurt. Using his left arm, he carefully sat upright. His left hand went to the back of his head and came away wet. Even without light, he knew it was blood.

A glimmer of light above drew his eyes upward.

"Benny!" It was Ashland.

"I'm..." His voice squeaked, his throat dry. He swallowed to clear it and tried again. "I'm down here!" he shouted as everything became dark again.

For a moment, he heard and saw nothing. Then the light returned, far brighter this time.

"Benny? Are you down there?" Ashland's voice called from above.

"Ashland! I fell. I'm injured!" he called back weakly, the effort causing pain.

All quieted, the light dimming but not completely. Benny closed his eyes, attempting to focus and keep the fear of the darkness away. When he opened them, it was brighter again. A rope descended from where the light was shining, running along the angled stone blocks above and dangling down to the floor. A moment later, someone began to climb down the rope. Benny saw boots braced against the angled stone blocks as they descended into the dark space. As those boots pushed from the blocks to shimmy down the rope, a face emerged from the darkness.

Brock landed on the floor and looked down at Benny with a smile. "I'm glad we found you, Benny. Good job locating a place to hide from the bacabra." Brock turned and yelled up toward the light. "Tie the rope off and send everyone down! We found a place to hide for the night!"

51

A shock of cold washed over Benny, causing his chest to contract. The brief loss of breath caused him to gasp before air began to fill his lungs. A shiver ran down his spine, and sharp pangs of hunger raged within his stomach.

"There you go, all healed and as good as new," Ashland smiled as she rose to her feet.

Brock held out a stick of dried beef. "Here's something to eat."

Benny accepted it with one hand, holding the other up to shield his eyes from the bright light Ashland held. "Thanks."

He bit into the meat, chewing heartily as they helped him to his feet. Turning, he saw Cam deftly drop down the rope to land on the stone floor.

"That's everyone," Cam said.

Benny turned toward Brock. "What happened up there?"

Brock shrugged. "Ashland scared them away. Apparently they don't like light."

Glancing at her, Benny squinted at the brightness of the light in her hand. "Where'd you get that anyway?"

"It's a rock charged with the last rune we found before the book was destroyed." Ashland shrugged. "The *Chaos* charge made it into a bright light."

Brock ran his hand through his hair and glanced toward the opening in the ceiling. "I think we know why people stay away from this place. I am sure that the pack of bacabra is responsible for the reported disappearances."

Sinclair chimed in. "They might not be evil spirits, like in the stories, but we sailors know to stay away from this place."

Tenzi nodded in agreement.

"This leads somewhere, Brock," Parker said from across the room.

Benny turned toward Parker, who stood beside a framed doorway at the far end of the room. Other than the hole above, the doorway appeared to be the only way out of the storeroom.

When Brock walked over to the door, Benny and others followed. As they approached, Ashland's light streamed through the opening to reveal a long corridor, fading to black beyond the glow of the light.

Brock turned toward his companions. "Since we're stuck here for the night, I think we should explore a bit. However, it might be dangerous, so be careful. Don't touch anything you don't need to touch."

Heads nodded in reply as he took Ashland's hand and led them through the doorway, following the light in her other hand.

Walking a step behind Brock and Ashland, Benny had a good view of their surroundings. A glance toward the floor revealed insects scurrying into cracks, escaping those who had invaded their habitat. Benny paused as he passed an open doorway and glanced about the room within. Dusty skeletons lay strewn about amongst broken furniture and crumbling pottery and nothing else of note. Turning to continue down the corridor, Benny wondered about the people, curious to know who they were and how they had died.

After passing two other rooms, both empty other than broken shelves and debris, the corridor ended. Two stairwells stood before them, one rising up into the darkness while the other descended into the inky-black depths of the stone structure.

"This place is creepy," Benny muttered.

Brock glanced back at him and nodded. "It's like walking amongst graves. I can almost sense the poor souls who died here, lingering as if they refuse to pass on."

"Which way, Brock?" Parker asked.

"Let's try up first," Brock led them up the stairs.

Upon reaching the top, they found a small room with a dusty painting on the wall. Fallen stone blocks beyond the doorway prevented further advancement.

Brock spun about. "Dead end. Everyone back down."

Formerly at the rear of their procession, Cam led them down to the hallway. Once there, Brock and Ashland led them down the other stairwell. The air grew noticeably cooler as they descended, a pervading dampness surrounding them. The dank surroundings, deep underground, reminded Benny of when they had been captured in the basement of the Sol Polis Citadel. He prayed that they had no similar experience here.

Brock reached the bottom of the stairs and opened a heavy wooden door that creaked in protest. Beyond the door was a long corridor with tattered tapestries hanging on the wall, fraying to the point where a breeze would send wisps of thread floating toward the shadows. Doors lined the hallway, most closed. The open ones revealed small rooms, each with a single bed and little more.

"It appears to be servant's quarters," Parker commented, the sound echoing in the quiet hallway.

The door at the end of the corridor protested even louder than the last, creaking noisily as Brock pulled it open. He led the group through to another stairwell going upward. They found another corridor at the next floor, this one blocked by a collapsed ceiling. Turning, Brock led them up another set of stairs to the upper level. Again, they found these stairs capped by a small room, this one with a broken statue, the bronze turned green with time. However, nothing blocked the doorway on this side. Stepping through, Brock and Ashland's bright light led the party into the next room.

The moment Benny stepped inside, he knew they were in a throne room. Although the collapsed ceiling left half of the space buried, he noticed rows of wooden benches that disappeared into the darkness. The broken relic of an ancient throne stood upon a raised platform at the fore of the room, drawing all attention. A skeleton rested upon the throne, the garments of the dead man now almost nonexistent, leaving the dusty bones bare but for a smattering of threads and spider webs. Other skeletons lay scattered among the benches and aisles, some bare and yellowed while others wore leather armor and dusty metal plates. The opposite side of the chamber was impassible, buried beneath tons of fallen stone blocks that split the room in half. Benny glanced toward the ceiling above them and realized that it had collapsed until the rubble in the center of the room supported the massive stone blocks above them.

Stepping into the room with his eyes on the throne, Brock spoke softly.

"Everyone be careful. The ceiling above appears shaky."

Walking beside Ashland, Benny followed Brock toward the throne – a beacon in the ruins, calling to him. When they climbed onto the platform, they had to duck as they neared their destination. The fallen ceiling stood just less than six feet above the floor, almost touching the legendary throne.

Brock looked at Benny. "Do you have any ideas?"

Benny squatted to examine the old dust-covered throne. Beneath a thick layer of dust, he could tell that it was of wooden construction, with a padded red velvet back and seat.

When he circled the throne, Benny tried to discern anything odd. He noticed something carved into the wooden chair back. Taking a deep breath, he blew hard at the surface and sent a puff of dust into the air. When the dust cleared, he found a carving gracing the back panel. Above the arc of a rising sun were three runes etched into the wood – the familiar symbols of *Order* and *Chaos* straddling another rune, unknown to Benny.

"Have you ever seen that rune before?" Brock asked, pointing toward the symbol in the center.

Benny shook his head. "No."

"Me neither," Ashland added.

Benny's eyes narrowed as he stared at the runes and sensed something odd about the symbol for *Order*. After a moment, he noticed something odd. His gaze flicked toward the *Chaos* rune and found the same issue.

"Brock, look at this," Benny said.

Brock edged closer as Ashland held the light so they could see.

Pointing, Benny explained. "See the rune for *Order*? It's not normally solid in the middle. Where's the diamond? The *Chaos* rune is missing the same element, normally in the core of the starburst."

Brock squinted at the runes before looking at Benny. One eyebrow raised as he set his staff down and reached toward the throne. Placing two fingers on each rune, he pushed. There was an audible *click* and the rear panel slid down. Brock glanced toward Benny again, sharing a smile. A rush of pride welled-up inside and Benny's thoughts of feeling useless were now a distant memory.

Brock wedged his fingers into the gap and pulled. Benny held his breath as the panel slid down to reveal a hidden compartment, its contents the fruition of their quest. The worn black leather covers of two books waited within – books that contained secret knowledge that might prevent the end of humanity.

Unable to resist himself, Benny eagerly grabbed one book as Brock reached for the other. They simultaneously opened the books and began to inspect their contents. Ashland leaned over them, holding her bright light closer.

"What is it? Did you find something?" Parker shouted from across the room.

Without responding, Benny examined the writing in what he held and found a series of dated notations. Flipping through the pages, he observed more of the same throughout the book and quickly determined that it was a journal. He glanced over at Brock's book and saw the same writing with even later dates. Brock flipped through his book and stopped when he came across a separate note tucked within the pages. He carefully unfolded the brittle paper and read it aloud.

"These journals contain proof of *The Hand*'s treachery and the abominable acts they performed in their greedy pursuit of power. Thanks to a Ministry official who had the integrity to place the greater good above his own personal agenda, they have been thwarted and were rendered unsuccessful in their gambit. With the Ministry's strength greatly diminished, my men were able to take Sol Polis and stamp out the last remnants of this plague. They'll not find a foothold within Kalimar again as long as I breathe. Even beyond my death, the threat of this proof should help to keep them in check. This proof and the power of truth within the Emblem Throne will continue to provide Kalimar the upper hand."

Brock paused, glancing up at Benny before continuing. "Should anyone find this, it means that I am dead. Should *The Hand* be behind my demise, I beg you not to let it go unpunished. Regardless, this proof is now yours to wield, for the words within are more powerful than any sword. The Keeper of Truth, King Tallinor of Kalimar."

Benny thought about the words. There were secrets within these journals – secrets persuasive enough to protect a kingdom, secrets someone would kill for.

<h1 style="text-align:center">52</h1>

With a firm grip on the rope, Brock pulled himself up the sloping stone and emerged from the hole, stepping into the tall grass surrounding it. The bright sunlight hurt his eyes after spending the night in the ruins below. He held his hand over his eyes to shadow them as he surveyed his surroundings.

In the sunlight, it was easy to discern the mound he stood upon to be the ruins of an old citadel. A quarter mile to the west stood the wall where they had set camp the prior evening. Turning about, he gazed over the Sol Mai Ocean to the immediate east, its bright blue waters waiting below the cliff that the castle had been built upon. To the south lay the bay along with the bulk of Sol Limar, which lay in ruins. Brock tried to imagine a bustling city, full of life. It was difficult to do given its current state.

Shifting his focus to his companions, he found them examining their surroundings, as he had done. Puri finished coiling the rope they had used to descend into the ruins and shoved it into her pack. He was thankful that she had brought it. Things would have been far more difficult otherwise.

"I think this one is still alive."

Brock turned to find Benny bent over a prone bacabra, the beast sprawled across the rubble of the fallen wall. As he walked over, Brock recalled striking the bacabra in the head with his staff. Stepping close, he knelt and placed a hand upon its back.

Through the thick black hair, Brock felt the animal's chest rising and falling. During the attack, the bacabra had been ferocious and frightening. It felt odd to see it sleeping peacefully, now appearing like an oversized dog. Memories surfaced as he recalled numerous stray dogs he had befriended back in Kantar. When he would happen upon a stray, he would often offer the animal food or water. Over time, he had even named many of them. Now seeing the unconscious bacabra in a new light, he felt sorry for it.

Brock spoke as he stared at the prone beast. "I want to try something. I need everyone to clear away except Cam and Puri." He turned toward Cam. "I need you to stand behind the bacabra with your swords ready. Parker, please have an arrow ready as well. However, nobody is to attack unless the bacabra attacks first. Got it?"

Cam and Puri nodded and moved into place as they drew their weapons.

"Got it." Parker responded, pulling his bow from his shoulder as the others moved away.

Are you sure about this, Brock? Ashland sent to him.

He closed his eyes. *It's something I must do.*

With his hand still resting on the bacabra, he slipped into meditation. The calm, coolness of *Order* was soothing as the symbol and its blue aura began to fill his mind. Reaching out, he stretched his awareness toward the bacabra, wondering what he might find.

Chaos raged throughout the animal, intermixing with the *Order* he had expected. He searched harder and found two angry red spots, far hotter than the rest. Pulling hard at the *Order* within the bacabra, he first attacked the two worst zones. The tiny storms of red symbols began to unravel, dissipating until they matched the jumbled mess of *Chaos* and *Order* that existed throughout the beast.

Exerting as much of his will as he could muster, Brock attacked the *Chaos* with the bacabra's own force of *Order*. The pressure of the effort was intense, but the *Chaos* eventually began to change. Rather than unravel, the small red symbols began to draw together, clustering into a single ball. The effect accelerated until a calm blue field of *Order* surrounded a single focal point of *Chaos*. The pressure eased, and Brock realized that he would be able to do no more.

He opened his eyes as the bacabra shook with a chill. When it opened its eyes, he yanked his hand back as if he had just touched a hot oven. Almost stumbling in his haste to back away, he watched the animal with no idea of what to expect.

"Everyone remain calm," he said softly.

The massive creature stood and shook itself as if wet. Its head turned toward Brock and large brown eyes met his. The tail, as thick as Brock's arm, began to wag as it moved toward him. The bacabra's mouth opened, its massive tongue lashed out, and a slobbering lick swept across Brock's face. He stepped back, sputtering and wiping the saliva away with his sleeve.

The bacabra moved closer and nuzzled against him, nearly pushing him over. He laughed and scratched it between the ears as he would any other dog. This one just happened to be five feet tall and weighed four hundred pounds.

With a smile on his face, he looked around to find the others staring in amazement.

❧

Brock felt her returning.

"Everyone remain calm," he said again. It had become a theme around her.

Seconds later, a massive dark shape burst from the brush ahead. The bacabra shook its head, causing the dead goat in its mouth to lurch violently from side to side. She set the goat down on the road and stepped back with her tongue hanging out as Brock approached.

Brock laughed, at her behavior and at the sense of pride that oozed from her through their bond.

"Good girl, Wraith."

The oversized dog's tail wagged so vigorously that her entire body shook in excitement. Brock walked past the goat and gave Wraith a hug as he scratched behind her ears. He let go, and the huge canine turned and bolted down the road, hopping playfully from side to side as she ran. He turned to find Puri with her knife out, dressing the latest gift from Brock's new pet.

"That's the third animal today, Brock," Benny said. "With your gigantic dog around, we shouldn't have problems finding food"

Brock laughed. "She's just a bit enthusiastic."

Benny stepped close as they resumed their trek north. "Are you sure we can trust her? I know she seems friendly now, but will that change?"

Brock nodded. "You guys have made your concerns clear, and I understand." He tried to explain. "It's hard to describe, but I'm... connected with her now. I can sense her in my head, and I get an impression of what she feels, what she's thinking. That's how I know when she's coming back even before you see her." Brock's hand squeezed Benny's shoulder. "Trust me. She's now just a loveable, oversized dog. If I sense any change in her, I'll let you know."

Benny nodded. "All right. I trust you."

Ashland sidled up to Brock as she took his arm in hers. "She sure adores you, which I can understand. I just hope she likes me too. I'd hate for her to be jealous of me."

Brock laughed. "Yeah, I can see how that might be concerning. I'll do what I can to prevent it, but I don't think it's in her personality. She seems too happy and playful to take you as any sort of threat."

Ashland leaned her head on his shoulder. "I'm glad. Although, it will be hard to share you with her. I'm used to having you to myself."

He kissed the top of her head, her brown curls of her hair tickling his nose. "Thanks."

They rounded a bend and the trees thinned to reveal rolling fields. Not far beyond, the road split with one path continuing north and the other heading northwest. Sol Polis waited to the west, across the open fields that lay south of the city, or what remained of it. With the sun now low in the sky, Brock found himself faced with a decision. Thoughts of what they would find at the city made the decision easier. Instead of pushing onward and reaching the city at night, he would rather camp here and arrive at the city during the day.

He turned to address his friends.

"Let's find a spot to camp along the edge of the wood. Tomorrow, we'll break camp at first light and head toward the city to find a ship as we discussed. Once on the water, we won't have to worry about running into the Horde."

Without argument, the others scattered in search of a suitable location to stay the night.

Brock and Ashland remained on the road and stared over the open fields. Laughter took him when he saw a black dog hopping and twisting playfully through the long grass. Ashland hugged his arm tight, her laughter joining his as they watched Wraith try in vain to catch a moth that flitted about in the evening air.

~

Leaning against Wraith, Brock relaxed on the grassy turf. He felt the slow rise and fall of her ribcage against his back. Curled up beside him, Ashland's head lay in his lap as he paged through one of the journals they had found.

He and Benny soon determined that the entries in the journals took place four centuries earlier. However, they still hadn't discovered the author's identity or why the journals were so valuable.

At first, the notations appeared mundane, covering visits to cities and meeting people unknown to him. Indirect mentions of the use of magic drew his attention, but offered no detail in the early pages.

Now reading in the dim light of dusk, Brock discovered that the author had journeyed to Sol Polis under a request by the Ministry with the task of developing new uses for *Chaos*. The writer believed *Chaos* to be the key to a more productive society. When details behind the author's research began to emerge, Brock's interest greatly increased.

"Benny, listen to this," he looked toward his friend. "The man writing the book described himself as a Master Ecclesiast and Master Arcanist, able to wield both *Order* and *Chaos*. He notes that some individuals could use one ability or the other, but it was less common than those who could wield both. In all cases, the people who exhibited an ability with just one of the two forces showed a lesser strength than those with both abilities."

Benny's brow furrowed in thought. "Aren't you and Ashland among the most skilled healers at the Academy?"

"Yes." Brock nodded. "Varius told me that we were the two strongest

Ecclesiasts the school had seen in generations."

"And both of you can wield *Chaos*," Benny said, prompting Brock.

Brock nodded as he realized what Benny was inferring. "Good point." He thought about it, considering what they knew. "And both of us are stronger with *Chaos* than Tipper or Libby, who can wield *Chaos* but can't wield *Order*."

Benny's eyes narrowed. "I wonder if the Ministry realizes that they are limiting their ability to field effective healers by weeding out *Chaos* users."

Brock thought about what Benny had said. The discrimination against *Chaos* users was hurting the Empire more than he had thought.

"What else have you found?" Benny asked.

Brock's gaze shifted back to the book. "Apparently, the author was trying to prove a theory. He was searching for a way to create a *Chaos*-induced effect that lasted a lot longer. In fact, he hoped to produce a permanent effect."

Benny whistled. "Wow. Could you imagine it? That would be a huge advantage for anyone who had access to it."

Brock considered how devastating it would be to have an army filled with soldiers permanently charged with a *Power* rune. Nothing could stop them.

He refocused on the pages but found the writing now impossible to read in the dying light.

"We'll do more reading another day," Brock said with a sigh. "It's dark, and we all need sleep."

Brock grabbed the loose sheet of blank paper he had torn from the second journal. Opening the folded paper, he stared hard at the image marking it. While in the destroyed throne room, he had used a crumbling piece of debris to rub the symbol onto the paper, copying it from the etching on the Emblem Throne. Although barely discernable in the dying light, the diamond-shaped rune intrigued him. He wondered what the symbol meant. Realizing he wouldn't find out tonight, he folded the paper and used it to mark his progress before closing the journal.

A glance around the camp revealed everyone else already asleep. After a long day on the road, Brock couldn't blame them. Twisting around, careful not to wake Ashland, he laid his head on Wraith's back. With his eyes closed, his thoughts turned to what they needed to do next.

53

The scene surrounding Sol Polis was grim. Numerous party members had to pause and retch miserably from the stench of rotting flesh. Wraith didn't like it any more than Brock did. With her ears flattened and tail down, she displayed nothing of the playfulness of the previous day.

Avoiding the city, they skirted around it as wide as they could en route to the harbor. The buildings outside the city walls were in shambles, damaged and burned. Bodies littered the streets, many torn to shreds, demonstrating the wrath that the Horde had laid upon those who lived there. The previously elegant towers of the citadel appeared a mess, with one tower collapsed in a pile of rubble while the others were scorched black. The bleak image of carrion birds circling above was the only sign of life. If anyone survived, they had fled by now.

Reaching the shore, they turned north and realized they had no choice but to pass through the mutilated bodies lying between them and the docks. Occasionally they would stumble across a dead banshee, but for each of those, there were scores of dead men and women and children. Many of the bodies were partially devoured, which made the scene even worse.

As they approached the docks, hope sparked within Brock at the sight of one lonely ship still afloat in its mooring. Stepping over and around the corpses strewn along the long wooden pier, he led them toward the ship. Sinclair's pace quickened, passing Brock with an eager look upon his face.

When they neared the vessel, Brock noticed that the ship sported two masts. Despite being a fair bit smaller than *Star Dancer*, it was sizeable enough for their small group. Besides, it was their only choice.

With the ship floating twenty-feet out, they had to pull on the lines to reel it toward the dock. It drew close and Sinclair took a running jump to grab ahold of the rail. As he climbed over, Tenzi followed. Soon, they were laying planks across for the others to board.

As his companions crossed the planks, Brock looked back to find Wraith staring at him from halfway down the dock. Her ears were back, tail down. Did she think he would leave her?

"Come on, girl!" he called and clapped his hands.

Her ears popped up, and she bolted down the pier toward him, the dock rumbling beneath her approaching weight. Brock scrambled up the planks just as the last of his friends cleared them. When he reached the ship, he turned as Wraith leapt from the pier. She landed on the deck and knocked Sinclair down with a glancing blow. The startled captain rolled over and blinked at the hulking dog standing over him.

The man flashed the dog a nervous smile. "Well, then. Welcome aboard *New Spirit*."

Wraith's tongue lashed out at Sinclair's face and gave a lick that left the man sputtering. Everyone laughed at the captain's plight, their spirits buoyed with the joy of finding a ship and at being away from the dead city. With the dark days spent in Kalimar behind them, they set sail for a new horizon.

54

From the rigging high above the deck, Parker watched Tenzi closely as Sinclair called orders from the quarterdeck.

"Unfurl topgallant sails! Hoist the yards!"

Copying her motion, Parker unwound the line and began pulling it downward. When the sail hit the stop, he tied the line off. A nod from Tenzi confirmed he had done it correctly. She began a quick descent down the rigging with him following close behind.

Upon reaching the deck, he looked toward the foremast to find Brock and Cameron making their descent. Those sails were also unfurled and rippled in the wind.

Sinclair turned the wheel, and the ship began to come about. The rippling grew more rapid until the sails snapped full. The ship gained speed, accelerating as it crossed the bay toward the breakers. Parker glanced back and gazed upon the ruins of Sol Polis. Although he knew what to expect after the attack on the city, he doubted that anything could prepare him for such a massive sense of loss. He closed his eyes and whispered a prayer for Pinkus and Agatha. Recalling how Niles had died from the banshee blade, Parker added his name to the list. He wiped the moisture from his eyes and blinked to clear them.

The peaceful blue waters of the sea seemed the same as always, oblivious to the death and struggles of man. He envied the sea for a moment.

His gaze then landed on Tenzi. He often found himself looking at the short blond. She intrigued him.

"So, what's your deal with Sinclair anyway?"

She turned toward him, squinting in the sunlight. "My deal?"

Parker shrugged. "Well, you obviously went out of your way to help and protect him when he was hurt. I know he's your captain, but I think your loyalty goes deeper."

Tenzi glanced toward the quarterdeck, where Sinclair stood with his hands on the wheel.

"I guess it won't hurt to tell you," she said, her blue eyes shifting to meet his. "I grew up near the docks in Sol Gier. My mother died during birth, so I never knew her. I lived alone with my Father, who worked at the docks. While not a big man, he was strong. He also had a temper, which grew worse when he drank."

She paused and gazed out over the water. "When I was twelve, he came home late one night to find that I hadn't made him dinner. I tried to explain that he hadn't given me money to buy food, but he wouldn't have it. He beat me pretty bad. As I lay curled up in my own blood, I decided I was done with it and done with him. It wasn't my first beating, but I had decided it would be my last."

She glanced toward Sinclair as she continued. "I grabbed my stuff and snuck from the house prior to first light. Since I'm marked with a *nauticus* rune, I decided to head for the docks to find a ship. I picked one and shimmied up the line tied to the dock. Once onboard, I hid in an empty barrel in the cargo hold.

"It was later that day when I was found. The sailors brought me to the captain, declaring me a stowaway." She paused, thinking. "I knew that a captain is the king of his ship and that his own rules apply. I also knew that stowaways were often killed or worse. I told Sinclair that it was a chance I was willing to take. I explained that I had no other place to go, no family or home to claim. He decided to wait to kill me, instead putting me to work scrubbing the deck. Days and weeks passed. Ports and cities came and went. Still, he continued to say that he would wait just a bit longer. As the months passed, my jobs changed and soon he no longer mentioned having me killed. Over the course of years, sailors came and went. Five years after my flight, I had become the most senior crewmember of *Star Dancer*, earning the right to be first mate and steer the ship. That was two years ago."

Parker listened intently before replying. "So, Sinclair has become a bit of a father to you, then?"

Tenzi shrugged. "I guess so. He's certainly treated me far better than my father ever did. He relies on me and values my skills and opinion. I guess I found a home aboard his ship."

Parker nodded. "I understand. You're quite skilled at sailing, so I can understand how he values you."

Tenzi smiled. "Thanks."

Parker stepped closer. "He's not alone. I also believe that you're an incredible woman."

The smile slid from her face as she gazed into Parker's eyes. He experienced a twinge of trepidation, fearing that his advance might be unwanted. Throwing caution aside, he pulled her close and bent for a kiss. The softness of her lips intertwining with his gave him a rush and his pulse began to quicken. As their lips parted, his eyes opened to look into hers – pools of deep blue that mirrored the surrounding sea. His arms were around her back, hers around his, and he became aware of her body pressed against him.

"You make me feel so alive," Parker said in awe.

She smiled. "It will take a few days to reach the garrison at Hipoint. That gives us some time to get to know each other."

A grin spread across Parker's face. "I'd like that."

Three marvelous days later, their destination was in view. While Parker was aware that time was critical, he found himself dreaming of sailing on endlessly. His time with Tenzi had been special, and he had relished every moment.

There had been just enough cabins on *New Spirit* for each of the four couples to share one and still leave one for Benny to use alone. Of course, Sinclair had claimed the captain's quarters, taking it at night while Tenzi and Parker manned the deck.

Somehow, Wraith was able to wiggle down the hall and into the small cabin that Brock and Ashland shared. Parker expected that it was diffi-cult to move about when the huge dog was in their quarters.

The practical side of him was aware of their food running low. They had made the most of the stores found upon the ship, having to toss less than a quarter due to spoilage. What remained was still enough for the three-day voyage and beyond.

Parker stood beside Tenzi upon the quarterdeck, waiting for Sinclair's signal to climb the mast. As they sailed up the bay toward Hipoint, he looked on in curiosity. Over a year had passed since he had last sailed into an unfamiliar port and this one was unique in numerous aspects.

The city was built upon a steep grade that overlooked the sea. The result was a long set of stairs running up the center, connecting a series of tiers occupied by houses and shops. A single ship currently occupied a mooring beside the long pier dividing the harbor. Unlike the other coastal cities he had seen, this one had no wall surrounding it. Thank-fully, Hipoint appeared safe and healthy. There had been an unspoken fear that they might arrive and find it also destroyed by the Horde.

"It's strange to see a port city without a wall," Parker noted.

Sinclair turned toward Parker. "She's a new city. Can't be more than a hundred years old. They didn't build a wall because she has no enemies. At least, none who would come from the sea." His eyes flicked to Puri, who stood below with Cam, Brock, and Ashland.

Parker nodded his understanding. The Tantarri were considered the only Empire enemy these days. That is, until the Horde appeared.

As they drew closer, Parker was able to identify the walled palisades atop the plateau above the city, marking the reason they chose this desti-nation. The visual realization of their goal made it seem more real and left him sad that their sea voyage was ending.

Sinclair turned toward them. "Get to your marks. We have a ship to dock."

Tenzi nodded and moved away from Parker to grab ahold of the rigging.

Sinclair called out. "To your marks. Let's get those sails drawn!"

Brock and Cam scrambled to the foremast rigging, scaling it with ease. Parker gripped the rigging and glanced up at Tenzi as she raced up the mast. He released a sigh began to climb after her.

~

Parker glanced back toward the ship and found Tenzi at the bow, staring back as the ocean breeze teased her blond hair. Their eyes locked one last time as he waved before turning to follow the others through town. While crossing the dock toward the stairs, he reflected on their last conversation.

"Please come with me. We belong together," he had pleaded.

Her hand had reached up to cup his cheek. "Dear, Parker. I'm sorry, but Sinclair needs me." She glanced toward the captain. "We have a mission of our own. For now at least, I belong on this ship."

"But what about love?" he asked. "What about me?"

She smiled sadly. "I do think I love you. However, your friends need you. We have a war to fight - one we dare not lose."

He leaned in to kiss her, sending every bit of sweet emotion he could muster into the kiss. It was urgent, yet tender, lingering for a time. He pulled his lips away and opened his eyes.

"What of the future?" he asked.

"If there is a future, come find me." She gave him a sly smile. "We'll make something of it."

He nodded. "If I live, I'll find you. Don't give up on me."

Her smile widened. "I don't give up so easily."

He stepped away, the last to leave the ship. Waving goodbye to Sinclair, he crossed the planks and left her behind. He would hold the image of her at the rail in his mind. That, along with the three days they had shared on the voyage, would have to suffice until this war was over.

Breaking from his reverie, Parker began climbing the stairs up into the city. People ahead cried out in amazement and fear as Wraith hopped up the stairs ahead of Brock. Parker couldn't help but smile. He expected that anyone seeing the huge dog would be startled. His gaze returned to Wraith, and he realized that he had begun to think of her as a dog, not as a bacabra.

Reaching the first tier of the city, they crossed the street past two rows of buildings and began ascending the next set of stairs. Parker's found his thighs burning from the seemingly endless steps that rose from the docks to the plateau. Pausing for a breath, he looked down to view the three tiers below. Swinging his gaze upward, he counted three more to reach the top. Resigned to the task, he continued upward.

When they reached the top, he turned to find a crowd gathered on each tier below, pointing up toward them as they discussed what they had witnessed. He suspected that each conversation began with Wraith. Her presence made it difficult for their party to pass unnoticed.

"Parker," Brock said. "I think it best if you and Cam approach the garrison. You both have parents with recognizable names. It'll give you a better chance to convince them of the truth."

Parker nodded. "We'll see what we can do." He nodded at Cam. "Are you ready, big guy?"

Cam nodded, "Let's do it."

Parker turned toward the garrison, its palisade walls built of logs sharpened to points, planted in the ground and aimed toward the sky. He and Cam crossed the road and angled toward the gate. As they approached, the two guards outside the gate stood tall in an obvious attempt to look as imposing as possible. Parker sighed inwardly, fearing the worst. He knew how these types tended to make themselves seem important with the intent of proving they were above you.

"Hello, Master Paladins." Parker smiled as he and Cam stopped before the gate.

"Hold there," a guard with clean-shaven scalp commanded. His *Order* rune appeared lonely on the bare expanse of his forehead. "State your business."

Parker donned a serious expression. "We have urgent news for your captain. News from Sol Polis."

The man glanced at the other guard, a tall woman with short clipped dark hair. The male guard stared at Parker with doubt in his eyes.

"Where's your message, then?"

Parker held his hands out, shrugging. "Given the urgency of the situation, there was no way for an official to craft one. Instead, my message is verbal. Therefore, I must speak with your captain."

The man's face clouded. "If you think I'm going to bother the captain because some young whelp wants to tell him a story, you're crazy."

Cam spoke. "Sir, do you know of Cassius DeSanus?"

The man shrugged. "Yes, we know who Captain DeSanus is. Why?"

Cam thumbed at his chest. "I'm Cameron DeSanus. Cassius is my father. Like him, I've been training to become a Master Paladin. The urgent message we have is related to the reason I left the Academy before my training was complete."

The man looked Cam up and down, examining him. "So you say. Do you have any proof?"

Cam reached for his hilt. "I do." He pulled the sword free.

Both guards stepped back and drew their weapons.

"Easy," Cam said. "I'm simply showing you the rune on this sword, which was my Father's until he gave it to me this past summer."

He held the blade flat before the two guards as they cautiously moved closer for a look. After seeing the rune, they stepped back.

"How do we know you didn't steal it?" the woman asked.

Cam's face darkened and he appeared close to losing his patience. Parker stepped in to take over.

"I also have a father who you will know. His name is Cedric Thanes, Chief Advisor to Archon Ringholdt." Parker reached into his pack and dug out a folded piece of paper. He held it out to the bald guard.

The man read it before showing it to the woman. After receiving a nod, he handed it back to Parker.

"You two wait here. I'll be right back." The male guard turned and disappeared through the small service door in the palisade wall.

As Parker pocketed the writ he had been given when raised to Academy Apprentice, Cam sheathed his sword. Two minutes later, the door opened as a third Paladin emerged.

This man had shorn brown hair and a well-kept short beard. His silver-plated gray leather armor marked him as a captain.

"I'm Captain Torreco. What's this all about?"

Parker moved closer and gave the man a short bow. "Captain. We've just arrived at the docks, coming from Sol Polis." Pausing for a breath, he prepared himself for a poor response. "I have grave news. The city has fallen, completely overrun. If there were any survivors, it is but a few. I seriously doubt Archon Ringholdt is among them."

The man's face clouded. "What? Are you daft? Who would attack Sol Polis? We have eyes on the Tantarri and would know if they attempted to leave their lands, especially if they brought an army."

"This might sound a bit outlandish, sir. However, it's true." Parker swallowed hard, glancing at Cam. "The Banished Horde has returned."

55

Brock viewed the exchange between Parker, Cam, and the guards while standing just down the road from the garrison. When the third man began to shout and wave his arms about, Brock decided to intervene.

With staff in hand, he jogged toward where Parker and Cam were standing. As he drew close, he heard the captain accusing them of thinking him a fool. He then shouted for them to stop wasting his time. The female guard glanced toward Brock. Her eyes grew wide and she drew her sword.

"Captain! Look out!"

The captain paused his rant to look toward Brock and alarm raised in his eyes. His weapon was out in a flash.

"Bacabra!" the captain shouted.

Brock stopped and looked back at Wraith, who was following him. When he held his palm toward her, Wraith stopped, sat on the road, and tilted her head in curiosity. He turned toward the Paladins and grinned.

"You men are mistaken," he shook his head. "This is just my dog, not some vicious bacabra."

Brock glanced back and waved Wraith forward. Excited, she ran until she drew alongside him. He glanced at Wraith, who was matching his pace, before again addressing the Paladins.

"However, if you try to harm me, she'll certainly not be so friendly."

The two guards warily backed against the wall, but the captain held firm. His eyes narrowed, and he eased his sword back into its scabbard.

"I guess she doesn't appear vicious like a bacabra. Her eyes aren't red, either," the captain noted. "Still, I've never seen a dog that huge." The man's eyes remained fixed on the giant dog.

Brock came to a stop a stride away from the man. "I bet if I came here yesterday and told you I had a dog this size, you'd think I was lying."

The man scratched his head, nodding. "Yeah. Probably."

Brock smiled. "But now that you see it, you believe it?"

The man nodded again. "How could I not?"

As Brock scratched Wraith behind the ears, her tongue hung lazily to the side and her eyes drifted closed at the attention.

Brock turned back to the man. "So, when my friends tell you that the Banished Horde is back and has decimated Sol Polis, you call them idiots who are wasting your time. You don't believe it because you've never seen the Horde in your lifetime."

The captain stared at Brock for a long moment. "I get your point."

Parker pleaded with the man. "Please, sir. Just send someone on a horse to Sol Polis. If what I'm telling you is false, it will cost you nothing but one man for a week. However, if our story is true and you do nothing, it could cost thousands of lives."

The captain's eyes shifted toward Wraith and then back toward Parker.

"Very well," the captain nodded. "I'll send a man. If it checks out, we'll have to act. If not, I will find you, and you'll wish you'd never met me."

"Fair enough." Brock nodded. "I'll also tell you that this isn't our only stop. By the time you catch up to the Horde, they'll probably have overrun most or all of the eastern provinces. As our forefathers did two hundred years ago, I plan to gather whomever I can and face them on the Tantarri plains. They will have to cross the plains at some point. Expecting them to arrive there in early spring, we'll be there and we'll be ready."

The captain stared at Brock for a moment before bursting into laughter. "You had me for a moment there, boy."

Brock glanced toward Parker and Cam, whom both shrugged. He addressed the Paladin Captain. "Captain...what's your name?"

The man calmed his laughter. "Torreco. Gavin Torreco."

"Captain Torreco. I urge to you to take this seriously until proven otherwise. I plan to amass an army who will face the Horde on the Tantarri plains when that object..." Brock pointed up at the white sphere in the sky. The three Paladins looked up toward the heavens. "Appears in the evening sky. Whether the Holy Army joins us is up to you. I'm afraid this fight is too vast for any force you can muster on your own. We must band together, or we will all die."

Brock turned and walked away. Wraith caught up to him, loping along calmly, mirroring his resolute mood.

56

Left with just enough coin to pay for supplies, they opted to restock and head west rather than stay at an inn in Hipoint. Brock doubted an innkeeper would allow Wraith inside anyway. Although he was quite fond of her, she presented a challenge in numerous practical ways.

As the town and the garrison shrank into the distance behind them, Brock slowed to allow Puri to catch up. He drifted closer to her and addressed the Tantarri woman when she turned toward him.

"I need your help, Puri."

She raised an eyebrow. "Interesting. You have done quite a capable job with very little of my help thus far."

Brock smiled. "Thanks. However, I do need it now."

She nodded. "Very well. What can I do for you?"

He glanced at Cam and then back to Puri. "Can you find the mine we saw a few weeks back?"

She looked at him, her confusion apparent. "Mine?"

He nodded. "Yes. The canyon with the wall spanning it, where the men chased after us on horseback."

Recognition lit upon her face. "Oh, that. Yes, of course I can."

Brock nodded. "Good. Can you find another route to it? I'm looking for a way coming in from the south."

She squinted as she considered what he proposed. "I believe so.

There must be a way for they had set men to wait for us along this road, east of our position." She nodded, seemingly convinced. "The western mouth to the valley cannot be the only way."

Brock stopped and stared her in the eye. "I need you to figure it out. I know you can do this. It will help because that's where we are heading next."

Cam's brow furrowed. "Why should we go back there?"

Brock smiled and he resumed walking. "I'll tell you tonight, once we set camp. I'm sure everyone will want to know what's next and why."

An awareness in the depths of his mind tingled. Wraith was returning, a sense of pride coming through their connection. He scanned the road ahead as he searched for her.

Seconds later, the shrubs to the inland side of the road began to shake. Wraith emerged tail-first as she backed into the road. In spurts and fits, she pulled her prize from the brush and onto the gravel.

Sitting beside it, she waited for Brock and the others to arrive. As he drew closer, he was able to identify the bloodied animal as a wild boar. He approached Wraith, scratching behind her ears as he rested his forehead against hers.

"Good girl," he said softly.

Wraith's tail wagged and her eyes narrowed in pleasure of the attention. He turned toward his companions as they gathered around the kill.

"It appears that Wraith has caught us our dinner. Let's search for a spot to camp. Sunset is less than an hour away, so we have to stop soon anyway."

His friends nodded and began to filter off the road in search of a campsite.

Brock turned toward Puri and Cam. "Can you two dress the boar while I search for something to use for a spit?"

Puri bent and drew her knife, not wasting any time. Brock smiled at Wraith and gave her a hug before he went in search of a strong stick.

. . .

"If this works, it'll be incredible," Ashland said, leaning in close.

Brock nodded and turned the page. "Definitely."

Unsurprisingly, Benny's curiosity drew him over. He sat on the log beside Brock. Ashland was sitting at Brock's other side as she read along with him.

"What did you find?" Benny asked with an eager edge to his voice.

Benny's curiosity knew no bounds. Brock smiled and explained their findings.

"The author of the journal had a theory about creating a permanent effect from a *Chaos* charge. He termed this concept *Infusion*, which involved the use of *Order* to bind *Chaos*. He believed the net result would be weaker than a normal use of *Chaos*, but the effect would last far longer, possibly forever."

Benny's eyes grew wide. "Of course. It makes total sense." He looked at Brock, excited. "Has he documented any experiments?"

"Not yet, but I'm sure it's coming. Hopefully, we can learn more as we continue to read his notes."

Brock turned to find Benny staring blankly into the surrounding darkness. The gears turning in Benny's head were almost audible as he came to grips with this revelation. After a long moment, he jumped up in front of Brock.

"You and Ashland need to find out how it works!" Benny's hands waved about in excitement. "This is big, Brock. Really big!"

Brock laughed. "Fine." He waved Benny off. "However, we've run out of light, so we'll have to wait until tomorrow. Reading under the firelight leaves much to be desired."

The agony of waiting was apparent on Benny's face. Dejected, he circled the fire in search of a spot to sleep for the night. Brock smiled as his gaze followed his friend, deciding that he found Benny's predictable nature comforting.

A glance about the camp revealed Tipper and Libby sitting together on a blanket, talking quietly. Cam and Puri shared a seat on a log as they stared into the fire. Parker sat near Benny as he stared into the flames, likely thinking of Tenzi. Brock understood how Parker felt. He'd desperately miss Ashland if they were separated. The very thought of it made his heart ache. He put his arm around her and kissed her forehead. Closing his eyes, he thought about the task before them.

What they were about to try was risky, perhaps more crazy than attacking the banshee hideout. That venture had cost them dearly, with some of his companions paying with their lives. However, the plan had succeeded despite seemingly impossible odds. This time, there were six fewer people among his small group. Did that make the odds even more impossible? What might it cost them this time?

57

Brock followed Puri's finger, intensely searching where she was pointing. Careful to keep his head low, he nodded to let her know he saw the bowman. There were four archers along the top of the wall, each pacing a section. Beyond the wall stood the guard barracks, now dark in the long shadow of the tall wall. Men sporadically entered and exited that building while the other buildings remained static. A stable and a small shed lingered just beyond the barracks, totaling eight buildings within the compound.

A few minutes later, people emerged from the tunnel below the far cliff. Aligned in single file, they marched toward the stone buildings tucked further back in the holding. Armed guards walked beside the prisoners, herding them toward their destination. This process continued for a while, surprising Brock with how many people were held captive. The sun dipped below the western horizon as the last prisoners completed the trek from tunnel to the buildings. As darkness fell over the compound, all became quiet.

Brock tapped Puri on the shoulder and motioned for them to retreat. When she nodded, he gave Benny's cloak a tug and turned to follow Puri. They crouched as they snaked through the boulders back toward the trail. Once beyond view, they broke into a jog with Puri in the lead, Brock in the rear.

After running a quarter mile, they crested the rise, and their camp came into view. Brock smiled when he saw Wraith rise, her tail wagging in anticipation. It had taken him a few attempts to get her to stay and let him go alone. Even then, he could hear her whining behind him as he ran up the trail to get a look at the mine that doubled as a prison. An hour had passed since then, the last hour of daylight.

"I've seen what I needed to see," he announced as he drew close. "The plan remains the same. As I expected, the building nearest to the wall is the guard barracks. Just beyond is the stable. The four buildings in the back house the prisoners. I estimate about thirty guards within the compound. However, if things go as planned, we'll only have to face a few of them."

Parker's gaze flicked toward the others, then back to Brock. "Are you sure we need to do this, Brock? It seems pretty dangerous."

Brock nodded, his position was firm. "Yes. Everything we've seen and done thus far has aligned with the Tantarri prophecy. There's one piece left, and this is it." His eyes scanned those before him. "We found the journals in the Emblem Throne. We healed the wound by closing the doorway the Horde was using to reach Issalia. The last remaining task from the prophecy is for us to free the truth. What's behind that wall is a truth that the Ministry has been hiding, holding captive." He felt driven to intercede. "Those poor people are imprisoned simply because they are Unchosen, forced to work in that mine for the remainder of their lives for reasons they don't comprehend and are unable to change even if they did. I can't leave them to such a miserable fate. Regardless of what anyone believes, being Unchosen is not a crime."

Ashland stepped beside Brock, gripping his hand as she spoke. "I agree with Brock. Regardless of what you believe about the prophecy, we should help these people. We have the means and surprise on our side."

"All right." Parker nodded. "I hope your plan works. There are only eight of us while they have at least two dozen armed guards."

Brock smiled. "That's where you're wrong. There are nine of us if you count Wraith. We also have *Chaos* on our side."

"I hope you're ready, Tip. It's up to you now." Brock squeezed his friend's thin shoulder. "Don't get caught."

In the starlight, Tipper's nod was barely visible "I can do this, Brock."

As Tipper snuck off into the night, Brock turned toward the others.

"I assume you all remember your part in the plan. Cam, Puri, and Parker, I need you to get past the wall as quickly as possible. Just be sure not to look at the light."

Quiet responses told Brock that they knew what to do.

"Parker, how many arrows do you have left?" he asked.

"Seven."

Brock knew Parker was running low on arrows, but he had hoped for more. "It will have to do. Try to make each shot count, and be sure to take out anyone with a bow. We can't have arrows raining on us while we are defending ourselves against swords."

"Don't worry, Brock." Parker replied. "I know what to do."

Brock turned toward Libby. "All right, Libby." He lifted his shirt, exposing his stomach. "Use your fear and charge me up."

He took a series of calming breaths as he waited for Libby to tap into *Chaos*. When her eyes began to glow red, he looked down at the black rune drawn on his pale skin, lit by starlight. The rune glowed bright red, pulsing before it began to dim. Queasiness arose within him as his stomach took a turn. The weight of his body pressing downward lessened to a fraction of what was normal, but he didn't become overly floaty like when Ashland had used the same rune on him. He had chosen Libby to make him lighter, hoping for a lesser effect with her weaker ability. Thankfully, it worked. Although he now felt far lighter than usual, he didn't have to worry about floating off into the sky.

"Thanks, Libby." He set his hand on her shoulder. "Now you and Benny need to stay here with Tipper when he returns. If all goes as planned, you three can bring our packs when the place is secure."

Brock turned and stared in the direction where Tipper had vanished into the night. He took a long, deep breath in an attempt to calm his nerves. Everything hinged on Tipper making it to the wall and back without notice. His eyes scanned the prison wall, spotting a bowman stationed near each of the four glowlamps lighting the top of the structure. Getting past those men and the wall was just the beginning of their gambit. He prayed that the plan he and Benny had hatched would work. It had to work.

58

Cam waited beside Puri, focusing on the task before him. He found that her strength and conviction made him more confident.

Someone approached, marked by the soft crunching of boots on the sand. As Tipper emerged from the night, Brock addressed him.

"How did it go, Tip?"

The white of Tipper's toothy grin glowed in the starlight. "It's all ready. Hit it halfway between the gate and this end."

In the darkness, Cam could barely discern Brock nodding in response. "Brilliant job, Tip. Now, hang here with Benny and Libby. Ashland will be back soon."

Brock turned toward Cam, gripping his shoulder. "Cam, you're up next. Make the shot count because you'll get just one chance at it."

Cam nodded and turned toward Puri. "Are you ready?"

Puri nodded, drawing her sword. "Of course. I am Tantarri. I am always ready."

Cam hefted the sling Benny had made for him and began jogging toward the wall. He could hear the crunching of Parker's boots to one side with Puri's softer footsteps sounding on the other. He expected the men on the wall would hear them coming. As long as they were beyond the light of the glowlamps, it wouldn't matter.

As Cam neared the wall, he began twirling the sling. After practicing with it for an hour, he was confident he could hit the massive target. As it spun faster, the sling began to make a whirling noise.

"Something is out there!" A man shouted from atop the wall.

The two men on the south end of the wall stood alert, bows drawn as they stared into the night. Cam hoped to be close enough to release the sling before they spotted him. As the wall drew near, he gauged the distance. Just a few more steps.

"Over there!" A man on the wall pointed toward him.

Cam gave one final swing, released his grip on the sling, and launched the heavy rock toward the wall. The moment he released it, Cam dove to the side. As he rolled in the sand, an arrow bounced off the dirt where he had been standing.

A *crack* sounded when the rock struck the wall. The structure shook, a shiver running along its spine before it collapsed. The south half of the wall imploded, blasting dust high into the air. Without hesitation, Cam and Puri ran into the billowing cloud of dust.

Parker slowed when he saw Cam begin to twirl the sling. Drawing an arrow from his quiver, he nocked it on the bow and began seeking a target. A man atop the wall shouted when he spotted Cam. As Parker ran forward to get close enough to take a shot, the man lifted his bow and pointed it toward Cam. Parker stopped, took aim, and fired. The man on the wall fired his arrow, staggering backward a moment later with an arrow through his chest. A thunderous *crack* sounded, followed by the rumble of the wall collapsing beneath the man.

Still running, Parker angled toward the gate and the part of the wall that was still standing. The two men remaining atop the wall ran toward the collapsed section. Lifting his bow to take aim, Parker shot at the closer man. The arrow took him in the throat and sent him tumbling backward and out of sight. The other man slowed when he saw it happen, his eyes falling on Parker as he lifted a bow.

Parker drew another arrow, nocked it, and shot it toward the man as quickly as possible. The man fired back, their arrows passing each other as they sped toward their targets. Parker's arrow hit the man in the stomach, causing him to double over, fall to his knees, and tumble from the wall. Parker's left shoulder involuntarily jerked backward, twisting his body and forcing him to stagger backward a step. He glanced down at his chest and saw an arrow fletching just inches from his face. It felt strange, even numb, as if he were dreaming. The world tilted, his head in a fog. He blinked, trying to comprehend what was happening as he fell to his knees and everything went white.

Ashland focused on Cam as she ran, waiting for him to launch the rock at the wall. When he began twirling the sling, she stopped and stared at the rock in her hand. She closed her eyes and used her fear to seize *Chaos*, noticing that it was easier each time she did it. A crack sounded, followed by a thunderous rumble that shook the canyon and informed Ashland that the wall was collapsing. Drawing in *Chaos* until she thought she might burst, she opened her eyes and poured the stored energy into the black rune scrawled into the pale stone. A familiar wave of exhaustion washed over her as the rune began to glow bright red. She averted her eyes just as an impossibly bright light burst from the rock.

Holding the rock above her shoulder, Ashland ran toward the cloud of dust swirling above the collapsed wall. As she neared it, she wound her arm back and tossed the rock as hard as she could. Like a shooting star, the blinding light sailed through the dust cloud to land beyond the rubble.

She spun about and blinked at the darkness, waiting for her eyes to adjust. A shape took form in the open dirt field outside of the wall. Changing her direction to head toward it, she soon realized that it was a person lying on their side, their back facing her. She slowed to a stop and used her foot to roll the person over, ready in case they tried to attack. A gasp of shock slipped out when she recognized Parker with an arrow sticking from his chest.

Brock allowed Cam, Puri, and Parker a significant lead. As Ashland ran to follow them, he sidled up beside Wraith and scratched the huge dog behind the ears.

"This is it, girl. You and me."

He hopped onto her back, landing lightly as he straddled her. With his reduced weight, he wondered if she even noticed him. He tucked his staff under one arm and wrapped the other around her waist-thick neck. Adrenaline surged through his veins, and his heart pounded as if it might burst. He took one last breath and shouted.

"Now, run!"

Wraith bolted after the others. Running as fast as a horse, the over-sized dog quickly closed the distance. Brock saw Cam launch the sling and the wall collapse into a pile of dust and debris. He flew past Ashland as Cam and Puri ran into the dust cloud. A moment later, he and Wraith followed them into the swirling airborne debris.

Up and over the rubble, Wraith emerged from the dust into the prison compound. Brock pulled to one side, turning her toward the guard barracks. The night lit up when Ashland's light bloomed, making it easy to locate his target. As Wraith neared the building, Brock brought his feet up onto her back and pushed off. With a strange sense of light-ness, he sailed impossibly far, his momentum carrying him over fifty feet to land on the roof of the barracks.

He scrambled to slow himself, dragging his staff against the roof tiles to create resistance. Stopping at the peak, he reached into his coat pocket, pulled out a chunk of coal, and began tracing a rune on the apex of the roof. Shouts came from inside as the guards raised the alarm. Brock had expected that the rumble of the wall falling would wake them and leave little time to act.

When the *Heavy* rune was complete, he closed his eyes and seized the surrounding *Chaos*. After drawing it in, he opened his eyes and focused on the rune. It began to glow with a crimson light, pulsing before dimming. The front barracks door opened as a loud crack echoed through the canyon. Before the fourth man could emerge from the build-ing, the roof gave.

Brock jumped from the plummeting roof as the center beam of the peak drove itself toward the ground, suddenly many times its usual weight. His leap launched himself out, beyond the three men who had just cleared the building, and flipped as he sailed high above their heads. Before Brock even landed, he heard screams coming from the ruined barracks. The three men who had escaped turned to face the building as dust and debris blasted from the open door. With their backs to him, Brock spun his staff to strike the nearest man hard against the head. Not having enough mass to remain stable, the recoil of the strike caused Brock to spin and stumble.

As the man crumpled to the ground, the other two turned to face him, their swords drawn.

Squinting to keep the dust from his eyes, Cam slowed as he navigated through the airborne debris. When he heard one of the bowmen coughing, he drew his sword and angled toward the sound. Light suddenly illuminated the dust cloud and revealed the silhouette of a man trying to regain his feet. Cam scaled the pile of crushed rock with leaping strides and swung hard, his blade whirling as it struck the man a fatal blow. Not slowing, Cam and Puri scrambled down the pile of the rubble and ran into the compound.

When Cam emerged from the dust cloud, the compound sprang to daylight with Ashland's bright stone landing just a few strides away. Puri stood beside him, searching the lit compound yard. Cam spotted Wraith ahead as he broke into a run toward the barracks.

When he neared the building, Cam saw men stumbling out the back door. He ran toward them with his sword ready. As the fifth man emerged, a loud crack sounded and the roof collapsed, sending a blast of dust and debris spraying out the open doorway. Distracted by the imploding roof, the men turned toward the barracks and left the opening Cam needed.

With a broad slice, he cut across the backside of the nearest man. The other four turned around with swords ready. Seeing one man holding his hand up to block the light, Cam swung low and sliced through the man's leg. As the man fell, another swung at Cam. Dodging the strike, Cam spun to see Puri lunge out and slice the man's sword arm off at the elbow. She slashed and opened another man's stomach from hip to hip. Puri cried out as her opponent fell to his knees and tried to push his entrails back in. When Cam turned toward Puri, he saw the fifth man yank his sword from Puri's stomach. A rush of anger gripped Cam. He swung hard and his sword exploded into the man's mid-section, nearly slicing him in half. Still filled with anger, Cam turned and stabbed the one-legged man through the chest. Realizing that all five guards were dead, he turned toward Puri and find her on her knees, holding her stomach. Blood covered her hand and seeped to the ground. Her tanned skin had turned pale, her lips blue.

Her eyes met his, the pair locking gazes for a moment before she collapsed to the ground.

～

Brock kept his back to the light as he faced the two men. They advanced toward him and he backed a step. A black blur struck the man to his right, slamming him to the ground. The other man glanced toward Wraith and Brock reacted, crouching and launching himself high into the air. With a hard downward swing, he rotated and his staff connected with the swordsman's skull as he flew over him. After completing his rotation, Brock landed softly on his feet.

He turned to find the man he had hit lying face-down in the dirt, unconscious or dead. A glance toward the other man revealed Wraith standing over him with his throat torn open. His gaze sweeping across the yard revealed no other movement.

He moved closer to Wraith and gave her enormous head a hug.

"Good girl."

"Brock!" Cam came running from around the ruined barracks. "Come quick. It's Puri!"

59

———

Brock stared at the ruined barracks and found no portion of the outer walls remaining intact. Only small sections of the building still stood higher than his head. The entire roof had fallen inside of those walls, the tiles of the roof shattered into small pieces. He still heard occasional moans from survivors, but he had no idea how to get them out. Part of him wished they hadn't had to kill these men, but it was a small part. A far larger part of him hated them for what they had done to the poor, innocent people they had held captive.

He turned to find Puri and Cam carrying an unconscious guard over to the ruined barracks. They sat him upright beside the other survivor, his bound wrists behind his back as he leaned against the broken wall. Cam stepped back and slipped an arm around Puri. The adoration shone in Cam's eyes when he looked at her. Brock thanked Issal that he had healed her before she had lost too much blood. It had been close.

Shadows crossing the light drew his attention. Wraith was hopping about, anxious as she led his companions into the compound. It had taken a bit of coaxing to get her to go find Ashland, but he was happy to discover that the effort had been worth it.

As his friends approached, Brock noticed blood on Parker's shirt and skin showing through the hole within the crimson streak.

"Are you all right, Parker?" Brock asked.

"Yeah. I thought I was dead, but Ashland saved me." Parker smiled. "I'm hungry enough to eat like Cam now though."

Brock smiled at the reference as he turned to find Benny, Tipper, and Libby approaching with everyone's packs.

"Tipper, Benny," Brock called out. "Can one of you dig some food out for Parker?"

"Puri needs some food too," Cam announced.

As Benny dug through his pack for some food, Brock pointed toward the ruined barracks.

"You were right, Benny," he said. "Increasing the weight of the beam at the peak of the roof brought the whole thing down."

Benny nodded while handing chunks of dried meat to Parker and Puri. "I can tell. You sure don't mess around, Brock." He shook his head in wonder while staring at the ruined barracks. "The building is just a pile of rubble now."

Brock turned his attention back to their prisoners. "Ashland, can you please heal these two men? I'd do it, but I'm a bit exhausted right now." The fight with the guards, followed by healing Puri had taken its toll on him.

She nodded. "Sure, Brock."

Kneeling beside the first man, she put her hand on him and closed her eyes. A moment later, the man trembled and began to breathe rapidly. However, he did not wake. When she healed the other man, his eyes opened and he gasped for air.

Brock smiled. He wanted answers.

"I'm so happy you're awake," Brock casually said to the man. "What's your name?"

The man glanced around with fear in his eyes. "Um…Terrance."

Brock moved closer to the man. "You're lucky, Terrance. I'm giving you the opportunity to live, and I won't even subject you to torture. I just need you to answer a few questions."

Brock crouched and locked eyes with the man. "However, my big friend here and this Tantarri woman both know a thing or two about inflicting pain." He gestured toward Cam and Puri, hoping they would do their best to look menacing. "If you don't cooperate, I'm afraid we'll have to see what they can dream up."

The man's eyes appeared haunted as they flicked from Cam, to Puri, then back to Brock. "What do you want to know?"

Brock smiled. "Good choice." He stood upright and swept an arm to his side. "What is this place? Who runs it?"

"This is a mine," The man replied. "*The Hand* set it up. I work for them because they pay well. There's a lot of gold to go around."

Brock squinted. "They mine gold here?"

"Yes. There are gold deposits. They mine it and send it off to mint it into coins." He paused, looking around. "I'm starving. Can I have something to eat?"

"I'll get you some food after you answer my questions," Brock glanced toward his friends then back to the man. "You mentioned *The Hand*. Who are they?"

The man shrugged. "I can only tell you what I know." He glanced toward the unconscious man beside him. "He works for them. His name is Tom Gambo. Another man, a Master Eldarro, he works for them, too. He was here with some woman from the Ministry a number of weeks ago. She departed soon after, but Eldarro stayed until he and a number of the guards left to pursue someone." He paused and stared at Brock for a moment before continuing. "*The Hand* has a network of people working throughout the Empire. They send us new prisoners from time-to-time to replace the ones who die."

Brock thought of what the man said. *The Hand*. The name reminded him of the mark he had seen on Samson, Varius, and Eldarro. He moved close to the unconscious man and tipped his head forward. In the light coming from Ashland's charged stone, he spotted the same mark at the bottom of the man's hairline. He stepped back, leaving the man's head drooping at an odd angle.

The guard was telling the truth, a truth that was now becoming clear to Brock.

"Do you know why *the Hand* is doing this? What's their agenda?"

Terrance shrugged. "Gold I guess. Most of the prisoners are Unchosen. I always assumed they use them because nobody will miss them when they're gone." He paused, his brow furrowed. "Oddly, some are marked with the rune of Issal. I asked about that once, but they told me to shut up or leave without my gold. I shut up."

Brock's eyes widened. "There are prisoners marked with runes? Are you sure?"

"Yeah." The man nodded. "We get one or two a year."

This news intrigued Brock and he decided it was time to see about the prisoners.

"We need to open those buildings back there." Brock pointed to where the prisoners slept. "Where are the keys?"

The man glanced toward Gambo. "He should have them. If not, they're buried in the barracks."

Brock glanced toward the ruined barracks behind the man before looking down at Gambo. He bent over and searched the pockets of the unconscious man. After hearing a jingle, he pulled a set of keys from an inside coat pocket. The man then began to stir. When Brock stood, Gambo raised his head and blinked in the light. His gaze drifted up until he saw Brock's face and the man's eyes grew round.

"That symbol!" Gambo exclaimed. "Why are you marked with that symbol? It's evil!"

Brock smiled a humorless smile. "Can't you tell? Look around you." Brock spread his arms in a welcoming gesture, but lacking any sense of the sentiment. "Surely, you can see for yourself. Your worst fears are coming true." He crouched down and leaned close, looking into the man's eyes as he held his open hand out. "You might be a member of *The Hand*," Brock squeezed his hand into a fist, "but I am the fist, the fist of *Chaos*. I'm going to crush your plans. *The Hand* will pay for what they've done here."

60

R ubbing at weary eyes, Brock tried to shake his grogginess. After a draining and emotional night, the two hours of sleep he was able to get in left him tired and wishing for rest. However, that would have to wait.

He motioned for Wraith to sit, and scrambled atop a boulder near the mouth of the main mine tunnel. With his back to the cliff wall, he faced the crowd assembling in the shade before him. Beyond the congregation, the morning sun brightly lit the western section of the compound and remains of the wall.

As he waited for the crowd to settle, he noticed a few still eating their meal. Upon discovering that one of the buildings was a mess hall, they had located the prisoners who were the camp cooks and set them to making a massive breakfast. Many of the prisoners even went back for seconds, eager to eat more than their typical allotment. Amazement appeared etched on some prisoners' faces, while others reflected doubt, unwilling to believe that they were free. Many would absently rub at their raw ankles, now free of shackles for the first time in months or years.

As he waited, Brock gaze drifted to a girl his age sitting in the front row. Salina smiled at him, tears filling her dark eyes again. He still couldn't believe she was here. Salina couldn't believe she was free from her bonds. When she disappeared from the Academy the prior year, Brock had assumed she had quit and gone home. After all, that was what he was told by Academy leaders. When Salina explained that they had kidnapped her at the beginning of winter break, Brock recalled the carriage that had almost run over him and Ashland while in Fallbrandt. The girl had likely been inside the carriage, on her way to this forsaken mine.

When the cooks emerged from the mess hall, Brock decided it was time.

He cleared his throat and prepared to speak. Benny had explained that his voice would carry from this spot, the sound guided by the alcove of rock walls behind him. Speaking with force, but not quite yelling, he tested it out.

"Can everyone hear me?" Brock's eyes searched the crowd. "Someone raise your hand in the back if you can hear me."

When three hands along the rear of the assembly popped up, he nodded in satisfaction. After taking a deep breath, he released the air in a long exhale to calm his nerves. He was unused to addressing large groups. The audience of a hundred people before him felt daunting. His stomach began to churn, yet he forced himself to speak.

"Good morning everyone." He began. In truth, it was a good morning, surely the best morning the prisoners have had in years. "I am very sorry for what you've had to endure here. As you may have figured out, you are now free. Your captors have been disposed of, and there is nothing stopping you from going off to live your own lives."

Cheers rang out from the throng with tears flowing again as they hugged each other. Brock remained patient and allowed them enjoy the moment before he continued. After a minute, he took a breath and resumed.

"However, I also have bad news to deliver." He wished it were otherwise, but the truth was all he had. "A horrible war is coming. A dark force of incredible strength has come to Issalia and has already swept across Kalimar. I know for a fact that this force destroyed Sol Polis, the largest city in the Empire, in mere hours."

He paused, trying to pace the message. "I expect that you all have heard of an ancient enemy known as the Banished Horde. It may seem like the stuff of legends and fairy tales, but they are real and they have returned. I've seen what they can do. It is the stuff of nightmares, not legends. The death and destruction they leave in their wake is horrifying."

Brock's gaze skimmed over the crowd before landing on Ashland. She nodded when their eyes met. Confidence rushed over him and he continued.

"This unstoppable force will continue across the continent in their quest to kill every man, woman, and child. It's just a matter of time before everyone is dead and every city is destroyed."

He paused again, dreading this part the most. "So, enjoy your freedom for the moment. Your life is soon going to come to a bitter end. I'm sorry."

He stopped his speech to allow the gravity of it to sink in. For a long moment, shock held the audience hostage.

Salina stood and shouted. "Why even free us if this is our fate? Can nothing be done? Won't the Holy Army stop them?"

Brock mentally thanked the girl for her spirit. He had counted on someone to do it, for he could not lead them to salvation alone.

"From what I've seen, the Holy Army stands no chance. They are outnumbered and out-powered." He maintained an intense expression as his gaze swept across the crowd. "You see, The Horde is made of banshees."

Everyone had heard of banshees, likely thinking them nothing more than tales of fancy.

"Yes, I said banshees." He nodded. "They are real. We have seen them and have even fought them. We lost some good people in that fight." He thought of Lars and how he missed his friend. "At ten feet tall, each has the strength of many men. They use fear as a weapon, along with long sharp talons that can tear your face off with a swipe. There could be thousands of them."

Brock saw the previous hope he had given them fading fast. He hated to do it like this, but he needed them and could not afford any hesitation.

"However, there is one thing that might turn the tables in our favor. There is one thing that might stop this dark army and save humanity from extinction."

He paused, waiting for it. Again, Salina was the one to speak out.

"What is it? What can we do?"

This was it. This was his moment. Brock raised his arms and held them open.

"You can join me and form the most potent army ever known."

The expressions of those standing before him appeared baffled. Salina shouted again.

"What are you talking about? Look at us. We're not fighters. Some of these people can barely walk."

"True." Brock nodded. "However, each of you can be worth a hundred fighters. This is because most of you, like me, have the ability to wield magic. The magic of *Chaos*."

Perplexed looks and mutters shifted among the crowd. Needing to impress them, Brock decided that a demonstration was necessary.

"Watch this." He jumped down from the boulder.

When Brock shooed Wraith toward Ashland, everyone backed away as the giant dog walked past. He had counted on that reaction, because he needed the space. Withdrawing a chunk of coal from his coat pocket, he traced a rune on the face of the rock and closed his eyes. The storm of Chaos raged around him – a storm he dove into, wrestled, and captured, absorbing it. After opening his eyes and charging the rune, he scrambled backward as it began to glow.

A loud crack sounded and shards of rock sprayed in all directions, falling just short of the front row of spectators. The boulder then began to rise until it stood on four stone legs. Scraping and grinding sounds echoed throughout the complex as the boulder rumbled toward him. Before everyone ran in fear, Brock approached the rock, and placed his hand on it.

"See what the power of *Chaos* can do?" He stood beside the rock, patting it as it stopped beside him. "Using this magic, I brought this rock to life. It is now my pet, willing to attack anyone I set it upon or protect me from anyone willing to do harm. This is but one example among many things *Chaos* can do. This is what you can learn if you let me teach you."

Brock scrambled up the creature's leg and climbed upon its rocky back. "I know quite well that this world has treated Unchosen poorly. I was one of you, born Unchosen." The crowd was silent, their full attention directed toward Brock. "I have discovered that you all were subjected to living your lives as Unchosen because the power of *Chaos* resides within you. Some people know the truth, and they've been trying to hide it. They fear this magic, afraid of what *Chaos* can do. Because you have this inherent ability, they established laws designed to keep you down in the fear that you might discover this power within. A group known as *The Hand* has gone even further and locked you away in this prison, where they can control you and prevent you from ever discovering your abilities."

Brock searched the faces before him, seeking a spark. He needed to make them angry enough to fight. "I say, damn them all. Sure, we could seek revenge and use *Chaos* as a weapon against the men and women who have chosen to deceive us and cage us. However, is that what Issal would have you do? Is it right to abuse this power by harming others for such selfish reasons? Wouldn't that just prove your hateful captors correct and confirm their motives?"

Brock paused again and allowed them to consider the dilemma. *Now to provide them direction.*

"Another option is for you to join me and use this power to stop this demonic army. You can help me save the innocent men, women, and children who will surely die if we do nothing. We can prove our value to the people of the Empire by saving them. We are their hope because we are the only ones who can do it. Perhaps, we can then live the full lives that they have previously denied us. Who is with me?"

The canyon was quiet for a long moment. Brock waited nervously, hearing only the eerie sound of the wind whistling in the mine tunnels behind him. With a look of determination on her face, Salina ran toward Brock, climbed onto the living boulder, and stood beside him. She turned toward the throng and shouted.

"Let's do this! If what Brock says is true, we can be something, something special!" Her fierce brown eyes swept across an audience who stood before her in still silence. She then thrust her fist into the air. "Let the Unchosen be the saviors to mankind!"

A deafening roar rose up, the sound echoing off the canyon walls. The newly freed prisoners jumped and cheered while pumping their fists high. Every single one of them.

Brock realized that he had done it. He had freed them from their bonds, only to bond them to himself. He had them, and he hated himself for it.

61

———————

The hinge squeaked as the door opened. Brock didn't have to look up to know it was Ashland. He sensed her approach, similar to how he sensed Wraith's presence on the floor near the bed. Choosing not to respond, his face remained buried in his hands. A warm palm rested on his arm, but he showed no reaction.

"What's wrong, Brock?' Ashland asked. "It worked, just as you planned. I thought you'd be happy."

Removing his hands from his face, he sighed before responding.

"I manipulated those poor people. They don't understand what will come, what they will face, but they bought into it."

She stared him in the eye. "You told them the truth and nothing else. While your methods may have been a bit dramatic, they are understand-able given the circumstances. We don't have time for them to debate the issue. Our only chance – their only chance – is to commit immediately and begin preparing for the Horde."

Despite knowing that she was right – that he had no choice but to do as he did – it didn't make him feel better.

"How many will die because of me?" His voice was a whisper.

Sympathy reflected in Ashland's eyes as she cupped his cheek. "Oh, Brock. I realize that this is hard. Yes, many will die in what is to come, but you can't look at it that way. Would they have lived if you hadn't freed them from this prison? If you did nothing, these people and thousands of other innocents would die at the hands of the Horde. This way, they at least have a chance."

She leaned in and her lips met his. He closed his eyes and embraced the warm rush. As their lips parted, he opened his eyes to look into hers.

"Remember, you did give them an option," she said. "You laid the truth before them and they chose to join you and fight back. It was their choice to make. Now that they've decided to follow you, your job is to prepare them so they have a chance. Do your best and we'll see what fate decides."

Brock stared into her wonderfully blue eyes and marveled at his luck in finding such an incredible woman.

A knock on the door caused Wraith's head to pop up and look on in anticipation.

"Come in," Brock said.

The door opened and Benny and Parker peeked into the storage closet that Brock and Ashland had claimed as their private room.

Benny entered, holding the door for Parker as he spoke. "We finished taking the inventory of food stores in the cellar."

Brock nodded. "What did you find?"

Parker responded, "The cooks believe we have enough food to feed everyone for five or six days. With the guards gone, there are about twenty fewer mouths to feed, so that helps as well."

Benny nodded. "It appears that the mine gets food delivered several times each month. The next wagon is due the day after tomorrow."

"We need that delivery to show up so we can remain here for a bit," Brock worked through the plan in his head.

Parker smiled. "That's not all. We found something else."

Brock arched a brow in question. "Well, what is it?"

Parker glanced at Benny, who was nodding. "There are casks of ale. Four of them. Apparently, it was for the guards."

Finding the ale was a bit of a surprise. Considering what was coming, they could use some ale and a little diversion. Brock forced a smile, showing what he hoped was enthusiasm.

"First, let's work on getting things cleaned up around here today, and then we'll have some fun." Brock nodded toward the door. "Tell them we'll break the ale out at dinner. Tonight, we celebrate our freedom."

Everyone smiled, seemingly happy to have cause for celebration. Brock tried to focus on the moment, focus on today. He feared what tomorrow might bring.

NOTE FROM THE AUTHOR

I hope that you enjoyed The Emblem Throne and are looking forward to the epic series conclusion in *An Empire in Runes*. In addition, check out the series prequel, *Rogue Legacy*, which reveals the truth behind key events in the Issalia's history

If you are willing, please consider leaving a review on Amazon, Goodreads, or your favorite book commence site. Reviews help us independent authors immensely.

Best Wishes,
Jeffrey L. Kohanek

For my latest book updates, sign up for my author newsletter at www.jeffreylkohanek.com

BOOKS BY JEFFREY L. KOHANEK

Runes of Issalia

The Buried Symbol: Runes of Issalia 1

The Emblem Throne: Runes of Issalia 2

An Empire in Runes: Runes of Issalia 3

* * *

Runes of Issalia Boxed Set

* * *

Heroes of Issalia: Runes Series+Rogue Legacy

* * *

Rogue Legacy: Runes of Issalia Prequel

Wardens of Issalia

A Warden's Purpose: Wardens of Issalia 1

The Arcane Ward: Wardens of Issalia 2

An Imperial Gambit: Wardens of Issalia 3

A Kingdom Under Siege: Wardens of Issalia 4

* * *

Wardens of Issalia Boxed Set (April 2014)

* * *

ICON: A Wardens of Issalia Companion Tale